TOXIC

THE BLOOD LEGACY SERIES
BOOK FOUR

KENYA GOREE-BELL

EDITED BY
VIRGINIA TESI CAREY

To the ones who love doesn't fit into a perfect box.

For you mom, always for you.

AUTHOR'S NOTE

YOUR MENTAL HEALTH MATTERS.

This is a DARK ROMANCE featuring a VILLAIN HERO. He will not be redeemed, he will not grovel or ask for forgiveness.

CWs: Please be aware this is a DARK ROMANCE with a character with a personality disorder characterized a psychopath. The hero in this book is mean and cruel to the heroine, so if your feelings are easily hurt by mean words please pass on this book. YOUR MENTAL HEALTH MATTERS.

Other more serious CWs: The hero is a villain and does villainous things like murder; manhandling (groping) of FMC, Kinbaku- sexual rope play, graphic violence, kidnapping, stalking, imprisonment, Virgin kink, Hemotolagnia - blood play, breath play, intimidation of FMC by MMC, OTT, yelling, profanity, hunting of FMC by MMC, voluntary leaving (running from a crazy mfkr), pushing sexual boundaries, heavy dub-con, patient abuse not on page, talk of SA, coercion, rough penetrative sex, rough oral sex, killing, blood and gore, ambiguous consent, light drug use (weed), talk of criminal enterprises as a way of life. This list may not encompass all of the CWs. Mental Challenges but not used as excuse for bad behavior. Medical abortion as a preventive measure (on page). Death of parent. light Dollification. Hemotolagnia. Forced confinement of a mentally changed individual. Suicidal ideation on page. Talk of suicide on page.

There is a scene of violence against the FMC in the second 1/2 of chapter 15. This may be extremely upsetting to some readers. I advised severe caution reading this if you were ever a victim of violence.

This is a work of fiction for entertainment only. The sexual practices in this book should in no way be used as a guide for real life safe sex practices, BDSM or Kinabku. I advise you if you want to explore these practices you should join credible organizations or reach out to ethical professionals.

This book is called TOXIC for a reason.

JAPANESE WORDS & PHRASES

Please note this list are the translations and are close approximations if not out right translations because the Japanese language is gendered and has just as many nuances and inflections as English. as much as possible I have included as much explanation as possible.

- I love you - Aishiteru yo or I like you as Sukidayo.
- Beautiful - Utsukushii is the direct translation but you'd often hear people use *Kirei* instead which is more like sayin pretty. So you can use Utsukushii for when a person see's someone for the first time and is captured by their beauty.
- I love your taste - the words coming from a man would be Omae no aji ga daisukida

- Mine or you're mine - the words coming from a man would be Omae wa ore no da.
- Please forgive me - the words coming from a man Ore o yurushitekure.
- kawaii chef chan - pretty chef.
- Chīsana hato — little dove
- Nante kotoda would be something like what have you done!
- Nante kota : would be like what happened?!"
- Korewa taihen da :would be like Oh this is bad.
- yoi - good
- onnichan - older brother
- niichan- younger brother
- ii ko da ne — good girl
- Coming - Iku
- Your wet - nureteru
- Don't cum or hold it - Gaman shiro
- Lick it - namete hoshii
- Lick me more - motto namero
- Want it in - irette hoshii ka
- Feels to good - kimochi ii
- Feels good I can't hold on any longer - yabai, gammon dekinai
- Breast - oppai
- Dick - chinchin
- Pussy - manko

- I want to fuck you- orewa omaeto fakku shitai
- Nasty - yarashii
- Kiss me - kisushite

PROLOGUE

Hisashi ~ 14 years old

Crick, snip, snap. I look at it the feathers a beautiful and soft dove at least that is what Kana said the last time when I finally manage to keep one of the doves she wanted alive.

Silly mother is all upon arms about it. Probably because she couldn't or wouldn't figure out a way for Kana to keep her little pets without them flying away.

I promised I wouldn't hurt them again and it was only a little lie. I had to make it so they wouldn't fly away so tinier breaks here and there then wrap their broken legs with pretty tape. Mission accomplished.

"Arigatō, Hisashi-Oniichan." her sweet baby voice whispers to me when I pull the bird out of my pocket and give it to my three year old sister.

"Ahh, little dove, I like you very much." she snuggles the bird close to her kimono.

After giving her a solemn bow I leave her suites. I'm not allowed to be here. Mother doesn't want her tainted by my influence.

Silly woman, Don't you know I've always been this way.

"Yessss, perfection." He whispers. *"A perfect boy just as father says. a genius."*

"Hai," I mutter to myself knowing that she has her spies and has told any who see me muttering to myself to slap me full in the face. I can control it now but when I was smaller I was far too careless so I faced severe punishment. More so when father was away.

That's when my Monster first came. Grabbing the hand breaking and several fingers on one of my minders.

"And I will do it again." He soothes. "I will keep you safe always."

CHAPTER
ONE

H isashi

WATCHING THIS LITTLE BITCH, I stroke my hard as a brick dick.

Idly, I contemplate whether I'm going to fuck her within an inch of her life, then kill her or choke her to death as I fuck her. The possibilities are endless.

"Fuck her dead corpse," *He* whispers. "Fuck her dead corpse."

Impossibly, I get harder. Like I said, possibilities.

Strands of a ballad fill the auditorium and Santiago saunters out onto the stage, taking the stool that was placed in the center stage, dragging it to the right side of the stage and starts strumming his guitar. The song has various women in various states of swoon but the one he can't keep his gaze from is Dr. Mimi Love-Spencer, who the town affectionally calls, "Doctor Everything". She's always there when you need her and recently took the position as the head of the Women's and Infant's Center at the Shelby-Love Medical Center.

From where I'm sitting in the cloak of darkness, I only have a view of her profile, but even from this distance, Dr. Mimi's affection is obvious as she stares at the rock star is apparent.

I should warn Santiago, Love women are dangerous. From that crazy ass scent that they wear to the curve of their pussies, they lead to a man's ultimate destruction. It's best to get them out of your system rather than be ensnared in their web.

My brother Kiyoshi, a sadist on his best day, is already too lost to his obsession, Krie Love, the head chef of The Camillia. I'd have thought a man as brilliant as he would have learned from my mistake. No. He's caught no differently than I was years earlier. He claims to only want to destroy her brother for hacking into Creative Chaos. The company our cousin, Akchiro, entrusted us to run. How that transformed into her spending every night at his home. I don't know, but I know it doesn't bode well.

Watching as the audience gives ovation after ovation, I watch Taylor Love sashay her curvy little ass out onto the stage, beaming with pride at her proteges. She takes in the crowd as the lights go up. Stepping farther back into the shadows of the balcony alcove just as her gaze rises, taking in the balcony, I watch as the cast link hands paying close attention to the way Santiago's much larger hand engulfs hers. Rage pulses in my chest. "Kill him. Make her suffer," *He* incites.

"Soon," I whisper, watching bow after bow. The need to sever the linked hands crackles inside me. That he would dare touch what is mine won't be borne. He needs to fucking perish at my hands. His death beneath my scope, the blade of my Kanta, or my unrelenting grip, is the only thing that will satisfy *Him*.

"Patience." The stage quickly fills with parents, friends, and family of the performers as they take pictures of the kids. Soon Santiago frees himself to jump down, joining Dr. Mimi and the child that is obviously his son. He takes the baby, and they make their way through the throng to the vestibule where the reception is being held.

I lose interest in my second mark momentarily. Only his open devotion saves him for the moment, that and the fact that soon I will have the answers as to his true dedication to the little doctor with whom he secretly fathered a child.

Again, my attention turns to my little bitch. Her head thrown back, exposing her neck, a delicious torment for me as she laughs delightedly at some nonsense one of the teens surrounding her says.

Enjoy your time, little dove. I'm coming for you.

It's well past midnight when she finally emerges from the Shelby-Love Arts Center. She's busy looking at her watch. She has her phone up to her ear.

"My flight leaves from Birmingham at eight a.m. I think instead of taking a quick nap, I'm going to just drive up and stay with Xander-Rafe Leroy and his sisters tonight and have one of them take me to the airport. I don't know, though."

She pauses, listening for a moment before assuring the person on the other line, "I already packed. My bags are in the rental." She stops looking around for the car I had moved hours ago. She opens her bag, searching around for her keys. I had one of my people relieve her of them while she was prancing around the stage after she directed from the booth.

"I'll text when I get back to New York." She looks around the nearly empty parking lot. There is a maintenance van which I'm standing just to the left of that's obscuring my Maybach.

I step out of view as her gaze sweeps past me unseeingly. Her situational awareness has never been great. I almost pity her. Almost.

Hot anticipation that's been ten years in the making slices through my body. My dick hardens at the prospect. That fucking vanilla rose has me biting back a growl, and she's not even cleared the front bumper. It's not that the scent is overpowering. No, my body is just too in tuned to it. I don't know what they put in it, but it must be formulated to match them all differently. I smell the same scent on her cousin Krie, the chef who has my older brother enthralled, and it has no effect on me. Yet, as Taylor approaches, my dick primes, my knees threaten to buckle from the way she smells. She has me salivating. Another reason to punish her pussy.

"Take her," *He* demands. "Now."

I can hear her approaching me, assuming her rental is on the other side of the maintenance van. Just behind the back doors of the darkened van I watch the disappointment spread across her beautiful face as she takes in my Maybach. Turning back to the parking lot, her head moves from side to side, looking for the rental.

"Now, I know nobody stole..." I'm already on her, snatching soft curves against me. My black gloved hand smothers her shocked gasp.

Her legs lose their strength as the chloroform starts taking effect. Dragging her ass back to the trunk, I press the fob making the trunk swoosh open. Removing my hand, I let her breathe clean air.

I don't want her unconscious. I want her to experience it all. Every bit of her treachery will be atoned for. Beginning tonight.

Hoisting her nearly limp form, I lay her in the trunk. She's fighting, but her movements are sluggish, and her aim is off. She swings, catching nothing but air before collapsing in a heap of frustration. She twitches, trying to make her legs work, to no avail.

Beautiful broken doll. Her legs twisted and useless, her head still has just enough mobility, but she's turned away. I can't have that. Twisting and twisting the mass of soft, luxurious curls in my fist, I make her look at me.

"Little bitch," I whisper in my native language. Her head jerks around. "Little bitch," I whisper in English for good measure. For a split second, I think I see relief before sheer, unadulterated horror bleeds into her eyes. She tries to get up.

"Shh." I cover her mouth and nose with the chloroform. I want to see her eyes. I want her to know it was me. It was always me. I've watched. I've waited while she's gone on with her life like I meant nothing to her.

"Like *we* meant nothing to her," *He* hisses. "She'll be punished for that, too."

All in due time.

Savagery almost makes me come. I'm not a boy, though. I pull myself back, savoring the ache of anticipation, loving the way she struggles beneath my grip, trying to dislodge my hand. I press harder, knowing I may bruise her. Unfortunate but I can't help if she won't be reasonable.

"You will stop hurting yourself," I command.

She stiffens, her nose flaring. Her eyes cloud. She is looking dazed, but I want her awake. I want her to fight. I remove my hand. Looking down, I watch as she takes deep inhales to clear the fog from her brain.

"Welcome home, wife." I smile down at her, watching as she rears back trying to put distance between us like she's terrified of me. The one who's watched over her, kept her safe, despite her demanding my face and the great dishonor she served me. I who did nothing but cherish her for as long as I was able. The man she shared her firsts. I would have given her the world. She's proven she only deserves the hell I shall visit upon her ass for her treachery.

Ignoring the twinge of disappointment, I laugh at how easily she's played into my hands. I slam the trunk down on her. I hear the muffled scream as I make my way over to the driver's side of the car.

Sitting behind the wheel, I turn the ignition. The roar of the engine sparks a panicked cry from the back that I can hear over the local radio station's R&B.

Turning off the music I've loved since the moment she introduced it to me years ago, I watch the camera I placed on the roof of the trunk to see her every moment.

I watch and listen to the sounds of her banging on the trunk. She tries to maneuver around the trunk space to get to the lights, but her useless legs prevent her success. She screams in frustration. Rage and pain play out on her face as she tries to fruitlessly inch her body around to reach the lights. Her screams of despair give way to cries and soft whimpers of defeat. Finally, tears stream down her face in rivulets as the anger gives way to fear. She tries to take breaths to clear her mind. I know she'll tell herself she just needs to calm down. Easier said than done when your biggest fear manifests in the flesh, ready to tear you asunder.

She hyperventilates. Watching with detached interest, I watch her struggle. Sick satisfaction has a smile playing at the corners of my mouth. Vengeance is a beautiful, delicious fuckable thing made real for me at this moment.

Unable to catch her breath, she passes out. Her head lolls from side to side. Tears track prettily down her face. She's always been a beautiful crier.

Driving at a steady pace, I make my way to my estate. The road is dark and winding. The modern Samurai mansion hidden behind the gate.

"Home at last. She's ours to do as we will," *He* crows with malicious delight.

"She's mine," I grit, pushing back against the mind monster that's been my constant companion for as long as I can remember.

"You both belong to me now." *His* quiet assertion is all that's needed. We both know it's true.

SHE'S STILL NOT AWAKENED by the time I take her to the room where she'll learn how to be a good, dutiful wife to me.

"You must harden yourself. You are weak where she is concerned," *He* warns as I lay her down on the bed made special for her.

"I already have," I hiss, not in the mood for *His* fucking admonishments. I'm in full control. I long since realized *He* is not the one in control. I am. Only allowing *Him* to come out to play because for a while there *He* was all I had before her, then after her betrayal. *He* deserves a reward, but I will never allow *Him* free rein again. This time *He* could kill her. *He's* been jealous of Taylor from the start. Hated the influence she had over me. For a while he'd been pushed so far back and not in the deadened way medication makes me feel. No, with her *He* was just asleep. The ways she spoke to my soul filled in the ragged, jagged places. Then she left me, betraying me in the process. Now she will pay.

I watch her for long moments as she sleeps off the chloroform and the fright causing a panic attack. Like many times before, she's blissfully unaware of me watching over her. She sleeps like an angel, deep with no sins marring her beauty with frowns. Her curly hair spreads out on the pillow behind her in a thick, kinky mass. Her dark skin shines in the darkness cast blue under the moonlight, shining down from the glass ceiling that flows into a wall of windows. The room under brighter luminesce is her favorite royal purple, but in my way, monochromatic. I find too many color variations stressful. I don't expect her to appreciate my efforts, at least not right away.

"Mmm," a soft moan slips from her plump lips. Her breasts rise and fall under the black wrap dress she's wearing that's hugging each of her bountiful curves and gets my attention. I'm salivating to touch them, to slide my dick between those plump mounds.

"Fuck," muttering, I pull myself away from the temptation that is my treacherous little bitch. Heading into the bathroom, I start the bath. Take out the soap. I don't trust myself around her.

I'm still not quite sure of what I want to do with her. Fuck her? Definitely. Choke her? Already got all the various devices to implement that particular torment. *Kill her. Kill her. Kill her.* I know the thought is not my own, just as I know *he* will have no peace until *He* eradicates *His* competition.

"We play first." Taking great care, I add her scents I purchased months ago from her cousin Crimson's apothecary. I've made it my business to become acquainted with every Love. There are hundreds of them. Undaunted, I've made a complete family tree. None have gone beyond my notice. She will have nowhere to run, no succor, no solace. She is mine to torment. My vengeance screams for her body, her blood, hell, her very soul. I will not be appeased by anything less. He won't. Her face is only the beginning.

Going back into the darkened room, I unknot the belt holding her dress closed. I slip it from her body. I take her bra and ease down her shapewear. Her soft belly pops free with a carefree jiggle and it takes everything in me not to bury my face there. "You won't be needing this anymore. I'll make sure to burn it," I mutter to myself.

She's all softness when I sweep her into my arms and stride into the bathroom. Vanilla-rose permeates the air. She's buried her head in the crook of my throat. Soft puffs of her breath tickle me as I test the water with the tips of my fingers. Shifting, I put her in the bath.

"Ah." She wakes with a start. Her eyes are round, big and luminous like those of a cartoon kitten, deceptively innocent. Her pupils, still dilated, expand a mere fraction.

"Hisashi?" My name is a high squeak. She squeezes back against the back of the bathtub to cover herself in a pointless attempt to hide herself from me.

"One and the same," I tell her, scooting to the opposite side of the tub, so I can more fully enjoy the view. The bubbles covering her are white iridescence against her lovely brown skin. One knee is bent slightly to spring out to escape, or another attempt to hide from me. I can't tell, nor do I care. There will be no escaping or hiding, she will find that out soon enough.

"W-where am I?" She looks around frantically, taking in the lavender marble floor, the glass ceiling, the full wall of windows just beyond where she sits ensconced in vanilla-rose.

"Our home, wife." Angling more toward her, I take my time rolling up my sleeves. She watches me in silence. I let it drop between us like a veil of mystery. I don't owe her anything anymore, but my wrath and vengeance are so sweet my body quakes even in this moment to mete it out. "She never deserved you," *He* whispers with insidious seduction.

"Hai," I say, drawing her attention. "You will remain here for the time being," I have to add to cover my slip. I don't need her screaming and having a breakdown on me because of my *Monster*. Oh, I fully expect them to meet, but it will be on my terms, not *his* or hers.

"Where is here? Wait." She raises a bubbly hand. "It doesn't matter. I have an entire life I need to get back to. My writing..." Her words come to an abrupt stop when I move. Pushing her to sit up fully, I start moving the sponge in gentle circles on her shoulders and back.

A smothered gasp escapes her lips as I smooth the sudsy, soft mesh over her breasts, taking my time with her gorgeous nipples. The tips harden, making me bite back a groan. She fucking slays me.

Moving lower, I cover her tummy, skipping her center, moving down to both thighs and feet. Dropping the sponge, I plunge my hand into the water.

"Hisashi, no." Her hands are shaking wanting to stop me.

"Your eczema is too bad for you to be in here too long. The more you fight this losing battle, the worse the effects will be on your skin. Should your skin become inflamed, I will have no choice but to add the results of this misbehavior to your already extensive punishments."

As soon as her hands fall away, my hand finds her soft pussy. I use my fingers to clean her. Diving my other hand in, I clean her other hole. She gasps and I have to bite back a groan when I meet the resistance of both her pussy and her ass.

"Good girl." Rising as I praise her, my heart hammering double time, I take a long plush bath sheet and hold it out for her.

I help her stand on wobbly legs.

Taking my time, I take the thick creamy vanilla-rose lotion she loves so much, smoothing it on her thick curves. Getting down on my hunches, my face is level with the soft thatch of curls hiding her fat, pretty pussy. Her clit barely peeks through. Lust fills me as I inhale the musk of her and the vanilla-rose.

She holds herself so still. You'd think she was under threat of my fists. I'd never hit her. Hurt her? Only when she wanted me to. Later, I acknowledge

I'm not sure what happened when I released the monster.

"Fuck her," He growls, chomping at the bit. *He* can't wait for *his* taste.

"Brush your teeth," I snap, striding from the room.

"Get in the bed," I say when she comes in, not bothering or trusting myself to turn from the window and the view of my Japanese garden and get any closer.

Watching her reflection through the windows, her hips swaying, her body gleaming from head to toe, she slips between the sheets. She did her face routine, as I suspected, when she took longer than brushing her teeth required.

"I wish you a good night, wife," I tell her, not trusting myself to go near her. In fact, I take a step back before I stop myself. My brother, Kiyoshi, would die of shame to see me hesitant to face my own wife. "I have some appointments for you tomorrow." I wait until her shoulders sag in relief.

"Then your punishment begins." I give her a brief bow, ignoring the look of abject terror on her face, and I leave.

CHAPTER
TWO

T aylor

"THEN YOUR PUNISHMENT BEGINS."

It's my fault I let my guard down. I knew better. I knew it was only a matter of time before he'd come for me. He never asked for a divorce. Never divorced me, as it was his every right to do after what happened. I knew he'd been lying in wait. But I let the years and the false assumptions he'd moved on, as the press reports of his dating various socialites indicated, to allow me to play with my life.

I sit in the palatial bed looking up at the crescent moon shining down on me. I love stargazing. It inspired much of my writing to be themed around perseverance and hope. Now, I can't muster anything other than dread. He didn't kill me immediately, like I thought he would. But that gives me little hope. He's a monster who likes to play with his food. Proved that the first time we were together.

He's not the same man I knew. He is a monster of an entirely different breed. A poshly, cold monster. His dead eyes flicked over me, taking me in, cataloguing every difference. I'm smaller than I was when we met when we had that whirlwind of a love affair before it all went to hell.

I saw appreciation, lust, no love. Was it ever love the first time or just an unhinged obsession? His need to own me?

Sleep is elusive. I'm caught up in the memory that started like a dream come true and ended in horror and blood.

Tokyo (ten years ago)

"You must use your best Japanese," Alexa, my graduate advisor, whispers to me as we enter the ballroom of the reception welcoming new students on fellowship at Sophia University. This is a black-tie event sponsored by the university so the elite who donate to the scholarship fund can feel good about who they are giving their money to. The elite from all over the world send their heirs here for the business and engineering program. If I hadn't been raised to know God made me perfect, I'd be terrified, but having love and confidence poured into me from an early age, there is no gaze I will shy away from.

"Mochiron," I say brightly. We both know my Japanese is better than hers. That's why the tall blond has been clinging to me the last month since my arrival.

"Yes, of course." She blushes prettily. She's been here for a year and has been nothing but kind to me. However, she, like many others, tends to underestimate me when they hear my southern lilt.

I squeeze her hand, letting her know there are no hard feelings. We share a smile before releasing each other's hands. Public displays of affection, even between friends, are still frowned upon by some, though Sophia University is probably the most progressive of all elite universities in Japan, the board of trustees and the administration aren't nearly as egalitarian.

This is the elite of Japanese society. She whispers, "Be careful. One wrong word or flirtation will have you back on a plane to the States by morning." Onlookers would never guess her dire warning from the way her cheek dimples highlight the hint of rosy blush she chose tonight.

We both look rather elegant. I have on a light lavender empire waisted formal gown my aunt made me with the help of my younger cousin Summer. When the ten-year-old showed me the design, I was so excited. She's a genius when it comes to design. My aunt and uncle are okay with indulging her hobby since my aunt also enjoys making clothes, as long as she stays focused on being a vet like them. It's a family tradition of sorts. Every second son in the Love family has been a vet since the time of Emancipation. Since they didn't have a son, they figured both of their daughters would fit the bill. My cousin Valentine is already in vet school down at Tuskegee. But something tells me Summer, for all her sweetness, will not follow that path without more of a fight. And why should she? I think, looking down at this gorgeous creation she created. She is gifted.

"Wow." Alexa tilts her head up toward the ceiling that looks like a fairy wonderland. Lights twinkle across the expanse of the high ceiling mounted on mixed silver branches that cover the broad expanse then cascade down to the side of trees that run along the side of the room. Other trees are sprinkled throughout the room save for the area designated for the dance floor, the tables strategically placed under each.

"We should mingle," she whispers.

I can see several other students amidst the throngs of millionaires and billionaires that fund our education. Captains of industry already grooming their next corporate citizen. There are even members of the imperial family here as well as other royalty. I see the king of Morocco with his tall, beautiful wife making their way toward us.

I resist the urge to grab Alexa's hand for support. Remembering the years of etiquette my mom taught me, I give them a slight curtsey in deference. "Your Majesties," I murmur, waiting as Alexa does the same.

"Taylor Love?" The queen asks warmly.

"Yes, ma'am." I can't hide the surprise in my tone.

"I guess Thomas and Lilly didn't tell you about the time they spent at our home," Queen A'isha muses, looking at me indulgently. "You were very small and a toddler at the time."

Dismayed, I shake my head, laughing a little. "No, ma'am. They don't really talk about their work," I tell them knowing they know full well why not. My parents on paper are diplomats and maybe Mom is to some extent but my father, Thomas Love, was much more before he took a desk at the State Department.

"It's all very well. We couldn't miss the opportunity to introduce ourselves after the great service your parents paid to our country," the king tells me, scanning my features before adding, "The resemblance to your father is uncanny."

"It's the dimples," the queen coos like she wants to squeeze my cheeks like she must have done when I was little.

"And how are the princes and the sultana?" I ask, having no memory of the boys who must have been only a few years older than me.

"Ahem." The king presses his mouth in a thin line that somehow makes his handsome face even more handsome.

"They are pursuing careers as movie producers," the queen says primly. By the shift in energy I can tell this is an ongoing battle between them.

"Khadesia is entering her freshman year here at Sophia University," King Khalil says proudly.

"May I introduce my friend, Alexa?" Not wanting to leave my friend out of the conversation, I extoll all her virtues mainly of helping me navigate this new environment. I needn't bother; they probably had dossiers on everyone present which is why they made a beeline to me when I arrived. It's obvious they knew I'd be here.

After a few more pleasantries we meet more impressive titles. Though advised to mingle separately to foster more individualized interactions, I can't help but appreciate Alexa's presence by my side.

"Ladies." One of the advisors of the program garners our attention as he approaches. He's a dapper gentleman. I forgot what subject he teaches. I've met all my professors in the theater department.

"Honda, sensei," Alexa answers as we both bow to the man.

"I have your seating assignments." He hands them to us, bows briefly, then pivots to find the other students.

"What number do you have? You know it's based on the rank of the host family," she says, showing me she has table ten.

Flipping the card over, I hope that it is further down the line. Not that they still wouldn't be wealthy or even billionaires, but it wouldn't be the emperor's table.

Hope whooshes out of me, along with my breath. "Table two," I say, showing her the card.

"Wow, the people who sponsored your fellowship are second only to the imperial royal family in power. Wealth, they most assuredly, outrank them since they barely have three hundred million between the lot of them. So, think of them as you would the royals," Alexa says, giving me the information just as the dinner chime is sounded.

An attendant silently comes to stand at my side while another appears beside Alexa. I place the card in his white gloved hand and follow closely behind him as he leads me to the head tables. A sea of faces follow me as I approach. The king and queen of Morocco's table is to the right of the emperor's table. I breathe a sigh of relief, thinking that's where I will be sitting. It makes the most sense.

I swallow back my surprise when he passes that table, and another Black girl is seated in the guest seat by the king and queen. So that must be table three. He moves with fluid grace around table one making sure not the show them his back. Mimicking his movements, I follow close behind.

Finally, we come to the table. My gaze is so trained on the attendant I'm following I nearly miss that he's stopping to reach for my chair.

"Allow me." A deep voice catches my attention. I look up meeting the inscrutable face of the most handsome man I have ever seen. A brief smile ghosts his lips as he bows slightly indicating that I should sit.

I move with the grace my mother taught me and slip into the chair he holds out. He pushes me up to the table in a smooth movement. The table is circular with about eight people present. There is no way to tell where the head of the table is.

An older handsome gentleman is to my left and turns an indulgent smile on me. "Welcome Taylor-san, as our honored guests. We are very happy to have you join us." Several heads bow around the table in acquiesce. I notice an elegant woman who bows her head but keeps her gaze cold and unwavering on me. She's looking at me as if I am not only beneath her but that my presence is an affront to her very being.

"Hmph," the man clears his throat with a pained glance at the woman, who clears her expression immediately. "I am Takeda, my wife Mrs. Takeda." The woman nods with a fake smile. "And sons, Kiyoshi," he gestures to a young man across from me with a stoic expression that gives nothing away, "and Hisashi." He indicates the man who held out my chair.

"How are you enjoying university?" Hisashi asks in perfect English obviously the designated host for me this evening.

"I love it," I tell him turning toward him. "It's very challenging."

"Theater is challenging?" Mrs. Takeda scoffs, bluntly dismissing me. "Our last fellowship recipient was in the nuclear science program."

"Mother," Kiyoshi snaps. Immediately the table quiets.

"It's alright," Mr. Takeda says in a placating fashion. "We wanted to help someone in the arts this time. And I for one couldn't be happier with our choice. Taylor we've heard many great things."

The table affirms with cheers and raised glasses. Even the austere Kiyoshi breaks a little smile my way.

"Indeed," Hisashi says for my ears only. "We can't be all business with no arts to elevate us to a higher plain."

"Arigatō," I say softly only for his ears smiling at him.

His eyes move from my eyes to my lips, darkening for a brief moment.

"Yes, well, you say thank you, like you were born

here. How long did you study?" He asks, turning back to the table as large.

"We lived here for four years when I was ten," I tell him.

He looks at me for a long moment, then nods approvingly. I don't know why that sends rays of warmth through me. Why should his approval matter? Yet for some reason it does.

I can't help smiling as I say, "I'm sure your English is much better than my command of your language though."

He nods. "We started lessons at the age of three. It's a requirement that all Takeda heirs be fluent in various languages."

I can't stop the way my brows arch upward. "How many languages do you know?"

"Hm." He presses his lips in a way that seems contrived, practiced. "At the moment, twelve — English, Arabic, Mandarin, French, Spanish, Swahili, Igbo, Russian, Urdu, Hindi, German, and Korean."

Snapping my mouth closed I stare at him in awe.

"Kiyoshi and my father know more." He waves his hand dismissively as if his accomplishment pales in comparison to the other men in his family. "My older cousin who will be the Takeda, possibly more than they. Yet, I can sufficiently muddle through a meeting or two," he says modestly.

"I think you're amazing," I say. He just stares at me

for an unnerving moment before he shifts to finally focus on the soup course.

Immediately I cringe. "I-meant knowing so many languages." I sound like a country bumpkin. Jesus let there be a spontaneous sinkhole and swallow me up and save me from this mortification.

He slowly places the soup spoon down quietly turning back to me. The onyx fire of his gaze traps me, weaving a web of titanium around me. I'm utterly lost.

"You will dance with me later." No smile. He's not asking. He waits as his demand sinks in. I swallow the lump that's formed in my throat. I squeeze my thighs tightly against the zing of pleasure that settles in my kitty cat at his sudden change from dinner companion to thinking he's the boss of me.

His glance down tells me that he didn't miss my reaction.

My nod and "sure," is met with a dark smirk before he turns back to the soup course.

The rest of the dinner passes with light small talk and polite inquiries about my focus on theater. The interest is real and except for Mrs. Takeda's opening remarks everyone makes me feel welcome.

I don't know what I expected when the dinner is over. It was not for Hisashi to give me a brief vow and disappear.

There's more mingling as the orchestra sets up. Soon the strands of music fill the air.

"Hey how did your dinner go with the Takedas?

They normally only sponsor fellowships for engineers and computer scientists," Alexa asks, sidling up beside me.

"Takeda-sama says this year they wanted to help out in the arts. Mrs. Takeda wasn't pleased," I whisper so that only she can hear. "As for the dinner, it was nice. I sat by the youngest son, Hisashi. He asked me to dance."

"Woah." Alexa pulls back and gives a wide-eyed look then grins like the cat who ate all the canaries, not just one. "They are gorgeous. Introduce me to the older one," she urges.

"I will if I can find them in this crowd again." I look around trying not to make it obvious I'm looking for anyone in particular.

"This is my second one of these. Someone will dance with you. As for Hisashi, he's in his doctorate year of computer science. He already owns several patents on proprietary software. He's said to be reclusive and only seen out on rare occasions like this." Alexa drops all the tea on this man like she's an obsessed groupie.

"Wow." Looking at her smirking, I say, "You really did your homework."

"Well." She gives me a smug shrug. "My fellowship is in computer science. I never see him in the department though. He has his own lab and everything."

"Ladies." Two young gentlemen come up beside us offering their hands to lead us on the dance floor.

Music fills the room and I'm caught up with partner after partner drawing me into one whirl around the room after another.

"I'm sorry, I need a break," I say to a young man who comes just as my fifth partner walks me back to the edge of the dance floor. You would think we were in an eighteenth-century salon with suitors lined up to find their next wife instead of an evening for scholars of one of Japan's most premier universities.

He bows giving me a rueful smile before he goes on to someone else.

I have long since given up on seeing my handsome dinner companion, assuming I mistook his meaning of me dancing with him. I thought it would only be him and immediately. Pushing down the disappointment I make my way to the ladies' room.

The other women smile briefly as I enter. Most are fellow scholars like me who are finding a brief respite. Some are lounging on the settees in the lounge while others use the facilities. After my ablutions I check my make-up, thankful for the online tutorials helping me apply just the right amount so I can master the flawless no make-up look.

Applying my gloss, I listen to the chatter among the other girls.

"All the real business is being done in the back rooms." One girl twitters.

"Yeah, by your second year you should at least have an apartment or something. Agatha Thorncastle is engaged to a guy she met here," her friend chimes in.

"That's just because she's a Thorncastle from *the* Thorncastles and her family is as rich as the Shipmoores. The best our impoverished asses can hope for is to be set up in style while we attend school here. I haven't heard of anyone who isn't wealthy already snagging one of these guys long-term.

My heart drops into my stomach as I busy myself adjusting my dress and slipping my lip gloss into my pocket. Is that what I was to him? Just a warm body he could amuse himself with while he pursued his doctorate. Maybe that's why he didn't come back, maybe he found someone else or met an heiress.

I catch my reflection under the light and blush harder. Even though my skin is dark, the undertones make my cheeks rosy when I get upset. Never seen a Black girl blush beet red then you haven't met me. Thankfully no one notices as I make my way out of the bathroom.

On one side of me is a darkened corridor where I'm sure girls are auditioning in hopes of becoming girlfriends to the elite. In front of me is the ballroom, which I've had enough of thank you very much. To my right leads out to the gardens.

Deciding I could use a breath of fresh air I head toward the ornate double doors leading outside.

Thrusting them open I take a deep cleansing

breath of the jasmine and cherry blossom scented night air.

"I'm glad you finally decided to join me, Taylor-chan."

"Eep." I nearly jump out of my skin at the sound of the cold low voice coming from the shadows right before a heavy hand drags me into the dark alcove.

CHAPTER
THREE

T *aylor*

~

"DID YOU HAVE FUN TORMENTING ME?" he demands, whispering low in my ear. His hard body is pressed against every curve of my body. I feel a very distinct hardness pressing into the small of my back as he dips down whispering his menace into my ears.

His ragged breath causes warm puffs of air to tickle my lobe. I can't stop the accompanying shiver. His hands pressing just beneath my breasts tighten pressing me closer to him.

"Answer me," he growls.

"I-I umm... yes." I did have fun. Why lie about it? His hand curls into a fist bunching my dress. What happened to the gentleman who was my dinner companion? He's morphed into someone I don't know. I whimper. It's not from fear I belatedly realize.

My experience with men is nil. Still, I know this is not normal. This intensity is not what I'm used to. My parents are passionately in love but this? The edge of violence, coupled with my reaction to his ferocious focus on me, is so unnerving.

"You left. You said I would dance with you then you disappeared." My answer seems to appease him — a little. He releases my dress and starts to smooth circles just beneath my heavy breasts. Each brush of his fingers against the skin of my lower breasts has my body responding, my thighs clench as the ache from earlier returns with a vengeance. My nipples harden to an almost painful degree. They press against the silk chiffon as if begging for him to pay them the same attention as he's giving my upper tummy. The night air brushes against me heightening my senses. It takes me a moment to take in his words.

"I thought you'd follow me," he says in a grumpy way that indicates I should know what to do in situations like this — sneaking away from a gala for five hundred, Alex.

"Being a shortie makes it hard for me to find people in crowds." I shrug in a self-deprecating way.

He spins me around his eyes intensely roaming over my body from head to toe then back again before coming to rest on the twin protrusions begging for his touch. "You're perfect," he says, dragging his eyes back up to mine. "Absolutely perfect. May I kiss you, Taylor-chan."

My 'yes' is swallowed by his groan as his lips cover mine. He tastes like cinnamon and smoke. My toes curl as his soft lips drag over mine from side to side. His hands cup my face just beneath my jaw. He angles my head back.

"Open for me," he whispers.

I do. He claims me. His tongue delves into my eager mouth. His possession is no less intense by his gentle thoroughness. Wrapping my arms around his neck I draw him closer.

He groans, pulling me tighter, our bodies touching everywhere. I can feel the hard press of his dick as he lifts me to make our bodies fit. With one hand holding my waist and the other one beneath my body he holds me effortlessly, like my curves mean nothing against his incredible strength. I melt.

Losing myself, I don't resist as he takes my mouth like he owns me, hell like I owe him money. His tongue sweeps in. Tentatively I touch mine to his. A guttural groan rocks between us. Moisture blooms between my legs in an attempt to water my thirsty flower making it ready to be plowed by him. I press closer, forgetting everything — getting caught up and losing my fellow-ship and reputation, the fact I've never done anything remotely close to this, the fact we just met, and I know nothing beyond his name, his mom is mean as hell, his brother is aloof, and his dad is the peacemaker. I didn't even know he was in the doctorate program until Alexa told me. Those thoughts flit through my head but they don't take hold. It's like I can't catch them, it's like they are wisps of dandelions flying by on a spring day back home when I used to visit Shelby-Love, a brief distraction.

He deepens the kiss sucking my tongue into his mouth. Always a quick learner, I mimic his earlier actions. I sweep my tongue in the warm cavern of his mouth. Soon we are battling, sucking, savoring. He makes me take him. I suck on his tongue as he thrusts rhythmically into my mouth.

His dick kicks and I can't help rubbing against his throbbing hardness. It's like his body is the answer to every question my body has. His hard chest presses against my breasts, assuaging the ache there, while still holding the promise of more pleasure. His hard thighs against my soft ones are a foundation to build the sensual heat permeating from us. His strong arms hold me like it's nothing letting me know he's got me through this and if I want, he'll see me through to the end.

"And what will that end be silly, little girl?" I can almost hear my mother ask. "Being set up as some rich man's plaything? You were made for better, Taylor Miranda Love."

I pull back as the cold realization of what I'm doing drops over me like an ice bucket challenge.

"I'm sorry. I can't do this." I tap his shoulder, simultaneously pushing away at the same time.

His hard angular jaw flexes as he looks down at me. His onyx eyes hold a mystery only known to him.

"You don't have to apologize. Ore o yurushitekure." He bows, taking a couple steps away. Coolly closing his jacket, covering the bulge in his pants, his eyes unwavering he asks, "When can I see you again?"

Focus. I shake my head. "Umm, I don't that's a good idea," I hedge, the near miss of what I almost allowed with a complete stranger scaring me more than that *Exorcist* movie my cousin, Joi conned me into watching that one time. "I only came tonight because it was basically a requirement of the fellowship. The courses here are rigorous. I-I'm... my time is going to be spent writing and directing plays for the fall and spring season."

Why do I feel like I've been called into the principal's office? Why is my heart hurting at the thought of disappointing him?

"Give me your phone," he demands, holding out his hand in such expectation of my acquiesce I feel a compulsion to put it in his much larger hand.

His fingers close over it. He scrolls to my contacts. "Call or text me. If you need anything, I will be here for you. I won't lie and say I want to just be your friend, but if friend is all you can allow for now, I will play that role — for now."

Handing the phone back, his hand closes over mine. There is nothing gentle about him this time. Just short of bruising with the phone trapped between us he draws me close then closer still until our size difference is once again obvious. I curl into myself unable to withstand his intense scrutiny. He bends down whispering in my ear, "Know this, little dove, you are mine. Not will be. Are. You are mine. I will watch over you. I will take care of you. Always."

After pressing a kiss to my temple he releases me taking his warmth. I shiver but I know it's not from the loss of heat. Uncurling, I look at my contacts seeing what he put his name under: H✍.

Two weeks later...

"These are for you", the resident assistant says as soon as I enter the lobby. The fragrance of camellias and roses greets me as I walk up to the desk. There is a black card attached already opened by Ms. Nosey, here. I take it out knowing it will just have a monogrammed H in the center and nothing else.

Sticking it into the back pocket of my jeans, I give her a brief smile. "Thanks." I ignore the inquiry in her gaze. We are not friends. I have no friends here, only acquaintances. Alexa and the other fellowship students are cool, but most of them are in business and technology. All the people who get me are my fellow theater nerds. Only difference is our focuses diverge in a way that makes me doubt my chances of having my play picked as the one selected to be produced.

American theater's vision is one of hope and resilience, the cultural vision of my eastern colleagues is different. They believe in the cold reality of life when more than often despair prevails. Tragedies are often the theme. I've been admonished by my professors that I need to get with the program. I try to explain to them that my people prevailed through despair, Black Americans believe in overcoming adversity. Respectful as they are, they still have little patience for what one termed as a Pollyanna view of life that is trite at best.

Dropping my bag on my bed, I put my flowers on the desk. The others are starting to wilt and need to be thrown out. This man has my room smelling like a rose garden. The flowers began the day after the gala and continued every three days. He texts every morning at five a.m. The time I guess he gets up wishing me a good morning. Then again at night. He left me to the work I insisted came before everything. I'm sure he was busy with his. Every morning and evening, I respond out of politeness. At least that's what I tell myself.

How can I miss someone I've only met once? He left a massive impression kissing me the way he did. Making my body feel all kinds of naughtiness I've never had time to explore.

I can't help but think he found me gauche. He's the

scion of the Takeda family, one of the Tokyo elites. He obviously knows his way around a woman's body and I'm sure he could tell. I didn't know what I was doing. He must find me incredibly provincial. Naivete is cute but can become boring or irritating to the more experienced set. Maybe sending flowers is his way of slowly pulling away.

"If a man really wants you, you ain't gone get rid of him," my great-great aunt, Mama-Pete used to say when she sat on my grandmother's porch as they gossiped about some unfortunate girl chasing after some man. I never forgot that little nugget of wisdom.

Taking that into account, I put my new batch into fresh water. New determination fills me, thinking of how I can't allow a few bouquets of flowers to sway me. I grab my phone, texting him for the first time.

Me: The flowers are lovely. You don't have to keep sending them.

The reply is quick and the to the point.

H💍: You're welcome, little dove. I will.

I can't help but ask.

Me: Why?

Another quick reply.

H💍: You said you were too busy for more.

Several seconds go by as I read his words over and over the realization dawning that he's taken my words to heart. Working within the parameters of what I insisted I needed at that moment. He's letting me take the lead. As ludicrous as that sounds it causes warmth to fill me. He listened.

My fingers seem to move over the keys of their own volition.

Me: I know you are busy too.

H⟡: I will make time for you.

Me: 🫠I have to get to work. My professor hates my work so far. 😞

H⟡: I'm sure he's an idiot.

Me: LOLZ he is a four-time Kishida Prize winner.

H⟡: Don't let anyone make you doubt yourself, little dove. Learn from them then make it your own.

Me: I needed to hear that. Thx.

H⟡: I will always be here for you. Now get back to work, then rest.

I DON'T QUESTION how he knows exactly what I need. Over the course of the next few weeks our text conversations after my last class of the day become an integral part of my routine. I come to yearn to hear his voice instead of just his words. I make my biggest mistake one night, one that changes the course of my life or I think so, little did I know I never had a chance when it comes to Hisashi Takeda.

Me: I forgot how you sound.

H⟡: Really?

Me: Kidding

H: Did you forget how I look as well?
Me: As if

LATER THAT NIGHT as I'm snuggling into my bed for the night, my phone chimes and it never chimes. My parents and family FaceTime. I look at the icon seeing the familiar *H*. "Oh my goodness," I whisper to myself. Sitting up higher I croak, "Hiyo," trailing off feeling really silly and awkward.

"Taylor-Chan, I'm calling to wish you a good night since you've forgotten my voice." His voice sounds like thick caramel wrapped in sex and darkness. I can't help the shiver that makes me squeeze the covers closer.

"Hisashi, I was just being silly. I hope I didn't take you away from your work," I say, knowing he's told me how intense and delicate this program he's working on in association with the university and Takeda Industries that will revolutionize pest control worldwide without using dangerous toxins.

"I like the way you say my name, little dove." His serious tone fills the line. There is something I've missed I realize. He calls me little dove. He adds chan. He wants me to reciprocate. In the time I've been here the language has not been an issue, it's the nuances of tatemae. The unspoken language that you need to learn. What is not being said.

"I like the way you say my name too, Hisashi." His low chuckle makes my toes curls and pussy clench.

"Hai, little dove." I melt like a popsicle in the hot Alabama sun. His next words undo me.

"I need to see you. It seems I too have forgotten your face. Your lovely voice makes me want to see you again."

Immediately I regret my decision. What if I fall apart in his arms? The last time I came so close to forgetting myself entirely. Now he's had time to learn me. We've spent weeks texting back and forth sharing so much from what we ate that day, to books we like, down to his preferred software and hardware.

"We can FaceTime," I offer.

His silence tells me that's not what he wants. I can almost hear the recrimination in his voice when he concedes. "Let me know what time is good."

"I know you get up at five a.m. but I'm not up until seven," I tell him, mad at myself but still happy I am keeping some of my boundaries in place. I see a weakness I have when it comes to this man that I've never experienced with anyone else. It's not that I am a prude or ultra-religious. The way Hisashi made me feel nearly a month ago at the gala was so unique. Almost soul shattering. I can't lie. It changed me, challenged me, made me confront a part of myself I'm not sure I'm ready to see yet. That a man could do that to me. Had me shook. My foundation crumbled under his kiss, and I begged for more. Loved every moment of it until cold reality doused me. What will happen if I let him touch me again? Will I let him mold and shape me into someone I barely recognize? His pretty little toy ensconced in a Tokyo high-rise awaiting his every pleasure. The uptick in my heart rate lets me know that weak girl inside me would love it.

"As you wish, little dove," he speaks. And I can practically see him banging his head on a headrest or pillow in frustration.

"Unacceptable," Minamoto-sensei tells me, intense disapproval clouding his face.

"I will endeavor to do better, Sensei." I bow three times with my hands cupped in front of me. I have never failed at anything, least of all my writing.

"Too fanciful, nearly ridiculous in its execution. You cannot continue with this theme in your work, Love-san."

Heat flushes my skin. The humiliation is no less because of the in-office meeting. I'm sure the news will have spread. This is a competitive fellowship no different than those of STEM despite what Mrs. Takeda may have thought. The arts at this school are just as cutthroat.

"I will do better, Minamotto-sensai," I promise, head bowed.

"See that you do," he says boredly.

Bowing again I leave. Making a beeline out of the building I do my best to keep my composure and it works until I find myself walking straight into a deluge of rain. Looking up I let the cold rain cool my hot face as tears spill down my cheeks. I don't know how long I stand there until my shoulder is bumped.

"Oh, so sorry." I needn't have bothered apologizing, the person just throws up a hand and jogs into the rain.

Hair plastered to my head I know I'm going to catch my death if I stay out here. It's too slick out here to ride my bike to my room. "You're hitting on all cylinders, Tay." Muttering the sarcasm, I curse myself for not looking at the forecast.

My mind was tangled with the play I'm writing and the developmental meeting I had this morning. Hisashi did his best to calm me earlier over FaceTime, but I could barely concentrate on his words. It just so happens that the seven a.m. time I insisted on is just after his work out time. The last couple of weeks of seeing his body drenched in sweat as his tee-shirt clings to his beautiful body have been an exercise in agony. Today was leg day so he had on a double layer of shorts that did nothing to hide his muscled thighs and bulging dick print.

I may have even let a "Lord have mercy" slip much to his dismay and my embarrassment.

I hurried off the phone after wishing him a good morning.

Darkness dips around me and I feel my phone buzzing in my pocket. I know it's him but I can't risk answering it in this downpour. He'll understand me calling him later. The times of our calls have long since stretched beyond the time of the gala.

I have even fallen asleep a couple times on Face-Time with him, only to wake to see him reading having never hung up.

"I like watching over you," was his reply, and I thought it was the sweetest, most amazing thing.

I'm about a block away from my dorm when a sleek diamond black Rolls Royce comes alongside me. My tummy dips when it slows down coming to stop several feet ahead of me. I'll have no choice but to walk by or cross the busy thoroughfare. My brain scrambles as I try to figure out how I can politely decline the ride.

The driver gets out, opens a huge umbrella, and comes around to the back passenger side. I stop when a tall figure gets out with a long black coat draped over his arm. I know before he turns toward me who it is. I could never forget that tall wiry form, the length of his arms, or those hard thighs.

Taking an involuntary step back when I see the dark anger on his face, I can't figure out why relief and fear mingle inside my chest. Something in me tells me to stop moving, not because I feel assured, it's like prey trapped under the gaze of a predator who has her locked in his sights.

Anger and fierce determination are in every line of

his face, every step he takes my way. When they reach me, there is finally a reprieve from the storm raging, but why do I feel I'm about to be swept up in a tsunami? Hisashi takes my bags then wraps the heavy coat around my shoulders, wrapping a long arm around me, pulling me into his side.

Slowly the three of us make our way to the Rolls Royce. The driver expertly maneuvers us around to open the door, getting no one wet. Both men wait as I get situated in the luxurious confines of the car, doing my best trying not to soak the interior. Hisashi slides soundlessly in beside me.

Seconds later the driver slips behind the wheel. We pass my dorm.

"Um..." My head swivels looking as we zoom past my room.

"Quiet, little dove. You will let me take care of you." He drags me into his arms, stroking my drenched curls. Too emotionally and physically tired, I let him.

CHAPTER FOUR

T *aylor*

◆

WE ARE STILL ON CAMPUS, but it is an area I've never visited. The lobby has a doorman. Immediately, I can tell this is where the wealthiest students live. The foyer exudes luxury and exclusivity. After a whispered exchange with the driver, Hisashi leads me to the elevator. He walks close to me but the touching and pulling me into his arms like in the Rolls Royce is gone.

Shivering in the elevator, I miss his warmth. We are both silent, standing apart facing the mirrored interior of the elevator. The ride up is swift, but I can't take my gaze away from his sleek masculine form. He exudes sensuality and dark menace. The polite dinner guest may as well have been a figment of my imagination. The smooth lover of that night is gone as well. The kind, curious about every aspect of my life phone and FaceTime companion is gone as well. How many faces does he have? All those other people were the outer layers. Something tells me this dark, inscrutable stranger is the true Hisashi Takeda.

The doors swoosh open to a loft style apartment that could compete with any *Architectural Digest* layout. The entire skyline is illuminated in the ceiling. There is a wall of floor to ceiling windows. It's obvious that's where his lab is if the array of computers and whiteboards are any indication. The area has no chairs, only standing desks and one ergonomic ball with a base.

"Sit," he instructs, pointing to the gaiken. I sit. Before I have a chance to bend to remove my shoes, he gets down on his hunches. He cups my left foot his hand pulling my shoe off. Then switches to the other foot doing the same. He turns the shoes upside down looking at me while he does it, pouring water from them his expression bland before sitting them upside down on a drying rack.

"You'd prefer to drown than call me," he tsks, his disappointment pulling his beautifully cruel mouth down in a severe arch.

"N-no—" The look he shoots me makes me snap my chattering lips closed.

"Stand-up," he snaps rising. His tone brooks no

argument but I don't like it. Slowly, I rise but no sooner than I do is he stripping my clothes from me.

"Woah." I hold up a trembling hand staying him. He drops his hands clenching them at his sides. "I got it. Can you get me a robe or something?"

"Hai," he says. Striding away, his jaw flexes like I've insulted him or something.

I realize my mistake the moment I try to unbutton the first button. My hands are trembling so badly I can hardly control them enough to get them to my shirt. My fingers are so numb I have to squeeze them hard a couple of times to bring feeling back into them. Precious seconds pass before I finally get the first one done.

I'm just finishing the second when he comes back with robes and towels. He hands over mine. I look up into his somber expression, nodding, moving my hand from the shirt.

He makes quick work of my blouse, pulling it from my jeans. He gives me a towel to cover myself, turning me away from him unsnapping my bra. My breasts feel heavy when they fall free. Shrugging, I let the lace prison fall down my arms. Reaching around he takes it adding it to the pile.

"Turn around, please." His voice sounds disconnected from the moment like he's trying to hold himself apart.

When I move back around his fingers slip into my waistband, unsnapping my jeans. I suck my belly in when I feel his breath on me as he drops down to work them down.

His eyes are locked on my plump tummy. He pauses when he realizes I'm not wearing panties. He bites his lip, then his gaze skates up my body and his eyes meet mine in a brief hot moment before I make myself look away. A blush is burning my cheeks. I press my freezing hands to my face. I should have warned him. I don't know how I forgot.

"I'm sorry," I whisper, horror clouding my every word.

"I'm not," he mutters to himself but I can still hear.

Slowly, he pulls the wet material down my thighs until it reaches my feet and I'm able to step free.

Rising he tosses the wet jeans on top of the other material. "Don't worry. I'll have the staff dry clean them and have them ready by the time you're ready to leave.

"Follow me, please." He's not seen to any of his needs. I follow him to what I immediately realize is his bathroom.

He stops at the door. "Everything you need is here." He waves me inside.

After I step past him, he steps back, and the door closes automatically. The room is immaculate. If cleanliness is close to godliness, then surely, he's going to heaven. Sleek counters and a multi-head shower head's platinum sparkle are offset by steel gray stone.

Placing the robe he loaned to me on the bench near

the soaking tub, I look longingly at it for a moment thinking how I wished I didn't have to wash my hair but knowing I can't risk not taking care of it tonight.

When I step in the alcove, the water automatically comes on. A heavy spray hits my body in a massaging beat. "Ohmygoodness," I moan in rapture, making a slow turn to let the water hit aching tired muscles I didn't know I had.

I recall telling him how often I wish I had a better shower than the dorm issued one. If I knew he had what I longed for I would've already come for a visit and finagled a way to stay over. I giggle a little to myself thinking of how I can make the excuse in the future. His whole set-up is divine. The ultimate bachelor pad.

I pause pumping the unscented but thick soap into the soft brand-new sponge he placed on the inset shower shelf. He seems very comfortable with me in his space. He must have guests all the time. I don't know why but realizing I'm one of many dampens my mood. Why that is when he never made me promises, makes me feel a little sick. He only said I was his. He never said he was mine. Typical man. I wouldn't be surprised if he had several "mines".

After washing my body the necessary two times, I take a skeptical look at the shampoo and the conditioner. Not having a choice, I depress the button twice to get a generous amount. I sniff then sniff again. It smells exactly like mine, I realize as I rub the lather into my hands and hair. I wonder of the chances of a Japanese billionaire using the exact same shampoo and conditioner that I, a Black American fellowship student, uses. That would be none.

Were the dossiers they received that thorough? Did he know my cycle? Good because I needed all the help I could get with that wonky monster.

After rinsing the conditioner and moisturizing in another unscented thick body butter, I pick up another robe off the warmer as I go over to the sink. In the inlaid counter is a toothbrush the exact replica of the one I own, and my preferred toothpaste. A knock has me turning to the door, answering, "Come in."

He steps in freshly showered and shaven. He's wearing black silk lounge pants and a long-sleeve black t-shirt. I snatch my head back to the mirror when I see the way his dick is swinging with every step he takes in my direction. Taking in my blush and wide eyes I cast my eyes down just as he comes to stand beside me. "I thought you might need these for your hair."

"Thanks," I say, looking into the basket placed before me. Inside is a super soft cotton pj set in my size which is not even found in this country.

"Where did you get all these?" I ask. Again, the exact products I use.

"I made some calls." He shrugs. "There is an American military post here you know." Yes, I know, but it's not close. He'd have to make that call a while ago. Not today.

"When you're done, we'll eat." He gives me a small smile reeking of self-satisfaction.

After twenty minutes of detangling and moisturizing, I defuse my hair just enough so that it's not dripping. Normally I wouldn't put any heat on my hair at all but I'm already freezing. Going to bed with my head wet has never been my thing and after the drama of today that's the last thing I want.

Taking a last-minute look, I notice how my nipples protrude through the material. I pull the robe around me, so I don't risk poking his eyes out.

"Have a seat." He stands as I approach the sofa. The seating is deep. The material feels like velvet but is actually a brushed cotton or soft linen, obviously custom. The seating is so deep should I sit all the way back with my back to the cushions, only my ankles would reach past the edge.

I resist the urge to curl around the soft pillows and sleep. My grumbling tummy will probably have something to say about it as well.

The aromas wafting from the steaming dishes have me sitting up straighter. He places the dishes in front of me before disappearing behind a wall I assume houses his kitchen. He comes back out with empty bowls, cutlery, chopsticks, and spoons.

Placing all the items between us to allow me to pick what I prefer to use, he sits beside me and starts serving me. First, he spoons a thick creamy soup into a bowl and hands it to me. "Arigato, Hisashi." My trembling smile draws his gaze. His attention remains on me for a moment, but he doesn't press me.

"Iie, iie." He waves away my thanks. "Eat." He takes his soup, blowing it to cool it a little before covering it with his gorgeous lips.

I turn my attention to my own food, bringing my spoon to my lips. I blow like he did and the moment I do I'm in heaven. It's delicious. Never one to be shy to eat my hunger kicks in and I waste no time devouring the savory combinations of clams, mushrooms, and other delicious things I can't name or be bothered to ask my host. All I know is I love this soup.

When I'm done, I dab both corners of my mouth doing a double take when I see the arrested look on his face. Shoot. Did I break some cardinal rule?

It's not shock or dismay in his eyes though but appreciation. His mouth quirks a little on the side. He hands me another bowl with rice, opens several containers that smell just as fragrant and lovely as the first, and adds them to small plates in front of me. I think it's a waste of dishes but who am I to complain when the food is top-tier?

I giggle when he hands me each new item, the calamari edges are crispy and garlicky, the braised vegetables have a tangy sauce I've never tried before. "I never liked duck until just now," I say, humming around the succulent meat that's been barbecued.

"It's so good," I add for emphasis, and he gives me more.

I needn't worry that I'm outeating him though. This man can put away some food. He eats twice as much as I do and that's a conservative estimate.

I'm stuffed and we've barely made a dent in all the food. "I'm so full," I tell him, taking a sip of the sparkling water.

"Good, I've been worried if you were getting enough to eat with your schedule and the offerings of the campus cafeterias." Taking up the dishes and shaking his head "no," when I attempt to help, he adds, "You could've been having this all along."

"The cafeteria has great chefs. We get a lot of variety," calling after him I pull my robe tighter snuggling into the ultra-deep sofa.

I'm full, close to being sleep drunk when he comes back taking the corner. He stretches his legs out.

"Come here, Tay-chan. I will hold you now," he says with a quiet intensity that has me climbing over the cushions and settling against his hard chest.

"You smell so delicious." I breathe against his chest. He smells toe-curling good, like tobacco, flower, citrus, and something almost like cinnamon.

"If you say so," he scoffs a little, burying his head in my hair. "Now, you smell like my next best meal."

"Boy, hush." I giggle but I rub my hand up and down his arm. Then I look up into warm onyx eyes and whisper, "Thank you for picking me up."

"You're going to see very soon, little dove I always will. You're welcome." He bends his head down. "Give me those beautiful lips."

I want to tell him he's the one with the beautiful lips but he's already kissing me with long intoxicating pulls. My toes are curling now, my insides are clenching. Soon, I'm turning as much as the position will allow so that I can get more of him and give him better access to me.

His arms tighten around me as he angles his mouth over mine taking the kiss deeper. His tongue licks into mine. Not needing to be shown what to do this time I suck on his tongue like he taught me before. He groans rubbing my back in encouragement and praise. My answering whimper has him drawing me higher over his body until we are aligned.

My body is flushed with his. His hardness presses against my pussy and I can't help my body's reaction. He feels so good, so hard. He feels like mine.

Slowly he rocks against me, assuaging and intensifying the ache. I'm slick with need. I press kisses along his jaw. His aftershave has me craving more of him. His touch has me ready to beg for the unknown promise his body is tempting me with.

Hands stroke down my back until he's cupping my bottom pulling me against him. The way he fits against me is perfection. I grind against him.

"Hai, like that little dove. Give me that pussy." He kisses me in encouragement pulling back to look at my face. I want to bury my face into his chest and neck again.

I feel too open to his assessing gaze, too vulnerable to his demands.

"You're so beautiful to me." He pulls me close, taking my lips. "So lovely in every way," he tells me before dipping his head in my neck and sucking the skin there in strong steady pulls.

"Mine," he growls low, making me shudder as he rubs against me. I'm so close. I know the feeling, but I've never had the feeling with anyone — only alone. I'm scared. What if it's weird? What if he can tell I never — Would it matter? Is it a turnoff? I'm almost twenty. I never regretted anything more than I do right now.

Figuring I should just do it, I lean further into him. He takes my offering like it's his just due. Right before he pulls away, he sits up reaching inside his pants to adjust his erection. Before giving me a rueful look.

"I can see your mind working a thousand miles an hour." He scrubs his face. "I'm sorry. You've had a hard day." Rubbing his hand through his hair, he makes it stand on end.

Reaching out I smooth it down. He grabs my hand kissing my palm. "Will you stay?" His eyes are beseeching me in a way the man can never allow himself to.

"Yes."

He takes me up the stairs into the bedroom. I've

never felt this close to the stars except when I was at the observatory in Birmingham Southern College or at the Space Center in Huntsville when my parents took me home on visits.

His bed is in the center of the room. A blue so dark it may as well be black.

"You love the stars." My voice is hushed. This room seems like a sacred space for him. The bed is elegant and smooth like him. The wood is smooth dark teak or mahogany. I can't tell in the low luminescence. It's a traditional low frame sitting on what looks to be a solid wood frame. The mattress loft gives it a height. It comes to just below my thighs. It smells like him but more intimate. There is a low table beside the bed with nothing but a single book on it. The room is minimalist. No clutter. Everything meticulously put away. Hidden, whispers in the back of my mind. Yet what would he need to hide from me? I'm no one to him. *Yeah, he totally came out in that downpour for no one,* whispers my overeager for something more inner me.

"They bring me peace. Have since I was a child." He looks at the stars, his face awash with the peace he speaks of and pure, unadulterated joy. Then he turns back to me. "You can rest here. I still have some work to do. There's a headscarf on the table." He's already moving to the stairs missing the way my mouth falls open.

I want to badly to ask him to stay. And do what?

63

"Well, goodnight," I say, letting the words trail off almost sounding like a question.

"Goodnight." He gives an absent wave, his mind seemingly on his work.

I pull the thick cover back. Falling back on the pillow, the crush of my curls reminds me to tie my hair up.

Just as I knot it at the top I hear his low voice. He's talking to someone. I almost stop breathing just so I can hear what's being said. Even though his dialect has changed, it takes me more than a few seconds to pick up on what he's saying in the rapid-fire exchange.

Finally, I catch chichi and know he's talking to his dad. Something about taking medicine. Is he reminding his father to take his medicine? Then he wouldn't be any different than me and Mom getting on my dad about taking his high blood pressure meds and him grumbling he's tired of getting up at night only to have me snap back that he better or he won't be getting up at all.

Soon the quiet and twinkling stars in the night sky have me drifting off to sleep.

I'm not sure what wakes me. A sound, being too comfortable — despite finding an excellent featherbed my extra-long twin is nothing compared to this enormous piece of heaven.

Flipping the cover back, I immediately miss the warmth as I get up from the bed and head to the lower part of the loft.

Hisashi is still working seeming so focused on his work as I walk up to him.

"You should be resting," he says, not looking up from the code he's inputting at a speed defying pace..

"I will when this is done." Tucking my hands under my arms, I'm already second- guessing myself.

He types one line of code after another one with ease. I watch him fascinated, though I understand none of what he's doing.

"Where?" I'm feeling brave now that those all too knowing eyes aren't boring into me.

He pauses.

"Where will you sleep?" I hurry to ask before I lose my courage.

"There is another room off the kitchen. But I'll probably take the sofa. It wouldn't be the first time."

I can tell by his demeanor he's not changing his mind. I feel like he's dismissing me.

"I miss you not holding me," I blurt out, cringing. I turn away mortified, but he tugs me back.

"Come here, little dove." He pulls me onto his hard thighs. His arms cage me in as he starts typing more code. I listen to his heartbeat and his swift movement over the keys.

My head is fully turned into his chest when he whispers, "Come, let me put you to bed." Shutting down his computer, he pulls me to my feet. He pushes me ahead of him as we take the stairs.

He tucks me into the bed pressing a kiss on my

brow. When he moves to leave, I grab his hand. His fingers curl around mine for a brief moment before he disengages.

My heart feels like it's caving in. I turn into the pillow, embarrassed by his rejection.

The bed dips on the other side. Hisashi slides under the covers to the center and pulls me closer. He whispers, "I'm going to keep you," as he curves his long body around mine.

And he did.

CHAPTER
FIVE

T *aylor*

~

As I watch Hisashi's driver pull up my hands twist
nervously. The cold chill in the air whips around my legs. I
feel it all the way up to my bottom in this dress I have on.
Hisashi steps out looking every bit of the heir to a billion
Yen fortune. He's attired in a black tuxedo with a
midnight blindingly white dress shirt. The cut of his
jacket is cut high and severely to fit his tall frame. The only
hint of color is the thinnest of royal purple stripes in his tie
and his cufflinks that sport cubed purple diamonds. It is a
subtle acknowledgement we are together.

My dress is black velvet with a chiffon overlay

studded with purple crystals. It's the most stunningly expensive item I have ever worn. If it weren't for my concern of not wanting to embarrass the man who'd come to mean more to me than anything besides my family and my work, I would have refused this far too generous gift.

The tickets to the opening night of the theater would have been enough, but then he said, "You will be my family's guest." When he whispered later as he held me, "family," meant his entire family, including his parents and his cousin, the official head of the family, I would have fainted were we not already in bed and him holding me closely.

"It's time for the world to know you are mine, little dove." He pulled me under him then. Kissing me in longing, drugging pulls. That night we came so close to finally making love but for the innumerable time he pulled back even though my eyes stung in frustration when he got up to take care of his needs. The next morning, I woke with him cupping my mound possessively as he did every morning since our first night together. I let him hold me. I felt so safe with him. He's never pushed. Even when his needs obviously overwhelmed him. I don't know how the situation got away from me. It's like he's waiting for me. I know he is. I want to say I'm ready and to a point I am but there's something that makes the hairs on my neck rise when I allow myself to look past the fascination I have for him and get a peek at his intensity. Obsession, my mind whispers.

"You look beautiful, Tay-chan." He bows deeply after he comes to stand before me. Smiling I return with my own, "You look very handsome too, Hisashi." Stepping behind me he ushers me to the car. I slip inside. The privacy glass is already up. As soon as the door closes behind him, he leans over me cupping the back of my head. He draws me close to him. His lips are a soft welcome.

"I missed you," I say when he pulls back. Reaching up I swipe away the lip gloss staining his lips. It would be considered very unseemly for him to show up with lip gloss on his lips and would probably cause a minor scandal. Not to mention make his mother dislike me more than she seemed to the night of the scholar's gala.

"Good." He smirks with a roguish tilt of his lips. "Now you know how I feel every moment you leave the loft."

"I haven't been back to my dorm room since the night of the baby tsunami." Now he really chuckles shaking his head.

"That wasn't a tsunami. I hope you never have to see one." He lifts my chin then. "But if you do, I will keep you safe." The promise in his words makes me believe him. I know he will.

"I believe you." Leaning in, I want to reassure him of my faith in him.

He clears his voice. "You better." He turns to face forward. "Otherwise, the next hundred years would be very awkward."

I can't believe my ears. He's talking about forever. "Very." I scoot as close to him as I can, tucking my arm under his and resting my head on his shoulder.

"Courage," he whispers, as he helps me out of the Rolls Royce. Lights flash all around us and soon they intensify when they see who is with one of the scions of the Takeda Dynasty. Murmurs are added to the flashes as the members of elite and very homogenous Japanese society notice the lone Black girl entering their ranks.

Hisashi leads a step ahead of me but there is no mistaking we are walking together. He even moderates his stride, so he doesn't leave me. As we approach the rest of his family, I see several amused looks, one from his father, a tall, beautiful, svelte older woman who's accompanied by three equally handsome men, whose younger selves I've seen in several pictures among Hisashi few pictures.

Takeda-sama looks on with kind indulgence. His brother, Kiyoshi, looks on with curiosity but no malice. Their mother, however, is livid. So much so that her cheeks burn red with anger and her eyes flash with so much animus I almost take a step back.

"It is so good to see you, aunt," Hisashi addresses the obvious matriarch of the family. "I have been very remiss in not coming to visit, my studies are not even significant enough to excuse this failing. You must forgive your thoughtless nephew." He bows deeply to the woman.

Her smile is gentle. "Hisashi, you know you are my most favored nephew." She quirks a look at Kiyoshi. "And even my own sons can learn several things about your excellent manners and consideration. Now, who is this young woman you have brought for me to meet?"

"Dear aunt," he says with all sincerity and a gravity that is lost on no one. "May I present for your consideration, Taylor Love from Washington DC. Her father Thomas Love is a former ambassador to our country and her mother, Lilly is a philanthropist." He bows deeply and I follow. Speaking clearly I say, "You honor me, Lady Takeda."

There is a hard pulse. Rising to the shocked silence I watch the expressions on every Takeda's face as they take in the fact that Hisashi isn't just introducing me as his girlfriend. He's declaring his intention to marry me in front of his entire family.

The breath is sucked out of my body, it takes everything in me not to look his way. Now, I realize he wasn't just saying sweet things. He meant every word. *"I'm going to keep you."* The fact that I'm not afraid, I'm not thinking I'm too young. Somehow, I know he will make it alright. We will make it work.

"You've always known your own mind, nephew." Lady Takeda nods her assent before turning on her oldest son's arm and leading the family into the theater.

I glance at Hisashi to see him looking at me with unhidden emotion. Dark intensity is electric between us. We can't touch but I want more than anything to touch him right now. I want to kiss him, love him, give my body to him.

It's not until we are seated and the house lights go down that I feel his strong hand covering mine, his fingers slip between mine.

"I didn't tell you earlier Tay-chan because I knew you would overthink it. I meant what I said when I said you were mine. I want to be yours too."

I squeeze his hand in return. "You already are."

THE RIDE back to his loft is quiet and intense. There was almost a scene with his mom demanding he come visit them tonight. It was already past eleven, so he told her he would be by tomorrow after he and I got back from an excursion.

Hisashi, his father, and brother had an intense closed in conversation outside of the car. From what I gather from the people passing and trying so hard not to be seen looking at the intense conversation was so out of the norm.

The thick glass kept me from hearing a clear word. I could to some degree see Hisashi was having to fight for us. His brother seemed the one with the most intensity. Their dad rounded on Kiyoshi at one point with his older brother countering saying he was deluding himself and it would all fall at his feet. He threw up his hands barely giving both men brief barely respectable bows before storming off.

Hisashi gets in the car cold and silent. He doesn't look at me but out the window, his jaw working hard like he's trying to bite through a jawbreaker.

The car stops, he turns to me his eyes almost dead. "I'm not in a good place. I will have Kogi take you back to your dorm."

"No," I say. "I want to be here for you." I reach for him, but he takes his hand away crushing my feelings in the process.

"Taylor, you will go back to your dorm," he says, opening the door stepping out into the night.

"Hisashi—" He slams the door in my face.

He may as well have hit me. I sit there stunned for the entire trip to my dorm.

My mind doesn't even come back to me until the car stopping registers. I don't move when the door opens. I keep my eyes trained in front of me. "Take me back, please. I don't even have my key," I say.

"I have my orders, Miss." He holds his hand out to me.

"So, what happens when I walk back in the dark in this dress and heels?" A big meaty hand curls in frustration. "I thought so," I say with a smugness I don't feel. This is a terrible manipulation. And I kind of hate myself for it. Not to mention I'm doing the very thing I'd been admonished to never do — chase a man. It doesn't matter that he's hurting. He didn't want me around.

I can see the driver is on the phone calling him. I resolve just to get my keys and go back to my dorm. What happened between his brother and dad changed something in him. Did they remind him that I'm not rich, obviously not from their culture. He knows who I am and everything about me, down to my preferred soap. If their opinions can shake him at this stage, then we definitely won't last a century like he claims. It was nothing but daydreams and butterfly kisses.

He's standing outside with my keys and backpack when the car pulls to a stop. I don't wait for the driver. I open the door, watching his eyes flare when I hop out, storming over to him.

"Don't call me again." Jerking my backpack out of his hand, I reach for my keys attempting to tug them away.

His hand covers mine. "Stop," he says with a harshness I've never heard from him before.

I still.

"Just stop, okay?" He sounds so anguished. I turn my hand over. He cups mine with his keys trapped between us. Pulling me behind him, he leads me to the elevator as we enter the building. He seems uncaring if anyone sees us holding hands in such an intimate manner. This is not his way and definitely goes against the tradition of his strict family. But then seeming to get himself under control, he releases his grip but keeps my keys as the elevator dings. Shoving them into his pocket he nods me on ahead of him.

The elevator ride to his loft is vastly different than the last time. We stand as far apart as possible. The air is charged with an energy I can't decipher. It's like it's taking everything in him to keep himself from exploding. In the time apart he's changed into workout clothes. Into a tight-fitting Henley and long fitted workout pants; he has loose basketball shorts over them.

I'm standing in the corner, and he's braced his arms behind him gripping the handles seething looking at me through the reflective glass. The doors open with a quiet hiss into the gaiken of his loft.

"If you didn't want me to come back—" My words halt when I see he's on his knees before me. He takes my shoes off, placing them neatly in the place that's now become mine. His head is level with my belly. "Ore o yurushitekure," he apologizes roughly into my tummy. His head buries there. "I just don't want to hurt you, Tay-chan. Not by accident. Never on purpose. Do you understand?" He looks up at me, his eyes pleading.

I nod. "I know there is a little darkness in you," I start.

He scoffs, muttering, "Little."

Spearing my fingers through his hair, I tell him, "I

want all of you, Hisashi. We all have bad days. I don't just deserve your good days. I want to be there for your bad days, just like you were there for me on the baby tsunami day." Bending, I press a soft kiss on his forehead.

"You have no idea what you're saying," he hisses, nuzzling the breasts I've put too close to his face.

"Show me." Hearing the challenge in my voice, I almost take it back. I don't know what I'm doing. He's never touched me beyond holding me at night. I've never seen his body naked nor he mine. I wait a beat, swallowing back the trepidation clawing at the back of my throat telling me to stop before I embarrass both of us with my inexperience.

He waits a beat. Then he's pulling the material of the bodice down freeing my breasts. Moving closer, it's like he inhales me. Like he wants to savor this moment. He stretches his mouth covering one whole areola, while his other big hand covers the other.

My face heats. I freeze. My fingers tremble when I place them on his shoulders. Briefly, I wonder if he can feel the way they are shaking. Can he tell I'm scared?

My knees nearly buckle as he worships my breasts. Sucking them in tandem then pushing until they mesh to suck them together. He licks and laves me.

My tummy dips. My pussy clenches begging to finally be filled.

"Please," I say, watching him from my position

looking down at the way he's loving on me. My fingers are now flexing, urging.

With one last delicious suck he lets them pop free. They are dark brown looking like chocolate morsels. My nipples stand out in attention begging for more and it doesn't seem like he can resist because he's back at it licking them, lavishing pleasure upon me like it's his mission.

Cupping his head, I hold him there wanting to sink down on the floor. When I try to, he cups my bottom coming to his height bringing me up with him.

"Wrap your legs around me, little dove," he commands, holding my bottom.

Doing as he instructs, I wrap my thick thighs around his lean waist.

When he starts walking, I feel every inch of him rubbing against my soaked pussy.

"Fuck, little dove. I can feel how much you need me to fill this sweet little kitty up."

I guess he figures we won't make it to the bed because he lays me on the sofa.

Falling back, I bounce. My heart hammers. I don't know how I feel about my first-time making love being on my boyfriend's sofa.

He pulls away looking down at me. His eyes rake over all of me. Wanting to squirm from the heat of his gaze, I force myself to be still, to draw on the confidence drilled into me by a mother who taught me to love my curves and my unique beauty.

His eyes get hotter as he takes me in from crown to tummy. I feel beautiful as I see how hard he's getting by just looking at me. Like I am everything he ever wanted to eat in his life.

Grabbing the arms of the dress he tugs it down my arms. I help him with a little shimmy when he reaches my torso, happy to be free of the built-in shapewear compressing my curves. Down and off he drops the dress like he didn't just spend thousands on the couture piece.

"We're going to talk about you never wearing panties," he growls, his eyes trained on my thigh-high silk stockings, tracing up the juncture of my thighs to my nest of curls. His eyes look at the soft hair covering me. His jaw works. His hands curl into fists like he's trying to hold himself back.

"The dress had a built-in bra and shaper," I try to explain.

"This is not the first time," he reminds me running his hands from my ankles to thighs. "I think I'll let you keep these on." He nods to the black silk encasing my thighs.

Leaning over me, he brings his hard body flush with mine. "This is the point of no return, Tay-chan. If you give yourself to me tonight, if I give you all of me. It will be forever. Tell me now."

He dips his head close to my ear. "But I can't promise I will honor your request, little dove if you try to deny me. You see, you already own my soul." He tugs my ear sucking my lobe in his mouth making me shiver.

I should know better. I should not be saying yes to this. It's too fast. He's too intense. But my brain takes a backseat to the warmth in my heart and the hot need in my body.

Turning my face, I meet his lips. Spearing my tongue in his mouth, I make him groan when I tangle my tongue with his. His mouth covers mine. With gentle pulls, he draws me further into his mouth, savoring me. I swept away like I've only read about in books before now. His mouth is warmth, he tastes like mint and smoke. Our tongues battle and suck, the intensity lessening to a savoring. Pleasure makes me moan. My heart seems to fill with an emotion that can only be adoration. I adore him. He feels like mine, and I am his. I know more than anything I want to be his in every way. I want Hisashi to have all my firsts.

He settles between my legs. I feel him pressed so deep and hard against my pussy but it assuages nothing. He's only making me ache more. I arch my hips. His dick is so hard through his pants. I try to grind. He shakes his head. "I need your words, little dove."

"Yes." Squirming I try to feel more of him. Deeper. I need him deeper. He strokes his still clothed dick between my slick lips hitting me just where I need him to. I'm so sensitive. I feel so alive. I crave this. Him.

"Look at the way you're wetting me up," he says, looking down where our bodies meet. He angles me up, so I can see him gliding. I can see his hard dick rubbing against my saturated curls. His pants glisten with my essence. I should be embarrassed, but the sight only makes me want him more.

"So wet for me." He slowly rocks. I meet him stroke for stroke. Gradually I pick up my pace, unable to stop if I wanted to and I definitely don't want to. He meets my eagerness with his own.

"Come for me pretty girl, so I can taste your come." His words trigger my immediate response. I come soaking him. He groans before bending and drawing my thigh over his shoulder.

His mouth is hot as he covers me, burying his face in my curls. He sucks my clit into his mouth with a slow tug, swirling his tongue in a deliciously filthy way. Heat rushes to my face as I think of how exposed I am to him. My whole sugar cake is in this man's face. I cover my face, embarrassed beyond belief. "Ohmygoodness," I squeak. He's going lower and deeper. He's licking inside me. I squeeze my legs, trying to close them.

A sharp smack on my outer thigh makes liquid gush from me and a rough "Iie," and he shakes his head in the negative. "Don't hide this beautiful kitty from me, little dove. Let me kiss her, pet her, fuck her like she's begging me."

My lower tummy clenches in anticipation of his words.

"Orewa omaeto fakku shitai," he says against my eager flesh. But I need to get you ready for me.

I want him to fuck me, but I don't use his words. Instead, I let my legs fall open giving him all the access he wants. I'm his to do what he wishes. And it seems like his only wish is to please me.

He licks into the opening of my pussy over and over before pushing my lips together and sucking them as one. The sensation of pressure against my trapped clit makes my eyes roll, little shocks of pleasure turn into a crescendo when he releases my little nub and starts flicking it with fast swipes of his tongue. The pleasure is so intense I try to back away, but he holds me down pressing my belly making me take his vicious tongue lashing. My body explodes in a sharp piercing orgasm, I'm screaming his name like a chant and curse.

"Hi-sha-" The strangled plea of my words is cut off when he claims my lips making me taste myself on his lips. His mouth covers mine. His kiss is a claiming. Almost brutal in its primal ferocity.

"Do you give yourself to me forever, Taylor Love?" He asks when he finally releases me. His eyes hold an intensity that both frightens and exhilarates me. "Hai, Hisashi Takeda, I'm yours forever."

His eyes light up with a fervor like I've never seen. "Even though we haven't said the words, you are my wife now. I will take care of you. I will honor you for as long as there is breath in my body."

He cups my face placing a gentle kiss on my lips before rising. He stands pulling his Henley over the hard ridges of his torso, up over his head, finally freeing his hands and dropping it to the floor.

It takes me a minute to realize what I am seeing. It's not until he bends pulling down his basketball shorts and pants together that I get a clear view. My breath catches at the sight of the most amazing clash of colors of jade and purple, black and red for each viper brought together in a full body tattoo.

Beginning at his ankles, twin king cobras twist around his body in an intricate pattern. The one leg is covered in jade and purple, each scale delineated and made to look as if it is constricting his long, muscled limbs. The red and black is much the same. I lean closer to see platinum around each scale, highlighting the pattern. At his waist, the serpents intertwine, overlapping in a dance of passion or battle. It's clear it's left up to the observer's interpretation. I decide I want it to be a dance of passion. They drape over his shoulders, their broad heads reared back with fierce snarls meeting in the center of his chest, their fangs bared as they are fighting for dominance. Their eyes gleam with ferocity. Yet I still think it's a battle of love, or at least I want it to be.

The only part of him not marked is his hard jutting dick rising high past his navel, listing a little to the right.

"Wow." I snap my mouth closed, looking up into

his serious gaze. He seems to be waiting. "May I see your back?" His back is a myriad of colors; jade and purple, black and red for each snake. The pattern is so intricate, yet you can clearly see each serpent, though their bodies are locked together. They are one, but clearly two, different entities.

"Wow." The awe in my voice is obvious. I never thought I'd date a guy with tattoos, let alone marry one with full body art.

"How long did it take?"

He turns back, his dick losing none of its hardness. He gives me a cryptic smile. "Too long."

"Why am I just now seeing it?" The fact that he's been sleeping beside me for over a month and I never saw even a hint of it is a little unnerving. I thought nothing of him coming to bed in his pajamas that covered his entire body.

"It is an old school Takeda tradition. Only our wives see our tattoos. No one is allowed to see us like this outside of our family unit. It is forbidden." My eyes round, my heart thuds. He is so fucking serious.

His expression intensifies. "If you think about leaving me now, think again, Tay-chan," he says coolly. There is an undercurrent of something — more of a deeper, unhinged quality to his words, making the hairs on my nape rise. My hind brain sounds the alarm, but I have no intention of leaving him.

"What if you change your mind? Forever is a long time." Not for a minute do I doubt my loyalty. "Loves stick." Like my daddy always says. "People get divorced all the time." I give him a challenge of my own. He's not the only one who can demand assurance.

His heavy hand presses between my breasts, pushing me back until I'm lying on the cushions. "Takeda's don't. Ever."

He follows me down, his face holding an almost scary intensity. "I knew what you were to me from moment I first laid eyes on you."

"What's that?" I manage to squeeze the words out as he settles heavily between my thighs.

"Forever." He takes my mouth in a long drugging kiss that leaves me panting.

I pepper kisses along his neck, sucking his skin into my mouth. Running my tongue along his bristly jaw, nipping his skin with teasing little bites. I kiss the hard angular planes of his cheeks, his eyelids — everything I can reach. I have this mad desire to show him he was right to place his trust in me. Right to make me his forever.

Long fingers squeeze and plump my breast. He moves lower, kissing the soft sensitive skin between my breasts. I know it for what it is. A promise. He will take care of my heart.

My body responds by curving into the heavy length of him straining into me. He's notched his hard, hot length at the slick entrance of my pussy. I want to feel all of him.

"Please." Running my hands down the hard planes of his body, I want him, I want him to make me his in every way. I'm still scared, but I'm ready. I've never felt more ready in my life. His back muscles ripple beneath my questing fingers. I grab his hard butt, urging him closer. Fear hammers at me, but I push it aside. I want to be brave for him.

"Shh, greedy girl. I've got you." He grips my face, making me look in his eyes. His intensity steals my breath.

"Keep those pretty eyes on me, little dove. I want to see it all when I make you mine." He takes his hand, slipping it between us, grabbing his dick, guiding it in.

Pain sears when he presses into my barrier. I'm ready, but his dick is too big. I feel like he's about to split me in two. I can't stop the panicked cry escaping my lips or the way I flinch.

He presses and stops. His eyes spark with a dark ferocity, meeting mine. A smile pulls at the corner of his mouth. "I knew it."

He thrusts hard past the thin barrier of my virginity.

"Ahh." Tears leak out of the corner of my eyes, rolling into my hair. The sharp burning pain has me bucking, but he presses onward, pinning me to the sofa, making me take every inch of his driving length, refusing to let me move or try to further unseat him.

"Shh, it's okay." He presses a little kiss to the top of my forehead. The only indication I have that he's affected at all is the little hitch in his voice when my muscles spasm around him.

"Fuck." He bites back the curse. Looking at me, his jaw flexes as he fights his instincts and his darkness to allow me the time to adjust to his massiveness.

"It hurts," I say. My feelings hurt from the way he held me down and made me take him.

"It supposed to," he growls. "Pain, blood, ecstasy, wife."

He shifts. I gasp at the pain. "So take it like a good girl." Slowly, he withdraws until I can feel only his head at my entrance. "I promise by the time I'm done making your little pussy mine, you're going to love everything I do to you."

He looks down between us. "Look how you've bled all over my dick like a good little virgin." He rubs his fingers around his dick where he's wedged over my pussy lips, taking my arousal blood and starts massage around the tender flesh of my clit. "Bleed kitty, bleed."

"She's stretched so prettily around my dick," he praises. My muscles clench around the head. Rocking against him, my hips chase his fingers and the sensations he's wringing from me.

"So wet for me. That's right, fuck me," he commands, making me realize that's exactly what I'm doing pain forgotten. He watches me slide up and down on his dick. My ravaged flesh glides along his hard, blood-soaked dick. His fingers flick faster and faster until my thighs stiffen as I orgasm on his fingers. It's like before, but more intense because my muscles aren't just squeezing air, but the head of his dick stuffed just at my entrance.

"Yoi," he murmurs with a coolness that's incongruent with the moment. I watch in what seems like slow motion as he brings fingers stained red with my essence and virgin's blood to his mouth and sucks them clean.

"You taste like," he looks away for a moment before spearing me with a look full of unmitigated lust, "mine."

Pulling one of my legs high over his back, he braces a strong arm high above my head and surges inside me. Pure fire slams through me as he drives his hips hard into me. My breath catches and I don't have time to catch it before he bottoms out, withdraws, and slams into me again. I'm beneath him with softness beneath me. The juxtaposition of my situation is not lost on me. He's fucking me relentlessly, giving me no quarter on a softer than a cloud surface.

"Tay-chan," he snaps, drawing my attention away from the confused thoughts spiraling through me. "Eyes. On. Me." Every word is punctuated with a thrust of his hips. He's demanding my complete submission. He doesn't have to say it. I know it by the overwhelming, all-consuming expression on his face. My entire focus tunes to him and his need. Soon it becomes mine. I rock up into the forceful drive of his hips, opening myself to take all he's giving me.

"Ahh," I gasp when he hits my spot. Heat flushes my chest. My face heats. I've never felt that sensation before, but I know I want to feel it again.

He stops, reaching for a throw pillow putting it beneath me to angle my hips up.

He's right there now. Writhing, I press down working my needy pussy on his dick. I'm so close.

He bows me up and starts pumping his heavy dick in me at a bruising pace. "Look, how well, you're taking me," he praises as I fall over the precipice of the ecstasy he promised.

"You wouldn't know I just split you open by the way you're taking my dick, Tay-chan. I like that so much, little dove." He fucks into me, over and over. Driving me past one orgasm into another one when he reaches between us again thrumming my clit until I'm crying with pleasure.

"You're mine." Pressing his body flush with mine driving into me with fury, his hips grind hard against my soft curves. "Forever." He thrusts hard, deep into my womb, filling me with his dick, jerking as hot jets of his come fill me to overflowing.

Heavy pants fill the air. The heady smell of sex, the mix of my perfume, and his cologne permeate the air. Trying to breathe as best I can with his body on top of me and his dick feeling like it's in my chest, I want to keep him close but he's too heavy.

"Hisashi?" I pat his shoulder.

"Hm?" He buries his face in my neck like he has no intention of moving.

"You're crushing me, babe." He freezes, then raises his head. His eyes are cool, assessing. All emotion seems to be wiped from his face.

Dread slowly crawls around my heart like a spider. Did I make a mistake? Was this some type of sick joke?

Before that thought can fully register, he dips his head and his face changes back to one with feeling. It's like he took off a mask. Or did he put it back on?

"Sorry." Pressing a kiss to the tip of my nose, he slowly eases out of me. I suck in a little air at the burn.

He stands not bothering to cover himself. "Don't." He shakes his head slightly when I try to curl my legs up to cover my nakedness.

"Eep." I grab his shoulders as he scoops me up. He hefts me higher striding over to the stairs to the loft, taking them two at a time, carrying me like it's nothing. I kiss his neck loving the fact that he can carry me.

"I'll be back," he says, leaving me in the bed.

"I'm going to mess up the bed," I say, feeling self-conscious wondering if the bleeding stopped and worrying about all the messiness from our lovemaking covering my thighs, coochie, and tummy. I know how fastidious he is.

"Don't worry about it tonight." He's already heading down the stairs when he replies to my worry.

Unable to relax I'm still in the same position when he comes back.

TOXIC

"Lie back, little dove." He sets a basin and a glass with water and a bottle with pills on the bedside table.

Doing as he says I rest back looking up at the stars letting the whole night rush over me.

"Why were you so upset earlier?" I brave to ask. "Were they reminding you that you are too far out of my league or something?"

"No." He doesn't say anything else for a long time just cleans me in a pensive silence. "They reminded me. You're out of mine. They know I'm not worthy." He tosses the pink stained towel into the basin then opens the pill bottle taking out two and handing them to me along with the water.

"For the pain." He waits until I take them then gets up coming around to the other side of the bed.

He pulls me into his arms tucking me into his chest. He kisses the crown of my head. "I almost let the truth of their words force me to do the right thing — let you go. Then I saw you standing there looking beautiful, mad as hell saying never to contact you again. I knew then I would be selfish as well as unworthy because I won't give you up and I will kill anyone who tries to take you from me."

"Hisashi, no." I rise cupping his face. Shaking my head. "No one is taking me away from you."

The fierce protectiveness, edged with tender obsession twists my heart. I know he means it.

T aylor

~

STRONG ARMS TIGHTEN around me as I shift in the early morning feeling a hard pressure against the crease of my bottom.

"Hm," he groans grumpily in my ear. "Stop moving." Shifting himself, he causes the thick head of his dick to press against my slick entrance.

"Fuck, Tay-chan how are you so wet for me already, babe?" Pressing in he doesn't stop when I gasp from him stretching me to fit around his dick, instead he reaches in front of me and starts working my clit.

In an embarrassing short time the head is distended, slippery and drenching his fingers. "Hisashi," I whisper, pushing back taking more of him inside of me. It hurts so deliciously. I can't seem to stop myself from seeking more and more of the sweet achy sensation he's evoking in me.

"Yes, love, take your pleasure from me." His other hand reaches for my breast, squeezing one, then the other. "So fucking pretty. So fucking mine." The possessive tenor of his voice has me clenching around him as he beats up into my pussy like he's trying to own it. I love what he's doing to me. I start moving, meeting his rhythm. "Yes, that's right," he whispers, his filthy sweet nothings in my ear. "Fuck me back."

He fingers draw swift spirals over my clit pushing me hard over the edge. "Ohmygoodness," I gasp, shuddering as my climax claims me.

"Hai," he growls, "such a good girl coming so hard for me, little dove." He thrusts hard spilling hot come inside of me. He holds me so close kissing the shell of my ear. "You're so it for to me, little dove," he whispers.

"Well, you're good to me, so there's that." Bending my head, I reach for the hand resting on my breast bringing it to my mouth for a kiss.

He cups my cheek turning my head to face him. "We're getting married today."

I sit up unable to hide my surprise. "Today? What about our families?"

He sits up, pulling his knee close to his body and draping his arm over it. "I let you see my tattoo. It's forbidden. Far more so than anything you can imagine. If I wasn't going to marry you immediately to protect you, then I would have never taken you last night." He rakes his hand through his hair, ruffling it. I don't try to pretend I understand.

"We can have a more formal ceremony later with both our families, but we are getting married today. Everyone will know you saw my tattoo, Tay-chan. They probably already believe it so." He stands, then holds his hand out for me. "Come, let's shower. We have a long day."

Three hours later we are Mr. and Mrs. Hisashi Takeda even though I'm terrified of the anger and disapproval. I decide to do as my husband says, "You can't live for other people, little dove. That way is the path to misery."

No. I decided to live for us.

Later that night as he rubs my feet that are sore from walking all over Tokyo to take care of the getting marriage business and the fun day he planned. Taking me to get bubble teas, street sushi, and a food tour of all the best hideaway spots in all the city. He even took me to a little kabuki theater that was exclusive and only had a select few people there.

"Thank you for this day." I smile over to him. My feet seem to be swallowed up by his big hands with long elegant fingers working the knots out. I can't help but moan when he works one particular ache out I have in my arch. His fingers work up through between my toes. My eyes roll in pleasure. "This is bliss."

"I would think last night was bliss," he comments wryly.

Pulling my foot back I sit up then crawl over the cushions until I'm half lying on top of him.

"That goes without saying, Mr. Takeda." Wrapping my arms around his neck I sink into his hard body. He settles me more fully on top of him. "Aishiteru yo," I whisper, knowing it's not common in his language to say the actual words, "I love you". I decide I will tell him as often as possible because it is the truth. I love my husband.

He pulls back his eyes warm, tangled with a subtle darkness I've come to find almost comfortable. This kind of regard would probably frighten another woman, but I find myself preening. "Aishiteru yo," he says in a way more musing than I expect it. Then I realize he's mulling my words, my love over and over. Finally, he nods as if coming to a conclusion he's trying to rationalize. "Yes, you love me as I love you, Ms. Takeda," he states as if he's trying to make this be so when it actually is.

He pauses looking me over. "You've had a very tiring day."

I nod, a slow smile spreading across my lips. He's taking such care with me. The urge to tell him that I'm not that fragile builds inside as I see the indecision playing over his face.

"Are you still sore from last night and earlier?" I'm already shaking my head.

He catches the movement. He starts slowly dragging my leg closer and closer then scooting up until he's sandwiched sideways. In one sweep he pulls me until I'm straddling him.

His eyes track to my lips where I have the bottom captured between my teeth. "You're sure?" Reaching up he pulls it free replacing it with his fingers.

"I'm sure." Whispering, I lick my tongue out swiping the firm pad of his thumb. He presses the digit into my mouth.

"I don't know how gentle I can be. I'm not a gentle man when it comes to you. Suck." His eyes darken when I comply. I feel his hardness hot and throbbing between my thighs.

"Tay-chan," he groans when I rise to adjust him against my sex.

"Hisashi," I barely have enough time to tease right after he's pulled his thumb free and his mouth is covering me in a soul stealing kiss. My eyes roll back in my head. Undulating on his hard as fuck dick, I try to ride the storm he's creating in me. He lets me. In fact he's urging me on, gripping my bottom moving me so that I'm hitting his dick at the right angle with each circle of my hip.

"Yes, that's it. Take what you need," he whispers against my neck sucking the tender flesh in his mouth. He draws on me in strong pulls. I know he's marking me in a way everyone can see. Why this makes me hotter and needier I don't know. All I know is if I could get in his skin I would in that moment.

Long fingers reach between us grabbing a handful of one breast and his other hand urges me to ride harder. He takes a nipple tugging it between his thumb and forefinger then rolls.

My body shakes. The orgasm has me clutching and burying my face into his neck sobbing with the intensity of my release.

I barely catch my breath before he's unzipped his pants, sliding my panties off, flicking them away like a gnat and is driving into my pussy with teeth snapping intensity.

"Now, it's my turn, little dove. You're going to learn not to give me everything I want," he says, angling one thigh so he can drive higher, pressing our bodies closer so that he's hitting my clit with every hard press inside of me. I can't be made to care. It feels too good.

"It's what I want," I gasp as he hits my spot making stars dance behind my eyelids.

"Look. At. Me. Wife." My eyes snap open feeling him close his hand around my throat. His teeth are gritted. Barely banked emotion akin to rage burns hot in his gaze. "See me, Tay-chan. See—"

"Hisashi." The harsh heavy shout of his name makes me freeze. My heart seizes. He presses his head against mine.

"Hisashi." This time it's said with aggrieved urgency. Our gazes meet. The message is clear as water. Don't say shit.

Slowly he disengages. Standing, he adjusts his still painfully hard dick in his pants before turning to his brother who obviously has a key to his apartment. The only way anyone can get up here is with a key card and a fingerprint scan. Hisashi told me earlier today that he would see that I was outfitted with everything needed to have full access to his life in the next couple of days. He made it sound way more monumental than just keys and check cards though.

"Brother. I apologize for not greeting you downstairs." He bows slightly, using tatamae letting his brother know he doesn't welcome his intrusion.

Speaking silence is as pervasive as the smell of sex.

"I have tried calling you since noon." Harsh words have my husband stiffening immediately. Kiyoshi's true feelings bleed through the room by the way all politeness falls away not tatamae no, his words are cold unvarnished honne.

"Gomen-nasai." Hisashi bows a little deeper. "What's happened?"

The entire atmosphere has changed. Sitting up, I look over to his brother. His eyes flick over me, his jaw hardening for a moment. He inclines his head. I bow as best I can from this awkward position. My whole face heats, shame has me turning away. Hisashi's eyes cast in my direction and his face hardens, eyes glinting onyx, face a cold emotionless mask. I almost want to jump to Kiyoshi's defense. He doesn't know we're married. Me being a gold-digging slut and not good enough for his brother is probably firmly solidified in his mind.

Never have I wanted the floor to open up and swallow me whole more in my life.

He takes us both in and I hope he can't see that much of me. But who am I kidding? He can see, smell, and nearly taste the sex we were just having in the air. I want to wave my finger showing him the platinum band his brother slipped on my finger and wave it like Suge Avery saying, "I'm married now."

He closes his eyes for a moment, then presses his fingers between the bridge of his nose, exhaling. "Father is dead." After a moment, he continues. "The wake is in an hour. Mother is only waiting long enough for us to return to the estate. Hurry."

Hisashi pivots, heading toward the stairs to the bedroom. Taking them two and three at a time he disappears into our bedroom.

Awkward silence follows. Kiyoshi comes over to where I'm sitting. He looks around the apartment then over to me. His gaze slides to my right before his face flushes and he turns swiftly. My gaze follows to where he was looking. Mortification explodes in my body. My eyes burn with embarrassment.

Quickly I grab the panties, balling my fist around them.

Swallowing, I stand clasping the offending object in my hands to hide them. "Maybe I should pack a bag for him."

"Hai," agreeing he nods not looking my way.

"I'm so sorry for your loss," I manage. "Your dad was lovely to me."

He turns to me then, looking at me for a moment his eyes softening for the briefest moment. "Hai, he was."

Bowing I turn.

"Taylor-chan." My heart thuds at the familiarity in his tone. I turn. He hesitates. Then his face hardens into a stoically cold mask. "You need to be gone before he comes back."

My heart drops the full thirty seconds I stand there looking at his broad back. Turning I run up the stairs. My heart is beating so hard, I think it's going to burst from my heart. Why would he say that? Demand that I leave his brother at a time like this?

"Hisashi." I burst into the bathroom and stop. I can't tell him what his brother said. I can't have my introduction to his family be me causing a rift between him and his brother. They'd already had words over me last night.

Who'd have thought that the jovial, kind scholarly man I chatted with last night would be dead today. What happened? I knew my questions would have to wait. Hisashi doesn't even know.

Looking at him, I can't help but go over to him. He

stops after pulling on his black slacks. I walk over to him wrapping my arms around his waist. He rests his head on the top of my head hugging me. He's rubbing my lower back like he's trying to comfort me when it's obvious he's the one hurting.

"I know my brother probably told you to leave. You probably should—"

"I'm not leaving. I'll be here when you come back home," I cut him off pulling back to see red rimmed glassy eyes. He's been crying.

The corner of his mouth lifts. "I was going to say —" he cuts me off sighing so hard his whole body expands. Releasing me he swipes both hands through his hair making me release my hold on his waist. Stormy gaze meeting mine, his lips press into a hard line. "I was going to say I know you should, but I'm a selfish motherfucker, little dove. I can't — won't tell you to leave, but I should. I. Just. Can't." He sounds gutted.

"Hisashi—" he cuts me off kissing me with a hard claiming of his lips. The hard sweep of his tongue makes me gasp with its possessiveness.

Reaching up I circle his neck pulling close. The kiss gentles until we pull apart. His anguish is palpable.

"I'll be here," I promise.

For a moment he hesitates, then nods. Together, we go back into the room. He finishes getting ready, taking a black formal man's ceremonial kimono out of his closet and putting it in a garment bag. I pack his overnight bag with his toiletries and underwear and change of clothes.

I follow him down the stairs bowing in return to both men as they depart. As they look at me as the elevator closes both their gazes scream different messages. Hisashi, be here for me. Kiyoshi, get out.

Weeks later...

My mouth is parched. I know I've failed my classes. Those are the thoughts drifting in and out of my mind. If I even have a mind anymore. At least nothing beyond the fact that I'm dying.

Hisashi has been gone for days. He's forgotten about me this time. The last time it was a whole day but as soon as he came, he cleaned and fed me. He made sure everything was nice before he brought me back here to tidy me up, tying me in intricate kinbaku knots bringing me to orgasm over and over again. This time something's happened to him. I don't know if I should be happy or afraid.

Maybe people noticed I've been gone. He promised to let me go back to class then he got paranoid thinking I would run away from him. "I can't lose you too," he said, his eyes taking on that unhinged light again. He only got quieter when I promised him I wouldn't. Then went stone cold silent when I begged him. Punished me when I told him he needed to get some help. He made me beg for it as he edged me for hours.

"Tell me, little dove, what help can anyone possibly give me that you're not?" he whispered as he slid slowly in and out of me making me clench around his length as he taunted me making the kinbaku knots tighten against my sensitive flesh in delicious torment.

When he asked me nearly a week after his father passed away, if I wanted to explore rope play with him I said, yes. Not just to soothe my increasingly erratic husband, I was genuinely intrigued. Hisashi is an amazing lover. I could tell he was using it to deal with his grief and I was happy to be there for him in any way he needed. He showed very little interest in talking about his father's death. Flat out refused to go to grief counseling. I could take from his non-response that a Takeda would never. Not just from fear it may get out but from what he said. "It is not our way." Leaving it at that.

The Takeda way was to push through, suffer, push all the pain down until it was ground into the dirt. Never to be spoken of again.

I knew a little about that. Loves did talk to each other though. Taking advice to just pray about it. Family elders scoffed about telling folks our business when anyone of the younger generation talked about going to therapy.

So, I understand where Hisashi's family was coming from, but I'd hoped he'd share his pain with me. Instead, he buried himself in his coding programs for the first few days. Looking back, I can see his mood gradually changing over that time.

A week later he started tying me up. Soon things began to blur. He wouldn't release me. I started to panic. He'd soothe me with food and sex. So much sex.

"I can't lose you," he'd say, holding me afterward. In truth I didn't want to leave him. "You'll leave me now, if I let you go." He never believed me when I promised I wouldn't. I figured I was suffering from Stockholm Syndrome, but can you have it if you weren't kidnapped? If you voluntarily stayed when he warned you, you should have left?

I know I shouldn't blame myself. I begged him to let me go days ago when he said he had another emergency. He looked disheveled and even fearful when he came to pepper me with kisses.

"Babe, brush your hair," I whispered when he gave me water, rice porridge, and fruit.

"I will." Promising, he looked harassed. "I'm going to let you go."

"Why not now, babe?" I asked softly.

"Not now." He pressed the softest, saddest kiss on my lips. "When I come back." Getting up fishing for his keys, he left me in the room off the side of the kitchen behind his dojo. I'd been coming to work out with him in the room beyond having no idea he had a secret room until he brought me back here the first time for rope play. Here I was thinking it was our own little red room. No, ma'am. It was so much more than that.

He confessed he'd been exploring kinbaku since he was a teen. He was able to use the practice to focus and explore the darker side of his nature.

My husband was a pleasure torturer. A sadist. As chilling as it sounds, it didn't deter me until I realized his father's death affected him much deeper than I realized. In his effort not to lose me, he's slowly killing me.

My tongue cleaves to my mouth. I gag, my throat spasming. I have nothing to swallow. My lips crack. Tasting blood my throat attempts to swallow. The blood paints my dry, cracked lips, seeping on my tongue. The taste is a harsh brackishness, it makes acid rise as my tummy rebels. Hot bitterness presses hard in my chest.

I'm crying, eyes burning with tears I can't shed. Sounding like a small frail, whimpering animal, I'm listening almost removed from the pathetic sounds I make as I listlessly try to pull free. Skin chafing from the rope burns break against the jute making them bleed again.

I whimper against the pain. I really feel like I'm going to die any minute. My nose stings. I can't even bring myself to be mad at him. I should have listened to his brother. I should have called Kiyoshi when I noticed he'd not slept by the third day. I knew I was out of my depth. He needs help, but I just didn't want him to be mad at me. Now, I'm trussed up like a turkey about to die from dehydration in a secret room I didn't even know my husband had. This is what I get.

Something's happened to him I know it. He would've never left me alone this long. The last time he came back after they'd spent all day at their family estate interning his father's remains and handling his will. They'd met with lawyers after that well into the night. As soon as he came back, he apologized, taking care of me. It was embarrassing because I'd soiled myself. I just couldn't hold it anymore.

He said nothing hurtful only kept saying how sorry he was. I didn't want to speak to him anymore after that but eventually I broke because his anguish was so palpable.

"What is really going on with you?" I pled with him.

"I'm fucked up," was all he'd say.

Blinding light streaks across the room. I can't see anything. It's not Hisashi. The crisp citrus and spice are nowhere near the smoke, cedar of him.

"Korewa taihen da" the low, pained question of what has he done is not answered by me. Gentle fingers touch my forehead pushing my head back. "I see you're still alive, beautiful." The low soothing tones of Kiyoshi make me squint to see his concerned face.

"No worries. I'm here," he murmurs. Within seconds he's cutting away the bindings holding me.

He finds out very soon and from my ragged scream they are practically melded to my skin.

Though outwardly I don't make any sound, inwardly I scream form embarrassment when this pristine man sweeps my filthy, soiled body into his arms. He lays me on the bed, disappearing. Exhaustion tears at me. I have no energy to do anything other than fall into the darkness of sleep. Hours or seconds later, I don't know, I'm jostled awake.

I gasp when he eases me into warm water. He gives me ice chips to melt on my tongue as the blood saturated jute rope then falls from my body. My body is so tired, too spent to care that my husband's older brother is giving me a sponge bath.

He dries me and puts me in the bed. His phone chimes. "The doctor is here," he tells me, leaving. Mortification fills me again but I have no energy to care beyond the internal shame.

He shows the female doctor up into the room and disappears. Coming back, he brings in a large duffle laying it at the foot of the bed then leaves again.

"Ms. Love, I'm Dr. Ishii," she tells me taking items out of the bag. "Can you tell me what happened?"

"M-my —" I stop my throat still too sore to really talk. Hurrying to give me more ice chips she sets up an I.V. Not being able to find a vein in my arm she has to settle for one in my hand. After securing the butterfly infusion and setting the saturation, she turns back, her eyes clouded with deep concern. "I will ask questions.

Do you think you can nod and shake your head yes or no?"

I nod, grateful I don't have to talk. Even if I could, I doubt I'd get through the entire interview without crying.

"Were you sexually assaulted?"

I shake my head and even add a broken, "No."

She nods though I can see she doubts me.

"Do you need a pregnancy preventative?"

I shake my head no. I got an IUD the week we got married. It was copper, so it lasts ten years.

"With your permission I'm going to check and dress any wounds."

After I nod the affirmative, she makes quick work checking and treating the rope burns and abrasions.

"I'm leaving you with pain medication. You are to stay in bed until you finish this I.V. of saline and electrolytes. You are only to go to the restroom. I will leave Mr. Takeda with instructions for your care. Be well, Miss Love."

"Takeda." She pauses as she picks up the bag. "Pardon?"

"It's Mrs. Takeda," I say in a reedy voice. "Hisashi Takeda is my husband."

"Sign this," Kiyoshi tells me a week later.

"No," I snap, tossing the papers on the floor. "Tell me where Hisashi is."

"Hell no." Shaking his head, his face is just as cold as it was the first time I asked and he refused.

"I'm his wife I have the right to know what you did to him." I stand feeling strong enough to finally confront him.

"He nearly killed you," he says the hard truth. It feels like a blow.

"H-he didn't mean to." My voice sounds small to my own ears.

"Don't you think I know that? I told him he wasn't ready. He wouldn't listen. He had to have you. You wouldn't listen." He walks away putting distance between us. "Now look what's happened."

"I just want to see him." I cover my mouth when the sobs escape.

He swings back his face ashen with shock. "You can't be serious. Let me be very clear, Taylor. My brother almost killed you. If he doesn't get help, he will succeed the next time. Do you understand? You can't help him. It's out of your hands. He's ruined your chance of the fellowship. They have you listed as dropped out. Did you know that? Your parents are scouring the country looking for you. They've met with me and my cousin, Akchiro twice. This can't go any further. You need to go back to the States and get your life back. I will do all I can to help you but my brother is out of your life. We can't help him." His voice sounds like it's breaking.

Bomb after bomb falling from his lips makes me realize just what kind of mess my life is right now. I am trying to see a man who almost killed me while my parents are heartbroken looking for me.

"What are these documents?" I sit back down picking up the papers.

"Hisashi made you the executer of his estate. This power of attorney gives us, his family temporary power of attorney if you go back to the States. You will be well compensated for all you have been through."

I hesitate, not wanting to give up on him. "I don't need any compensation. If he wanted me to be the one in charge, there has to be a reason," I say, looking at the tall figure looming over me like judge, jury, and executioner.

He sighs his face not lessening in its hardness one iota. "My brother would be ashamed if you were not taken care of. It would cause him no small amount of shame if we abandoned you. Would you have this, Taylor?" Heat infuses my face at the thought of my proud husband facing more pain because of me. Shaking my head, I listen as he continues dropping more devastating news.

"He was out of his mind with grief and in the midst of a mental collapse when he signed everything over to you. My mother is threatening to have you arrested for fraud because of this. She will win, Taylor.

She has many friends." He rubs his forehead like he's finding all of this so tedious. "She is moving to have your visa rescinded as we speak. It is only my promise to meet with you that is staying her hand."

For the first time I really look at him seeing the dark circles under his eyes. He's lost his father and his brother for the time being. The thoughts of my fellowship have long since fled my mind. I missed too many assignments being locked away as I have. But my visa? I could be expelled from the country, jailed, hidden in a black site.

"What's his diagnosis?" I ask.

His expression hardens. "He's never been officially diagnosed."

I cant my head looking at him. "But you have an idea."

"My father did. He worked very hard with Hisashi for many years to teach him how to be around people. He was doing well." He breaks off not meeting my eyes. It's obvious his loyalty to Hisashi won't allow him to say more.

"Then he met me," I fill in the blanks.

"The moment he met you he felt alive in a way he never had before. He told me you made him feel things. He'd never felt things before you, Taylor-chan. He started to think he didn't need anything other than you." Dismay gives over to despair. There is no accusation in his words but it's obvious that he feels as if I had the opposite effect on Hisashi. I was not good for him. I was very bad for him. My love for him almost killed us both. The responsibility I feel that moment is crushing. I just wanted to love him. Never hurt him.

Crushing hurt and disappointment lance through me digging harder than the jute rope of over a week ago.

"I promised him —" I shake my head what does it matter. Would he even remember my promise? He was probably out of his mind with delusion and grief.

Taking the paper I sign on the line with the X by Responsible Party ignoring the tears splattering on the page.

CHAPTER
SEVEN

H *isashi ~ Present Day*

UP CLOSE SHE'S MAGNIFICENT. I don't let it change my course. The vengeance my pretty little bitch deserves will be meted out with the same precision that I create algorithms that have made Takeda the most powerful conglomerate in the world. My extreme — some would call obsessive focus has allowed me to pioneer tech to modernize farming to rid the world of famine to inclusive AI that has made the use of tech more available to those in under-serviced communities. Not everything I've done touches on altruism. No, I've helped my family create a monopoly that in chip making using alloys instead of raw minerals.

Our lab made cobalt will make blood tech obsolete in a year. Then all major tech companies who don't want the blood of children on their hands will have no choice but to use ours. My cousin, softened by his wife Flower's heart, called me personally to solve this problem with the incentive that this was the last thing he'd require in order to free my mother and sister from his imprisonment. He even said I could hold the patent. I have no doubt it was Flower's way of being fair. Akchiro, like all CEOs, wanted to keep the patents created by scientists and computer scientists owned by the company. I could see the way his mouth twisted in derision at the idea. It was obvious it hadn't been shaped by him, but his diminutive, beautiful little wife. That she is a relative through marriage to the woman I married is not lost on me. There's something about all of the Love women that has the ability to ensnare men.

Stepping inside the room, I close the door listening for the click, not relaxing until I hear the beep that lets me know only my retina scan will unlock it. How she manages to sleep so soundly is beyond me. She should be up cowering in the corner. The memories I've been able to recover of those last days, say she should be climbing the fucking walls.

I was the reason for all those nightmares she had was I not? The countless nights watching her toss and turn. I heard her scream my name and the word, 'No', hundreds of times as I watched over her as she slept.

"Taylor, get up," I snap. Irritation eats at me. I watched her most of the night until I had to make myself sleep knowing I must be strict about my regimen.

"Why does she get to sleep while you suffer? Make her suffer. Make her bleed," He demands, but it's faint.

My monster no longer rules me. I respect *his* place in my life now. Fighting *him*, I learned only made *him* stronger. It wasn't until *he'd* insidiously slid in and took over nearly costing me everything did I gain a healthy respect for my monster.

"You're jealous," I murmur.

"Taylor." Getting louder makes her head pop up. A mass of crushed and tangled curls makes my mind and my body harken back to those many years ago, waking up with my head buried in her hair when she'd been too sleepy to get her bonnet or when her headscarf slipped off in the night. Bonnet betrayal she called it.

She stretches then stops. Freezing in place her eyes dart around the room until her whiskey brown eyes set on me. Her arms drop from where they were suspended mid-air.

"Hisashi?" Her tone is more concern than fear. Concern for me, I don't know if I should be offended or amused.

Ignoring the question in her tone, I give her a mocking bow. "Get up. We need to shower."

She hesitates. In three quick strides I'm over to where she sits in the center of the bed.

Her soft flesh gives as I drag her from the bed to stand before me. Spinning her around I frog march her into the adjoining bathroom.

"I just bathed last night." She sounds like she's pleading.

Stopping at the water closet, I open the door. Her gaze meets mine and I keep my expression impassive. Stepping past me, she goes in. I close the door behind her waiting until she's done before taking her over to the chaise lounge. "Lie down."

Going over to the towel steamer, I take two towels from it, tossing them between my hands to cool them.

Watching as she eases into the S curve of the chaise, I resist the urge to bend her over it and drive inside of her luscious heat.

"Open." Trembling thighs spread at my command. Dropping my eyes to the lush curls of her pussy my mouth waters wanting to bury my face in the thick abundance hiding her from me. There will be no fucking hiding from me this time. Placing the towels over her lower half, I leave them there to prepare her. She squirms but says nothing more.

Forcing myself to turn from her I go over to prepare the shaving cream. I am very deliberate as I mix the foam I had made special for her. It's the vanilla-rose she loves so much with a little touch of menthol to make the shave clean. When the foam is thick, I walk over to her not bothering to hide my erection.

Laying the towels beside her, I take the brush. I paint the rounded curve of her lower abdomen below her navel, the little dip in the crevice that's tucked away right before the rise of her mound where all that lovely hair is. I cover every inch of her pussy with the creamy foam.

"Damn," I groan, looking at my handiwork. The contrast of the white foam against her beautiful brown skin has my dick pearling. "Don't," I say when her legs start closing. "Don't mess up my creation. I'll be forced to spank your pussy before I'm ready. And if I spank your pussy, I'm fucking it." I watch her stiffen. Her legs fall back open. What I don't say is I have every intention of fucking her. In fact, she'll be begging me to. Only she won't be rewarded that soon. Her punishment happens first.

Leaving her spread open for me, I sharpen the strop. Fifteen times on the front and fifteen on the back I swipe my straight razor on the strop. Holding it up, I watch light dance across the blade. Fascinated as always by my blades I imagine it gliding across her skin with precision. Though the desire to see her bleed is dampened by the feeling of causing her any pain or marking her skin more than I already have.

Going over to the chaise I kneel between her legs reveling in the pressure on my knees. I almost want more pain to heighten the experience. Pulling back her soft flesh I make a steady downward stroke of the blade removing her hair. Biting my lip I make another pass. "You're being such a good little bitch, for me," I growl. Her tummy sucks in at my words.

I can smell her pussy the way it blossoms under the heat of my regard. I meet her gaze when I finish the top half. "Hold your thighs."

I press the mound of her fat pussy taking my time stroke after stroke freeing her of hair. Moving to the indentation of her thigh I swipe. She flinches. A thin line of blood trickles from her satiny flesh.

"I'm sorry." She rushes to apologize but I'm already shaking my head.

"Very bad girl, Taylor. That will be ten swats," I tsk, continuing.

She barely breathes while I continue to work. Ignoring the blood, I'm extra careful denuding her plump little lips. Moving lower still, I take hair from both her holes.

I place more warm towels over her newly bare areas. A little tinge of blood mars the pristine white of the towels and I shake my head. "You should have stayed still."

Taking the towels, I toss them into the towel dispenser.

"Up," I say, walking her over to the shower. Turning it on to a temperature shorter than the one of hell I know she loves I start to disrobe. Her eyes round but she knows better than to say shit to me.

"Inside." Nodding, I wait to let her go before me. I pump and emulsify the shampoo spreading it over her hair. I push my dick into the crevice of her ass.

She's changed shampoos since we were together but says nothing. She's not surprised that I have her products.

"What kind of husband would I be if I didn't provide what you needed?" I answer the question she doesn't ask. "But I'm not really that to you am I, Taylor?"

"Hisashi—" she cuts off when my hands tighten in her hair harder than they need to.

"Don't fucking speak, little bitch." My teeth clench so hard. My erection gets harder at her gasps. I trained her well. Easing my grip in I begin to massage her hair, washing away sweat but none of the anxiety.

"Turn around." Tilting her head back into the spray I rinse her hair. Adding conditioner, I work it though her thick curls, allowing her tresses to drink in the emollients.

"Bathe me." Stepping back, I give her the room to get a loofah. She lathers it with my soap. Watching as she inhales familiarizing herself with the scent she once loved on me, I tilt my head trying to figure out the emotions playing across her face. I recognize it as one as a boon companion these many years — longing. Rage gathers around my being drawing me taut. No. She doesn't get to feel that let alone express it. Not after what she did. Broken promises. Lies. Disappearing like a wraith. Broken vows. Betrayal.

She reaches out with the loofah. I snatch her wrist watching as she winces, watching as it falls from her fingers.

"Use your hands, like a good concubine." Nodding she swallows, stepping back briefly to pump more soap into her hand. Rising to her tiptoes, she lathers my neck, shoulders, then chest.

Refusing to move, I force her to move around me washing my back. She kneels moving to my thighs. She comes back to the front doing the front calves working her way up to my dick. She takes me in hand washing my dick in firm strokes sliding my sensitive foreskin back exposing my head dripping with precum. She steps closer circling my middle slipping her hands between my ass to clean me there.

"Fuck," I mutter, stepping out of her reach and under the spray dismayed at how quickly she got control of the situation.

"Finish. I'll await you in the room." I don't bother looking her way. If I do my plans would fall to ruin because I'd only end up fucking her. I need a moment to get myself together.

I feel like I've run a marathon by the time I reach the room. I moisturize my body using the time I know she's detangling her hair to calm my raging libido.

Making sure she has everything she needs ensures she doesn't take that long. Her curvy little body is smaller than when we met but her belly still has a sexy curve, her hips round out to support her bountiful ass in a way that has me salivating. Big breasts tip with flat nipples I can't wait to suck to hard points sway with a natural sag.

"On the bed." My voice is hard and my dick is no less so as it juts past my navel. Her eyes widen with fear probably recalling how much it hurt when I took her pussy all those years ago. I know she's not had any lovers. I've seen to it myself.

I almost relish in telling her, how her need to fuck could have led to the untimely demise of her would be lovers if she dared to break her vows.

I'm feeling a little generous just thinking about it, so I don't get too upset when she takes more time than necessary getting in the bed.

She lies down like a corpse which I'm not the least disturbed by as I circle the bed. Her hands are in tight little fists balled at her sides. Legs melded together like keeping them fused together will save her from me slapping her pussy the ten times I promised.

She did an amazing job making her body gleam so prettily for me, the smell of the vanilla-rose body butter creates a Pavlovian response in me. Come drips from my dick.

"Not yet. Punish the little slut first," my monster whispers, clamoring to come forth.

Climbing onto the bed, I resist the urge to straddle

her head and fuck her face. Instead, I move between her legs spreading them wide.

"Such a fat, pretty ass pussy for such a bad girl." Reaching down I press my finger against her clit, already protruding from its hood. Slick with her nectar, it's slippery and begging to be sucked. She arches like a ballerina on pointe into my touch. She should be scared. She rides my hand instead.

"A bad disobedient, little bitch," I snarl, drawing back slapping her pussy.

"Hisashi," she screams, her body undulating with pain and pleasure.

"A lying, needy little slut," I growl, adding two more swats to her plump mound.

"Ohmygoodness," she arches away, her pussy glistening, weeping with want.

Who am I to deny her? Or *him*?

"No running from me. Take your punishment like a good girl," soothingly I urge. Smoothing the sting away. As soon as she relaxes into my touch, I give her five hard swats in succession. Tears leak from her eyes and wetness seeps from her pussy. My hand is drenched. Bringing my hand to my mouth, I slowly lick her essence from palm to fingertips. Taking my time meeting her glassy gaze, I dip each into my mouth, sucking her delectable juices from my fingers. I feel come rushing to my head. "Fuck," I growl, biting back a groan. I missed this.

Rage comes at what she's denied us. Reaching

between her legs, I play with her pussy, making her squirm against my fingers as I ruthlessly bring her close, then closer still. She's right on the precipice when I say cruelly, "So easy, so quick to come for a man you ran from."

Before she can respond, I slap her pussy right on her quivering clit. Hot spurts of her girl come douse my hand. Plunging two fingers into her tight hole, I press into her G-spot finger, fucking her into another drenching orgasm.

"Ahh," she screams unable to form words, her breath catching, her body seizing as I manipulate her into another orgasm.

Her come is all over her denuded pussy, mound, and lower tummy.

"Fuck her into the mattress. Make her tremble. Make her weep," Monster whispers.

"No." Despite the massive pressure in my dick I refuse to give her any part of me right now.

"Feast, then."

Silently I nod. That I can do.

I fall upon her with ravenous hunger taking long swipes along her soft rounded belly, licking her clean.

Taking my time, I do the same with her mound trying to pace myself. I press my aching dick into her down comforter. She tastes so fucking good.

"Mine," I say, looking up into her eyes.

"No motherfucker, ours." Lowering my head, I bow my head at *his* words indulging *his* delusion.

Tugging her fat lips into my mouth one at a time I suck them individually then together, letting her clit hide. Delving deeper, I circle the perimeter of her clit deliberately giving it no attention. Lower, my tongue finds its home licking the nectar of her pussy. Wrapping my arms beneath her thighs I hold her in place as I bury my face in the soft, musky sweetness of her. Her pussy is a paradise of pleasure, and I can't get enough. Nothing tastes better than my woman fresh from a shower.

Taylor's writhing turns to pumps as she fucks my face in tandem with my tongue fucking her pussy. Slipping two fingers into her tightness again I piston them into her as I move to suck her engorged clit into my mouth.

I draw on it like I need it to live. Maybe I do. I suck that little hard motherfucker, flicking it over and over with my tongue. She cants her hips riding my tongue. Looking up into her gaze I pull back licking from hole to clit, then again then following with a sharp little nip, suck, and flick. I grin wildly, unrelentingly flicking as she comes again. Her body convulses, her thighs tremble clamping around my head. I bury my head laving her slick plump flesh.

I stay soothing her with kisses, soft sucks followed by harder ones when the need to mark her overtakes me. "Oreno da," I tell her again and again, lest she forgets to whom she belongs.

She looks away then. Anywhere but at me. The

man who is worshiping her. The one who's watched over her.

"*Ungrateful wretch. Snap her neck,*" Monster grumbles.

Instead I rise above her. Looking at her, I watch as her eyes round with fear as she takes in my size.

"No, it wasn't a figment of your imagination then or now, little bitch." I quirk a smile taking myself in hand.

Her legs are spread, her pussy soft and puffy from my attentions. Purpling marks speckle her thighs from my stubble, marking her. Burning lust surges inside, watching her breathing pick up, in fear this time. The sadist in me rises in anticipation.

"Open your pussy for me." Slowly, her hand reaches between her thighs. She pulls back the soft flesh of her lips, giving me an unfettered view of her pussy. There is no part of her hidden.

"Good girl," I say, looking at the pussy I just licked, finger fucked, and sucked, making her come again. I stroke, lost in the sensations of memory of what I wrought just moments ago.

She wants to touch herself but no, this is for me.

Her nipples are pointing high begging to be sucked. I'm almost tempted to suck them again. Soon. I stroke thinking of how soft they were. The cushion and soft give as I plump them. She's so fucking soft everywhere. I feel my nut rise. My ass clenches as I see her press her clit with her finger and bite her bottom lip.

A hot spray of come jets from my dick painting her breasts and belly. I aim lower watching come coat her pussy covering her hand where she's opening herself for me.

"Lick it clean," I tell her. Reaching down, I push it into her. Smear it over her mound, tummy, and breasts. I sweep it up her neck and into her mouth.

"That's all you get. You will wear my come today."

Standing from the bed, I leave her while I still can.

EIGHT

isashi

STANDING outside Kiyoshi's office I can hear the muffled conversation between him and our cousin, Akchiro, The Takeda, the head of our international conglomerate. Normally, they talk on a weekly basis. Recently it's become two or three times a week since the little chef my brother's been preoccupied with younger brother took it upon himself along with his friends hacked into our local arm of Creative Chaos, causing millions of dollars of disruption to our production lines.

The only thing saving the boy's life is the fascination my brother has for his sister, the owner and head chef of The Camellia, admittedly the best restaurant in the state. In the weeks that have followed my alarm about his behavior has grown. Now we're being threatened with a strike, a boycott by employees we've made every fucking accommodation for.

The atmosphere at the plant has been very toxic since our first failed meeting with the employee leaders. Each head of department has just given me their reports on each department's outlook. There doesn't look like there will be anyone crossing the picket lines. We have made every good faith effort to accommodate them. In our last meeting, there was no contention. We were very close to an agreement then and in less than twelve hours everything fell apart. We've had no contact or answers as to what changed. No one needs to tell me foul play is afoot. I relish what I'll do once I find the culprits. Yet, none of the searches are turning up anything. We have the message boards monitored and eyes all over the plant—still nothing.

The network of players who are instigating this has learned from their last endeavors, which leads me back to Krie's brother and his friends. I hope for his sake, I'm wrong because there will be no mercy this time. I don't care how much his sister begs my brother or how well she pleases him. He's got his one and only pass.

When silence falls, I knock briefly before letting myself in. Stepping before my brother's desk, I bow briefly. He acknowledges me with a slight dip of his head. I can tell without him speaking and his face remaining a stoic mask that he's still disappointed in my behavior from the meeting with department heads. I know my temper got away from me as we tried to negotiate with these knuckle draggers. I refuse to give face to people we've given a better quality of life than they've had in generations.

"As I said before, brother, the people here are ungrateful. They don't want to work, and they will never accept us as leaders. They would rather work for the very people who were exploiting them and will continue to once we are gone. We should encourage the Carrington brothers to relocate their plant and let these people rot. They've shown what loyalty means to them—nothing," I tell him watching his impassive face.

He nods then asks, "What will we do once they label us as failures? How quickly would we be demoted? Regulated to some third-rate factory in the middle of nowhere. Creative Chaos is the leading chip manufacturer in this country on the cusp of being number one in the world. The word will spread like wildfire, our reputations ruined. No brother, we will fix this." He pins me with an unwavering stare. "We don't quit."

"We are only here because Akchiro is too weak to say no to his wife." I scoff at him reminding him of how precarious his own position is if he allows the chef to continue to lead him.

"Need I remind you because of his weakness for his wife, he didn't kill us?" He tilts his head to the side, looking at me squarely. He knows better than anyone what our father's death cost us. Shame eats at me. Though he's never blamed me, I know I left everything for him to handle. He didn't have me at his back.

"Fuck him. He's giving face. You would have peeled Akchiro's face off and fed it to his wife." Swallowing back the acid in my throat, I grit out, "And that's why he's unworthy. Now, I wonder if your chef is not having a similar effect." Taking no quarter, I let him know the disdain I have for his weakness.

"Well, we can't all capture and imprison our pets now, can we? How long are you planning to keep this one, brother? I hope you're feeding her. You know you have a terrible habit of breaking things. This one will be missed. I would advise you to tread carefully and make sure no harm comes to her."

My face clouds with fury. I can't hide my reaction. The only indication he shows that he knows he's gotten to me is the slight lift of one brow.

"She's not being hurt. She's free to go whenever she wants," I grind out through clenched teeth.

"Liar. You're never letting her go," Monster chuckles maliciously.

"Stockholm Syndrome doesn't count, Hisashi," he reminds me. All taunts aside, I know he's serious.

Fuck, I'm serious. My brother knows how obsessed I am. He knows better than to try to reason with me. This has been years in the making. Coming to the States is my perfect opportunity to get back into Taylor's world. No more watching from afar. Trips back and forth from New York to Tokyo. No this proved perfect. Still, he has no room to judge.

"You're one to talk. Using a minor infraction to bring a woman to heel? And you dare judge me. She has nothing to do with her brother and his friends. Yet, you saw the prime opportunity to get her to bend to your will. So, who is breaking people, brother? Not to mention this whole situation is going to blow up in our face the moment the Tatsumoto syndicate finds out that the princess is being usurped by a mere cook." I can call him on his bullshit as well as the repercussions to the entire family. Shaking my head, I finally get to the reason I came into his office in the first place.

"Bubba T texted me saying he wants to open the line of communication. He said we are being done dirty — his words, and he wants no part of it because we've been more than fair."

I continue telling him all the necessary details relayed by one of the few good actors in this entire situation. Bubba T has his hand on the pulse of this plant. Even in my highly critical assessment he's proven to be an excellent manager. My brother listens impassively as I relay the information.

"Very well, we will meet and hear what he has to

say and see if we can get any relevant information on those who seek to harm this company." It goes without saying what the retribution will be. Thaddeus and his friends did something so brazen; headlines were blaring about it. This however is being orchestrated with stealth and will be handled just as silently. I can tell he is actually looking forward to it. I'm salivating.

Bowing I leave my brother's office. Heading down the long expanse of hallway leading to my office opposite his, my mind pulls to the way I left Taylor this morning.

When I'd looked on her, she'd fallen into an exhausted slumber. Glancing at my watch, I hasten my steps. I have thirty minutes before my next meeting.

"Mr. Takeda." My gaze tracks to my assistant, Siobhan.

"Yes." The deep dimples in her face give her an adorable look reminding me of another dimpled beauty, she's all seriousness though. "Bubba T called while you were out. Says he has new information."

"Thank you, Siobhan." I incline my head. She bows, making me bite back a smile at her effort. We don't require our American employees to adopt our social norms, but when they make the effort, it shows a certain level of respect.

Walking over to my desk, I stand raising the hydraulics until they're high enough. Pressing a button, I lock the door to my office. I prefer work standing. Entering my password, I watch the screen bloom with the image of Taylor.

She is looking out of the window. I notice the tray of food beside her has gone untouched. Switching to another camera, I can now see the pensive expression on her face. She's been crying. That's no surprise.

"Who gives a fuck? She's lucky, you're allowing her to live." The monster inside scoffs fast, losing patience with the situation.

"Calm the fuck down," I say out loud. We're alone, the door is locked, so I don't have to worry about anyone barging in and seeing me have a conversation with myself. "We expected this. We took her and threw her in a trunk."

"It's the least she deserves," He mutters. *"Let me have her."*

"You almost killed her." I shake my head. "No way."

"That was because you tried to keep her all to yourself. Selfish motherfucker," He hisses.

"She's my wife." More tears fall from her eyes and my heart threatens to cave in.

"Ours." The emphatic reply is jarring.

My intercom buzzes. "Yes."

"It's Bubba T," Siobhan says.

"Put him through." Not for the first time I think of the waste of the company having landlines but I know my cousin finds this the most effective way of spying on me and my brother. I know the phones aren't just monitoring our calls but everything in the office. I'm not stupid by far. The tech he uses to watch us I hold the patents on. I could put a stop to it, but he's made it more than apparent that if we step out of line my mother and sister's lives are forfeit.

"Ayyye, Mr. Takeda," the deep voice of Bubba T fills the line.

"Bubba T." I grimace at the gross familiarity the people here insist on.

"Yes sir, we got a pretty good lead on the new leak. Seems like it's those kids again. Got 'em on camera and everything."

"You are very effective Bubba T, send me everything you have," I say coolly.

I work steadily for a few hours, having watched the video that seals the fate of not only Thaddeus Love and his friends but of the chef, Krie, who my brother seems so taken with.

It brings me no pleasure to be the one to show him the betrayal of the woman he's involved with.

The timer chimes as if on cue.

I take the medication out placing the syringe on the desk along with the alcohol prep. Though I normally take this at night, it's well past six p.m. and I see no end to my day yet.

Pulling out the tail of my shirt I rub the prepped pad over my abs.

"Coward. You don't need that shit. It kills your brain cells. That's why you couldn't stop the hack. Why you

couldn't catch them before they caused millions of dollars in damage to the production lines. Why you can't please Taylor. You need me, motherfucker. You need—" I press the pre-dosed syringe into the hallow space between my muscles and depress. *He's* quiet though I can feel the searing roar of *his* silent anger.

I learned a long time ago there is no way to truly silence *him,* and *he's* never really gone. The medicine just keeps *him* from taking over my mind completely. *He's* never liked that. Taking a backseat is not *his* way, but if I let *him* step forward and protect me, there will be nothing but carnage left in *his* wake.

I know *he's* my mirror, my Siamese twin, my protector, boon companion, but *he's* evil and though I don't put all my actions on *him,* I know I am the better of the two to face this world. I don't get to hide in my mind like I made the mistake of doing and allowing *him* to take over like *he* did when father died. *He* almost killed Taylor and I would have let *him.* I know better now to give *him* full rein. *He* can witness even participate however, *he* can never be in charge.

"Call me a coward all you like but we both know you can't be allowed to lead."

Putting away my medication and setting my calendar I turn my attention back to the tasks at hand.

My little bitch and my wayward employees. I tell myself there is no malice in my heart when I send Kiyoshi the video that will burst his little bubble about Chef Krie.

140

"It's no more than he deserves," Monster whispers. *He* still sounds sulky.

I don't respond to my monster, *he* feels threatened by anyone I have the slightest emotion for. Never mind my psychopathy only allows room for my siblings, mother, and now Taylor, though she's moved from emotion to an obsession. I won't allow tender emotions with her anymore. Not after her betrayal. I still bear those scars. She lucky I haven't killed her treacherous ass.

"Kill her. Fuck her dead corpse." The insidious whispers slide in and if not for my medication, I would act on this impulse. I'd fantasized about it long enough. Slowly strangling her until her eyes glazed over into the forever she promised. The one she lied about. I owe her little ass a killing, but I knew I couldn't do it. It would be too final. No. She doesn't get a path out of this entanglement, no, she will have to persevere. She will endure me as I suffer her.

Pressing send, I retrieve my jacket, making sure I am tidy.

Kiyoshi: Dinner tonight with the team

I roll my eyes. You'd think he didn't have a personal chef he brought from Tokyo, not to mention the one he made serve him in other ways.

Me: Hai

"I don't need anything further tonight," I tell Siobhan.

"Yes, Mr. Takeda." She stands giving me a differential bow. After returning her farewell with one of my own I move to the private elevator that is for the sole use of the CEO and COO.

The other executive suites are on the floor below us. Kiyoshi and I trust no one save each other. We know my cousin may have his spies, but we won't invite trouble by people whose loyalty cannot be determined beyond their ambition to rise within the ranks of Takeda.

Getting in my Maybach I pull up my phone. Taylor has moved from the sofa facing the garden. Her gilded cage has been stripped of all amenities except the basics of a bed and seating area.

Her head lifts as one of my trusted servants, Aiko from my family's home comes in bringing her another tray. She shakes her head. "I'm not really hungry, thank you though," she says to the older woman, who frowns and says in stilted English, "You must eat, ma'am. You barely touched your food earlier today."

"Yeah, well I've been kinda stressed. Do you think I can get permission to go outside?" She smiles hopeful to the attendant.

"But it's dark now." Aiko waves helplessly to the expansive garden. I haven't told them she cannot leave but my staff is not stupid. They are well aware the door is locked for a reason even if they don't know why.

"Tomorrow, then?" My eyes narrow at the hope she puts into her voice.

"Hai, maybe, miss." Aiko nods nervously, her gaze skating around the room as if she expects to be lambasted at any moment.

"You know what? Never mind, I will take it up with Takeda-san." She hurries to reassure the servant she never should have put in such a shameful position.

She's obviously forgotten herself. I will take pleasure in reminding her later.

"Spank that plump ass," he demands.

"Oh indeed," I murmur, pulling out of my executive parking space to head off campus and meet my brother and our team at The Camellia.

HOLDING the steaming plate in my hand I lean in to allow my retina to scan the entrance of Taylor's room. She sits up when I enter.

Not sparing her a glance, I move over to the wall of windows that face the garden. "Lights." Lumosity surrounds us at my command. "Come here."

Her eyes rake me from head to toe. "I'm not hungry."

"I won't be repeating myself," I say, removing my jacket, draping it over the arm of the sofa. "If you refuse, I will be forced to have a feeding tube placed." I don't bother to look her way. "Outdoor lights, dim." The garden lights with fairy lights strategically placed throughout dim. Areas of the garden are highlighted. The temperatures in the south allow for a beautiful Japanese garden. I also had some of the regional plants — camellias, posies, roses, flowering dogwood, and honeysuckle incorporated.

"Wow," she whispers more to herself moving from the bed and coming over to me.

She sits in the farthest corner of the sofa. "Not there." I ease back, making room on my lap for her.

She hesitates, and her gaze shoots to mine. I quirk an eyebrow, daring her to balk. I almost want her to. Any reason to punish her brings me unmitigated joy.

"You don't need a reason. She belongs to us," my monster nudges in the recesses of my mind. It's a gentle persuasion.

I like playing games with my little bitch though, so I say nothing, just let her fall into my web. Either way, I win. She sits, I touch her. She doesn't. I touch her — harder.

I have to keep her nourished this time, though. I won't make the same mistake.

Slowly, she's trudging like she's knee deep in the mud, we get down here sometimes after a torrential rain until she comes to stand between my thighs.

I have to bite back a groan when her plush scent greets me. She's clean, having freshly showered, though she hasn't left this room all day. Though I guess anxiety can make you sweat.

"You washed my come off you," I remark, pulling her back against my chest just where I want her. Now her ass is sitting on my rapidly hardening dick. I position her so that I'm nestled between her warm cheeks.

"You didn't say I couldn't," she quips before she can stop herself.

"No, I didn't," I concede. Reaching past her, I get the plate and silverware. I had the food precut to prevent any mistakes or accidental stabbing.

I fork some of the garlic mashed potatoes, bringing them to her mouth. She hums with pleasure, making my heart and dick jolt.

I don't bother to taunt her as I spear the brandy braised short ribs and feed those to her. By the time I move to the rosemary glazed asparagus, she's eating with gusto.

For some bizarre reason, my monster and I both relish in feeding her, even take pride in it.

"I'm full," she says at last, shaking her head. I put the plate down.

"You will eat the food my staff prepares for you. If you want something different, something perhaps from your cousin's restaurant like I brought you tonight, you will inform Aiko and she will get a message to me," I tell her calmly, though I know she was deliberately starving herself today out of petulance and I don't like it.

"Can't I just tell the room at large? I know you're watching me," she huffs.

"Unfortunately, I have a company to run. It prohibits me from watching over you as much as I like." Not bothering to deny the accusations in her words or gaze, I look her squarely in the face.

"Being worried when you'd next appear and do some crazy shit killed my appetite." She cuts me the meanest look she can muster.

"Ohhh, sweet little bitch, don't you know better than to use the word crazy? It's ableist." My soft words belie the deftness with which I flip her head over ass so that she's over my knee.

"We use person first language in this house." I give a single slap to her ass. "Crazy. Psycho. Pencil or eraser eater. Idiot. Stupid. Spaz. Nutjob." I highlight each word with a smack to follow. "Will not be even thought by you. I don't disrespect you and I will not tolerate being called those names." Heat flushes my cheeks but not from the effort I'm using. I know enough about myself to know when I've been triggered. Forcing myself to stop, I rub her bottom soothing away the hurt I caused.

She holds herself stiff but I can see the wetness between her thighs. I'd done a good job of not letting her nakedness get to me but seeing her response to the punishment meted out on her juicy ass has my dick pearling.

"Do we have an understanding?" I growl, dipping my fingers between her thighs running my fingers through the essence. Bringing my wet digits up to my mouth, I suck them clean.

She's still nodding when I right her. "I'm sorry." I

can tell she means it and is not saying it out of fear. She seems ashamed for saying it.

Giving her a brief nod, I move her back nestled against my chest.

"Some punishment. She should be on her knees." Ignoring *his* harsh, scoffing complaint, I continue with the aftercare. Rubbing the goosebumps on her shoulders I note the chill of the room. She had to be chilly today. She never complained to the staff. Probably thought it was part of her punishment.

Solace surrounds us as we both look out into the garden.

"Why am I here, Hisashi?" Her voice sounds small, yet I detect the barest thread of hope.

"I'm punishing you," I say simply, holding her until I feel her drift off.

Liar.

CHAPTER
NINE

T aylor

~

A KIMONO ROBE is on the bottom of the bed with a note on top of it. Crawling over to the edge I pick up the card.

Enjoy the garden ~ H

I don't know if I should trust anything he does at this point. He said unequivocally that I'm here to be punished. I'm not going to make it easy. I know from therapy and studying people with his particular personality that fighting is futile, he'll only become more obsessed, his purpose darker.

My only hope is to get him to see me as Tay-chan again and not some*thing* he gets to punish or conquer. Arguing with him is pointless. He had months probably years to plan this.

Me coming to Shelby-Love was a mistake. Writer's block be damned because a change of scenery had done nothing to help my loss of words. In fact, it only seemed to exacerbate it. I couldn't refuse FADE's request when he asked that I be the artist in residence. The kids were inspiring, to say the least. It's just that I can't fake it anymore. I'd barely pulled the show off. It wasn't even new material — not really. Despite the calls to come back to Broadway and rework the material for a new production, I know without a doubt it would be an epic failure.

Hisashi taking me was a blessing in disguise. Hopefully, I'll slip from people's minds and the expectation of me delivering something fresh, new, and innovative to the theater masses will be forgotten until I am truly ready. That is, if I ever am. If he ever lets me go — even live.

I have no doubts he hates me. Leaving him after we promised forever. Abandoning him after he lost his father. He doesn't care about my reasoning. I don't know if I do either. I have never forgiven myself. How can I ask him to forgive me when I can't?

My shower is quick. I make sure to use sunscreen since I'll be in the garden.

I'm just tying my kimono robe on when there is a

light knock on the door. "Come in," I say, as if I have a choice.

Aiko comes inside bearing a tray laden with food and coffee. "Takeda-san says you may like to have breakfast in the garden."

"Yes." Smiling at her, I watch her put the tray on the table in front of the sofa before going over to the wall adjacent to the wall of windows. My eyes round as she steps up to it, pressing her fingertip into a place that is smooth and indistinguishable from the rest of the panel from where I stand gawking. A panel lifts, she leans in, a beam of light pulses. She shifts as another panel emerges. This one has a keypad. Then she presses a code into the kanji pad that I can't make out.

The doors open disappearing into unseen pockets. Turning back to me she smiles sheepishly coming to pick up the tray again. "Follow me please."

I follow, the small realization that escaping this hidden Samurai mansion in the absolute nowhere of Alabama is going to be impossible. Retina and finger-print scans, hidden panels, not to mention I know he's watching my every move with hidden cameras. I wouldn't be surprised if he placed a chip beneath my skin. I didn't feel any raised areas but doubt that he'd make it obvious. Hisashi is brilliant. His cleverness has never been the issue. It will make my leaving him absolutely impossible.

The smell of honeysuckle greets me as I enter the

paved expanse of the garden. I can hear the water gently lapping around me, the birdsong is sweet to my ears. I don't allow that to lull me into a false sense of serenity though. No. If anything the very tranquility of this place holds a sinister reminder of his power.

No one knows I'm here. My family thinks I've gone back to New York. My parents are on assignment in of all places Osaka, Japan. I find it interesting that they are halfway across the world in the one place the Takedas hold the most power while I am under the control of Hisashi again. I know without research or wonder that he did it. He pulled whatever lever he needed and called in debts he was owed to have my father reassigned to Japan after nearly twenty years.

I'm sure he's set up all types of proxies to intercede if people start looking for me. I'm completely at his mercy until he tires or kills me. I'm under no illusions of what his intentions are. I owe him a blood debt for my betrayal to him. I know I do. I made promises. I swore to never abandon him. He won't care I was left with no choice. He won't care if I regret it all to this day. His only mission is to punish and seek revenge. I know this. Then why am I still hoping to reach him in some way?

"Mrs. Takeda?" I start at the sound of Aiko's voice. Making my way over to the small table laden with my breakfast I smile my thanks.

"May I pour for you, ma'am?" she asks, already taking the carafe. Having no choice but to smile and nod, I settle into the cozy chair waiting as she pours the steaming chocolate liquid of the mocha latte into a delicate porcelain coffee cup.

Taking in the elegant lines of the dish, it doesn't take me long to realize it's the exact pattern I chose when we got married. At the time it seemed silly. We were so young. I was sure we'd break them all in a matter of months. No, it was in the days that followed when Hisashi smashed them one after another looking at me with an almost placid expression.

I'd given up pleading with him after the fifth one.

"Is my sweet little wife upset?" he asked almost detached as he carelessly smacked the dish to pieces between us in the kitchen. I don't remember anything other than I'd told him to be careful when he unceremoniously dumped a plate into the water as I washed the dishes.

"No," I whispered, keeping my voice calm. Small. Helplessly I watched as he destroyed every dish of the hundred-and twenty-piece set.

"Is there anything else you need?" she asks, dragging me back to my present nightmare, pretty though it may be.

"No thank you." Hearing the change in my voice I can't even bring myself to fake smile. My hands tremble as I reach for the cup. Squeezing my hands closed tightly I place them back in my lap.

I stare at the filled cup for long moments my fingers clasped in my hands. The beauty of the day is lost. I hated I ever came out here. Hated I asked, no begged. Now, I can't even eat.

My breath shudders in and out like I've run up a hill ten times. Is this some type of trick? Is he going to constantly taunt me with reminders of our time together? The things that terrified me and made me fear for both our safety?

"Ma'am?" I startle, an eep escaping as I look at Aiko.

"Y-yes?" I look at her, my eyes falling to the cell phone she's holding out to me.

My hands are still trembling when I take it from her.

Hisashi's hard face is on the screen.

"Why aren't you eating?" he snaps.

"I was trying—" I start.

"No, the fuck you weren't. You sat there for damn near thirty minutes looking at a veritable feast and not touching it. Are you trying to antagonize me, Taylor?" His voice licks over me with malice and anticipation.

"No." Making my voice strong I answer eyeing the nearly congealed spinach and feta omelet. One of my favorite breakfasts.

He stares at me hard as I eye the food then looks off. I wonder if he's looking at me from another angle. I wouldn't doubt it.

"Somehow I don't believe you." He ends the call.

Seconds later Aiko returns. I didn't even think to

call anyone so caught up in his anger and the knots forming in my tummy.

After pocketing the phone, she starts gathering the dishes. "Mr. Takeda says you can try again later." She answers my questioning look with a sheepish expression.

I stand to follow her back into the confines of my room, but she shakes her head. "You can stay out here as long as you like."

Breathing with newfound relief I don't take my seat again but take in the garden from where I stand. Following the sound of the water I soon come upon a little bridge. Koi frolic below, slipping and sliding around the pond. I know they are considered good luck, but they are hideous fish. We fed some the day we went on our little wedding day excursion. We flung the pebble sized food into the water watching how they ate as if in competition. Such a day of soft perfect love.

Thinking of the soft life we shared, my heart squeezes, so many dreams deferred.

Feeling stupid for hoping for more, I linger among the flowers and foliage for long moments getting lost in the beauty of the blossoms. The southern sun starts making its presence known. Sweat makes my kimono cling to me. Needing a shower and unable to resist any longer I head inside.

The room is a blank canvas. Nothing. A gilded prison. Something tells me to rush through my shower because the door will be closed and my only source of freedom will be gone.

It doesn't matter how many hours I've wiled away in the garden, it means nothing if I'm locked away. I don't care if the late fall night is cooler, I rather be out there than locked inside. Yet, I know if Hisashi returns, and I've not showered he will insist on doing it. I'd rather not add to my torment thank you very much.

After a bracingly hot shower and moisturizing with my favorite vanilla-rose, he's obviously procured from the source, the Love Apothecary and my cousins, Crimson and Clover, I step into the main bedroom. The room is cool. There is another kimono robe on the bed, pink and purple dragon printed on the soft silk. Twilight is on the horizon, and I can see the first sparkling stars in the night sky. I almost want to squee. They didn't lock me in again.

Hearing his firm strides, my heart squeezes and other lower parts clench. Hisashi stops just at the entrance leading to the garden. He shoves his phone in his pocket. "Just in time for dinner." He holds out his hand waiting.

Unable to take my eyes off him and his sheer beauty I tread over to him slipping my feet into the sandals I used earlier for the garden.

His hand is hard, firm, and warm when I place mine inside of his. Tugging me behind him he leads me back to the small table. The table is dressed for two, but I know better than to attempt to sit in the chair opposite him. The bone china tableware is the same from this morning. My heart starts beating harder than before if that's even possible.

Pulling me into his lap, he says nothing of my stiffness. "I'd thought after you had time to enjoy the garden to your heart's content today, you'd be more receptive to eating this evening," he muses, reaching around me to fill the plate with fingerling potatoes, broccolini, and red snapper. More of my tantalizing favorites. I wonder if my cousin, Krie even questioned this special request because she makes it off menu just for me.

Forking some of the succulent fish he brings it to my lips. Opening I then close my mouth around the aromatic fish chewing slowly. It practically melts on my tongue but it could be paper. All I see is smashed plates, bowls, saucers, cups, and serving platters. Nicks in his skin and flecks of blood splatter on his clothes. My nose stings, tears slip free.

I cough chewing a fingerling potato. He stops placing the fork down and handing me water. "Why are you crying?" He sounds genuinely troubled.

"You mean other than the fact you kidnapped me and are probably going to kill me?" I scoff after taking a sip clearing my clogged throat.

"Yes, other than me kidnapping and not deciding whether I want to kill you or not, yet," he deadpans.

"Why are you using this tableware, Hisashi?" I turn to catch his puzzled gaze as he looks from the table to me then back to me. I can tell he's trying to place something in his mind.

"I-it was the one you liked," he states with a vagueness almost as if it's a question.

I swallow when his gaze reaches mine. He just looks — lost.

Despite everything my heart shatters all over again.

Lips pressing into a hard line, he shifts uncomfortably, his gaze shifting away, then back. "I found a receipt for the purchase — later. Then I remembered you liked it. You smiled and kissed my cheek, then ducked your head to apologize because that isn't my way — to behave so freely in public." He eases back from me, propping his arm on the arm of the chair, looking at me through half cast eyes. "Am I misremembering?" He waits as if in challenge, but there's more confusion and hope he's doing everything in his power to mask.

"No." I smile at him a little. I long to reach and touch that hard jutting chiseled jaw. I bite my lower lip hard. "Is that all you remember about them?"

"Ahem," he clears his throat then shrugs. "You took them with you. There was only the receipt. I made sure to get everything you liked and bring it here for your visit."

"Oh." I look around at the garden so similar to the one we spent so much time in on our walks. It's not similar I realize but an exact replica. The bed. Ours. Ohmygoodness. What is he doing?

"Hisashi—"

"You need to eat, Taylor." He sits back up grabbing the fork spearing the broccolini, clearing his throat. "I will replace the dishes if they upset you."

I catch his wrist. "No, I do like them. I just thought they were part of the punishment." Leaning forward I pull the vegetable off the fork with my teeth to chew.

His other hand snakes around my middle pulling me back onto his hard dick. "You will know when I'm punishing you, little bitch."

He makes me feel him pressed hard against my pussy as he feeds me.

"Done?" he asks when I shake my head at the mostly gone fish.

"Yes," I tell him, hoping I can get up without the evidence of my desire causing me further embarrassment. I know his expensive suit has a stain from my arousal.

"Now it's your turn to feed me." On cue Aiko comes and replaces my meal with his. Thin slices of Kobe beef, horseradish and ponzu sauce, and an array of vegetables. The broth is steaming. I dunk the meat into it using the chopsticks. Taking it out I twirl it around with the vegetables feeding my mean ass husband.

"If I knew you had this, I would have eaten this too," I grumble.

"I didn't want to risk it with the way you've been wasting food," he tsks just as his phone buzzes.

I know it's his brother or some other member of his family. No one else would dare interrupt him while he is at home.

He holds his fingers up to his mouth his eyes hard, letting me know a severe punishment awaits if I make a sound.

"Hai." His eyes trail down. My gaze follows. The kimono has fallen open. Reaching between us he pushes the robe open farther exposing my double D mounds to his gaze. The rapid Japanese and the nuance of dialect tells me it is in fact his brother or someone else close to him.

Idly he begins to stroke my breast as he talks and listens to the other person on the phone. My pussy clenches and floods when he thumbs my nipples. I'm clutching the table his dinner all but forgotten. My other hand is curled into his dress shirt. I could feel his hard length pulsing beneath my ass. It takes everything in me not to grind myself against him like some needy fiend needing a fix.

I catch the name Thad in the discourse realizing this whole conversation has something to do with my young cousin. A hard steady twist on my nipple has me creaming and so close to orgasm. I'm squirming and panting.

"I'll see to it," Hisashi affirms before hanging up and turning to me. "I'd like to finish my dinner now."

Ignoring the coldness of his words and his cool assessment of me I do as he bids. If he's aware of my discomfort or the reasons for it, he doesn't let that deter him from eating nearly every morsel I feed him.

"I'm done," he tells me. Again a servant, this time a man comes, replaces food with a whiskey decanter, two glasses, and a black box.

When he leaves, I pour the drinks as I know he expects in traditional fashion. I see the way his eyes flash in approval. Something inside — that needy little bitch of his, preens from his tacit approval.

He nods to the box. Opening it I see three neatly rolled cigarillos and a titanium lighter. I take one long slender joint out along with the lighter. Placing it on my mouth I notice it's cold. Lighting the bottom I puff. The florid aroma of weed fills the night around us. Blowing the smoke out I pass it to him.

Relaxing back he takes draws on it exhaling the smoke out of his nose, tilting his head back.

"Are all of you Loves bound by treachery?" The way he asks so casually takes me a moment to realize he's insulting me.

"It seems hacking our plant isn't enough for your cousin. He's determined to destroy everything we've built in this community never mind the thousands of jobs he's going to cost. He's used Krie's closeness to my brother to further his goals. Only now she's left to pay in full for his sins. It seems she no longer has to suffer that burden alone."

"What do you mean?" My voice trembles at his words. All of the heat rising in my body gutters as my heart is pounding in my chest, my ears. Tummy plummeting, I take in the dark cast of his face along with the sheer menace in his face.

"It's simple. Thaddeus Love's fate rests not only in Krie's acquiesce to my brother's desires but your compliance to mine."

Hisashi

"Tonight," *He* whispers.

"Tonight." Lifting my neck, I swipe the growing beard from my face with the blade of the straight razor. Quiet pride races through me. A decade ago, I couldn't trust myself with such a task. Too tempted to bathe myself in my own blood or that of others.

The deadness I felt was a companion for far too long. Thinking of the burdens I'd placed on Kiyoshi, all the grief and turmoil I'd left him to deal with alone. The guilt is still a constant companion. Inconvenient for one like me, a pure psychopath but the fallacy about us is that we feel nothing. The opposite is actually true for those we've connected with. We care too much. Have been known to love them to death. Once we have decided a person is ours, they are so — irrecoverably. For me, Kiyoshi, my sister, and the unfortunate little soul who is now my wife all fall into that sphere.

The myriad of times he's told me he doesn't blame me. The forgiveness I insisted on seeking to his chagrin and mortification. None of it ever feels enough to repay him for saving me. What I needed of him. I was an emaciated husk when he finally hunted down the shadow facility I was confined. Needless to say, the Sagumo Hospital for Mental Care no longer exists nor do any of the staff directly in charge of my *care*. The way my brother carried me, carried this family in the face of my father's death at his own hands, is something I will never be able to atone for.

Nor will Taylor's abandonment in the midst of it all ever be forgiven. I remind myself leaving the bathroom to go into my closet to retrieve a suit for this special outing.

Inspecting the custom black on black silk with invisible seams, so my hypersensitive skin won't feel the thread work, I draw out the slacks slipping into them. The tailored fit is exactly to my specifications, with the right amount of room for my dick. Leaving them open, I get the dress shirt buttoned and tuck it in along with my t-shirt into my boxers, then button and zip my pants. I look at the floor-length mirror, taking careful inventory. Perfection is a must for this evening. I want my little nemesis's experience to be exactly what she deserves — just a taste of hope before I snatch it back and leave her begging for what could have been.

After the careful assessment and making minor adjustments to my hair adding a bit more pomade to tame some errant locks of my jet-black locks, I brush it back making sure it shines.

After applying the citrus, smokey cologne I know she loved those many years ago, I grab my suit jacket, snatching my key fob off the counter so I can leave. I pause at the threshold of my bedroom. Midnight black silk sheets, a board framed teak platform as close to the floor without being a mat. Ten years of loneliness. Ten years of penance. No peace. Abandoned by the woman I'm about to give the night of her life.

I look away from the reminder of my failure and her betrayal closing the door behind me with an ominous click of what awaits when I return to this room alone.

"Keep her," he insists.

"Not yet. Soon." My words brook no argument. *He's* tamer now that I've had my injection.

He's quiet, trying to be good, hoping I'll let *him* out to play or lying in wait for me to lay down my guard or have a break, I've vowed it will never come. I have too many safeguards in place now; a brother who knows to never allow me to go down that road again. I'd rather die. I'd take that fucking blade from earlier and slit my own throat. My medication is perfect now that I've found the proper therapy regimen. I meant to prove them all wrong when they locked me away and I haven't failed yet. Well, not since, and I don't intend to. There is too much at stake like Taylor Takeda's delicious punishment.

Taking the knowledge, I stride down corridor after corridor going into higher levels into which I deliberately separated us into in case the temptation becomes too great. Like I said, safeguards. If the need to fuck her to death takes me. The very long walk to her set of suites will give me time to reassess and burn off some of the rage and lust I feel for her. Not to mention I thrive in darkness and she is the light. She is like a flower needing the sun and I'm a serpent wanting the cool comfort of his cave.

The path to her rooms blooms with natural light and though she hasn't been on this side of the door since I brought her to my hidden mansion, I can still almost smell a hint of her fragrance. I lick my tongue out as if to taste and there's just a hint of vanilla-rose in the air. I don't know what aphrodisiac they put in the compound. I've heard it whispered as witchcraft, not one to dismiss anything with my family history. All I know, on the Love women it makes men reckless. However, me taking her wasn't spurred by the scent it was written when she broke faith.

I don't bother to knock. This is my house. My woman. The door opens silently. Her back is to me. Purple amethyst against the dark umber of her skin is stunning. The material of the couture fashion by Summer Love hugs her curves like a lover. The back dips in a wide V stopping at the rise of an ass so plump you'd think she'd paid for it. The strategic cut almost but not quite hides the plump little roll of a love handle I can't wait to play with.

"Turn around, Taylor." My voice is rife with lust as I stand at the threshold of the door where I've come to lean. When she does, I see the trepidation in her eyes. She's wearing the earrings I bought, pink diamonds with a purple amethyst in the center.

They catch the light and her messy but elegant updo makes her look regal, if not a bit subdued. The front of the dress has a tuxedo heart-shaped outline over her beautiful breasts. Her plump, lovely form is even more lovely from the front. I want to kneel in front of this woman after worshiping her from the crown of her head to her lovely little purple polished pinky toes.

There is a teasing side split reaching just to her thigh. The way her skin glistens is as though she's bathed in an iridescent body butter but that is just the way she takes care of her skin. She's the loveliest little thing. I almost regret having to break her. But break her I shall. The choice is no longer mine. She made it for us both all those years ago. The taste of retribution too sweet.

"Fuck her. Fuck her. Kill now. Fuck her. Kill her. Keep her."

I watch the way her eyes take me in. Her chest rises and falls. The effect seeing me dressed like this has the same reaction in her as me seeing her is having on my traitorous body. Fearing if I step farther into the room we'd never leave, I jerk my head turning into the hallway. "Let's go."

She clasps her hands together approaching me, my diamond sparkling on her ring finger. I wonder why she's never taken it off or put it away. I shove any hope of why away. She knew I lived. She knew where to find me. My face hardens just thinking about her perfidy.

Big brown eyes beg me for things that she dare never ask. "I don't have shoes," she mumbles to me as she approaches.

"I'm keeping you barefoot for the present," I tell her, stepping back allowing her to precede me out of the room.

"Not pregnant?" she quips.

"Never," I say with all seriousness. Her head dips but not before I glimpse the hurt clouding her features. She can't possibly know why that can never be. I don't bother to tell her why even if we were like we were before. She doesn't deserve my story, definitely hasn't earned one fucking thing beyond what I decide to give her. The brownish red tinge on her high cheekbones has nothing to do with the light blush she's wearing. I've hurt her.

"Taylor—"

"I'm being punished. I know that." She looks at the beautiful gown wondering what the catch is.

"Well, we better get started then." I smirk, tucking her hand in mine leading her out to my Maybach ignoring the feel of her eyes on me and the odd pang in my chest. Fuck this.

"WHY ARE WE HERE?" she asks hours later when the driver pulls up to the Gershwin Theater. She didn't question when we boarded my private jet and had dinner served in flight. She ate everything I fed her and fed me in return. It took everything in me not to have her during the flight, but I knew we were already pressed for time this evening being made possible by an unexpected opening in my schedule.

"It's opening night." Quirking a brow, I get out of the open door on my side, holding my hand out to her. As soon as she emerges, lights flash and theater paparazzi start hurling questions one after another at the long-lost darling of the New York theater scene.

In the last several years Taylor has become one of the most successful theater writer directors in the world. Her groundbreaking plays have solidified her as one of the most gifted of her time. Her depictions of the human spirit rising through adversity through love and community highlighting the need for introspection and grace have catapulted her into a stratosphere all her own. In the last few years, she's been rumored to suffer from writer's block and has come under scrutiny because of it. The pressure for new work is evident even tonight as we navigate the throng of the press, several celebrities, and theater influencers.

"Taylor are you back to stay?"

"Who's your date?"

"Taylor is that an engagement ring?"

"Taylor are you working on another play?"

I can feel her tremble as I tuck her small hand inside my arm. "Don't give them the satisfaction," I say for her ears only smiling down at her with the smitten indulgence I've practiced for such events.

She looks beautiful. She's mine. So, there's not much effort I have to expend for the pretense. The obsessive possessiveness she elicits in me is coupled with a warmth I've never been able to effectively eradicate where she is concerned. Distance. Time. Self-harm — nothing has been able to exorcise Taylor Takeda from my soul. I intend to make her atone for that particular agony.

If I didn't know better, I'd say she was my everything. But your everything doesn't leave you in your darkest moment. Your everything doesn't eviscerate your forever. Your everything doesn't leave you flayed, tortured, and alone — a mere shadow of what you used to be. I should thank her and I will for fully revealing her true self to me; fickle, selfish, craven. There is no place in the Takeda line for one whose loyalty is so feeble. I must gird myself as I work to rid my being of my troublesome addiction. The delicate strength as she faces this throng makes my dick hard and my heart twinge. I may find myself in her thrall once again if I'm too lax in my treatment of her.

"You're right." Saying that on the heel of my toxic thoughts is almost like a confirmation until I look down and see the soft hope in her eyes. "I'm not going to let them get in my head." Those damn dimples are almost my undoing. Inwardly, I groan, forcing myself to look away.

"Hai," I say, leading her into the theater.

Sensing she'd rather not mingle with those attending the VIP, I lead us directly to my box.

"I didn't know you had a box here," she whispers when I show her into my private seats.

I give her a vague little smile. "Takedas love the theater." Giving her nothing more than the gentle reminder of when she met my family the second time, I don't dare mentally touch the aftermath.

I can almost taste the curiosity she's bubbling with. I could use this time to toy with her more but then she reluctantly drags her attention to the main house of the theater and the boxes filling with her theater colleagues. More than one has taken notice of me, recognizing if not me then the family I represent. I see several heads dunk looking at their phones in google searches. On cue people start leaning and chattering in the boxes around us as speculation mounts. My brother and I could be twins and no one outside of the small enclave of Shelby-Love knows about his dalliance with the little chef. I'm sure the first reports will be wrong. Yet soon the news will be out because I have given the Creative Chaos team permission to reveal our marriage if inquiries are made. There will be no more hiding for Taylor. I will make my claim on her in every way possible starting tonight. She is mine. Soon there will be no doubt.

She takes the speculation in stride as if she's not hidden her marriage for the last decade. Holding her head up she smiles at me brightly as if I haven't all but forced her here. She's better than any stage actress I have ever seen. I can't help but give her a smile in quiet acknowledgment. She plays the gossips against themselves and to her own advantage. Regardless of the speculation or how she's come to be here she's not letting me or them make her the victim. She made all of us her acolytes.

The house lights dim as we are all admonished to put away flash photography and our cell phones. Silence falls as the play of boys from the wrong side of the tracks with big dreams begins. I watch Taylor as she's riveted by the play, her eyes turning glassy when in the second act one of the teens dies trying to save someone's life in a fire.

I hand her my handkerchief as she dabs her swimming eyes at the end. We stand and give them an ovation. "Brava," Taylor cries enthusiastically with the rest of the crowd.

The lights fill the theater. We wait as people start to file out. Being in the theater with her for the first time in years I can feel how it's still so much a part of her. The very ability to witness the process feeds her spirit in the same way writing code and figuring out algorithms does for me. Though the two are disparate as any two things can be what they mean to us is the same. They give our life meaning. Such a simple fact is how we came to be in the beginning. Why we work so well for that little while how we still could if there wasn't so much darkness between us now.

"This is one of the best adaptations of this story I've seen." I nod, familiar with the story but only aware the book purported to be written when the author was a teenager.

She looks around, almost as if in a panic. "Can we go out back? I don't want anyone questioning me about my next —" she cuts off, cringing. She looks up at me, sadness clouding her face. "Is this part of my punishment?" With the accusation comes a spark of anger. Her little curvy ass dares to step to me, her mouth forming into a deliciously malicious pout as she hisses, poking a sharp fingernail in my chest. I back up, allowing a cruel smile to form on my lips to further bait her. "You brought me here to remind me of what I love and do what? Snatch it away?" she demands as my back presses against the velvet tapestry that lines the wall of my private box.

"It didn't cross my mind but now you've given me the idea. Arigatō, Tay-chan." I laugh softly at her fury. I like the way it makes my dick hard. She's even more delectable mad. In a smooth movement I reverse our positions pressing her into the wall. Circling her neck, I pin her to the soft textured surface. "Make no mistake, little bitch." Bending low, I whisper hotly into her ear, my tongue darting out tracing the shell of the orifice with my tongue. I feel the way she squirms, reveling in each twist of her soft little body as it brushes against mine. "When I punish you tonight, you'll know it."

Her breasts rise and fall against me. I inhale the sweet smell of her. Her eyes are wide with a touch of fear and raw passion as she watches my nose flare getting high on her scent. Punish her? As if sitting beside her the whole night was not a punishment for me. I could taste, touch her, or simply gaze upon her beauty like some lovelorn youth on his first date. Watching her experience the play was an exquisite punishment De Sade himself couldn't have dreamed of. She is every temptation. Everything I desire.

"Tay-chan," I growl, buckling under the sensations teasing along my stretched control, burying my face in the hollow of her throat. Pressing between the drenched vee of her creamy thighs, feeling that hot little pussy pressing against me. I pull the soft flesh of her neck into my mouth, tasting the fragrance and much of her skin beneath my tongue. Lost in her, I groan, snatching her close, grinding the heaviness of my dick into her soft flesh. I can feel how much she needs me buried deep inside of her. Her pussy pulsing against me is a plea for the pleasure only I can give her.

"N-not here," she pants, her small hand pushing against my lapels.

I look down into the luminous pools of her eyes begging for what her mouth won't. Any number of her theater fellows are milling about outside of the confines of this not so secluded box. Some uncouth person could pop in at any moment seeking to speak with her. To be found in such a fashion would tarnish her hard-fought reputation. Making a note to have guards posted next time, I nod stepping back to give her space.

Turning I adjust myself in my trousers, so my dick won't be so prominent.

"Ready?" I ask over my shoulder.

She looks flushed and beautiful. Nothing seems out of place. Reaching out, I use my thumb to rub away the smear of make-up beneath her lips.

"Okay?" The apprehension on her face gives me pause. I narrow my gaze on her as a nasty thought emerges.

"Do you care more about what they think you've been doing or who you've been doing it with?" My voice sounds deadly to my own ears, but I don't care, I won't apologize for who or what I am. She needs to know that now. Not that she'll have a choice once the news of our marriage is leaked.

"People have speculated for years on the source of my plays' funding. A nobody coming on the theater scene fully privately funded for her plays when she's straight out of theater school and a failed fellowship is the feeding ground for gossip." She shrugs.

"So rather than tell them you were married to a mental patient you let them think you were a slut?" I nod, rage making my Japanese harsh and cutting. Head shooting up she looks like I slapped her. The fact that she doesn't deny it only serves to make my point and my anger hotter.

"After you," I whisper with ominous promise not giving a fuck about her pride and reputation at the moment. Yet more to add to the arsenal of vengeance I have for her.

"You live here?" She looks at me in wonder when the driver pulls into the high-rise apartment building she lives in as well.

"I don't see why not." Flicking a nonexistent piece of lint off my silk pant leg I glance at her dispassionately as possible. "I own the building."

I have to hold back my laughter when her head snatches around to look at me in shocked horror.

"H-how?" Her voice sounds strangled, her eyes round with surprise.

"A real estate acquisition including several properties owned by the parent company when Takeda absorbed them." I blink like it's the most common thing on the planet which it is. Takeda is always looking for investments, so no one batted an eye when I orchestrated this purchase.

She settles back into the cushions of the car for the brief moments it takes for the driver to take the private car lift that securely takes us up to my suite.

Kogi opens my door and I step out, returning his bow of deference with a brief one of my own. Straightening my suit, I come around, opening her side. When her small cool hand slips into mine, the possessiveness I've managed to stave off up until this point falls like ash from a flicked cigar. I help her smaller, curvier body out, liking the way she barely reaches my chest. We are close, as close as can be without touching. When I breathe, it makes her hair flutter. *Fascinating. Fucking beautiful.*

I lace our fingers, interlocking them, feeling the tremble in hers. I can feel her eyes on me, but I know better than to look. Putting her body protectively in front of mine, I lean forward, pressed against her soft body for the retina scan. The lock clicks and double doors slide open.

We're now standing inside the glass surround of the penthouse elevator. "I'll show you the downstairs tomorrow." Pressing the UP button, I look down at the mass of hair I can't wait to loosen from its chignon, watching it fall down her lush brown curves.

Ten years. Ten fucking years and not another moment longer, He promises.

The glass doors open into a gaiken. Silently we take our shoes off, placing them into their perspective spots.

I stand back, watching as she takes in the room in front of her, the amethyst dress flowing around her like a sleek invitation for me to slide it off her and leave it in a puddle on the floor.

The New York skyline is on full display as we enter from the right, looking out into the entire penthouse below us. It's like our previous loft, amped up to the thousandth degree.

There is a wall of windows facing us. We're too high to have an open terrace, but just beyond the living room below, the enclosed garden is visible. She slowly does a full turn, taking in every modern minimalist detail of the room, the free-standing, floating library on the far left side of the bedroom, stopping when she sees the bed on a raised dais enclosed on both sides with jute rigging behind her facing the expansive wall of windows. *Ten. Years.*

I can feel my dick firming. Her eyes track down, seeing the evidence of my need for her. They dart to the bed — particularly the rope. I tilt my head to the side, my mouth kicking up on one side.

She steps back. "Don't move." Disobedient little minx does the opposite and steps back five more steps. My heart rate accelerates the moment I scent her fear and arousal. *Her pussy is dripping. He* smirks. Dirty motherfucker.

"Don't. Move," Enunciating, I hiss each word. I warn her. She's only inciting *Him* and me. She doesn't have a chance. Not when we've been such good boys for so long. We're salivating for a taste. Ripping my jacket off I toss it in the area of the bed. Rubbing the ache in my chest I watch her eyes track me like so much prey.

"We will fuck you where you stand, little dove. But run, please run," His words growl out. She starts back peddling in a little jog. I tsk, shaking my head, waiting. Anticipation ratchets up my spine like an illicit shock, one that's welcome. They didn't kill this part of me, not any part really — only made me stronger. The man who claims, the samurai who conquers, the monster who hunts, the demon who devours, the husband who claims every part of his wife.

Turning, she sprints across the room, heading to the bookcases, quickly disappearing behind it. "You want to play, little dove, let's play." Calling after her, I throw my head back, inhaling the scent of her fear and arousal. The air is thick with it. My dick stretches hard and ready. My socked feet are a whisper on the sleek teak floor. She's barefoot and her feet leave damp prints on my floor, leading me in her exact direction.

"Oh, little dove, I thought you were cleverer than that. Come, make me work for it," I taunt, not bothering to hide the sheer glee I feel.

There is really nowhere to hide in the open space, so I take my time. This is my lair. Like the monster that rides me within and twin serpents I wear on my skin, I stalk my prey. It's like I can even hear her heartbeat. Just as I turn into the shelves, I see a hint of purple and track to my left darting around.

"You have nowhere to hide, Tay-chan, but I like the effort," I praise, stepping into the dark shrouded alcove only to find the dress she hastily shimmied out of to fool me. I pull the soft fabric to my nose, inhaling the lovely fragrance of her. *Delicious.*

I turn at the sound of the ding. *"Smart, little dove,"* He whispers. But the elevator won't move without a retina scan. No one will ever have access to me in that way again, not even her — especially not my dear wife, I almost spit the words. So, she has no choice but to get off and try her luck somewhere in here where the monsters lie.

I've been patient, more Buddhist priest than man in the years I've waited to claim her, watching over her, keeping her safe. I tell myself a few moments more won't matter, but my body sings another song. It's not sweet and melodic. More of the discordant mix of base and clashing tremble in an ever-rising cadence rising to the highest crescendo in my chest.

Grabbing the dress, I inhale her scent again letting it engulf me in her essence.

"We shall bathe in her," He promises.

Closing my eyes, I groan against the ambrosia that is all her. She calls to me. Wrapping the garment around my neck, I'm ready to drown myself in her.

Striding over to the bed I almost miss her feet peeking beneath the layers of fabric. From my vantage point I shouldn't be able to see her beneath all black but one pretty pinky toe hits the light at the exact wrong moment but right angle.

"Noooo," she cries out kicking the air as I drag her near naked form out from beneath my bed. The demi bra is fighting for its life as her bountiful titties jiggle and shake as she thrashes trying to no avail to grab onto the bedsheets. She manages to pull a few with her as she struggles.

"Do you want me to fuck you on the floor?" I growl, flipping her little ass over like a rag doll. Her eyes should've told me what was coming but slut that I am, I was distracted by a flash of pussy, so I'm unprepared for the sharp kick she gives me squarely in the solar plexus.

My breath catches as the hard kick sends me back so hard, I bang my head on the teak floor.

"Ow." Rubbing my head, I see stars rubbing a goose egg. "I'm spanking your pussy for that when I find you, *wife*," I growl.

Gingerly, I climb to my full height, heading to the

sleek paneled wall behind the bed on the other side of the bookcases. Pressing the panel, the pocket door slides open, revealing the grand bathroom of the master suite. Lights mimicking daylight illuminate the room. There is a massive tub in the center, a shower along the wall with floor to ceiling windows with one-sided views for privacy. Since my involuntary commitment, I don't like being enclosed. The feeling of being trapped makes my monster rise to protect, and once he goes into that mode, there is no stopping him.

Taking a mirror, I turn this way and that feeling the goose egg Tay-chan left me with. "Well met, little dove," I murmur, getting an ice pack from the bath fridge along with a few aspirins. I place the compress on the little rise on the back of my head, tossing back the medicine with a quick swig of water from my filtered tap. Pride at her resourcefulness swells in my chest despite the pain she's caused me.

"Take it out on her ass," He grumbles, seeming to feel it worse than me. I take my time knowing she's tucked safely up here with me. She won't be able to find the stairs leading to the lower level unless I show her myself.

After the pain subsides, I'm back on the hunt. I retrace my steps going back to look under the bed, the closets lining the gaiken. There is a seating area alongside the bed with a very particular chair suited for pleasure. The area behind it is the perfect hiding place for a smallish, little ball of fluff.

Pretending frustration, I sit on the bed, raking my hands through my hair as if I'm at a loss as to where she can be. I know if I attempt to go downstairs, she will hide again. Standing, I walk as if I'm going back to the alcove by the bookcases.

I see a hint of movement just as I suspect. I take a few more steps in that direction before pivoting and rushing my prize.

Shoving the chair aside, I force her to track to her left. Another floor to ceiling window is to her back. Her breasts rise and fall as she takes rapid breaths. Her eyes dart around looking for escape before settling on me.

"Aht, aht, aht. I've caught you, little dove."

CHAPTER
ELEVEN

T aylor

~

A SLOW, vicious smile spreads across his face. My traitorous body melts as I watch his eyes darken knowing he's won. Thinking I can throw him off balance, I shove him as hard as I can pitching my body to the left.

For half a second, I think I'm free until I feel his hard ass hand snake around my neck snatching me back. My feet leave the ground when I take flight. The world tilts for a panicky second. My body is pushed against the cool glass of the window.

Breath rushes from my body. My head glances off the glass and my eyes smart from the sting. He is not being gentle. I don't want gentle from him. I want the real him. No careful lover. I want him to show me the monster that lives inside.

"I. Said. Don't. Fucking. Run." He kicks my legs open wide. A combination of fear and hot anticipation have left them feeling like Jell-O.

A smile of pure evil kicks at the corner of his mouth. He leans in so close his breath heats my skin, his tongue flicks out first tasting then sucking my earlobe into his mouth.

I can feel every inch of him when he presses in again. His dick is so hard. It feels so fucking good. A whimper escapes my mouth.

"I can smell your pussy, little bitch. What are you running for?" He sneers low into my ear sending shivers through my traitorous ass body. This slutty girl is weak for this man.

"I don't want this," I say, lying through my teeth not daring to look up into his all too knowing eyes.

"Really?" Doubt resonates around us like a blast warning the challenge will be accepted and tested to its fullest.

In one swift movement he's moving my wet panties to the side and sliding two of his fingers inside my pussy. He pumps and curls. Thrusts deep, pulling out to tease my clit with vicious promise. He pulls the two drenched digits out holding them between us, the evidence dripping from his fingers as viscous evidence of my lie before taking his forefinger and sucking it clean then pressing his middle finger between my lips and making me suck my essence off. He pushes it back far enough to test my gag reflex before slowly retreating.

"She says different, little liar." He gives me a rakish grin before his eyes cloud with menace. "Open." I do.

He sucks my flavor off my tongue in that kiss. I moan against the luscious devouring possession. I can't keep my breath he's taking it all. I moan against him needing more, so much more. Every time he's touched me has only primed me for more. I've been waiting for his loving for so long. My body is about to combust, and he's barely touched me. I can't get close enough to him. His scent is all-encompassing. I want to get in his skin.

His hand cups me and I nearly come from the pressure. I'm so caught up in the pleasure, I'm not ready for the hard smack on my pussy sending me to my knees when he releases me at the same time.

Hot shuddering spasms rack through my body. Tears spring to my eyes. A heavy hand wraps around my messy bun dragging me to my feet.

"I told you I would be spanking this hot little pussy for your defiance. The last person who kicked me, I fed him his foot." He looks up as if reminiscing, then shaking his head he looks at me his eyes hard. Cupping my chin, he says, "You're very lucky, little wife, I have use for you." His voice is so calm devoid of emotion as if someone else has slid in the place of the man whose eyes burned with passion a moment ago. The smile that blossoms is for me but not one I've seen from Hisashi before.

"Keep fighting. I like when you do that." His kiss is all-consuming, devouring, but cold, so chillingly erotic. He said to fight, but the moment I move my head, the hand clamped in my tresses tightens. He groans, leaning in, grinding. Fucking me with his clothes on. If not for the material separating us, he'd be inside me. I feel every tantalizing slide of his dick as he rubs against me. He aims himself to brush my clit over and over. I can't help but ride him. I'm his puppet. His doll to maneuver however he wishes. I let him use me. Meeting every movement, I'm so caught up that when the second orgasm slams into me, I'm calling his name, "Hisashi."

He holds me against the wall, muttering, in Japanese. I can't really catch it and assume I'm mishearing the words, "Not him."

"Hisashi," I say again.

He stills, eyes half-mast. He's panting. His dick is still pressed deeply against me. Stepping back, his hand finds my ruined panties, and he rips them from my body. The sting has me curling into myself. Eyes on me, he unbuckles, unzips freeing himself. His stiff, long staff rises high and hard between us.

Looking down, I watch as he fists the heavy flesh.

"Look at your husband when he fucks you for the first time in ten years." My eyes fly to his. Gaze dark with lust, hot with passion and more than a tinge of anger, he notches the thick head of his dick at my entrance. "Watch me split this motherfucker open, little wife. No, you put me where you want me," he demands, dropping his hand.

Watching as my trembling fingers circle his massive dick bringing it to my pussy lips, I bite my lip rubbing him against my aching slit. My heart is beating so hard. I'm scared. I remember how it hurt that first time. It's been ten years since a man has been inside me. He's not going to be gentle. He never was before. He hates me now. I know it with every fiber of my being. Still, I press down inviting him in.

"Fuuccck, little dove," he groans, his hand slapping hard against the window as he's easing the head of his dick into me. I can feel the window vibrate against the force of the blow but he's not hurting me. No, he is being achingly careful. Still, he's so big — too big for my tender flesh.

"It's too much," I whine, pressing my head back while trying to watch what he's doing.

"And you're going to take it too," he grits, his gaze tracking from my eyes to where we're joined. He bites his lips giving me no quarter.

I press my hand against his hard abs trying to slow him down, but he remains persistent pushing in with slow relentless pressure. The rasp hurts so good. I don't know if I want to push him away or pull him close and grind down on his big ass dick.

"Hi—"

"Shh," he hushes me. "I got you, little one." Lifting my leg, angling it wide, he presses in. Making the breath seize in my chest. My heart is thudding so hard my body is vibrating with it. It's like he's in my fucking chest.

"Breathe goddammint," he grits.

I look up to see him watching me, fierce intent marking his face. His teeth are clenched like it's costing him his very life to go slow.

Nodding, I exhale. My body relaxes. He slips deeper. Then a hard thrust and he's home, bottomed out inside me, hard and pulsing. My muscles squeeze and release, I'm so close. Another heaving exhale shudders through my body. I can feel the dense hair around his dick brushing against my clit. He's flush against me. The contrast is so evident. His tall wiry frame is pressing my soft, plush flesh against the cool glass. He's so hard everywhere, angry and I'm afraid. None of the differences are lost on me. Still here we are together sharing in the most intimate of dances.

"Good fucking girl," he growls, tipping my head back with his free hand as he takes my mouth. He draws my tongue into his mouth. He sucks and slides his own against mine. My pussy clenches loving the way he takes control. Impossibly he glides deeper. I gasp.

"So fucking wet for me," he praises.

Slow strokes eat up the distance as he fucks me

against the floor to ceiling window. His drives are powerful and almost punishing. He drives me up to my toes thrusting up inside me like he wants to fuck me ten years in this moment. Every drive of his merciless hips is making up for time lost. I feel him everywhere. My ass is slick against the glass sliding up and up with each thrust of his pistoning hips. His thighs surge powerfully up as he fucks me like his life hangs in the balance. I know mine does. I claw and cling to him seeking more of what I know only he can give. If I had to miss his lovemaking for his raw, senseless, fucking then it makes it almost worth it.

He's taking his time like he wants to savor every moment like it's our last. He commands my body. I can only hold on kissing his chiseled jaw, nipping his lips, sucking on his neck, hell anywhere I can reach as he pounds my pussy with impeccable precision.

His breathing is steady while mine is erratic. He's fucking like he's trained for this. His mission is to plunder and damn if he's not a pirate pilfering every bit of treasure kept from him these last ten years. I want to give it all to him in that moment. He doesn't even have to ask.

The orgasm is at the edge of my periphery, but I'm scared to ask for it. Is this the punishment? More edging? More orgasm denial? I bite back the plea hoping he'll take me over if I'm a quiet girl.

"I like the way you're sucking me in, little dove.

You kept this pussy so tight for me." His praise would make me preen if I didn't need to come so bad.

"Yes, only for you, Hisashi." I want him to see my loyalty. "I've been good."

"I know, Tay-chan." He finally moves his hand from my hair wedging it between our sweat slick bodies. Nimble fingers find my hard little nub and get busy making naughty little swirls around it. "Such a good girl for me." His soft words belie the hard way he's fucking me against the glass that has no give. Having no place to go I simply melt into him taking the full force of his merciless thrusts.

"Such a good little slut only for your husband, hmm?" He drives harder making my toes curl and my pussy shatter.

"Ohmygoodness, Hisashi," I cry as the orgasm is punctuated by the wet saturating sounds of my come hitting us both and splattering on the floor.

He doesn't stop, if anything my climax propels him higher, chasing his own release. Grabbing my other leg, he links them both over his long arms splaying me against the glass. I hold on to his shoulders for dear life.

His dick lends its own punishing torment of pleasure hitting every inch of me. My come is overflowing making us messy as he slams home again and again. All his anger, pain, passion, and the ferocity of his longing pours into me driving me into another orgasm as he cries my name as the hot jets of his release flood my womb.

His head drops into my neck as his body vibrates from our shared bliss. He doesn't stop his hips keeping the maddening pace as he rides his orgasm like a wave.

His eyes are half cast in that sexy ass way I love and he slows down but doesn't stop fucking me. His hips just slow to an erotic rhythm. I don't think he could stop if he wanted to. We are both caught up. This man has me wide open. I'm his to do as he wishes.

Eventually he slows to a stop.

Instead of sitting me on the floor he pulls me higher. I gasp feeling his dick still high and hard inside me.

"I have you," he mutters. Turning away from the window, he heads over to the massive black bed.

Still connected he falls back against the pillows with me straddling him.

He takes my lips in a soft languid kiss. We kiss in long, slow pulls savoring moments missed. Mine are of apology, his of longing. They are sweet, gentle pulls of lips and dips of tongue, learning each other again until they aren't.

I feel the tug once more sliding within us as if some dormant entity that's been asleep these ten long years has awakened in these last moments wanting every second missed of touching, and tasting this man erupts inside of me. My muscles clench and a deep ache blossoms in my body, demanding that I ease it.

Slowly, I start grinding on him.

"That's it fuck me," he urges. "It's been too long. I need more. I'm such a greedy motherfucker when it comes to you."

"Same," I say, looking down into the liquid onyx of his gaze.

Swerving my hips, I work myself up and down on his dick knowing I'm going to be hurting tomorrow but not enough to care in the moment.

I'm feeling every minute of those ten years we lost, too. I ride my husband just as nastily and with the same desperation as he did me. Bending down, I suck his tattooed nipple into my mouth, giggling when he gasps, and I feel his dick kick hard inside me.

"Oh, we got tricks?" he growls, making me sit up so he can press my breasts together, sucking both my nipples into his mouth as he drives up into me. I take him, moving my legs forward so I can rock into him over and over. Over and over, I slam my pussy down onto his dick. Each time is better than the last, but it's not enough.

Sensing my frustration, he thrusts up meeting me stroke for stroke. His fingers find my clit and he start massaging the slick tissue making my hips snap faster.

"Look at you riding my dick like a good fucking girl," he growls, his eyes trained on where he's flicking my clit. The whole measure of me in that moment is caught up in how good he's making me feel. And feel him I do. Every inch of him slams into me again and again. Low in my body clenches painfully as an internal orgasm shatters me following immediately after is the dizzying soul retching his busy fingers cause when he manipulates my clit into another intense climax.

Liquid flows from my pussy all over his hands and dick making me slick and messy.

"Fuck yeah." He pulls from me, spreading me wide, licking my pussy clean. He rises panting, looking down on me, his face a mess from his feast. Wiping his face he drags his hand sinuously down the hard planes of his torso until he cups his sac.

"Clean me, little dove." The seduction in his voice is irresistible.

Crawling to my knees I take him fully into my mouth, moaning when he thrusts down my throat fucking me slow. Cupping the now limp messy bun he rides my mouth, taking it easy on me. I lick him clean, loving every drop of our mixed essences. He tastes like mine.

"No." Pulling out he positions me on my hands and knees. Bending me forward until my face is buried in the duvet, he brings my hands behind me making me cup my elbows. "Stay here for me." Smoothing a heavy hand down my back his caress trails from the valley of my shoulders down through the crevice of my bottom until he's cupping my drenched, plump lips. Spearing two fingers inside he works me until I'm riding him on my own. So close. So close. Methodically he pulls free teasing me, torturing me.

I can't see but I feel him reaching. I still hear the slither of the jute. There is a pause. "Do I have your permission?"

I'm quivering. Terrified? Yes. Still wanting it? Definitely. Ten years ago doesn't enter into my mind. It wasn't his Kinbaku practice that hurt me. The reason behind his behavior was deeper than I imagined.

I pause long enough for him to shift as if he won't continue.

"Yes— you have my permission to use the rope, sensei," I hurry to add knowing how important it is to give him permission in this way.

The scene starts immediately when he slowly laces me from elbow to wrist. Once there, he inspects his work making sure he's not constricting me painfully. Taking the rope he wraps it over my shoulder crisscrossing my breasts. Wrapping around my back he twists taking it through my wrist again securing my hands in place then down between my ass cheeks splitting and crisscrossing over my pussy lips trapping my clit. The pleasure and intensity makes my eyes cross. "Ohmygoodness, Hisashi," I cry, bucking a little.

"I got you, little one," he assures me, securing the jute masterfully with no knots.

Rising he pulls me slowly suspending me in his strong grip as he slides home. My walls welcome him like a long-lost friend, clutching and kissing every inch of his dick as he splits me open like he promised.

"I wanted our first time to end like this. Thank you for letting me give you this pleasure, wife." He drives inside me, touching places that have languished for far too long. My body responds. I meet every hard plunge like the greedy little fiend that I am. He takes and I give. I give and he devours.

Hips slamming into me, his left hand explores my bound body. He tweaks and pinches my nipples to almost painful points until he smooths the soft mounds of my breasts with his hand then slaps them making them sting with pleasure. I squeeze him so hard in response I almost make him lose his seed.

"Uh, uh," he growls, snatching me close making me take more of him. "Take all of me." Thrusting up, he hits my spot like he never forgot where it lay. He pays close attention as he forces me into orgasm. "Edging you was never the punishment, little bitch." He grinds his dick in me, fucking me through the orgasm. I'm a rag doll. My body is his toy and he unashamedly plays with me. A heavy hand smooths over my belly dipping and swirling in my navel then working its way down. "No. Making you my cumslut is. You've come so prettily for me so many times tonight. Come for me one more time while I push this nut inside you. Show me you never forgot who you belong to," he whispers in my ear making me shiver. His dick feels like nirvana. Bliss rips through me. It's as if his words alone took me over the precipice then his fingers descend keeping me high and he follows me over the edge, his hot come flooding me again. Hot, sticky, filling me past overflowing. Still, I take everything he has to give, thanking him for the pleasure and the pain just like the little creature made for pleasure he sought to create.

I barely register him freeing me from the jute rope, wiping me down with a warm cloth, massaging my limbs, and tucking me into bed.

CHAPTER
TWELVE

T aylor

~

THE BED IS STILL warm when I wake a short while later. I have never been a good sleeper. My childhood was plagued by me never having a good night's rest. My parents tried all types of therapy and sleep studies. I only slept well with Hisashi. For about three years after my time in Tokyo it evolved into full-blown insomnia. I suffered through many sleepless nights, my mind plagued with worry for him and waiting to hear from his brother, whose communication was shotty at best.

Then one spring night I started sleeping. Then off and on I would have bouts of insomnia, but they were few and far between. My therapists said it was repressed trauma from childhood and what I went through in Japan. I didn't quite believe her. My trauma around Tokyo was less about the state Kiyoshi found me in but more about my worry and guilt around abandoning Hisashi. I don't downplay the horror of what he did to me, far from it. He nearly killed me. No matter how unintentional it was I suffered because of it yet I know down to my soul he did not intend to do it. I forgave him a long time ago.

I know he still seethes with anger with me for leaving. I'm not sure how much he remembers of that time considering the whole episode with the dinnerware. He was completely oblivious to why I was upset. It was more than clear to me he didn't realize he destroyed all of it with cold calculation.

It's eerily quiet. I sit up surrounded in darkness. Cool bamboo sheets glide over my skin when I get out of the bed. I go over to the seamless door leading to the bathroom. The door opens soundlessly. The dim light illuminates the bathroom as I pad over to what I assume is the water closet. Knowing my husband as I do I know he'll never have a toilet in the same room he showers. In that we are the same. A separate water closet was the reason I chose this building in the first place.

The fact that I qualified at the time was no mystery. I knew that Kiyoshi would pull any strings possible to keep me from having any reason to come back to Tokyo and making more of a mess of his brother's life. Not that I can blame him. They'd done a good job of keeping Hisashi safe for years before I came along. Then I came into his life and coupled with the heartbreak of his father's death a complete disaster ensued. I feel more than a little responsible even after years of therapy and understanding I was just a girl dealing with a situation so far out of my experience I could have never prevailed.

Heading over to the sink after I finish in the restroom, I wash my hands. It's chilly in here, I know he likes it cool. My nipples harden under the cool air. I look around for a panel indicating his closet. Everything is smooth. I press along the walls of the bathroom and find cabinets for toiletries, towels, soaps, even cleaning supplies but no closet.

Heading out to the massive bedroom suite I go back to the area we entered and opposite the gaiken I find the panel. There's a beep when I enter. "Well, there goes the element of surprise. I enter and the closet is massive as expected. There is every season represented with whites, grays, blacks, tans, and the occasional forest green here and there. These are his comfort colors. Nothing to trigger him. I notice the fabrics are soft and natural.

Taking out a neatly folded t-shirt, I frown. It's going to be a tight fit and I'm going to stretch it out of whack, but I didn't see luggage packed for me, so it's not like I have a choice.

Just as I suspected his t-shirt pulls tight across my breasts making my nipples poke out, hugs my tummy, stopping just shy of my coochie. Having no choice, I stretch the fabric over my knees so it covers my ass- barely. The bottom curve is still exposed. Oh well. It can't be helped. That's what he gets for bringing me here in the first place.

I already know he's not up on this level but when I see the stairs leading down to the lower floor I hesi- tate. Is he working? Seething?

My daddy didn't raise no coward though, so I take the stairs. My mom also didn't raise a fool so I try to be as quiet as I can be in case he's in a mood. How come I feel like one of those silly girls in one of those horror movies as I make my way down the stairs? Midway down I almost turn around but then I see the main level of the house and I'm compelled to continue. My toes curl on the cool marble cut in a chevron pattern before my toes sink into a thick rug. I wiggle them into the nap. The expansive sofa is facing the floor to ceiling window leading out to the enclosed garden.

He spared no expense creating this haven for himself. The entire room feels like a refuge. I wonder if he even uses it. The space is a serene oasis. Walking around I take note of Hisashi's minimalist style. Noth- ing's changed in the time we've been apart.

After making a circle I find the smooth curved wall leading to a dining room, passing that I see an eat-in kitchen that leads to indoor terraced Japanese garden.

It's beautiful. There is even a bridge and a koi pond. There are twin budding cherry blossom trees with a bench sandwiched between them.

I turn from the beauty, my heart twinging remembering our many walks when he said he needed to get out and touch grass. He always seemed to treat the time away from his bank of computers with grudging reverence. Like he was torn between two mistresses. I'm glad he's found balance.

I come back around to the living area. I know he won't be found unless he wants to. Hisashi loves nothing better than a hidden room and seeing there is no open office space out here I know he's hidden away. I head for the stairs then see a glimmer of light to the right of them.

Stepping around the stairs I follow the barely lit path. It's not hidden if you're familiar with the penthouse. It opens into a whole different area this more beautiful than the last and comfortable. Another deep sofa. The light was coming from a muted TV, so thin it looks like a projection. The room is still dark but when the sun rises it will be filled with sunshine as it faces the east.

I can imagine being cuddled and watching my favorite shows or theater productions. Too late to snatch the thought back I want to kick myself. I'm forgetting why he brought me here in the first place and it wasn't to cuddle my silly ass. No, it was to punish me, and make me beg for his dick.

Shaking my head in disgust I swing around to head back up the stairs. I see the door behind the sofa. He's not even fully closed it.

My heart slams in my chest. Walking on silent feet I move over to it. The door is ajar. It's not an office, it seems to be a security room. I stop just inside trying to make sense of what I'm seeing. Hisashi is sitting before a bank of CCTVs. His serpents are on full display on his back, their bodies in a fierce battle of dominance.

There are cameras aimed at every part of my life. My apartment that's several floors down from this one. He has a camera in every room. There's another four covering the house I rented in Shelby Love that I didn't get a chance to move out of yet. There's even one in my car.

There are labels on the ones that are dark. DR. AHMED'S OFFICE, PARENTS, THE KANDIE SHOP, THE CAMELLIA, THEATER.

He doesn't respond to my gasp. I step closer watching him benignly watching my life. There are also other cameras for people associated with his family or the company. They are also dark, except the one trained on my cousin's Krie's house and his brother's Kiyoshi's mansion and several for the Creative Chaos chip plant. There are another two labeled THADDEUS LOVE one for car and one for dorm. Thaddeus' life hangs in the balance and possibly Krie's as well if my young cousin doesn't stop hacking and causing problems with Creative Chaos.

"Why are you out of bed, little dove?" He sounds tired.

"Why are you?" My response is a direct result of the fatigue I hear in his voice.

"One, I can't keep my hands off you. It took a considerable amount of my control not to slide back inside of you while you slept." The cool honesty of his words sends a shiver through me. His admission should scare or repulse me. Instead, I feel liquid heat pool low and deep. My muscles clench at the thought of him fucking me awake. I'm just as depraved as this motherfucker.

"Um," I clear my throat focusing on the bank of computers. "How long have you been stalking me, Hisashi?" Stiffening at my words, his hand flicks a button and then my face in the present fills all the screens.

"You're mine to watch over. To fuck when I please. To punish. I don't have to stalk what's mine." His voice is brutal and clear. We both watch the horror spread on my face on the screens before us.

I take a step back.

"Don't," he snaps. He manipulates another screen and my apartment fills every screen.

"You wanted to know when the company whose holdings includes this building became part of Takeda? It occurred about a month after I discovered you lived here." Slowly he turns to me. "I've always watched over what's mine. I won't apologize. Come here."

Something tells me if I run, and he goes to catch me this time he won't be gentle.

I step over until I stand between his spread thighs.

"Good girl." His head is level with my breasts, but his head is tipped down looking at my thighs. I resist the urge to squeeze my thighs close. Knowing how hypersensitive his sense of smell is I know he can smell my arousal. Cringing I shift uncomfortably. He grips my hips his hands covering the hem of the shirt. "I like you wearing my clothes." Always full of surprises he adjusts the t-shirt lower rather than up as I was sure he'd do.

"I-it's too small." I squirm. He leans in pressing his face against my rounded lower belly. "So soft, so mine," he murmurs, rubbing his face into the fabric inhaling deeply. My pussy slickens with moisture. He pulls back until his eyes are level with my now hard tipped breasts. "Who says?" All grumbly menace, he quirks an eyebrow.

"It's a fact." I shake my head at him failing to fight the little smile that plays at the corners of my lips.

"Hmm..." Leaning in he captures a nipple in his mouth softly sucking it through the cotton. His mouth is so hot and deliciously wicked as he tugs it. His hands tighten on my hips making me take the pleasure he metes out.

Once the fabric is saturated with my nipple pressed tightly against the fabric, he moves to the other repeating the process. His hot mouth covering me, long drags sending sparks of pleasure from my breast straight to my hot center. "You wearing my shirt is a wet dream, little dove."

Turning me, he sits me on his lap facing the screen and begins to narrate. "This is three years after you left me. It took me a long time to feel like myself again—" He hesitates trying to find the right words. "Find balance. When Kiyoshi told me where to find you I came here and watched over you."

The screen shows me coming home some random night after rehearsal for Charles the Tenth, a play I wrote a about a bootstrapping young man who fights his way to the top in business only to realize everything he's gained is pointless without all of the things he took for granted on his way to the top. It was hailed as a "Citizen Kane on steroids at the time, with a rural urban twist" by one critic earning me a Tony Award. I remember the pressure of the rehearsals, the grueling schedule, and several prima donna actors. I watch as I trudge into the apartment kicking the door closed. It self-locked I remember but I didn't even bother to check. I dropped all my stuff at the entrance. Though it wasn't a gaiken, I still used it as one kicking my shoes off bypassing my house slippers.

Shedding my clothes as I go, I head straight to the shower. The apartment was spacious for a one bedroom by New York standards, but it still would only take up barely a corner of this palace in the sky.

The camera switches to the shower as I head to the water closet. No camera in there. I wait to watch as I emerge stepping from the toilet, remembering how much I wanted to take a bath but didn't have the energy. It looks like I take the quickest shower in the world. After a quick dry and moisturizing I walk naked into the bedroom. I turn on my pink fairy lights, say a quick prayer, and dive into my bed. I sit back up after a couple of minutes. I take a water carafe by the bed. I touch it in wonder because it seems cool, I shrug it off and grab the bottle of generic Benadryl taking two then lay back down.

Minutes tick by and I wonder why we are just watching me sleep when I see a dark figure emerge from my closet. Jolting forward, I gasp as strong arms keep me planted on his hard thighs.

"What?" I turn to him, and he just nods back to the screens.

"Watch." He's not even looking at me.

I turn back. A tall wiry form I immediately recognize as the man holding me steps out of the shadows. He's dressed in a black hoodie with a ski mask and gloves. He paces around the bed several times. He's muttering in Japanese seeming to argue with himself. For long moments he simply gazes at my sleeping form.

Finally, he sits at the bottom of the bed holding his

head in his hands like he's an athlete who's lost a big game. He rakes his hair back and forth between his hands then looks at me. Even from here I can see the anguished longing in his face, I see it morph into anger too. His hands squeeze and flex as he fights an internal battle, I can only imagine is raging inside of him.

He shoots to his feet and stalks away. The cameras switch as he drops to the ground, doing what must be two hundred push-ups, followed by sit-ups and martial arts moves that are slow and methodical.

He strides to the shower making sure to close the door silently. He goes into the water closet. He jumps into the shower using my products.

"Jesuslord," I whisper, a tight knot forming in my throat. "How did I sleep through all of this?" I don't bother to look at him. I know he wants me to keep my eyes on the screen. I'm also scared of what I may see in his expression.

"It wasn't Benadryl. You were having so many problems sleeping — night terrors. It was affecting your work." The admission is so matter-of-fact. He actually believes he was in the right. I shake my head.

"You shouldn't have done that," I tell him.

"There's a lot of things I shouldn't have done. I did them. I'd do it again." Unapologetic to his mother-fucking core he manacles my throat. "When you promised me forever, it meant forever at least to one of us." His hand rests there as we watch him finish his shower and ablutions.

He pauses as he leaves the bathroom. In the bed I'm already tossing and turning clearly in the midst of a night terror. I'm thrashing, tears are spilling down my face. I don't know if the dream stems from the embassy attack when I was small or from my time with Hisashi but I'm lost in its throes.

Striding nude to the bed he slips beneath the covers gathering me into his arms. Immediately I settle.

I can feel my eyes widen. My heart stutters. How the hell did I lay there resting my head on his chest and not remember any of it? He lays there speaking softly in Japanese telling me a fairytale, rubbing my back.

A soft snore escapes me and in the present I blush embarrassed. He cups my head and seems to settle himself, but I can tell he's not sleeping but watching over me like he promised.

He fast-forwards a few hours. My sleeping body moves. Biting my lip, I watch myself move and stretch over his. He's a stone beneath me then and now as I watch the sleeping me wind and grind on his still form. My cheeks and body heat watching the cover slip low on my waist exposing me to the rise of my bottom as I masturbate myself on my prone husband. His hands are fisted on the sheets. Up and down and around my hips gyrate at an increasingly fast speed until it's obvious I'm climaxing.

"Hisashi," I hear myself moan as I come before

settling back into a deep sleep. Turning away from him, sleeping me curls into a little ball obliviously unbothered by the torture I've just wrought on the man I didn't know held me all night.

Hisashi lies there. His dick is tenting the covers. His precum is wetting the sheet. He eases out the bed, his dick raging and primed. He stands over my sleeping form and starts pumping his engorged length. He takes the precum from the tip slicking it down, cupping his sac. He fucks his fist his gaze burning with hot lust as he watches me sleep. Feet planted wide his hand rapidly strokes up and down until come erupts from him in a wide arc splattering the sheets, his chest, and his belly.

Going back into the bathroom he cleans his mess, dresses, presses a kiss on my brow, and leaves.

I sit in stunned silence, not sure of how I should feel. There is so much wrong with what he did but trying to make myself accept exactly how disturbing it is seems way more harder than it should be.

Moving back in the chair he pushes me to stand his eyes daring me to move. He stands and lifts me until my bare bottom is on the CCTV's console free space. His pecs jump making his serpents dance as he spreads my thighs stepping between them. They seem to slither watching me just as he does. "Are you afraid of me —what I'm capable of?"

I think to how he could have fucked me and have to ask, "Did you ever— umm?"

"Take what is mine?" His mouth kicks up in a nasty smile. He looks at me for a long moment before shaking his head slowly. "You saw yourself. Even in your sleep your soul recognized its life's mate. I didn't have to. Just as I don't have to take your tight little pussy now." Shifting he releases himself from his sweats, positioning his dick at my entrance. "See how eager she is for me?" He presses in stretching me. Instinctively I raise my feet to the console giving him more access. "Fuck yes." Driving in he doesn't stop until he bottoms out. I can feel his sac press against me.

"It's too much," I pant, feeling him deep within me hard and relentless. "It hurts." I shift trying to give myself a margin of relief.

"It's supposed to." He shudders. "It's hard for me too. I haven't been with anyone else in all this time either."

The hushed admission has me pulling back looking at him in surprise. His hard mouth slams down on mine. Like how dare I ever have thought otherwise. I didn't feel he owed me loyalty after the way I abandoned him. I'm not going to lie. I cried at times thinking about it especially when I saw vague speculations about him dating various heiresses.

"Never," he promises as he begins to take me in that tender rough way I love. "Never," he vows, looping my knees over his arms as he braces on the console, thrusting at an angle that teases my spot with focused deliberation.

"Never." Reaching out I touch his hard jaw my muscles clenching when it tenses, and he turns his face into my hand kissing my palm.

Minutes later we cry out together as we vault into bliss as one being.

Slow to come down, my thighs are shaking and achy as he eases out and helps me to stand.

Stepping back, he seems agitated raking his hands through his hair which is a mess now. He looks around lost as if he's given too much away and regrets it.

"You need to go now." He looks like he's struggling for control.

I step down hating the way he's pushing me away. Not that I expect more from him. Why would I? This whole thing is about vengeance.

I turn on Jell-O feeling legs swallowing back the trepidation and shame I feel for even asking, "Can I take the elevator?"

He'd already turned back to the CCTV, so when his head snaps back around to me I self-consciously pull the t-shirt over my lower body trying to hide the evidence of what we just did.

His eyes sweep over me. I turn before I can see his expression of triumph or disdain. I know I can't bear it.

He brushes past me. "Come."

Following his longer stride, I give a small prayer

that I don't drip our mingled releases all over the chevron floor and expensive rugs.

Thankfully we make it to the elevator without incident. In seconds I hear the ding and the door slides open. I hurry in. By the time I turn the door is already closing and I only get a glimpse of his retreating back.

CHAPTER
THIRTEEN

H *isashi*

~

SHIFTING the gears of my car I take the roads to my estate at a reckless speed.

Kill him. Kill him. Dismember him like we did Dr. Sagamo. He snarls.

If it were up to me Thaddeus Love would be in a ditch somewhere. Again, I have been overruled by my brother, cousin, and of course FADE and Ghadi Carrington due to their close relationship with him through FADE's wife Delightful being his cousin. Akchiro surprises me most when he had no problem with Avunculicide, with our father and other two uncles and retribution in their complicity of his own father's death.

Kiyoshi is enamored with his little chef, though he denies it. Killing the little motherfucker would be inconvenient but even he is losing patience with the situation. His punishment of Krie Love is not having the desired effect.

The problems with Creative Chaos continue. We are having a full-blown insurrection and it is getting worse every day. Thanks to him and Maria Shelby, also off-limits because she's under the protection of Angel Cruz a business associate of ours.

Pulling onto the path that leads to my underground garage I floor it. New York was three and a half days ago. This is the longest I have ever been able to keep myself away from her. Making it four was impossible. I barely got through the day without saying fuck it and coming home early. Unheard of and sure not to go unnoticed by my brother and the rest of our team.

I'm consumed with this woman. I need to touch her, feel those lush curves under me.

I waited as long as possible and still my excuse about going home to work rather than have dinner with them at The Camellia was looked at with speculation. For my brother's part I'm sure he thinks I'm trying to devise a plan to rid ourselves of this meddlesome activist. If only it were so simple. No. I have an entirely different Love to contend with.

"Yes," I depress the call from my home staff.

"Dinner is ready, would you like us to plate or wait until you get home," my butler, Hiru, says over the line.

"I'm pulling up now," I tell him pausing as the garage door slides back into the wall allowing me access. Lights of my subterranean garage illuminate the space. I pull beside a diamond black G-Wagon parking my car. Getting out I toss the keys to an attendant heading straight to my room.

As I enter, I notice a set of clothes has been laid out as I dry myself from the shower. Bypassing the dinner dress pants and shirt I opt for a more comfortable set of joggers and t-shirt and hoodie. I've had a long, hard ass day. I don't want anything confining me. Pulling on my clothes with an embarrassing amount of haste for a man who deliberately stayed away from his own wife for days on end, I force myself to slow down to a less eager pace as I make my way up the levels to Taylor's room.

Opening the door without any preamble I take in the darkened room, irritation eating along my nerves. The door to the garden is open. I gave permission for her to be allowed to go there whenever she asks. I push down the recrimination that she shouldn't have to.

She's lucky to be alive, He hisses malice etched in each word.

"Feelings still hurt from being smashed upside the head?" I murmur, heading out following her scent more than anything. It draws me like bait on a fishing line.

Fairy lights greet me. Dusk has descended. The garden is beautifully lit. I can hear the babbling of the water and the koi jumping as they eat their time dispensed food.

The smells of lotus and jasmine mix with the camellias and buttercups indigenous to the area. The bouquet is unique and alluring just like the woman I see sitting in a new kimono robe on the little bench. Her beauty makes me catch my breath as I see her curled up deliberately looking away from me.

Hostility rolls off her in waves. I don't bother to address her or her disrespectful lack of greeting.

Sitting at the table I wait a bare second before Hiru and Aiko bring trays laden with food.

I don't bother addressing the obvious, she knows what to expect. Still, she sits as the food is served. The servants attending us shift uneasily when it's obvious she's not joining me.

Such disrespect won't be countenanced by a Takeda.

"Leave us," I tell them in Japanese. With all calmness I lay my utensils down. Getting up I go into the room and retrieve the jute rope along with a little surprise for my naughty girl from one of the secret compartments I had made special for her room.

Saying nothing, not acknowledging her pique, I

stride over to where she curled away from me. I sit beside her.

"I—"

Snatching her over my lap before she dares to get another word out, I quicky bind her hands. Bending her over my lap I spank her ass without remorse. She bites back her cries until she can't anymore. She's crying and shuddering after I have sufficiently warmed her bottom. I didn't bother to count. She's going to be feeling my correction for a few days.

"You will never leave me waiting again. Is that understood, little bitch?" Rubbing her bottom and soothing the sting and reminding her of the consequence of her defiance with a squeeze here and there, I wait for her answer.

"Hai." Her words are clouded with tears which makes it hard to hear her.

"Hai, what?" Smacking her ass hard I snarl, low and hard in her ear as I press the clitoral vibe I retrieved moments ago into her wet pussy.

"Hai, sensei." Her voice is high and thready.

Positioning the device snugly against her clit, I take out my phone and pull up the app. I hit the lowest setting. "Look how prettily you slither for me. Like a good little cumslut," I remark, rubbing along her back.

"Now get up and be a good girl and I may let you come later." Dialing the app down I make her stand adjusting her kimono robe.

Taking her elbow, I lead her over to the table. "You

will eat your entire meal." Pushing her seat to the table, I untie her, going around to my seat.

Moments later my staff returns with salad. We eat in silence.

Once that is taken away, I raise an eyebrow at her.

"Ahem," she clears her voice. It sounds strong despite her recent ordeal. "How was your day?"

"Horrendous, for many reasons but the chief one among them is your nuisance of a cousin, Thaddeus." I lean back observing her reaction. "Tell me. Is fucking around in other people's lives a particular predilection for Loves?"

It was her turn to lift a brow, then she shrugs. "I didn't know what Thaddeus was doing but knowing him and Loves I would say it is our predilection to put an end to what we see as an injustice. I don't know if you've heard about our family's history from around these parts but we happen to specialize in it. So much so that our people have gone far and wide doing much the same in whatever community we ended up in. My cousin Justice was killed because his mom and FADE's were speaking out about the influx of drugs in their community. That was the same person who tried to kill FADE in this very town a few years ago." She says all this with her eyes shining with fierce pride. I feel that same pride hearing her talk until her next words register.

"If you have such a problem with your company perhaps you should treat your employees better instead of blaming an eighteen-year-old kid who's trying to help his community." She grabs her wine taking a sip her gaze lasered on mine for a hot minute before she lowers it trying to cover her reaction.

Punish that little bitch. He sneers.

Reaching for my phone I dial the app to low watching as she swallows. Holding the glass with great care she continues to take sips of her wine. Her grip tightens as the dial goes up. Her fingers tense, hand trembles, the other one on the table curls into a tight fist as she tries and fails to fight the sensations the device is creating in her honeyed regions.

"Care to add anything more to your assessment of my company?" The words drip with smugness as I watch her squirm battling the incessant pressure thrumming on her pussy.

"You h-have a problem with the truth?" she pants, her eyes glazing over with the impending orgasm.

"We treat our employees with respect and offer them a living wage. If your cousin had bothered to really talk to anyone who worked at the plant, he would have found the truth out in minutes. He knows the truth now, but he and his friends still insist on causing more problems hacking our message boards posing as disgruntled workers," I snap, increasing the dial up. "Now, you add his stubborn recklessness to your penance."

I feel the liquid splash across my face before her words hit me with equal ferocity. "You fucking bastard." She throws the glass at me for good measure, which thanks to my training, I dodge at the right moment before the crystal wine goblet smashes me in the head.

Turning the dial to the lowest hum I cross my hands over my chest. "When did you become so violent, little dove?"

The calmness of my tone raises her hackles. She sits up straighter paying close attention to my every move.

Strange malicious victory races through me when I see her swallow. I make her wait ignoring the liquid streaming down my face.

"Clean your mess, Tay-chan." I push back from the table giving her room.

Admiration floods my heart with the grace she moves to her feet. *Do a better job of punishing her ass, He* hisses. *Make her crawl.*

Ignoring him I watch as she grabs her napkin and comes over to me. Waiting until she bends down I grip her wrist hard enough I know it will bruise. I grit, "Drop it." In my gaze's periphery I see the white cloth fluttering to the ground. "Sit."

Opening the robe, my gaze drops to her exposed pussy with the vibe clamped there as she straddles me.

"Clean my face," I demand, turning the vibe on but otherwise not moving so she'll have to stretch her smaller curvier body against mine to reach her goal.

Soft curves press tightly against me as she begins licking away the evidence of her crime.

Wet laps of her tongue glide over my forehead, trailing down my jaw. My chin follows then up the other side. She moans as she reaches mid-jaw when I increase the pressure. As she gets close enough to reach my hairline, she's grinding her hot little pussy against me. She grasps my shoulders when she reaches my eyelids. A whimper escapes when her tongue slides along the ridge of my nose. She nips the tip before settling on my lips. She swipes my top lip, then sucks the bottom into her mouth.

Decreasing pressure, I claim her lips as my prize. "You're so wet for me, little dove." Her pussy is like a furnace pressed against me. She's soaking my joggers and I love it. My dick is wedged against her heat. She moves tangling her fingers in my hair her nails little daggers on my scalp. I almost react negatively but remind myself it's her holding me not someone trying to punish me for being neurodivergent. I lose myself in her taste and touch for the moment.

"Damn," I groan, pulling back looking down in those eyes that make promises but hold nothing but snares for one such as me. "You almost make me forget what this is about." I shake my head more at myself than her.

She has the fucking nerve to soften more cupping my cheek. "Would that be so bad?" She swallows, her vulnerability on display as unabashedly as her anger was moments before.

"Get the fuck off me, Taylor," I bite out, my heart hammering like I've run a fucking race. I want to leave more than I want to eat or fuck and that's saying something for a man who's getting pussy for the first time in ten years.

She defies me again resting her head on my chest. "Okay, let me catch my breath." She stays longer than she should. I can't tell if she's doing it on purpose, but I almost jettison her ass across the garden when she moves to get up but nuzzles and kisses my neck instead.

My erection is painful and insistent when she brushes it on her way back to her seat. She has her own tricks it seems. I'm so tempted to keep edging her as punishment. The need to make her eat supersedes my pettiness at the moment. Once she takes her seat more food is brought out. Lamb for me and shrimp for her because I know she doesn't like the meat.

The steaming plates sit before us. Opting out of talking more about my day, I allow us to pass the rest of the meal in relative silence. My silence is two-fold to give her a false sense of security that I am done with her and to make sure she eats every bite. I don't care if she's lost weight though I love her curves. I just don't want her being here the reason she's lacking nutrition. She is mine to keep. Mine to care for. I won't fail this time.

I learned later the state Kiyoshi found her in after breaking into his encrypted data on the situation. The noxious shame I feel to this day cannot be pardoned by not even Taylor. It is a dishonor I shall carry with me the rest of my life. Does that absolve her abandonment and what followed? No. But it is the main reason she still breathes. She should have never been allowed to be put in that situation. Still her vows meant something to me even if they meant fuck all to her. And for that I will have her face.

"When are you going to let me get back to my life?" She asks, lying her fork down after taking a few polite bites of her food.

"I don't know— probably never." Cavalierly I answer lying my fork beside my own plate, tossing the napkin down on the food and standing.

I hold my hand out. She ignores it attempting to step around me.

Snatching her ass back I gather her by the cascade of curls at her nape, holding her throat as I drag her recalcitrant form back to my chest.

"I will dog walk your ass the rest of the time I'm here if you insist on being a naughty little slut." Shaking her for good measure, I growl, "Is that clear?"

Jerkily she nods. "Now. Take. My. Fucking. Hand." She stumbles with my abrupt release but places her hand in mine.

She's not looking at me, but I can sense the fire in her. "I just want to go home."

Pulling her around to face me, I bare my teeth at her demanding, "Okay let's think about how that will play out. You go back to your apartment in New York with me mere floors above you, watching over you and this time you know about it. Then knowing the nights you don't have night terrors I was there with you climbing all over my dick? Or did you think this would be over? That I'd just abandon you like you did me?"

Shaking her head she tries to step back but I won't let her. "You have to let me go. You have to stop this."

"If you try to leave me, I will destroy everything you think you love. Everyone you know, everything you have ever touched will be burned to the fucking ground and I will make you watch." Watching as she swallows against the truth of my words, I wait for her to challenge me more.

Nothing. Her eyes remain bruised with the hurt my words cause, yet she says nothing.

"Take off the robe and get in the bed." Releasing her, I step back to give myself a moment.

"What did you think she'd do? Fold after one night in New York? Stick to the plan." He laughs.

"Shut the fuck up," I mutter, stalking into the room.

Methodically, I retrieve long ropes of jute, dropping them at the foot of the bed. Looking at her prone form, the anticipation and desire to tie her up dissipates along with her desire to leave me. Why this deters me making my heart feel heavier than it did when I discovered her gone, I shove down into the deep recesses of my being not even *he* can access, not wanting to deal with it.

Allowing my eyes to rake over her, I take in all the markings I took so much pleasure in visiting on her body in New York. Many of them are fading. Soon it will be like I was never there. Which is why I intend to leave a deeper mark on her soul just like the one I bear that she left me with. I ache for her. I've wept for her. I'll be damned if I stop before she does the same for me. She will bear my marks — body and soul I will fill her to overflowing with my seed. Every time she moves she will feel me in the deepest recesses of her body. It's only fair for she lives rent free in my mind. Am I not to have some recompense? It is not the way of the Takeda to let such a thing go unanswered.

"What you want doesn't matter. This is punishment not a courtship. I don't need your petting, only your pussy."

Mustering strength I didn't know I'd need I do what I must and set to tying my lovely wife up for the edging she's earned.

FOURTEEN

T *aylor*

~

HE'S VERY pensive looking out the window of the airplane. The way he's acting one would think I was the one who kept him up all night edging him. My body is still experiencing the aftershocks from his vicious punishment. It went on for hours as he brought me close to orgasm with his mouth, fingers, hand, even knee at one point, no matter how much I begged he wouldn't let me come. He was exacting binding me in the jute so that it hit all of my pressure points to elicit the highest arousal.

Afterward he praised and soothed me until my body calmed down. My body is still hyper-aroused and even the light breeze I felt as we got in the car as we left for his private jet was torture.

I went without panties because of the sensitivity. My nipples remain budded from all of his ruthless attention. Gripping my iPad, I try to focus on the novel that held me in a chokehold about a young man wrongly convicted coming to get revenge on the co-ed who had a hand in his incarceration.

My fascination with vengeance is not lost on me nor my interest in dark romance; basically, living one at the moment. Epic fantasy, another genre I love, has taken a backseat for now.

Still, I can't concentrate because my very own villain is sulking. Giving up I turn off my device rising from my seat. Opting when I woke not to provoke him further, I acted unbothered. Not a spark of realism, no shock. It seemed like the hour we spent apart as he went to get ready in his own room, he used that time to harden his heart against me.

Shifting I feel pressure low in my belly made worse by the increased blood flow to my coochie. She's mad because she's been left on read, literally by the motherfucker who turned her out. I need to use the restroom and alleviate this pressure.

Rising I take my tablet. He'd only returned it for the trip after letting me download more books. He also made sure to disable the FaceTime app and other communication apps. Bastard.

"Where are you going?" His gaze slides over me

languidly. Totally unbothered he turns back to his view of the clouds.

"I need to use the bathroom." No response to my dry words. A hard hand grips my wrist. An unrelenting grip with intense pressure around the soft tissue just below the bone makes me wince, but I don't let him see that.

"Don't touch my pussy. No one touches her but me." Pain shoots through me when I snatch my hand away.

"Too bad you couldn't make her come." Tossing the quip over my shoulder, I add an extra swish to my hips because I know he's watching me walk away. I ignore the low menacing chuckle as I leave.

"TAYLOR, this is the second event you've been seen at with Mr. Takeda, are you an item?"

"Mr. Takeda, what is your relationship with Ms. Love? Is it serious?"

Ignoring the paparazzi, we smile benignly at the crowd gathered outside of the Theatre Royal Drury Lane. Lights flash all around us as barrage after barrage of questions and accusations bombard our every step on the red carpet.

It's opening night of *Requiem* a play produced in partnership with my cousins Lovie-Belle Al-Rasheed and Flower Takeda along with her husband and the billionaire Shipmoore brothers, Porter and Bishop.

"Behave," Hisashi says as we approach the group.

"What, you're afraid they will put a stop to what you are doing to me?" I ask, smiling sweetly at him. He doesn't miss the challenge.

A possessively deliciously feral smile breaks across his face. He leans close to whisper, "I'll kill anyone who tries to take you from me. I have before. Never doubt it, little dove."

Leaving me to process that information, he faces his cousin, Akchiro first giving him a bow in deference. "Cousin." He turns to Flower taking her hand bowing over it and kissing the knuckles in all politeness. My brows hike as she gives him a brief hug afterward. Hisashi can't hide the surprised pleasure on his face nor does his cousin hide his disapproval or the low growl of admonishment to which Flower flippantly responds, "Family supersedes protocol, silly." Then she shrugs like she doesn't care what anyone thinks. Despite his words he can't seem to hide the pride and pleasure in his eyes as he looks at his wife.

"Taylor." Lovie-Belle pulls me into a hug. "I didn't know you were coming. If I did, I would have made room for you in our box — well, the Shipmoore's box."

"No worries, we have a box," Hisashi smoothly interjects, stepping closer to me so there won't be any confusion about our association. Someone from such strict cultural tradition would never stand this close to a woman unless they were intimate.

Lovie-Belle's eyebrows arch with interest, along with Flower's. The only person whose face is not a mask of curiosity is Akchiro. I can tell from the cool assessment in his gaze he knows our history.

"Let's go in," Bishop Shipmoore suggests in an authoritative voice.

"See you at the reception after?" Flower asks us as we get ready to diverge into our separate boxes.

"We've made other plans," Hisashi says far too smoothly.

He has no desire to have me spending any more time with my cousin and her fellow producers. It's clear to me he doesn't want to give me any avenue of escape.

Disappointed she and Lovie-Belle accept his words giving me hugs. With a hand at the small of my back he ushers me into the seating area. When I hear the lock click a shiver darts along my spine. My nipples pebble along the black silk of the dress I'm swathed in. Gathering the mermaid bottom I sit in the first-row chair. There is room for two more couples behind us in this particular arrangement. However, if any of the other couples came to chat they would be sorely disappointed.

"You were a very good girl." His voice is low, meticulously cold, sounding anything other than like praise. Why that creates the opposite of the terror I should be feeling is a mystery I'm not ready to examine at the moment.

Taking the hand I'm unaware I'm gripping the one armchair with, he laces his fingers between mine. My tummy drops at his careless affection. Does he not know he's breaking me? Does he care? Slowly his thumb strokes the fleshy area between my thumb and forefinger in a lazy caress. As he does every thrum if my heart intensifies.

Other than his original words he says nothing as the play starts. I had no idea what the play was about but I should have known with my cousin attached to it, it would have to be a love story. Lovie-Belle is nothing if not a romantic. Her own story with Prince Sadiq Al-Rasheed was nothing less in its headline grabbing epicness.

The lead in to the final act is so hot as the characters finally act on the sexual tension that has been pulsing between them since the start of their second chance romance. The whole theater is a hivemind, pulsing with the pent-up passion between the characters.

When the handsome Polynesian actor grabs the curvy Black heroine by the nape in an all too familiar move, I make the mistake of letting a soft whimper escape.

Hisashi's hands slip free of mine. My fingers grip the armrest. My hand on my thigh fists as he backs her into a wall pressing her against it.

A big hand covers my exposed thigh slowly climbing until it reaches the apex of my thighs.

"So wet, Tay-chan," he growls, his fingers slipping beneath the panties I decided to wear at the last minute tonight. "Wearing panties?" The low sexy chuckle has my pussy clenching to an almost painful degree.

"The split was too high. I didn't want anyone to get a peek by mistake." I recall the torture I felt having to wear them against my already tortured flesh, between last night then the spanking on the plane after I popped off then being made to sit in his lap the rest of the flight. I was a mess by the time we got to London.

"I would have spanked this motherfucker raw if anyone saw what is only mine," he growls stroking between my puffy, fat lips with his long fingers.

"Hi," I gasp. His other hand catches my throat stifling the sound, cutting it off.

"Shh, you don't want your cousins hearing what a needy little slut you are for me do you?"

Ohmygoodness, repeats over and over in my head as he pushes his fingers deeper curling them into my tender, tormented flesh he's edged all night and on the plane. He finger fucks me slowly.

"So fucking wet for me," he whispers hotly in my ear. "Listen how she begs. Such a good, pretty little pussy knowing who she belongs to."

He pulls back, watching me now. Viciously he curls

and presses, thrusts and curls. A whimper starts in my chest, building. I try to hold it back, knowing a scream is building and I won't be able to hold it back. Frantically, I shake my head — not telling him to stop. No, we are way too far past the point of retreat. I'm trying to communicate it's too much, all the edging. Just as the hard, spasming orgasm hits, he covers my mouth in his hand, furiously pistoning in and out of my pussy. The swipes of his thumb on my clit aren't needed but more than appreciated as shuddering I come all over his hands, the chair, the thick carpet catches a gush of my come.

"Get up." He doesn't wait, but drags me on trembling legs up the few stairs to the darkened alcove, pressing me against the fabric wall.

Kicking my legs open he unsheathes sliding his big dick into my wet waiting pussy hitting every inch of my walls.

"Mine." Thrusting he bottoms out. "Every fucking inch is mine." He pulls out slamming in again driving me to my tip toes. "She knows it, you know it, and by morning everyone in the world will." He draws back out this time excruciatingly slow.

Burying his face in my neck he drives in and out of my pussy chanting, "Mine" over and over. His fingers find my mound again, spearing a finger within he thrums my hardened nub.

"Fuck," he growls when my pussy clenches around his thrusting dick in response. "I like how she's sucking me in, trying to hold me inside." He keeps fucking me like his life depends on it. Our bodies slap against each other as I open myself up to more of his attention. Uncaring of those around us he drives inside of me clutching me close. I tremble as the orgasm rocks through me. Pressing my face against the wall I try to muffle my cries as I start coming all over him.

"Hell, yeah. Give me all of it. Come on my dick, little dove." He thrusts up hard, fucking me past the climax making me see stars as he takes me higher. Nirvana approaches as he continues even as his hot come bathes my insides with his decadent essence.

He holds me against the wall for long moments. His breathing is harsh matching mine. I can feel his heartbeat at my back. It's hard and fast. I know I feel like I've run a marathon so I can only imagine how he feels since he's done all the work.

"You're magnificent," he murmurs, pressing a kiss along the shell of my ear making me preen inside.

Easing out, he pauses at my gasp going slower, knowing how sensitive my body is.

Adjusting my dress around he shrugs out of his jacket wrapping it around my shoulders, making me realize he's had it on the entire time he had me against the wall. I wonder if it was to maintain distance or so any unlikely onlookers wouldn't get a clear view.

"Let's go, beautiful." I look down at the firm hand he's holding out, then up to eyes entirely wiped clean of emotion, wondering how so much passion can come from a man so outwardly cold. One who calls me beautiful as easily as little bitch.

Placing my cool hand into his warm one I allow him to lead me out of the box.

THE TAKEDA ESTATE, Great Britain

Hot water laps around me easing my sore aching muscles inside and out. Stretching, I allow the hot sudsy bubbles to cascade over my skin and just luxuriate. The smell of vanilla and rose waft around me. How he got Crimson to make him enough of the exclusive fragrance I'll never know. This formula is only for Loves and he has it here in his estate in the British countryside.

I'm so curious. Is he blackmailing her? Not Crimson. For as sweet as she is, she's not a pushover. She and her sister, Clover, run the Love Apothecary. Crimson is the compound pharmacist and Clover is the perfumer and together they make up the team who creates and market the little boutique pharmacy. How Hisashi gets the scent exclusive to only Loves is a mystery.

"Do you want a snack?" he asks though he's holding a tray with food and rosé. My tummy growls in response. "Sure." Canting my head to the side I try to gauge his mood.

Last night it seemed as if he was overtaken after

our passionate encounter. When we got back to his flat in London, he took his time lacing me in jute. My body sang and stung all at once as the bonds pressed and tightened against my erogenous zones.

Methodically he toyed with me as I sat bound and naked before him. Taking my hair down brushing it in long sweeps around my shoulders.

"I dreamed of this," he murmured, his voice in cold cultured Japanese that sends chills down my spine. "Of you like this — my pretty little fuck doll."

Trapped under his cold gaze I almost hated myself for the way my body responded to his cruelty.

Even now part of me wants to cringe at the way I let him fuck my mouth, use my throat. How I greedily took his come and begged for more.

In the end I did everything he demanded of me in his cold monster form, loving every moment. It's almost comforting when he's like that, the worst of him shining through having free rein, he knows me to the depths of my battered soul.

"Eat." Placing the bath tray in front of me, he tilts his head mimicking mine seeming to try to read the inquiry in my gaze before pivoting and going across the room.

Dragging a chair from the vanity behind him, he drops his long form in the chair, his eyes skating across my body. Gaze heating when he takes in the rope bruises, I can't tell if the look is one of pleasure or not. He almost looks jealous. I can't fathom why.

"Was last night pleasurable to you, little dove?" He crosses his legs and arms across his chest.

"Very much," I answer, taking sip of the 2012 Domaine De La Romanee-Conti.

"Hm, what did you enjoy most Tay-chan?" he muses.

"Why, so you can punish me by withholding it?" Taking a long sip, I shake my head. "Nope. Nopity. Nope. Nope." Placing the empty glass on the tray I take a grape and a strawberry popping them into my mouth one after the other.

A cool smile spreads across his gorgeous face. "Maybe I want to know what pleases you more, so you'll want to stay with me this time."

I pause swallowing hard to keep the fruit from choking me.

"So, you're not going to kill me, like you planned?" I push the tray away readying for the fight I know is coming.

Shoving the chair away he kneels beside the tub taking the sponge floating on the surface. Silent as the darkest part of night he starts smoothing the bubble ladened softness against my skin. "Only if that were the only way I could keep you by my side. I'd rather visit your tomb every day." Touching my chin he lifts my face, his eyes searching my own. "But that won't be necessary will it. You want to be with me."

Closing my eyes against the truth, I nod turning my face into his palm. I never wanted to leave him in the first place. I was forced to. Telling him that would cause a chasm between him and his brother. I know he probably wouldn't believe me at this point. He'll think I was just trying to say anything to keep him from punishing me.

"Thought so," he murmurs finishing my bath.

Stepping out I allow him to moisturize my body. "Addictive." Pressing a kiss on my tummy he rises when he finishes.

"I have a surprise for you if you're willing."

"Oh?" A small thrill of surprise has me quirking an eyebrow.

Pushing me in front of him he walks me into the main bedroom suite. There on the bed is several layers of jute.

"Okay?" I drag the word out. Him tying me up is no surprise but expected. As I round on him I stop. He's stepping out of his clothes. He nods to the garments he's laid out on the bed. "Being dressed enhances the experience."

Wordlessly I put on the clothes he's laid out for me. It's a pink two-piece catsuit. The sleeves are long reaching well past my fingers with thumb holes. It clings to every curve of my body piercing between my lower lips with tantalizing precision. I find myself having to stifle a moan of pleasure as the material molds to my body. Have I become so much a hedonist? Has he made me so much his creature? I know I am his. From the moment he claimed me in that garden I knew and now I am helpless to do anything other than acquiesce to his every desire. Hisashi Takeda has captured me, heart and soul, it is up to me now to take part in my own destruction or liberation.

Clothes covering nearly every inch of my body but accentuating every nuance of the already primed flesh he's teased near completion, I turn to his naked and primed body open to my every desire.

He's never offered himself in this way. So selflessly open to me. Trusting that I won't hurt him. Trusting I won't use the knowledge I have about his desires and weaknesses against him in the worst way.

The thought never reaches beyond the periphery of my mind as I begin to lace him in rope led by his solemn words. Beginning at his neck to string the jute along his torso overlapping and interlacing him in an intricate knot. Kinbaku is practiced without knots. I hit all his pleasure sensors careful of his sac and dick not to constrict blood flow but to enhance it.

When I'm done I look upon my handiwork. Proud that I followed his exacting directions. He looks beautiful. His dick rises high and hard from the nest of black hair at its base.

"Ride me, Tay-chan, but only if you wish."

Oh I wish. But first I wrap my still fabric encased body around his, sliding against his already cherry flushed skin.

"Tay—"

"Shh," I whisper, sliding slowly along his hard length. "Let me."

His body is so hard pressed against mine and I love it. There is not one thing about him that does not call to me. He is like a magnificent god in all his raging glory, conquering everything in his view.

I see the muscle working in his hard chiseled jaw as I take my time worshiping his body as he has mine so many times. Starting on his face I place gentle kisses all over not skimming his eyelids, the tip of his nose, cheeks, and lips. Those lush kissable lips of his are my undoing.

Our tongues tangle and slide.

"Tay— little dove," he sighs against my lips letting me devour him the way I like to. I suck him deep into my mouth fellating his tongue no different than the way he loves when I do his dick. He is all things delicious. I savor the vulnerability in his taste.

He gasps and surges against me, but I do not relent exacting my own petty vengeance as I slowly torment him gliding along the hard ridges of his dick. Muscles straining, he pulses against me. His massive dick brimming with precum.

I can't resist. I move back from the position which I've come to straddle him. Dipping my head, I take him fully into my mouth smiling when he arches, grinning when he begs. Oh yes, sir. The power I feel is addictive. I love having him at my mercy as much as I like him dominating me.

Feeling him in the back of my throat, I close my eyes taking him deeper holding him there as he tries but fail to arch deeper.

Pulling away I smile meeting his gaze. "Is there something you need, my love?"

"You," he says simply and without any hesitation.

Pulling away I slip out of my bottoms keeping the formfitting top on.

Straddling him I offer him my breasts. He sucks the taunt tips through the fabric making them stand out against the pink material.

"Lovely," he murmurs, his eyes trained on the evidence of his efforts of pleasure.

I return his smile climbing atop his muscled thighs. They fold under him as he presents himself.

"Have you ever subbed for anyone before?" I ask.

"Never," he confesses. "Only as an act of trust between you and I would I even consider it." I can see the struggle in his words. Him submitting to anyone is anathema to his very being. I file this back knowing what this is costing him. He would never.

Without hesitation I take his long thick length within me.

The words I utter are lost at the rough glide against my flesh. I can think of nothing but how good he feels inside me. He is mine as much as he says I am his. More so. My feelings aren't enhanced by my brain chemistry. No. Just regular-degular Taylor Takeda consumed by the man of her dreams, tortured, and broken as he may be.

I ride him like I'm seeking glory in battle. He feels delicious. I finish first and don't hesitate, pulling free just as I feel his release, taking him in my mouth.

CHAPTER
FIFTEEN

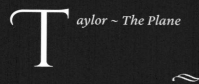

T *aylor ~ The Plane*

ACT 2 -Scene II

(*Setting*) *The asylum: Suro crushes the guard's hand and thrusts him away from Mia. As the guards cower Suro gathers Mia in close. After a few moments he opens the window with the clear indication of escape.*

Suro: It will be okay.

Mia: How do you know?

Suro: Because we have each other.

NEVER SO INSPIRED as I was by the performances in London, I work on my play for the first time in three years. I felt paralyzed and helpless during the pandemic. I thought going back to my family's home and helping with the launch of their new creative arts center would help me start to write again. It didn't take me long to realize how adrift I still felt. How much despair had caged me. I was walking in a cocoon of my former life. The one I managed to paste together after Hisashi. Still, I never felt the same after being torn from him. There was always something that felt missing. I knew even as I was being hailed as the next best thing since August Wilson that I was working on borrowed time. Soon it would all fall away once the quiet got to me and I had to deal with what I'd done. Leave the one person I loved most in the world in his deepest despair. No one walks away from that unscathed.

It's well past midnight but I haven't stopped writing since we boarded the plane. In fact, I asked Hisashi for a pen and notebook when we started on the way to the airport.

Hisashi seems more at ease now since the moment I re-entered his life. I'm not sure if it was the promise I made not to leave him or the Kinbaku scene afterward but he seems almost at peace.

Sighing, I get up from the makeshift writing desk I've made for myself. The interior of the plane is dimly lit. I gather the notebook and pencils he gave me. Why a pen would be detrimental to my captivity is lost on me. Hisashi forgets not everyone has the genius level deduction he embodies. I could have a hundred pens and still wouldn't even begin to know how to override the system to alert anyone of my kidnapping.

He's funny that way, assuming what comes natural to him is as effortless to others. I'm sure keeping company with his brother, cousin, and Ghadi Carrington has done nothing but further this thinking. Well, Mr. Techgenuis your wife's blessing is limited to her craft as a playwright, so I won't be MacGyvering my escape anytime soon.

Standing, I stretch my cramping back knocking out the kinks. "Ahh," I exhale, loving the stretch of my muscles.

Gathering my meager items, pulling them close to my chest, I head to the bedroom of the private plane. The term is all that is typical of this and most private jets. It's as large as Air Force One with the same type of security and high-tech amenities. The Takedas are known for their security measures, and none have been skimped on the plane assigned to Hisashi.

"To have me killed in such a dishonorable way would be a mark my family would never recover from," he told me unabashedly on the way to New York when I asked why he had such a supersize plane.

Making my way through the long deep aisle leading to the sleeping quarters I can't help the feeling of anticipation coalescing in my body.

Will he angry if I wake him up? I wonder heading down the corridor to the bedroom.

"Iie," gasped loud and in distress is the first thing I hear when I enter the room.

Frozen, I watch Hisashi fight for his life in the covers of the bed. I know he was exhausted. He hasn't slept in days. I noticed the dark circles marring his otherwise beautiful face. I know he still suffers from insomnia just like I suffer from the night terrors that have plagued me since childhood. The toll his work is taking is not lost on me. I know a lot of his behavior stems from the hacking and uncertainty this strike is bringing.

My gaze is glued to the scene before me as his long limbs struggle within the mass of sheets.

He fights. He flails. He screams in guttural Japanese threatening retribution. Maniacal laughter spills forth, promising, cursing, sneering only to be trampled by cries of mercy and heart-wrenching pain.

It's like my night terrors have returned only now made real. Every dream was of his imagined torture. What he'd been made to endure in the facilities he'd been placed. I know they were deeply hidden because the fear of the public knowing he'd been committed would have left a taint on the Takeda name. Guilt and fear haunted me for nearly a decade and were only alleviated by him— I realize now that I've seen the videos of how he soothed me while I slept. He was my solace even when I was his pain.

Suddenly, as if sensing me he sits up. Tears stream down his face. Anguish tears at every one of his features. His eyes well again and again. He so broken, beautifully so even in this moment.

"Tay-chan, help me. Please. I need you," he pleads, his whole face breaks as he's wracked with sorrow.

I don't hesitate. I don't think. Dropping everything I carefully carried into the room I rush over to him. Curling around him I wrap myself around him like I saw him do when I had night terrors.

Moments pass as he struggles. Eventually he settles. I kiss his back whispering, "It's okay. I'm here. Tay-chan is here."

He stills.

He flips us.

I'm underneath him, my throat is being slowly squeezed, and not in a good way. Not in the way I like. His hand is hard, his grip impersonal, cold.

"I've got you now, little bitch," he hisses in that cultured oddly detached voice he sometimes uses.

"Hisashi," I gasp on my last breath.

"No. No. No. No. No, little bitch. He's cowering from the rapists. He was SUCH a pretty boy. They couldn't resist him you know. They just had to take his ass," he hisses, licking a long swathe of wetness from my neck to cheek. "In the place you left him. The place he thought you'd come save him. But it wasn't you was it, little bitch but me. I was the one who kept him safe. Me. Never. You." He shakes me slowly, his voice almost lilting even as he slowly squeezes my life from me.

"I saved him as I always have even from his bitch of a mother," he whispers hotly in my ear. I feel the heat of his hardness pressing against me. I go cold. This is not my husband but a different person entirely.

"I saved him from YOU." He pulls back, his eyes black onyx orbs of coldblooded danger. "You broke him. I put him back together. Now you are back trying to break him again. I can't allow that to happen."

"No. No. I would never," I gasp as he squeezes, slowly methodically, relishing every moment in what seems to be killing me.

"Hisashi will n-never forgive you," I gasp. Dark spots dance before my eyes. "Never," I promise firm in my belief in a man who's never shared his darkest secret with me. Still. I know. I know.

"Liar," he rages. Teeth bared he snaps at me. Hatred and hurt mingled.

"You were supposed to be the one person he trusted. You left. He suffered. Now you pay, little bitch."

"N-no. I didn't want to leave. Kiyoshi made me leave. He said your, I mean Hisashi's mom would come after me, so he sent me away. I didn't want to leave." Pleading I feel his dick pressing hard against me. This version of Hisashi is getting off on my fear and pain.

Ignoring me he reaches down ripping my loungewear down beneath my hip.

"I don't give a fuck. You were never meant for Hisashi Takeda. You were never worthy."

My heart craters at his words. Surely Hisashi feels this way if this part of his psyche is capable of saying this.

Did he ever think I was worthy?

Still, something in me rebels at the words. He never treated me as anything other than cherished. He's always taken care of me, worshiped every part of my body, sought to give me everything I ever wished for. How could a man pampering me, pleasuring me, providing for me like this feel this way?

Shoving the vicious words away I call, "Hisashi."

My plea is caught on a gasp. Realizing then he was only toying with me I swallow my fear hoping it got through.

"He won't help you, little bitch. He's in his safe place letting me take care of things. He pushed himself past his limits when he allowed you to use the rope on him. That was not for you. Never for you. Not when you broke trust. Not worthy," he grits.

White teeth are bared and gleaming like the apex predator that lives deep within my husband's skin I didn't realize until now was so much a part of him.

"Hi—s—shi," pushing past the burn in my throat, pushing past the terror, pushing past the disbelief I call to the one who will save me.

Coldly he squeezes. "Too late, little bitch. You've hurt him enough. This is the first time since he's been free I've had to save him from the terror. *You* are the problem."

Stars dance before my eyes. The trapped air squeezes. I feel my heartbeat thudding in my ears. He's taking my life. I can't gasp. Words die on my tongue. Unbearable pressure builds up in my head. My eyes feel like they are about to explode. No air.

I'm dying.

The man I love more than life is killing me and my only thought is how it will destroy him when he realizes what he's done.

Forcing my eyes open in one last plea for mercy I force myself to meet his cold gaze. He is unrelentingly determined. I'm the threat that must be eradicated. I can almost respect his thinking if he were right. From his perspective I have brought nothing but hurt and horror on Hisashi. In *His* mind I need to be eradicated posthaste. Like yesterday. I may have proven my worth to Hisashi but not to him, perhaps never not to him. The protector. The guardian.

I pealed with my eyes even as I pour everything I have into my gaze. He will never relent. Gradually darkness crowds my gaze.

It's almost pleasant. For some reason I'm happy if the last thing I get to see is his face. Instead of pleading I focus on how much I love him. I don't even care if I live. All I want him to know is I love him with my whole heart.

I love you, Hisashi, my heart whispers. *I love you and your guardian. I love every part of you. You don't have to hide anymore.*

My vision darkens. His grip doesn't lessen — until it does.

I hear my name being screamed. My body being shook.

Hard hands grip my upper arms in a bruising grip.

"Tay-chan." Grief and disbelief mingle with the utterance.

Opening my eyes, I'm confronted with grief and disbelief. He thinks he's killed me. Not him— his guardian.

His visage is ravaged. "Taylor?"

My throat feels like it's been crushed. My eyes find his panicked gaze and hold it affirming what little life I have left in my body.

Dragging me close his body shuddering with sobs he cries out, "Gomen'nasai" again and again, clutching me to his chest.

Gasping I take long drags of air into my deprived lungs.

Listlessly I pat his chest trying to reassure him. "I-I'm. Okay." My bruised throat burns but my windpipe isn't crushed. I'm alive.

In the quietness he holds me. Stillness surrounds us as what happens settles around us like a cloak of darkness. It's like what my cousin Mimi told me about when her husband came back from deployment. The night terrors. Only with Hisashi his protector rose to do his job — protect him and eradicate the threat.

Unsure why I understand as I do other than the sheer volumes of neurodiversity and mental variance, I've read about since we first came together and trying to reconcile what happened between us. There is nothing new under the sun and a person's mind trying to protect him is basic human survival. I knew from the beginning I wasn't going to try to excuse his actions but understand them.

Eventually he moves away, leaving my body cold losing his heat. He doesn't go far but watches me as if waiting for me to react.

Screaming, fighting, cowering is all expected I suppose. Instead, I silently watch him as I slowly curl into myself. Watching, waiting to see if his guardian will emerge again.

Our breathing — his hard, labored; mine shallow, featherlike are the only thing breaking the tomb of silence.

Shattered, broken, alone on his knees he's looking at me like he's scared to touch me, afraid he's going to break me, kill me.

"You stopped him, Hisashi." Gathering the little strength I have, I push my hand forward grazing the long tendons of his.

"Iie." He snatches his hand away. Looking up to the ceiling of the plane he looks as if he's praying trying to find strength. "Iie," whispering hoarsely he bows his long body deep into himself. "Gomen'nasai," he keens, heavy sobs racking his body.

Long fingers tangle in his hair, clutching like he wants to rip his locks out.

"Stop it. Stop, Hisashi," pleading I sit up. A wave of dizziness makes me sway. A fit of convulsive coughing shakes me. I try to swallow back the sick rising in my throat only to fail miserably. I'm left a trembling mess by the time the episode is over.

Hisashi picks me up wrapping me in clean covers. Placing me on the sofa I've curled in so many times to read, he goes back to pulling the sheets from the bed.

Making quick work of it, he changes the bed replacing the soiled sheets and pillow with fresh new ones. Coming back to me he strips me down to nothing taking my dirty clothes adding them to the pile to be laundered.

"I need to shower, first," I tell him as he tries to put me to bed. Pivoting he doesn't hesitate.

Going into the bathroom he manages to start the shower still holding me. Steam fills the space. Still fully clothed he stands me up in front of him in the shower. He bathes me like I'm precious to him. Knowing my words will only bring him pain I just let him. Not bothering to tell him he doesn't have to be that gentle or slow.

"Can you stand for a sec?" I nod.

Stepping out, he rips off his dripping clothes sweeping me back into his arms. He grabs a few big towels.

Wrapping one around my shoulders he places one

on the bed. Wiping away the drops of water with the other he has me dry and warm in seconds.

He leaves and brings back lotion slathering it on my body in quick efficient strokes. By the time he's done I'm tired. When he reaches my throat, he pauses. His gaze lifts to mine and I see the horror of what he's done.

Reaching up I grab his hand shaking my head when he tries to pull back. "No, it happened. Neither of us is running this time." I lift my brows in confirmation.

"I *know* it wasn't you." I take his face in my hands. "I know." My voice is firm. I see the truth in his eyes before any other part of him gives me confirmation. He drops to his knees before me. He buries his head in my lap. "I'm so sorry, Tay-chan."

"I know." Stroking his still damp locks, I comfort him realizing for the first time how much in the throes of his illness he must have been the first time we were together and his guardian emerged. How much mental anguish and turmoil he'd experienced from his father's death.

His strong arms wrap around my waist hugging me to him. Long minutes pass with us like this. This moment with everything stripped away and nothing between us but our merged souls locked in the dance we chose probably before we even entered these forms, we find a semblance of peace.

He moves away his eyes not shying away from me.

Still, I can feel the cringe as he glances at my neck as if he can't help himself.

He moves so he's behind me on the bed. Covering me with the sheet he uses that as a barrier between us as if he doesn't deserve to touch me.

It's well past two a.m. I don't know how long the ordeal lasted or how long we ended up holding each other but exhaustion crowds my brain and the after-shocks of the traumatic experience we shared drag me ever closer to the bliss of oblivion.

Why I feel comfortable with a man whose guardian attempted to end my life and probably stills wants to try will probably take several dedicated therapy sessions to unpack. Still, in my heart I know Hisashi won't hurt me. He's already said as much. And now that he knows his guardian's intention, he won't let his guard down. If I know nothing else, I know how hypervigilant he will be going forward.

My body shudders and I realize he's not holding me. I don't say anything, just take one of his muscled arms and wrap it around my middle for support, reas-surance. I don't know why I do this, and I don't take time to figure it out. All I say when he tries to remove himself from me moments later is, "I know it wasn't you, Hisashi," bringing him back around me as I begin to drift away in his arms.

isashi

~

I HAD TO STAY AWAY. This motherfucker almost killed her. *I* almost killed her. *"Oh, no not this again. Don't go blaming yourself, now. I take full responsibility for almost killing your little bitch..." He* snickers like the shit *he* pulled was some sort of prank.

"You are not allowed to call her that anymore. In fact you are not allowed to even see her anymore, stay in your fucking corner." I watch in the mirror as he tries to emerge, but it takes little effort on my part to put him in his place.

"Don't," *He* pleads.

"Quiet," I snap, firmly closing that door. He's not a separate personality, he's my Id. The cruelest basest part of my psyche emerged to protect the frightened little boy who the world moved in opposition to when I was too young to understand how my brain worked.

My scholar father though he struggled to manage me, the same with my unfortunate mother who never had the capacity for much more than the competition she fomented between my brother and me. All that mattered to her was excellence. Having a child deemed defective by our elite society was anathema to her and to a lesser degree to my father who was at least willing to hope for the best for me.

Afraid of what I was capable of yet astounded by my genius he was torn between allowing me my interests as long as I did not hurt another.

He really thought my interest in Taylor was good for me and it was for a time. It was a healthy little obsession that kept me from pursuing her in other more dangerous ways. He and I both knew I was never worthy of her. Kiyoshi knew. The reason we fought that night by the theater was him reminding me of how I could be. For a brief moment I was strong enough to send her away. Then she came back and I was lost, helplessly lost.

She brought me more happiness than I ever thought possible. Then only anguish and abandonment. Still, she didn't deserve to die only the vengeance I sought.

"And you can't even follow through with that." He sneers.

"I'm not sure I want to. What you did was enough, *Monster*." Looking at my reflection I want to punch it, knowing the mocking sneer I sense but can't see because it's my hallowed cheek and five o'clock shadow that I see.

"We are not hurting her anymore," I state unequivocally getting my shaving kit together.

"Oh, so you're letting her go?"

Saying nothing, I text Hiru to come shave me. I don't trust myself with a razor. Not because of self harm proclivities but how my hands tremble from the lack of food from the fast I've been on.

"Sensei." I look up and nod to the man taking my seat. He steps past me to the sink preparing the barbering tools he needs to shave and cut my hair to a decent length. It's well past my shoulders and though the length doesn't bother me it needs a good trim.

I close my eyes as he wraps me in towels. "Mrs. Takeda has asked after you every day," he begins, giving me a detailed report on Taylor's activities as he shaves me from face to chin.

"She been writing every day on the new project. It's a new play. She seems to be very close to the end. She asks several times a day if you are to be expected and after your health. Ahem —"

I open my eyes at the way he trails off. "What is it?" I ask, waving him away wiping my neck clean myself waiting as he puts the soothing towel in its place before he moves on to trim my hair.

"Yesterday, she began her woman's time and she seemed to suffer greatly. Aiko assured me that it was nothing to worry about but today she seems to be worried and says that Mrs. Takeda is visibly upset and seeming to be in great pain." Hiru steps back already anticipating my actions.

I'm up and pulling on a Henley and a pair of joggers. Pulling socks on, I put my slippers on heading up the levels leading to her room.

Letting myself in to the almost too sterile room I see a spiral notebook on the bed along with several sheets of paper with notes in a neat pile. Beside it is a pencil pack.

The door of her bathroom is closed. Going over I knock. "Tay-chan?" I turn the knob and it's locked. I knock again. There is a click.

I open the door and Taylor stands in the door her face wane.

"What's the matter?" She's searching my face as much as I am searching hers.

"Where have you been?" Ignoring the slight accusation in her tone, I bow deeply to her. "Gomen'nasai, I had to take some time for my mental health." Deep shame at nearly killing her then abandoning her soon after eats at my insides like acid but I couldn't be around her until I was no longer a threat to her.

She continues to look at me with relief mixed with disbelief.

"What's going on?" I look past her but see nothing amiss.

Suddenly she gasps almost doubling over. Sweeping her into my arms I stride back over to the bed. Lying her down I see the bruises of two weeks ago have faded, but are still there. Still shaken by the damage I could have caused — may still cause — I step back a safe distance. She doesn't miss the action. She looks as if I'm hurting her instead of trying to protect her.

Shaking my head, I can't look at her. I've injured her beyond what should ever be acceptable. Still, she has forgiven me. Even said she knows it wasn't me. True. But I am responsible.

"What's wrong, Taylor?" I ask her firmly brooking no evasion.

"I got my period." She shrugs looking beyond me to the garden. "It's really bad. I'm bleeding too much. My cycle's late." She looks down at the linen duvet plucking nonexistent lint. "I-I think I'm losing our baby." The last part sounds clogged with anguish.

Stunned, I do nothing other than stare at her for a long moment. Getting my phone out I make a call. "I need you to make a house call," I say after he picks up on the second ring.

Less than an hour later, Lex Spencer is examining

my wife and it is taking everything in me to keep my cool as I watch from the other side of the room.

"Takeda." I meet his hard gaze. He nods me over. I go to the head of the bed and stand beside Taylor taking her small hand as she makes room for me to sit beside her on the bed.

"It's as you suspected though we'll have to have the lab to test the DNA to confirm it. Mrs. Takeda you suffered a miscarriage before your twelfth week. I'm sure if we did the math I'd say you were between six to eight weeks along," he says grimly looking between us. A rough sob escapes Taylor as she buries her face in my chest. Smoothing her riot of curls I murmur, "It's okay." I don't say any bullshit like we can try again or anything like that because it was never my intention to get her pregnant. Last I knew she had an IUD.

The worst thing I could do would bring a child into this world. I've never wanted children after the heartless cruelty I endured. Nature versus nurture always speculates about souls like me and in my case it was definitely both. My nature was to nurture a cold monster and I know I have the capacity for much worse. I could create an army of heartless sadists and psychopaths no different than my ancestors. It would break Taylor and that I will not do even for the Takeda legacy.

Lex watches as I hold her. He's not far off the mark from me. I hear his brother who died was the nice twin. Not this motherfucker. He's rumored to be as much a killer as healer when he was on the battlefield. Dr. Feelgood indeed. What an oxymoron. Still, I can tell his concern is for my captive wife.

"When can you replace her IUD?" I ask him over the crown of Taylor's head.

"Hisashi?" She pulls back, her luminous eyes filled with pain and betrayal.

"No?" I ask dumbfounded.

She shakes her head with a vehemence that stuns me.

Pain pierces my forehead looking at her.

"She wants our baby," He crows.

I'm robbed of breath as I look at her in what must be a stunned expression.

"You have plenty of time to think about it," Lex reassures her in a kindly fashion that is not lost on me.

"I'll see you out. Be right back," I tell Taylor disengaging from her. Pressing a kiss on her crown I show Lex out.

"What the fuck are you doing, man?" He rounds on me as soon as he clears the house heading to his G-Wagon.

"I'm sure I don't know what you mean?" Replying blandly, I cross my arms over my chest unbothered by the good doctor who has more than a few secrets of his own. Which is why I called him in the first place.

"Her. Neck." His jaw tics in a way that lets me know he's seconds from attacking me if I even give hint that I am mistreating Taylor.

"We play. I used a new cuff that wasn't broken-in well enough. We didn't realize until afterward," I tell him my chest tight from the lie and the truth.

"Happens." He nods in reluctant acknowledgement. "It must've been too big as well." Shaking his head he says, "You're asking for trouble having your wife be your sub. Lines are too easy to be crossed."

I can't argue with the admonishment. "Are you saying you think our activities had anything to do with her miscarrying our baby?" The words stick in my throat in a way I didn't fully expect as one who'd sworn off children.

"That was until she said she wanted them. You know you can deny her nothing." He snickers. *"Little dove wants our little doves."*

I really can't stand this motherfucker sometimes.

"No. Rough play doesn't lead to miscarriages, only abuse does," he assures me. "Breath play from over a week ago by the looks of her neck wouldn't either."

Opening his door, he gets in pulling it closed behind him. "Let me know if she changes her mind."

I watch until he leaves trying to decide how I'm going to tell Taylor I will never give her a child.

All those thoughts fly from me when I see how vulnerable and sad she is when I return.

"Hey, beautiful," I say, sitting beside her rubbing her back. She looks over her shoulder. "I'm sure I am anything but beautiful right now, Hisashi. Where were you?"

I know she's not talking about moments ago but the two weeks I disappeared after putting her in the car and instructing the driver to bring her back here.

"I needed to be in a safe space to work through my triggers and work through what happened during the episode." Telling her as plainly as I can I go through the debrief I did with my therapist.

"That took two weeks?" she asks rightfully skeptically.

"No." Pulling my hands away I tell her, "That took about three days in our beautiful home in the Osaka countryside."

"And then?" She sits up her eyes troubled and searching mine.

"I needed to atone for my actions." Grimly I explain, "I have to have consequences for my actions, or I will definitely repeat them."

"So, I guess for almost killing me you exacted some pretty intense consequences on yourself and your guardian," she muses sadly.

"Guard-guardian, what the fuck did you call him?" I'm utterly aghast.

"Your guardian. That's what he is. He rises every time you are threatened, perceived, or otherwise." She shrugs in a matter-of-fact way.

"Guardian. She called me Guardian. I'm starting to like this woman." He preens.

"He's a fucking monster, a monster. He is

Monster." I scoff at her. "This is fucking ridiculous. He almost killed you, Taylor."

I want to rage at her. I keep my voice low and as calm as possible. I grit my teeth when she only waves me away.

"He sought to protect you. Left with no other recourse he tried to eliminate the treat. You stopped him. Your guardian immediately ceded control as soon as you stepped up. Now that you know you hold the power in this situation you can no longer abdicate control to him or use it as a cop-out." Her gaze is all unwavering honey laced with steel. Her voice is strong.

Taking an involuntary step back, I digest information I've never been presented with in all my years of therapy and struggle. I own *Monster*, *he* does not own *me*.

Turning away from her, I look out into the garden. I think back to all the times when I took control back over as soon as I became aware just how out of control *he'd* gotten. The one and only time I was lost for an ostensibly long period was when my father died and I realized that Taylor had abandoned me. The darkness that surrounded me then started out as a warm comforting cocoon and fighting my way back was like a thick morass of bramble that clung and tore at my soul. Finally, I made my way out. Determined to never allow *him* to take control of me again and that exercise alone not only proved futile it was unnecessary. I was in control as long as I remained brave enough to be.

The revelation has me turning back to her with a new hope and determination. "I still have to be careful until I know I have full control." Holding myself rigid, I stand before her knowing I still don't trust myself to be this near her.

She nods pulling the cover up around her for added protection. "Why didn't you tell me?"

I'm already shaking my head. Pausing I tilt my head her way tsking. "You, know that is not our way."

"Well, you have to have a new way. Our life and our family need open communication." Folding her arms across her chest she looks adorable.

"Our family will only every be you and me, Tay-chan." I don't drop the harshness from my tone. She needs to accept it now.

"Hi-"

"No." I cut her off with a sharp slice of my hand. "I will not bequeath our child with this turmoil of a life. I will not continue the sickness rife in the Takeda legacy." The vehemence in my voice has her eyes widening.

"The legacy of your family is also one of genius," she says.

"And madness," I counter quietly.

"Maybe some of that can be offset since y'all aren't marrying your first cousins anymore." She shrugs like she just didn't say the most disrespectful ass thing ever, though somewhat true.

"Intermarriage has not been a thing for over a century in our family." I return, humor turning the corner of my lip involuntarily.

"That's not enough time to undo the damage. A little newness in the mix won't hurt." Another shrug.

"When did you decide you wanted to have my child? Was it before or after I almost choked you to death or left you here to bleed to death?" I drop cruelly between us relishing the flinch filtering across her face.

She exhales, shaken by my sudden attack. "The latter. When I saw all the blood, I realized what was happening. I never thought about having a family, not right now. Not before—"

"Because you left me," I cut in stating the facts unequivocally. No babies with a husband locked away in an insane asylum that you never even visited. I shove aside. I would have still been a danger to her much of that time. Still the abandonment and betrayal I feel is tearing at me like a vicious festering wound.

"Yes. And too young. I was just getting into my career and though you probably didn't have tough hurtles, there were still things you wanted to accomplish like getting your doctorate. When I got back here my cycles were horrible, so I got the IUD removed. Did you finish your thesis?" So before I came to watch over her, that's why I didn't know.

"I had to scratch it. Someone beat me to the patent while I was sick," I tell her adding when I see her face fall, "I created something entirely different that revolutionized pest control with sonic waves and another proprietary tech that monitors blood oxygen levels and more brain wave innovations." I preen at the wonder in her eyes as she looks at me. I can bask in the way her eyes light up when they set upon me for an eternity. I don't miss the emotion there though I do not trust it or think it is fickle. No, she left before, and she will again if given the chance. She will never have that chance. Taylor Love Takeda is mine.

Ours.

Which reminds me. "You may call *Him* what you wish. *He* is dangerous. *He* is part of me and therefore I am. I won't be spending time with you anymore until I have this under control." Seeing how the steely command in my voice is having no effect on her makes my ire rise.

"Seems unfair." How she can look at me without the horror that should accompany everything she's been made to endure astounds me.

"How so?" I step closer unthinking. To retreat now would make me give face in front of a woman whose esteem I earned. I stand my ground looking down at her though somehow even through the height difference and her sitting while I tower above, she is a regal as a queen. My equal in every way.

"You owe me recompense now, husband. Allowing your guardian to nearly kill me, getting me pregnant without my consent." She shrugs one shoulder. "You must make amends."

How the fuck did she turn the tables on me? I stare at her diminutive, clever form.

"Well played, little dove," He croons. *"Ohhh, I like her. Like her. Like her so much more now."*

"Very well," I sigh, looking at her. "What will you have me do?"

I know I'm in trouble when I see the slow smile spread across her face.

CHAPTER
SEVENTEEN

T *aylor*

~

Lights Darken ~ The End

Sitting back, I look at the last words I've transferred on the brand-new MacBook Pro Hisashi gave me, when he got tired of all the notes in disarray on the bed and me asking to use his laptop for research as I finished the play. I don't know how I feel about my first play in years.

Feeling inspired wars constantly with the feelings of will it be good enough or just some self-indulgent, trite bullshit better never to see the light of day. I don't have imposter syndrome, no. I am well aware that I am a gifted writer, rare and bold as one Washington Post critic said. Being out of the game a few years doesn't bother me either. No. The niggling feeling I have that I have to press down and not consume me is being even better than I was before. How do you top yourself? I should just do my best and hope for the best. Yet, I've never done that. I've always leaned into my gift. Shifted through the chaff to get to the best of the wheat, golden and strong ready to be fed to theater fans the world over.

A sick feeling settles in my stomach. I have to put my work away. Come back later when I have more of a three-sixty view and a better perspective. Distance is my best friend right now. I know I'm good enough and this play will be stellar with pruning. The excitement at the prospect of workshopping the play and bouncing ideas off the cast, so we can work any kinks out sneaks into my overtired brain.

Knowing I need a hot shower to calm down I pass by Hisashi's sleeping form.

It's well past midnight and he's finally fallen into an exhausted sleep after fighting his sleep for the past three days. I told him in no uncertain terms the lack of sleep will only contribute to a setback.

"I know, Tay-chan, I just need to watch over you," he said gruffly stroking my hair the other night. I wanted to argue with him or tell him to go back to his own room to sleep as he had the first few nights.

The selfish part of me likes the way he holds me, likes waking up in his arms, the way he strokes my hair and smooths it away from my forehead. He does this little thing where he twirls my curls around his fingers then slides his finger out making a spiral. It's the cutest thing, almost nothing really, but it's something I can't remember him ever doing from our time before. It's a new memory for this version of Hisashi and Taylor. Something not linked to the past. Like a new beginning.

After Lex left earlier, he finally napped for the first time. The bloodwork came back positive for fetal cells as we suspected, but after the mobile ultrasound he brought with him that he uses for rural visits. He assured me — well, us, even though I think Hisashi would've rather not have heard the news that we'd have no problem if we chose to pursue another pregnancy. And we could start as soon as we were comfortable.

Hisashi looked at me askance when Lex offered contraception as an alternative, which I politely declined.

He didn't come back for hours after he saw Lex out. When he did, he brought more clothes and a huge box of condoms, tossing them in the drawer at the bedside.

For a while he watched me work seeming content to work from home this week. The strike has slowed things down considerably. He doesn't talk or rage about it, but I know he's still terribly angry at his brother, Krie, and Thad.

He's not said anything more about me paying the cost for Thad's hacking which was never fair in the first place, I'd be quick to tell him. He codes counter measures into the Takeda system and then works on whatever side project that currently holds his interest when he gets bored. Watching him in his element is sexy. It's calming. Who knew being held captive by my estranged husband would be the catalyst for new words.

He's taking his atonement seriously though, doing everything I ask.

After returning from my shower, I put the laptop away. There has been no bleeding the last two days. I've always had short light periods and after the initial bleeding from the miscarriage, my cycle returned to normal. I'm still hormonal though, crying at odd times and not sure why other than the shock of losing a baby I had no idea I was pregnant with.

What Hisashi said about us needing to wait makes sense, if I told his ass that he'd be unmovable. We've waited long enough to be together. I know we need more time to get to know each other in this iteration of who we are as older more mature adults. We have whole separate lives we have to merge and not a small amount of trust to build between us. I know this, my mind knows this, but my heart after seeing what could have been washed red down the drain, is singing another tune entirely.

Telling him that would only further his thoughts of brokenness. I don't want him to carry that any longer. "God made you perfect," Mom would always say. "We are always learning and growing," my father would tell me when I made a mistake. They never made me feel like I was a disappointment or damaged no matter the nightmares I had or even when I told them I married a Japanese man from the prominent Takeda family and didn't tell them until the months after I'd returned to the States. They took me not being ready to talk about it at face value and let me go into the therapy I sought. They were always there, never pressing me with questions trusting me, though at times I doubted myself and the decisions I made, especially leaving him and never knowing where they'd sent him.

I know Hisashi never had that soft place. He needs to know I can be that for him. Despite it all, he's mine. I'm his too. We just have to make our way truly back to each other. His illness is not an excuse for his behavior, but neither is it a reason to abandon him.

Looking at the bed I approach. I stop, watching him. No night terrors from him but mine have come back with full force. He's held me through them all. His arms are my safety, my solace. He is my home.

Slipping beneath the covers, I snuggle close as I

can, not wanting to wake him. Settling in, I let sleep lull me.

"Hey, little dove." The cool cultured tones catch my attention.

"Shh..." He presses a long finger to my lips. *"We don't want to disturb his sleep. He's terribly exhausted. Watching over you. Keeping you safe." His* smile is wild and gorgeous — familiar.

"I won't if you're going to be good," I whisper under *his* finger.

"Oh, I plan to be very, very good to you little — one," He promises, mischief in every word.

I squirm back, trying to at least put space between us but I made a fatal mistake when I came to bed. I got right into the snare *he* laid. Was *he* awake the whole time watching, lying in wait for me?

"Uh, uh," He tsks, shaking his head, pressing his long, hard body between my legs. *"I owe you an apology. For — many things, Tay-chan. So many naughty things."*

Stunned, I look into solemn eyes. *He's* serious.

"There have not been many times in which I have misread the intentions of another in regard to our friend. I've always watched over him. I'm never wrong until now — and then, with you. How refreshing." Bending down *he* buries *his* head in my neck seeming to inhale me. *"Delicious," He* growls.

"All is forgiven. I told Hisashi as much. I don't know if you heard," I tell *him.*

"Oh, I did little dove, you called me his guardian. I've been Monster so long, his Monster at times too. I forgot I could be more. I could be so much more. You reminded me of that, beautiful. Arigato."

Despite myself and the possible danger he presents I find myself basking in the adoration in *his* gaze. I've gone from being called little bitch to beautiful by this part of my husband's psyche.

"Thank you for watching over Hisashi and protecting him when I couldn't," I tell *him*, bowing my head as much as I can in thanks. "Arigato," I whisper.

Before I can think, *he's* covering my lips. The kiss is soft in its worship. I press my hands on *his* shoulders to push *him* away. *He's* clearly not my husband, still a part of *him* but conscious and real and not Hisashi, yet I know *his* touch, *his* kiss.

He kisses me in long lingering pulls, beckoning, seducing, enticing. I sigh, so close, dang it. I almost — *he* pulls away, *his* eyes warm, a small knowing little quirk playing at the edge of *his* mouth.

"Magnificent. Let's keep this between us," He whispers turning from me in smooth liquid movements.

Soon Hisashi is throwing his long arm above his head unbothered in his sleep.

I lay there for a long time unsure of what I just felt. Remembering the slow seductiveness of words when he said so "many naughty things" and "then and now."

Hisashi didn't remember smashing the dishes

because it wasn't him, it was his guardian, the monster, his monster. The whole past unravels before me in a way that has me sitting up covering my mouth. It was never him. He was lost in the abyss of his mind. He had no idea. His guardian emerged seeing the perceived threat and pounced. Like a cat *he* played with the little dove *he'd* caught in *his* lair a little first.

I wonder if Hisashi knows. How much if anything Kiyoshi told him of the state he found me in. Probably nothing fearing it would further fracture his brother's psyche. I have to know. We can't move forward with him not knowing. I hesitate as the nagging thought takes hold. This could lead to me losing him forever.

"I ASSUME by the way you're set up to binge watch this ridiculousness that you're done with your play." Looking up at his stern expression as he stands before me in gorgeous austerity taking in my array of snacks, I turn my focus back to the projection screen set up in my quarters.

"For now, I'm letting it marinate a little before I make edits." I flick play on the Japanese anime and quickly become totally absorbed in the show about a blue-eye samurai.

"Whitewashing," he grouses, sitting down beside me taking the popcorn I'd placed between us to share and placing it on the low table in front of us then pulling me into the curve of his arm so I can rest my head on his chest.

"You haven't even given it a chance," I look up, telling him in a huff.

"I don't have to. Let me know when you want some real anime. I will be happy to supply you with my own library but in only Japanese; the English translation misses a lot of nuances," he says with an indulgence that is both smug and endearing.

"I'd love that," I tell him, shimmying my shoulders a little "But right now we're watching this one." Patting his knee, I can't help giggling at his irritated face.

We binge the show and despite Hisashi's overactive mind we manage to get through all of the episodes without him leaving in disgust.

"Let's go for a walk in the garden," I say as the servants come to clean. I'm never comfortable with people cleaning up after me much to Hisashi's amusement. I still feel uncomfortable with them knowing they tell him my every move, which his arriving so soon after the miscarriage started was a clear indication not to mention how obvious it was Aiko knew he was watching when she brought the food. They may serve me but their loyalty belongs only to my husband.

"Stop laughing at me," hissing to him over my shoulder, I lead him out into the garden.

"I'd never laugh at you," he says, just for my ears. "I simply find it amusing that a person with such abysmal cleaning habits would be upset with having staff."

Rolling my eyes, I guide him to the small bridge overlooking the koi pond. It is one of my favorite places because it affords you a clear view of the entire garden.

When I was first allowed to come out here, my goal was to find points of weakness. I should have known better. There were none. Hisashi created this fortress for one reason to make sure no one entered or left without him knowing their every move. Lex was the only person I'd seen here and that was just for an emergency. Though my movements are highly monitored, and I've not been given access to the entire estate I doubt Kiyoshi has been out here nor does he see his brother outside of work dinners. As for the possibility of this little dove being able to fly away that has proven to be an impossibility.

Once I gave that particular fantasy up, I was able to fully experience and enjoy the beautiful architecture, flowers, and trees he'd place here to honor the beautiful Japanese garden we visited. The sheer time and expense he went to recreate this particular memory makes hope stir in my heart, despite his continued aloofness and doubt. Only time will heal the breach between us.

After allowing the silence to fall between us for a moment I tell him, "Your guardian visited me last night."

"What?" He draws up so tightly it's like he's become a strung bow ready to launch an arrow. He turns from me, distress rippling through every tautly pulled muscle of his body. I can imagine how he's raging internally.

"*He* didn't hurt me. Quite the opposite, in fact." Hastily, I try to reassure him.

He swings back to me, his eyes raking me from head to toe. "How so?" He asks with deadly calm. I'm not fooled one bit. Trepidation ripples through me. I swallow against the welling anxiety.

"Well," I hedge, watching as his eyes flare with barely held annoyance. "*He* apologized for his actions. *He* took accountability but tried to make me understand *his* reasoning in trying to protect you."

"And you believed *Him*?" He sneers, his face hardening an impossible degree.

He waits for me to nod before he rips into me again. "Did it ever cross your mind *He's* just getting you to let your guard down so *he* can take greater advantage? Not call me when *He* actually kills your silly ass?"

"No." I shake my head, hearing the hurt in my own voice. "*He* only wants to keep you safe, Hisashi. You should know better from all *He's* done," I tell him so sure before, but now I feel a small kernel of distrust taking root.

"You should fucking know better, Taylor. *He's* jealous of you, always has been. *He's* never liked your influence. How you control me, make me weak, or so *he* thinks." He crosses his arms over his chest. "The next time *He* tries to contact you, I don't care what state I'm in. You call my name."

He skewers me with a hard gaze. "Frankly, I can't believe you didn't immediately call me last night. How long was *He* with you, Taylor?"

"N-not long." I shrug, my face heats calling me for the liar I am, and he doesn't miss the tell.

His hand whips out snagging my nape. "How. Fucking. Long?" he grits through clenched teeth his chiseled jaw working like he's grinding glass. The words that follow are just as bloody. "Did you fuck *Him*?" He shakes me roughly.

"No. Hisashi. No." I shake my head vigorously, back-and-forth guilt assailing me. Maybe not last night, but never? I can't say for sure. *He* apologized for his hurting me in the past like *He* was the one who fucked me and left me to die in the Tokyo flat.

Misreading my confused guilt, Hisashi grips tightens even more. "Something happened. You have this one chance. I have cameras everywhere, little dove. I will find out and you will be punished, regardless. The severity is all up to you."

"*He* kissed me. He wanted more, but I said, no." Looking him squarely in the face, I allow no hesitation to enter my voice knowing he will take that as deception. "I've never lied to you, Hisashi." The pleading in my voice makes me cringe.

Stepping back fast, he releases me making me wobble. Reaching out I grab the edge of the bridge for support. His nostrils flare. His gaze is trained on me. His breathing is labored as he decides if he will believe me and what my punishment will be.

"I didn't want it," I tell him, soft but firm.

"*He* is not me," he says wrathfully. "I know there are times in the past when you didn't know and for that you will be forgiven." He pauses, his gaze saying he judges me anyway for not knowing.

Okayyyy, not my fault motherfucker.

"Did you knowingly share me with *Him*?" I ask, suddenly understanding something about this dynamic I didn't before — sometimes they work together.

"Yes," he says coldly, unapologetically his face cast in a vicious mask. "For a long time I thought *He* was me. Just another braver, darker soul, without remorse, conscience, or any of the messy feelings that hold normals back. Eventually after therapy and medication I knew better. With lovers before you *He* was content to just watch. *He* was a silent observer. *He* knew something about you was different. *He* knew you made me feel. You were special to me. *He* wanted to see why you evoked those emotions in me. When my illness reared with father's death, *He* became stronger. Much of what happened during that time is lost to me." He looks away, then turns back shame etched in every hollow of his face, his eyes a chasm of pain. "Kiyoshi told me how he found you. I don't know if I did it or if *He* did."

"You didn't." I reach out to him, but he snatches away.

"You can't know that. Nor can I." Shaking his head he rips his hands through his hair. I notice how his fingers tremble slightly before they grip the locks in frustration.

"Then why did you come back to me? Take me from my life. If you know you could do that to me again?" I ask, my heart caving in.

"I'm better now. I have tools, medication. You are my fucking wife, Taylor Takeda. You saw my tattoo. You made a promise of forever." His mouth forms a hard smile. "And I will never let you go. I'm a selfish motherfucker. You're mine and you will remain mine until I part this earth. Even then I won't let you go. I will haunt you until you join me. And should you leave first I will join you soon after. There is no me without you. No you without me. I will allow nothing to come between us. I will not share you. Not with *Him* or anyone."

He means that unhinged shit. I can see it in the cast of his face, the way his breath harshens. I know it with every fiber of my being.

Stepping up to me, he captures my face between his warm hands. His long almost artistic fingers spear into my curls. "You will call me if *He* comes." The dark fringe of his spikey lashes draws my attention, and I get lost in him for a moment.

"I promise." My eyes sting. His face is ravaged. His soul is mine. I am his. My beautiful broken husband.

"We are so fucked up." Staccato laughter breaks from me. He chuckles a little bringing me deep in to the safety of his arms.

"We are." Resting his head on top of mine he holds me for long moments. The smell of honeysuckle, rose, and hints of the vanilla orchids surround us, the beautiful bouquet making promises to souls we dare not speak yet.

"Time for your little punishment." Pulling back his onyx gaze meets mine. He reaches down taking my hand in his, tugging me behind him.

"I didn't do anything." My protest is halfhearted at best.

"Hmm. Should I catalog all your trespasses? Refusing contraception. Kissing the monster. Staying up too late. Making me watch a ridiculous inauthentic anime."

Snatching me in front of him, he buries his head into my neck and growls, marching me to my doom. "Shall I continue? Shall I tell you what I'm going to do?"

"Yes," I pant, feeling him pressed against me.

"First, I'm going to worship your plush little body. Suck your nipples until they stand out. When they are glistening and begging for attention, I'm going to slide between them while I fuck your hot, naughty little mouth. Then I'll kiss a trail down your body and lavish your pussy with my tongue. After you come on my tongue, then I'll stop being gentle and fuck you hard the way you like. And if you ask really nice, I will fuck all my kids into your hot little snatch. Anything that spills, I'll push back inside of you and fuck you and keep fucking you until you're weak and too exhausted to remember any other kisses."

I'm liquid as he leads me to his exquisite brand of destruction.

H isashi ~ Paris

"STAY THERE," I murmur biting back a groan, my eyes skating over her freshly bathed, waxed, and moisturized curves. Tay-chan is so cute trying to hide her curiosity as her gaze tracks me as I walk over to the oversized jewelry box I previously laid on the dresser.

Taking the long black box over to her, I turn it toward her so she can open it. Whether her fingers are trembling from anticipation of fear, I can't fathom. I think I'd like if it's both. "Fuck yesssss," *He* snarls in agreement. We're barely on speaking terms, but in this we agree.

"Hisashi," she whispers, as she takes in the long glimmering ropes of diamond over platinum. Over a million diamonds cover the body necklace.

"Will you wear it for me?" I ask already taking the masterpiece out of the case. "You will barely feel it. Only the barest slide against your skin," I say, beginning at her neck overlapping the sparkling bands so that it drapes to the back. Placing a clasp there, I circle back to her, draping the length over and around her kinbaku knots.

"Oh, that's why you had them made so long," she muses, watching me turn her diamond body necklace into a masterpiece. She is my design. Diamonds crisscross her from neck to waist. She looks like she's corseted in diamonds.

Kneeling, I bring the chain lacing her at the dip of her waist, traversing the top of her thighs, looping through the center down to her slick pussy. Carefully I leave enough slack so that it teases not torments her sweet little bud as I pull the chain between the crease of her ass for the final clasp.

"A chastity belt?" She gasps, looking down at my handiwork.

Sitting back on my hunches, I look at the beautiful web of her diamond gift shimmering on her beautiful brown skin. "Why would I need to cage what's mine, wife?"

Captivated by the twinkle and sparkle caressing

her pretty pussy, I can't resist leaning in and tasting her luscious little cunt.

"Fuck, you taste good," I say between licks. In seconds, she's canting her hips and pushing that fat motherfucker into my mouth. I'm seconds away from pulling her to the floor and making love to her when the doorbell buzzes.

S𝐇𝐄 𝐋𝐎𝐎𝐊𝐒 lovely in the floor length Yumi Katsura red and black hand embroidered dress, it sets off her beautiful complexion. She can barely hold her excitement when the tailors come to fit her into the garment. They buzz around in a mix of rapid-fire Japanese like moths to her alluring flame. She stands gloriously in all her beautiful curves as they fit the silk chiffon and webbed lace to her body. Layers of fabric surround her as if she's sewn into the couture gown.

"Oh my goodness, Hi—" she cuts herself off seeing my quirked eyebrow knowing it is not my way to speak of anything in front of others. To my amusement she manages to keep her silence until the team leaves.

"*Beautiful, fucking magnificent,*" *He* murmurs in awe as she turns this way and that admiring herself in the long cheval mirror facing the room. She catches my unwavering stare and damned if she doesn't preen for me. My pretty little pet.

My length hardens in my pants. *Patience,* I tell myself. *All in good time.*

Soon there is another knock and in flows the hair and make-up team. Mindful of her curls I made sure my assistant knew to ask a for stylist proficient in natural hair.

Tay-chan sits quietly and more than a little nervous as they proceed with her make-up. Quelling the low simmering rage marked by the abject shame I feel in this not being the norm for her when it should be, I make myself watch at what should be the most mundane of experiences all the while furious at myself and *Him* that it is novel to her. All because I couldn't keep my shit together long enough to be the husband she deserved.

"Oh, don't be so hard on yourself. She ran," He attempts to soothe.

She should have. Turning briefly away, I remind him, *We almost killed her.*

"Perhaps," He concedes, drifting back into *his* dark place.

Focusing back on my pretty wife again I marvel at her beauty and her courage to want to deal with one such as me. "Deal with" was always what I heard. I was always the one who needed to be dealt with — my attitude, lack of emotion, troubling behavior. No one ever tried to understand me until Taylor. No one saw me. She saw past the billion-dollar facade to the man I am. The monster. Hers.

In much the same way she's allowing me to give her this surprise though I know she's dying to know.

Even with pretended calm I know she doesn't feel she lets them do their job. The whole time the curiosity in her eyes tells the story, she never could hide from me.

I can hear her questions without her having to speak.

Hisashi did you arrange this? Why?

I wouldn't answer even if we were alone. Why? I could say my atonement for not only the present but the past. Still, that wouldn't be the truth should she suddenly realize it, she'll have my face. Know truths I'm not ready to speak.

I don't indulge her curiosity. I just sit in the quiet corner of my Parisian penthouse taking my pleasure watching my beautiful wife be pampered.

Eventually they all leave.

"I will be back shortly," I say, moving into the suites' bathroom smiling when I hear her grumbling about mysterious trips.

"There's no one here," she says as we take our seats in my private box.

"Hai, it's just you and I," I answer, mindful of the echo. Though we are the only patrons, it's hardly empty. The whole cast and stage crew are here.

"Why?" she whispers looking at me her eyes wide with wonder.

"We missed the last night of the last performance because of your illness. So I asked them to give us a private performance tonight." Crossing one leg over the other I lounge nonchalantly against the plush cushions just as the house lights are dimmed.

"What?" The way she gasps. It's so adorable. Looking to the stage then back at me she mouths, "For me?"

"For you, I'd do anything." Nodding toward the stage, I lace her soft fingers between mine. "Shh, it's about to start."

We settle back and the curtain rises to August Wilson's "The Piano Lesson."

The luminosity of her gaze says it all as her head snaps to me, then back to the stage. In her gaze is everything I have ever lived for. If for no other reason than to see her look at me like she just did, as if I hung the fucking moon, the sun, and all the stars. I'd do it again. Buy out a theater, kill, maim it doesn't matter. A glance from her sears through my soul. For she sees me, knows me for the monster that I am as well as the one that lives within and she's not shying away.

This makes me think how things would have been different if I hadn't worn the mask the first time. Hid my true nature and frightened her away. Would she still have repudiated me? Ran away? Tried to melt into the landscape of New York?

"We will never know," He laments.

No but perhaps this time will be different.

"Let her go and find out," He taunts.

Fuck you.

Coward.

Turning my attention back to the play I squeeze her hand. A small reassurance to myself that for now she's mine. Right now in this moment she wants to be here. Soon, all that melts away. I become engrossed in Black Americana and what heritage, legacy and the sense of responsibility all current generations feel to the ones that have come before.

"WHERE ARE WE GOING?" Tay-chan gasps so prettily when I pinch her nipple making sure to capture it with the chain.

"You know better than to ask," I tsk, soothing the hardened nub with my finger.

"Now, people are going to see my nipple through my dress." Her complaint is cute.

"We better make them match then." Reaching over with my hand I pinch the other, making sure to soothe it as well.

"Happy?" Looking down at her, I let cruelty bleed into the word.

Impossibly she melts into me. Softened by the soft luxury and the play, she's pretty and pliant.

Her hand drifts up scraping my nipples softly before she pinches me in return. The sting goes straight to my dick.

"Little bitch," I growl against her mouth dipping my tongue in, loving that my kitten is learning she has claws.

"You started it." Her pout is all petulant cuteness as we pull up into the private entrance of Le Pre Catalan.

No sooner than we come to a stop is the driver helping her out and we're being ushered into the dining salon.

The room is at capacity and I'm not surprised at Taylor's shocked expression.

I wait until we are seated and given menus before I address the obvious question in her gaze. "I feel it's well pastime that we go out more."

"Going out is a movie at the cineplex. You brought me to Paris." She shakes her head like I'm being over the top.

"Thus going out among our set," I deadpan, turning my attention to the wine list.

"Lafitte de Rothschild," I tell the sommelier who nods approvingly then bows to us before taking the wine list.

"Still, I'm having the most fantastic time." She smiles prettily her thanks as the first course is being served. The way she always acknowledges people no matter their job humbles me. She taught me to see people I was raised to take for granted.

People from our set never acknowledge those that work for us. We simply take their service as our right. In the beginning, I thought it gauche until I realized that she actually meant it. Something shifted in me then. To say she makes me better is too trite a term, no. I'm not even sure I want to be that person. Will people ever be anything more than bags of flesh better left for dead to me? Hardly. But how I treat them matters to her, and she matters to me. Maybe the only one who does outside of my siblings. So, in that respect, my perspective has been grudgingly shifted. I haven't decided if I should hate her for that or not. She'll definitely be punished deliciously for any smiles I give.

"Hai, I did too," I return to her. "The play reminds me of your work, in fact, just as most of the critics say."

"Really? Have you read all of them?" She smiles tremulously, as if she fears what I will say. I can sense her tension rising at the possibility of a critique.

"No." Slowly shaking my head, I watch the disappointment filter across her face. "I've seen them all." Taking a sip of the wine, I let it wash over my tongue, savoring her shocked look more than the bouquet of the ten-thousand-dollar vintage.

"What — how?" She leans forward, her gaze searching my face for the lie.

"I have always found a way," I tell her, shaking out the napkin and lying it across my lap. "When your first play was picked up on Broadway. It was during the final run that I finally got the chance to see it." I leave out what we both know. While she'd been running in smaller theaters trying to get noticed I was being treated for my mental illness. Complete lockdown in an institution leaves little time for an excursion to another continent for theater performances.

"It became easier once I secured a place in New York." I let the words sink in.

"I didn't know," she tells me, worry spilling across her face.

"I didn't want you to know." I wave her concerns away, knowing why she worries. She acted like she was a free agent dating and the like. Thankfully for her sake nothing ever came from her admirers.

"Did you like pretending you were single?" Giving her a little wink, I nod for the main course.

"It was for appearances," she says, her eyes not meeting mine. She casts around for the words. "There were so many rumors about how I got financing and why it was anonymous. It got nasty. Marc Lukas, the critic, I don't know if you remember him. He died in a really bad car accident. Well, he panned Heart Less, calling it trite and too sentimental. He heavily alluded to me not having talent, and me being funded by some indulgent sugar daddy."

Nodding, I take another sip, savoring my words.

"Indeed. I remember quite clearly." Her head bobs and she spears her savory duck. Watching her lovely lips cover the tines and the way her white teeth pull the flesh from the fork, I wait, not wanting her to choke. At least not without my hands on her throat. Swallowing the food, she follows with the wine.

"I made sure he suffered before his car exploded." The duck has a delicious tang. *"Even sweeter after that little confession,"* He snickers, sliding back into the darkness.

Eyes widening as my words settle over her, Taylor looks around making sure we're not being overheard. "You did what?"

I shake my head. "I'm sure I don't know what you are referring to." Quirking my brow, I let her know to drop it. One never repeats such a thing. The other person simply misheard.

She visibly swallows.

"I will allow no one to hurt you," I coldly return with a negligent wave of my hand.

"Other than you, you mean." The pride I feel at her hand not shaking when she grasps her glass, after that little smart-ass quip could light the Eiffel tower.

"I save your pain exclusively for me, little dove." I chuckle, watching the blush warm her skin and devour the duck just as I intend to do her later.

"Make her bleed for her arrogance. Bruise her bottom for that cheek," He suggests. The suggestion has merit, but my plans follow a different path tonight.

. . .

SLOWLY I PEEL the dress from her body and toss it in a nearby chair. Vanilla-rose wafts from her skin. My flesh rises in response. The heady musk of her snakes around me like an aphrodisiac. Heat pulses through me, my dick presses against my zipper seeking freedom, wanting to bury itself into the depths of her tight pussy.

Her nipples are taut and beckoning, the diamond chain glinting prettily against the umber of her skin. With cool deliberation I keep my touch feather like, still I can't resist touching her. Her peaks are hard little juicy berries, the tips dark as the deepest blueberry and just as sweet.

"Pretty motherfucker." I dip my head pulling one then the other into my mouth. Come slips from my tip. This woman is going to unman me. Groaning, I lick a long trail between the valley catching the chain in my mouth. Tugging I draw her to me and taking her sweet lips.

She tastes like the champagne pear glace we had for dessert. "I think I'll drink champagne from your pussy one day soon," I tell her, dipping in to capture more of the taste. "Umm, Yum." Pushing her breasts together I suck her nipples as one until I hear her panting and feel her squirm against me. The way she writhes brings her against my hardness. With each brush I feel the chain.

"Do you like the way it glides against your pretty little body, Tay-chan?"

"Yes," she moans writhing in curves and jewels.

Stepping back, I nod to the bed. She has the nerve to sit demurely on the edge. Scooping her up I press my knee on the edge placing her in the center spreading her legs, not bothering to restrain her hands.

My eyes never leave her as I shed my suit. Climbing between her legs, I lean over her body. "There are many things I have required of you, wife. You've given yourself to me beautifully. Trusted me when you should not. Now, I will ask more. I need more. Will you give me what I need?"

She visibly swallows. "What do you need?"

Reaching over to the nightstand I take the ceremonial dagger from the table unsheathing it. "I thought long and hard about how I must atone for my sins against you. You will let me do this thing for you." I draw a thin line along my left clavicle.

"Hi—"

"You will let me." Slowly I continue with the other side until the line meets at the center of my chest.

"No." With a strangled cry Tay-chan reaches up to grasp my hand. Grabbing her delicate wrist with my other hand I make her help draw the thin line to the center of my chest.

"You once owned me here. You left and ripped my fucking heart out." My Japanese is so rough, so raw, her eyes widen. I release the dagger. Now only she is holding my life in her hands.

"Plunge it in and you can be free. You'll never have to worry about me again. You'll free us both." Spreading my arms wide, I continue, "I release you, but for only this life. In the next one, I will come for you again. And in the next and the next. We are for eternity, little dove. But in this lifetime, if you want to be free from me. End it now." The point of the dagger is sharp against the center of my chest. It's nothing compared to the agony in my heart. I can't live without her. I don't fucking want to. This is her only moment to be free. I can see in her eyes when she realizes the truth of my words. This is her only chance.

The knife moves a slow agonizing drag downward. My tumescent dick rises as pain, tormenting pleasure causes an affliction of lust to rise like a tsunami inside my body.

In that moment my little angel becomes a shepherd of the devil as her little evil ass continues down past my navel making me bleed from neck to dick.

Precum drips like a sieve from me. "Fuuuuck," I growl, watching my blood stream down my body in a thin trail. She's gone beyond what I wanted. Gave me what I didn't even know I needed. Taking the knife my little vicious one doesn't stop until she's reached my sac. I feel them draw up at the sting.

"Enough." Words catch in my throat with her hot little mouth covers my sac. It's so fucking hot. She licks her handiwork, slicing her tongue over the cut with a slowness that only furthers the torture. I have to grab the base of my dick to keep myself from shooting my load right then and there.

"Goddamn!" I yell. Her tongue slides around the base like a hot little serpent. Her head swivels this way, and she laps the trail of blood I started, but she happily continued. Rising a little, she licks up my length, playing with the cut with her tongue. Up and down she runs her tongue over me, getting me slick, then her mouth covers me, feeling like a damn furnace. My hips jerk fucking into the heated cavern. She downs me over and over, taking me to the back, not gagging, but I can see tears in her eyes. Honestly, I don't know if it's from her exertions or emotions. Her dimples deepen as she takes my dick in long sucks down her throat.

Tugging her head back I look into those big doe eyes. The eyes that a few short hours ago had me thinking I was her everything.

"You're so fucking beautiful." I shake her a little bit. Almost angry that she makes me more unhinged than I normally am. I take her mouth. I want to fucking brutalize her. Plunging my tongue inside of her mouth, I suck her deep, inhaling the vanilla-rose and the metallic flavor of my blood. I pull and suck her bottom lip into my mouth, then the top. I give her mine in return.

My dick thrums between us with a heartbeat all its own.

She pulls back burying her head in my neck sucking my blood then trailing her tongue to the other side taking from there too.

"I've created a vampire." My eyes cast down to watch her lips crimson with me as she follows the trail to my heart. There she lingers kissing the place I begged her to pierce me. End me she did not sealing her fate and mine.

"That was your last and only chance, little dove," I tell her. She looks up, unwavering. An empress draped in diamonds and my blood. "I know."

I take her down then into the white down comforter now smeared with my blood.

Pulling her thick, soft thighs over my shoulders I bury my head in her pussy. Tugging her lips into my mouth in tandem I suck. I use my tongue to fuck her pussy before going lowering and laving her bottom hole. She arches into my mouth crying when I spear two fingers into her pussy and ruthlessly finger fuck her. Her muscles clutch me as I work her driving her higher. Bringing her heels up she fucks me back meeting me thrust for thrust.

I press her spot just as she bears down. Rising I smack her pussy with the first jet of her come. She splashes so prettily against my hand as she climaxes, crying out my name in a way that has my dick hardening in anticipation.

Flipping her over, I shove a pillow under her hips. Straddling her hips, I hitch her up until her drenched hole is open to me. Spreading her pussy lips, I notch the head of my dick at her entrance.

"Head down like my good little cumslut." Pressing her head into the down comforter I drive into her hot tight pussy until my sac is flush against her. Her scream is muffled by the comforter. Sliding back, fascination has my gaze seared to the sight of my dick slick with my blood and her juices. The stinging pain creates an ecstasy that surpasses all understanding. Pain, pleasure, and passion manifest in a primal press of comingling flesh as I drive deep into the recesses of her lush pussy. My eyes roll back, my brain threatens to disengage as the sensations intensify.

She's taking me into another stratosphere. The jiggle and shake of her ass is hypnotic. The slip, slide, and slap of our flesh creates a cacophony of craving that resounds throughout the room.

"Hm?" I taunt her fucking into her when she whimpers. Splitting her pussy on my dick the way she loves. "Do you need more, little dove?"

Driving deeper I rise on one knee planting my foot on the bed for more leverage. Her pussy is speaking to me. "I can hear you begging, needing more of this dick. Do you need more pretty one?" My tone is sweet, but my hands are dirty motherfuckers when I ease them between her cheeks and start to play.

"Hi — eep." She breaks off in a yelp when I smack her ass.

"Shut the fuck up and take this dick, like my good little dove." Spreading her wider I angle down fucking her to the hilt. My sac slaps its own rhythm against her fat little clit each time I bottom out. Her walls squeeze me so hard I see heaven and my fingers play with her nub so slick with need I can barely find purchase.

"Such a good girl. So sweet for me. Come on my dick so you can lick it clean," I whisper roughly. Eager as ever for my command she does just as I say. She fucks me back every stroke, taking the pleasure she deserves as she spirals away on her own cloud of bliss.

Before she can crumble, I pull her to me. Her mouth already open takes every inch of my dick, sucking me down, taking every jet of come, the mix of her essence, and my blood down her hot little throat.

"Such a good fucking girl taking me so deep," I praise.

He growls in agreement.

CHAPTER

NINETEEN

T *aylor*

~

"I'M SORRY. I have to leave for a bit." No sooner than we get back to his samurai mansion of the south is Hisashi being called away again.

"Why? What's going on?" Dread quakes inside of me. All I can think of is Thad and his shenanigans causing more trouble for me and Krie. How he can be so cavalier about the pain he's causing his own sister is reprehensible. I always longed for siblings and my mom told me how devastated she was never to have any more kids. That's why my parents cherished me so much, doted on me. They made sure I had everything I needed, but never had a sense of entitlement. My father always made me know how important it was to give back in word and deed.

He looks down as he texts back and forth in quick succession before he looks up, his troubled gaze reaching mine, worry lining every aspect of his handsome face. "My mother has fallen ill," he says, his tone completely devoid of all emotion. It's as if he's shutting down his emotions in advance to protect himself.

"Oh," I say, searching his face.

I step toward him, and he immediately steps back. For a moment I think he's going to raise his arm toward me off. Barriers — invisible and seen are going up so fast between us.

Pushing the fear of rejection and maybe even bodily harm aside, I step closer. Muscles tic, his face hardens visibly, his jaw juts out, his teeth clench. Dead eyes watch me — daring.

And yeah, I fucking dare. I step into my own destruction.

"Hisashi." I shake my head a little, tilting my head to the side giving him a small gentle smile.

"I'm here for you. I'm here now." His eyes track to my throat where he can obviously see me swallow back the emotions threatening to break free.

I know his battles now for they are ours. Trust has been broken on both sides. Still his pain if it should be more than he can bear will be visited on us both. This time neither of us may escape. We have to face this together. And unlike last time, I know what I am up against. I know the monsters I'm fighting. The man and his monster. His mental illness won't win this time. Not if I have anything to say about it.

"Just go about your day, Tay-chan. I will see you when I return." He rakes his hand through the coarse locks of his hair.

"And will you return, husband. Will it be you?" He's still for a long time and it takes everything within me not to retrace my steps. He looks down at the ground for a long time and I'm almost certain there is a whole ass conversation going on between him and his monster.

Finally, he looks at me. His eyes aren't dead anymore, they are resolved. "It will be me." He steps closer. "Be careful what you ask for." With those cryptic words he presses a kiss on top of my head turning to leave.

I BARELY NOTICE the quiet slide of the patio doors sliding open. I can't see who it is but I know it's him. The staff would never come in through those doors. The room has low luminescence with just candlelight and the glow from my MacBook.

He towers over me in his bare feet as I sit cross-legged on the floor. Craning my neck, I look up to the hard visage of his face. The cruel cast eclipses everything soft that could have been there. All kindness and softness is wiled away. His nostrils flare.

"Hi," I say, closing the laptop and sitting it beside me. In one fluid motion he takes up residence beside me, though he doesn't respond.

Silently he takes in the room before him, the one that was supposed to be a cage I've made my own. He sighs deeply. "We leave tomorrow for Japan to go see what ails Mother."

Heart tripping, I move to get up from my position. Though I dread facing his mother again I still don't hesitate. I won't fail him this time. I won't have him face the possibility of losing his only parent alone no matter how horrible she was to me before. From her perspective I can see all she was trying to do was protect her son from what she perceived as a gold digger, wrong though she was. I get it.

He stays me with a hand on my shoulder. Shaking his head, he gives me a little smile. "Kiyoshi and I will be going. You will stay here." Relief and disappointment mingle as my mind plays out the various scenarios. If she's sick, they probably don't want to do anything to further aggravate her condition.

"Okay." I can't quite quell my disappointment at his words. I look anywhere but at him, not liking the feeling, any suspicion niggling in my mind.

Eyes narrowing on me, he watches me with unwavering acuity. "You are upset about me not taking you with me."

"N-no." Shaking my head, I hate that my heart has me making this about me. "Not really, you just took me to Paris, London, and New York before that, I'm fine," I hurry to add, looking at his darkening expression. "I know that your family comes first." With that I clamp my mouth shut, quitting while I'm ahead, feeling like a ruddy-pooh.

Impossibly he looks angrier. Reaching out he cups my chin with deceptive gentleness. "And just who is supposed to be my family if not my wife?"

"Your brother, sister, mother —" I stop at the slow shake of his head.

"Unto you I plight my troth, isn't that what your people say? A man shall leave his father and mother and cleave to his wife?" He chuckles bitterly. "Isn't that your tenant, wife? Don't tell me I know it better than you. Is that why it was so easy for you to do what you did? You never meant the words you insisted we speak. I told you what seeing my tattoo meant. I *told* you once you saw my tattoo there was no going back. I meant that shit then, I mean it now. It doesn't matter if a thousand oceans separate us. You are mine. Fucking. Mine." He gives me a little shake with those last two words.

"I know." Covering his wrist, I feel the way the veins stand out on his hand. His grip doesn't tighten or bruise, but he doesn't let me go, either. If anything, his eyes glitter with a maniacal light.

"I didn't want to seem selfish when you've done so much." Rubbing up and down his arm, I can feel the intensity vibrating beneath the surface. He's doing a good job of keeping his emotions reined in, but they are pulsing beneath the surface, calling for me to soothe him.

"See, that's where you are wrong, Tay-chan. I haven't done enough. Not nearly enough. I should have come to you sooner. I should have gotten myself together long before now. Been the man you deserved from the start—"

"No." Tears spill free. I cover his lips hushing those mean words. "Don't you dare. You had no control of that."

Curving his face into my hand he kisses my palm. "I should have, little dove."

"You couldn't Hisashi, you just couldn't." Coming to my knees, I press my own kisses to his face. I pepper kisses on his hard jaw and little pecks on his lips.

"We are here now. Let us be here now, babe." My hands grip harder, I feel the tensing flex in his in response. My heart drops, soul plummets.

He closes his eyes damning us for a hard moment with a negative shake of his head. The look in his eyes is final. We can't because he won't. I am his captive. His plaything nothing more. Too much has happened.

"Please." A dark abyss of onyx nearly swallows me whole with every misery he's ever experienced with all the pain and recrimination we still have between us and secrets—so many secrets he's still keeping from me because he hasn't found a safe place with me nor I with him. In that moment my heart is torn asunder by a truth I've only just realized. We haven't earned each other yet.

My hands fall. Crushing disappointment burns my flesh like I've stepped in a fire ant hill.

He pulls back regarding me through veiled lids, keeping his secrets close.

My mother said, "Trust broken is irrevocable." Breaking the promises I made when I saw his tattoo and our vows caused a chasm between us I fear we won't ever be able to come back from.

Scooting back I pull together the tatters of my pride and face him. "When will you be back?"

He shrugs. "I don't know." He looks at me, all emotion wiped away. "We don't know the full extent of her illness. My sister is frantic, and that is what troubles me. My mother would not lie to her about an illness, not only that my sister is with her every day. She says my mother was visibly trying to hide the signs of her illness. It wasn't until she fainted during a luncheon with Kiyoshi's fiancé that anyone was aware of her decline. This is why we must make haste."

"I understand. When are you leaving?" I ask, moving to stand.

"Tonight." A swift hand reaches out pulling me back down.

His mouth is a hard line. "You will not try to leave. You will not give the staff any problems with not eating. I will still be watching you and don't think any distance will prevent me from punishing you when I return if your behavior is not that of a good biddable wife."

"You are being ridiculous." Snatching my hand from his grasp I'm appalled by his awful words. "Biddable? This is not the eighteenth century, Hisashi. How dare you?" I rail at him wondering how I let myself forget for any length of time exactly who I'm dealing with. A man who's kidnapped me, keeping me from my family, organized for my parents to be sent out of the country and told not to expect me. He has me on lockdown twenty-four-seven at his every whim, fucking me at his will, dressing me like his little doll, and now demanding I be a happy docile, biddable wife.

"I mean every fucking word, *wife*." His words are heavy as granite falling between us like an unmovable boulder. His closed off expression tells me that there is no way I can win this but I don't care. How he can take me on such a lovely trip then act like this just because he has bad news from home is more than not fair, it hurts me.

"How about I will start acting like a wife when you start treating me like one." Nose stinging, I try to wretch my hand away. Impossibly he snatches me closer.

"You gave that up when you ran from me, little bitch. When you left me signing me over to that hell." The cruelty of his words bombards me like vicious little bombs.

"You're a big bastard." I feel bruises bloom on my wrist as I try to no avail to dislodge him. I tumble when he abruptly releases me.

"I knew my father as much as that may have pained him." He rises leaving me sprawled on the floor giving me his back raking his hands through his hair in the telltale gesture of frustration.

Pulling myself up to my feet, I rub my chafed skin. "He seemed proud of you the few times I met him. You dishonor him and us by doing this," I say to his broad back.

Whipping around he manacles my throat. "What the fuck do you know about honor, Tay-chan? You are a fucking coward who ran."

"Y-you almost killed me." Scratching his exposed wrist I don't miss the blood welling on his torn flesh. If he's bothered, he doesn't show it.

"We said for better or for worse if I recall. Keep fucking with me and we can make it true." His mouth kicks up with triumphant cruelty.

"Your guardian promised he wouldn't kill me. I doubt he'll let you." His grip tightens as I speak, but I can see the truth of my words. "You promised you wouldn't, anyway. I know you can't. You don't want to. You're just hurting and now you want to make me hurt. Make us both hurt because you can't deal with your shit." Stars dance before my eyes just as he releases me. Making myself stand on my feet, I reach for the sofa's arm to steady myself.

My breath saws in and out of me. Fear is the farthest thing from my mind. Anger rolls through me like thunder. "I'm not going to be your biddable little wife. I will be your partner. I will comfort you if you let me. When your father passed away, we didn't know any better. You've sought help since then. What did they tell you to do when you experienced trauma?"

He stiffens at my words. "To reach out to my therapist or someone I feel safe with."

Swallowing back the pain knowing I am not that for him at least not yet, I nod. "Then call them. Now."

He looks at me for a hard moment. "It's private."

"Go to the garden and close the door. If you want to see me and apologize after I will be here. If you don't or won't, then have a safe trip." Seconds tick by and it's like we're in a visual battle. Taking his phone out, he presses the keypad.

"Dr. Inoru, I apologize for the call at this hour, but I have an emergency," he says to his therapist. "Hai." He nods my way then turns toward the garden's double doors.

Watching as he goes out into the garden I wait until he closes the doors before allowing my shoulders to relax. The tension in my body is so tightly wound I feel like I'm about to explode.

I don't know if I'm in shock or still angry, probably both. Deciding a shower will calm me I head into my bathroom.

Seconds after I turn the spigot steaming hot water

pours from the shower head. Securing my head with a bonnet and a shower cap I step inside. Soaping the loofah, I let the warm soothing scent of vanilla rose envelope me.

Taking my time, I bathe my body twice then start my face routine in the shower. Feeling calmer, I do my entire face routine, not skimping on the products or skipping the steps. Not knowing how long Hisashi's conversation with his therapist is going to take or if he's going to leave without saying anything or even acknowledging just how fucked up his behavior was, I instead focus on what I can control — myself.

Taking his even calling the therapist as a small win, I go on to moisturizing my body. Walking naked into the closet, I pull on a pink cami and boy short set. It leaves my plump tummy exposed, which Hisashi seems to love along with the way the shorts ride high on my bottom. Not that I'm trying to entice his mean ass, but it's either this or be naked — he considers this loungewear and I should be grateful he's deigned to allow me clothes.

His moods are mercurial at best. I know I was pushing him far past his boundaries when I asked to start over. However, he gave me hope with the Paris trip. I should have known better. Whatever his bizarre agenda of punishment is having what we could have been must be on the top of his agenda.

I'll know better than to get my hopes up ever again. It's all cruelty. Teasing me with the promise of forever. He watched me for years devising his scheme of retribution. Yet, he expects a biddable little wife. Never happening.

I get in the bed, my eyes on his form encased in shadows as he seems relaxed back into one of the patio chairs as he talks to his doctor. That's his way. Never giving off the turmoil inside. His brain switching to protect him and slide the mask in place.

I don't feel myself drifting off as I read an epic fantasy tale in which the world is held in the balance upon the discovery of a fae king and his hidden princess.

A hard body presses against me. "Ore o yurushitekure," he whispers, covering my neck with a kiss. "I was wrong to allow my emotions to get out of hand. In the future I will reach out to Dr. Inoru and not bother you with this."

Sleep having fell away at his touch I turn in his arms shaking my head. "I want you to tell me what is going on. I —" I don't dare say it. "I want to be here for you. I just don't want you lashing out at me, hurting me." My gaze searches his face, and I don't expect any promises. I see the wounds in his expression. He touches his head to mine. "I'm so fucking sorry. For ever even approaching you at that gala. I just couldn't..."

I don't ask what. I was drawn to him from the moment I saw him. Something in him spoke to me.

Words seem inadequate. Cupping his face I meet his gaze. "We do this together."

"Together," he whispers, pressing a soft open kiss to my lips. I don't hesitate to open for him. He takes my lips in a soft apology. The ask for forgiveness on his lips hovers just there before we touch, firm, open, unhesitating. My answer matches. A sweep of my tongue touching, tasting, a welcome, also a plea; take me, cherish me, forgive me too.

In that moment I think he does a little.

Then later when he opens me to him I welcome him, letting him have me with a sigh and pull of encouragement as he pushes in with an exquisite burn making me gasp his name.

I'm lost in him and him in me. The fight is forgotten for the moment. Tools hopefully in place when we encounter this again. I know nothing will be accomplished unless we work hard together to use the tools his therapist has given him. The only problem being I don't know if he wants it to be me, the one he has to count on. I know I left, and that's maybe why, yet I feel there is more to his unwillingness to trust me.

As he holds me after as I struggle for words but let them lie on my tongue not wanting to ruin the tentative truce we've forged knowing full well I'll regret my cowardice later.

. . .

I DON'T KNOW why I insisted on coming with him to the private airfield he and his brother own. From the moment we woke this morning he has been so closed and cut off. Barely looking at me let alone speaking in one-word responses. He's back to his silent cruel self. I couldn't help but ask him if he was utilizing the principals his therapist told him to employ.

"Why yes, Taylor. As you see I haven't fucked you into the bed or used your body in any way to exorcise my trauma, I've not self-medicated or caused harm or killed a motherfucker so yeah, I think I'm on the right path, wife," he responded dispassionately taking a sip of his morning matcha, dead eyeing me the entire time.

Rolling my eyes, I said nothing more, leaving him to his fucking misery as I went to get ready, which he also took issue with.

"Anything can happen, Hisashi," I tell him with a look of exasperation. "My cousin, Krie, lost her parents a few years ago, so I have learned not to take anything for granted."

I don't mention his dad but he relents.

Now, I'm sitting here in silence as the car pulls up to the tarmac. I see the Rolls Royce in front of us and I know it's his brother.

"Is he why you didn't want me to come?" I ask, nodding to his brother's car remembering how he pressured me to sign those papers and get out of town. I know he thought I was bad for Hisashi. I'm sure that hasn't changed in the ten years that's past. I know he probably blames me for everything and will continue too if anything happened to Hisashi now.

"No. He knows about you. This was my decision," he says in clipped tones his gaze unflinchingly hard.

Nodding, I press my lips together so I don't dare ask him why — this is for family and he's made it clear by this decision that though I am his wife and his family, how far that extends to his real family I don't know. His brother urged me out of his life saying his mother wanted to have me arrested for goodness' sake. Was any of that true? I doubt we'll ever know. Kiyoshi and I haven't been in the same room for ten years and since I'm not invited on this trip, I doubt we'll be anytime soon. I can't dwell on what could be. I'm this man's literal captive for the time being.

"Take care of yourself while I'm gone." His gaze sweeps over me seeming to miss nothing of my angst yet not remarking on his. Cool as a panther and as sleek as the serpents that line his body, he withdraws from the car without a backward glance.

He's midway down the tarmac when I push open the door unthinking. "Hisashi," I call, running over to him. He catches me to him as I practically leap into his arms. I can feel the pounding of his heart through his suit as he holds me flush against him.

"Please be safe." I bury my face in his neck, kissing him there, knowing full well public displays of emotion are an absolute, not with his upbringing, especially with his brother looking on in his car.

"Woman," he growls into my hair. He pulls back for a second, his eyes a storm of emotion. Lips covering mine, he devours me. Inhales each breath before I can even think to take it.

My fingers spear into his locks. His lips on mine telling the story of his heart that his lips don't dare to speak out loud.

I don't blame him as I do much the same. Let my lips say what my mouth dare not say. I just kiss him, hoping to fortify him and take some of the pain away.

CHAPTER
TWENTY

T *aylor*

~

CHERRY BLOSSOMS MAKE the garden so pretty. I can't complain about anything for the two days that Hisashi has been away, except he's not called. He hasn't text me through any app or anything. I assume the situation is really intense there with his mom's illness. But I'm not sure I even want to talk to him. I'm still smarting from the fact that, though I wasn't deemed acceptable to go see my mother-in-law, my cousin Krie was allowed to go. I watched feeling like an idiot as she boarded the plane along with Kiyoshi, who I guess she's seeing now since I don't have access to anything outside of the limited use of the iPad Hisashi gave me with only access to him and the information he gave about her paying Thad's debt. Maybe she's his captive too, and he has no qualms about his mother knowing. Which is very likely since his brother has shown he has proclivities for kidnapping. It's probably a family trait.

I swan around the garden with plum wine I was able to cajole Aiko to give me. Since I ate and have been eating nonstop since he left she happily complied. I don't fool myself into thinking she's not text him for permission.

Getting out the iPad iMessage him

Me: YOU ARE AN ABSOLUTE ASS FOR NOT ANSWERING OR RESPONDING TO MY MESSAGES.

I send it off and wait for a response. Nothing. Bastard. I don't care if he does know his daddy. Motherfucker then. I'll tell him when I see him how over here, we are not as precise with our words we just let them hurl to match the sentiment we are feeling.

I pull up my notes app. Note: Find Japanese cuss words for my husband.

I kind of regret not learning any in my attempts to keep my dialect perfect for my colleagues and the elite set of people I was always around. They definitely were not using any slang.

The wind is nice today and the fragrance of the flowers is delicate and warm. Not overpowering. Pinks and greens remind me of my sorority. The whisp of petals floating around me like a fairytale or rather the precursors of the nightmare that I've found myself.

"Heavenly Father please heal my mother-in-law of whatever ails her." Giving the brief prayer, I feel a little better knowing I did my part in her healing. I don't worry myself of the fact she didn't like me or want me with her son. No mother would want what she perceived as a gold digger in her son's life especially one who had mental challenges. I don't blame her. The way things went down. She had no way of knowing that I wasn't out to exploit him in some way. I can't blame her for trying to protect him.

I don't like how they push me out of his life, but I understand why they did it. The fact that it left us broken and probably unable to repair ourselves is the problem. However, it is one we must acknowledge. They no longer have the power to keep us apart, only we do.

The ball is in our court. I just don't know if I even want to play with a person who can't even call and let me know if he is okay if his plane landed or not.

Trying to focus on the story I'm reading, I give up after a quarter of an hour knowing I won't be able to focus. Shoving the device away I debate shutting it off. I had it on pretending to read when I was really waiting on his inconsiderate ass.

Grabbing the bottle Aiko left I pour a hefty amount of the plum wine into the glass until it almost reaches the rim. I guess I'm going to try to get a hundred on this test. I giggle feeling the effects before I take a sip of my refill.

Out of nowhere FaceTime pops up with K emblazoned on the icon. My tummy drops thinking it's Kiyoshi.

All I can think for a split second before I press the button is that something happened to Hisashi.

"Hiyo," the singsong hello greets me as a beautiful face fills the screen.

"Hiyo," I whisper arrested by the person that is Hisashi's younger sister.

"Hi, Taylor-chan," she says in English far superior to my Japanese. "I'm, Kana." She gives me a little bow that I return. I wait watching as her cheeks flush. "How are you?"

"I'm fine. Is Hisashi okay?" I ask, unable to hide the fear lacing my voice.

"Oh, Hisashi-oniichan is very well and on his way back to the U.S. with Kiyoshi-oniichan and Krie-chan." Her gaze skates around for a moment as if she fears being overheard. She leans in. "I must speak with you. You must forgive me." She bows solemnly.

My heart plummets, my chest feels as if being cleaved in two as I watch all friendliness flee her face and her expression turns somber.

"Okay." Bowing to her, I wait, knowing she's going to swear me off her brother. Only there is no way I can do that. Not to mention I don't want to. I know they probably think we are terrible for each other and I may have ulterior motives, but not one iota of that matters. They couldn't keep us apart then. I can't get away from him now. How do they solve the problem of my being held in his samurai mansion? Are they going to send an extraction team? I'm pretty sure knowing him as I do, he has every eventuality figured out.

"Hisashi-oniichan likes you very much." She adds the heart sign so there is no misunderstanding of her words. Japanese elite rarely, if ever, use words like "love." The most you will get is I like you or I like you very much to convey words of love, adopted during the Meiji Period where a lot of western mainly conservative Victorian societal norms had a great impact on the culture and still lingers to this day.

Still, I am left without words at her pronouncement. I am a useless being staring at my husband's sister, wondering how she dares be so bold with a person she has no association with.

"Um." I bow, because what else do I do at such a pronouncement? "Did he tell you this?" I watch as she bows more out of habit than anything else.

"He confided after an incident with Krie-chan that he had a person who he likes very much. I have been to his suites of rooms many times since he's been gone. You are the only person on his wall. It is not a bad wall like Kiyoshi's, it is only a Tay-chan wall. I know it can only be you." She smiles warmly. "He deserves this happiness with you, Taylor. You must be very, very patient with him. He's endured much." Her eyes dim briefly before they lift to mine, glistening. She wipes an errant tear. "Promise you will."

"I will promise to try," I tell her, my heart, chest, and throat tight.

"Hai." She bows to me.

Returning the gesture I watch the screen go black, disbelief rioting through me like an errant wind.

To say this experience is getting wilder by the moment is an understatement. His sister was so far off-limits when we were together before he barely mentioned her beyond saying he had a sister.

Now she's calling asking me to have patience.

Many more sips of plum wine later I'm incensed just ruminating on the facts. His sister called but he couldn't be bothered, she asked for patience, and I had to implore him to get help.

I didn't ask to be here. I was going about my life fine unknowing of his constant interference. Now I can't unknow it. Even if I am able to pull the tatters of my life together after what he's left behind I won't be able to be free of him.

By the time I enter the bedroom, I'm not even bothering with a glass anymore. I take the bottle to the head. Miserable, alone feeling unwanted and bereft, I drink the last bit watching nothing play before me on the screen.

In this moment I hate this place, this life, and the man who forced me into it.

TWENTY-ONE

isashi

"It all leads back to Thaddeus Love and his best friend, Mariah this time. They alone hacked the message board; the other kids who helped them all are in the clear. We are tracing the IP addresses as we speak. They did a better job of scrambling the signal but just like bomb makers every hacker has a signature. This is theirs. They often work as a team," Yumi, whose excellent performance in the Love matter has garnered her a promotion, informs me.

I read through the report. "Take everything to Takeda-sama." I give her a hard stare unwilling to reveal how at odds my brother and I are over his lover and her younger brother.

Knowing also how protective he is after the stunt my mother pulled is another reason why it would be better coming from a neutral source.

Bowing she leaves without another word walking like flames are licking at her heels. I'm sure in my current mood I give the impression that I'm a demon from hell. The last few days have been a torrent of emotions, something I chose to keep from Taylor. I know my brother's not fairing much better.

A previous conversation still leaves me stunned. *"Do you want her?"* He asks in a gentle way. *"I know you went out your way to tell her about my Yakuza princess as she put it."*

It was then I knew he was lost in her not that I'm anyone to judge. I don't know when I lost myself again in Taylor.

"You've never been found, poor thing." He chuckles. *"You've been locked in from the start. All this seeking of vengeance even I knew it was a bullshit excuse to have her back under you."*

"Fuck you, Monster," I sneer, focusing on finishing my work now that I feel some semblance of my sanity returning. Now I can go see her without the event of the last time repeating. New challenges rose out of this trip home. Now with my mother, brother, and possibly sister at odds, all are looking to me take over the navigation we as a family have to undertake to fully free mother and Kana, though what Kiyoshi will have to say about that is still to be decided. Mother's behavior to Krie was unexpected, maybe her confinement played a factor in her rashness. Her brazenness was astounding. She's been out of sorts since the thing with us and our cousin transpired, now that we know the truth, my brother and I are left without an enemy at least not the one we thought.

Sitting out the medication on my desk, I set to administer it wondering why I haven't shown Tay-chan the process.

"You still don't trust our little dove," He answers what I already know.

Will I ever? The moment I do, I will be waiting for another betrayal. Leaving was not enough, no. Her actions nearly ended me. I can't leave myself open to her again. My heart cannot take it nor my mind. What will be left after will far surpass anything she has ever experienced from the Monster. The monster inside that is unvarnished Hisashi Takeda is far more terrible. Unleashed after such an event will lead to her complete annihilation, neither of us will survive because how could I ever go on knowing I harmed my little dove. I don't trust myself to trust her after what she's done. That may prove to be the death to us ever getting past our history but to give in and lose risks something far greater — our very lives.

It's not like I blame her for being unwilling to watch over me in the condition I was in but the rest?

No. She made promises, understood fully what seeing my tattoo meant, knew what our vows meant, ran, repudiated me then tipped it off with the ultimate betrayal.

Unease and the lingering misgivings I have haunt me as I administer the shot. Going home being so deep in the mountains of Osaka and the reminder of what I endured while in others care always leaves me ravaged in some way emotionally.

I know even as I put away my medicine, adjust my clothes and gather my laptop not thinking about anything other than my wife as I transverse the path to get to her.

Let's just say how she greets me is not at all what I expected. The fucking door is not only locked it's barred.

"I guess this is your little way of taking your power back." A low mean chuckle crawls up my throat as I stare at the door I had made special to keep her in that she's now locking me out.

You can't make this bullshit up. She really thinks she's about that life. She will as our younger staff often says, "Gone learn today." Southerners and their collo-quialisms, you have to love it.

"Aiko already informed me of the copious amount of plum wine and my best whiskey you've been drink-ing. I see it was a mistake because now your little ass has gotten brave," I add, shoving the blocked door for good measure. She must have somehow moved the custom-made sofa I bought from Joybird. I guess inebriation has given her extra strength.

"Fuck you, Hisashi," I hear muffled through the frame.

"Oh, definitely," I promise, leaving.

It takes me about five minutes to make it to the garden. My stride is unhesitant as I enter the garden, grab the chair from the table from which I fed her from my hand just a week prior. Stopping several feet from the glass door, I heave the motherfucker with all my strength through it, splintering the glass into thousands of pieces.

Satisfaction licks at me as I hear the crunch of shattered glass under my boots.

"You were saying?"

I don't bother looking for her. Heading over to the closet where I keep all my special toys, I pull out long lengths of jute, toys, and clamps. Oh we are in for a fun night. I had not anticipated it being as such. I was ready for holding and soft whispers into the night with long lingering kisses that eventually got hotter until I found myself sinking into her soft flesh.

However, if my little dove needs correction, I will be more than happy to oblige.

I toss my arsenal of pleasure on the bed and go in search of my wife.

I don't so much as find her but catch her. She's trying to sneak out over the glass wearing a pair of Ugg slippers. As much as she tries to tiptoe the distinct sound of the glass crushed under her soft padded shoes can't be mistaken.

She's just past the door when I catch her little curvy ass. Reaching out I grab the cami top with one hand and belt her waist with my arm. I hear the harsh rip of the sheer material when I snatch her back. It's in tatters, hanging in sad wisps from her when I heave her soft body up pressing her against me to protect her from the sharp shards. "Nice try, little dove."

I ignore her kicking and verbal abuse — she's literally calling me everything but a child of Buddha.

Silence is my shield as I take her squirming, flexing, twisting form to the special room making sure that I retrieve the ropes from the bed on the way.

It's not a dungeon but a light airy space. The ceiling is open with rays of sun shining down like a halo blessing the experience. The walls are soft white damask with a dove and serpent motif I thought very fitting for our personalities. She always being in flight from me hunting her. The ropes and pulleys are all whites, purples, blacks, and light grays.

I wanted the opposite of the one I had in Tokyo. We are bathed in purple light as soon as we enter. The suspension cords hang from strategic posts throughout the space. I'm only interested in the center hooks, the ones from which I will dangle my little dove.

Rather than ignoring her words I let them wash over me, fuel me as I make intricate knots. "Coward-ass motherfucker, psychopath, terrible husband, mediocre lover, bitch-ass kuso yarō no baka tare." A smile spreads across my face despite her feisty words.

"I thought I wanted you docile and sweet. I see now that was the young me. The one without life experience. I see now I like the bad bitch perking up inside of you. She's easier to punish. Keep it up." I smack her ass in appreciation. She settles a bit, but I can feel the strain in her taut body. She wants to fight. I like that shit.

Plumping her down in the center of the thick black tatami mat, I slip the ropes in place to muffle her around her mouth. "You will tap three times if you are pushed past your limits," I tell her.

I hide my smile at her already tapping. Gripping the curls at her nape, I tug her head back so that I see those pretty eyes.

"So are we lying, Tay-chan?"

Shaking her head vehemently, she spears me with a glance that almost has me doubting — almost. I file that away and get to work. I secure her feet first.

This will be an inverted position. Tripling the rope three times I secure her feet from ankles to calves. Then taking the jute, I do the same to her waist and torso only to backtrack and re-secure her ankles. Pulling the jute taut, making sure to erect her spine to keep her stable, I circle her neck and mouth, making sure the rope is secure and unslacking for her safety. I bind her hands at the wrist behind her locking them against her spine.

The pose is reminiscent of "The Lonely House on Adachi Moor," a famous depiction of kinbaku. Once I have her bound, I lace the rope through the pulleys.

Slowly, I hoist her until she is hanging upside down, her head level to my waist. Her pretty already weeping pussy at my mouth.

She looks divine suspended so beautifully before me. Kneeling before her, I search her gaze. Pupils blown, I see she is reaching her limit.

"How are we doing, little dove? Tap thrice if you need relief." Placing my hand within reach of her bound hands, I wait for her, speaking in soothing tones.

"I have neglected you in this because I was afraid when I should have trusted your strength." Seeing her eyes flare, I know I have tapped into the answer. My sweet little dove not only needs my loving rough touch, she needs to be bound, made to submit to my cruelty. I didn't trust myself. I wasn't ready to make her fully submit. Now, I see the lie in what I took for comfort. She needs this as much as I do.

"I have been remiss in your correction — no more." She closes her eyes against my words. Noticing the slight relaxing of her shoulders, the deep exhalation and the flare of her nostrils, I know I made the right choice.

"Taylor." My voice is hard and clear. "Are you willing?"

She knows she holds the power. I will unlace her the moment she says.

I know she takes her time to torment me. Ever so slowly, she nods her head. Instantly my dick presses against the seam of my pants with even harder purpose.

Rising, I capture my bottom lip between my teeth, drawing blood as I take in her beautiful form. The ropes cut gently into her lush curves. Placing two fingers between the rope and her flesh, I make sure nothing is tearing her delicate skin.

Taking two steps back, I grab one plush thigh and spin. I spin and spin. Watching her body catch the purple light, loving the way she's inverted. I'm not ashamed to admit I love her being at my mercy. The level of trust she's giving me — after all I have done is simply incredible. It almost seems like love. I can't allow myself that delusion, though. I thought she truly loved me once so much, so I showed her my sacred tattoo and gave her words meaning forever in my culture and hers, then lost three years in an asylum thanks to my little dove. I push those thoughts away before they cloud my purpose, focusing instead on the task at hand — kinbaku.

I twirl her slowly and she spins like a ballerina dancing on a cloud, only one that has been suspended by rope. Art and eroticism meet in a sensual dance.

I stop her after the fifth rotation. Her hardened nipples beckon me. Clamping them, I watch as goose bumps rise on her skin, the way she captures her lush lips between her teeth. I spin her again. Her body in motion is hypnotic, grace, and beauty. Tied she's supposed to be at my mercy, but I feel like an acolyte.

Reaching out to touch a smooth calf, I stop her.

"Shall we see how you lie, little dove?" Already I see how slick her pussy is. Leaning in I inhale and dip my tongue between her lips for a taste. "You'll pay for your little lie in the beginning. Know this, you'll never be able to hide from me. You're mine don't you know that?" Trailing my finger over her drenched mound, I tap the sticky sweetness bringing my glistening fingers to my lips and sucking them clean.

"So fucking sweet," I say, burying my face into her exposed pussy. I don't even have to bend as I taste the delectable nectar of her.

I hear her muffled cries as my tongue slides over her exuding clit. I take my time, not wanting to rush. Her pussy lips pout like they're mad at me for neglecting them for so long. Who am I not to make amends? Dipping my tongue as deep as I can in between them, I lick and lave until they are thick and puffy, then the benevolent motherfucker that I am, I suck them both in long pulls. Leaning back, I drip onto them, making them glisten. Then I do it all again.

"Such a pretty fucking girl," I groan before diving back in. She tastes like everything good in life. All I missed in ten years of being separated and unable to touch her as I wished. She's everything I'll ever need.

I bask in the beauty that is pushing her higher and higher to reach her passion.

"So good, pretty girl." Stepping back, I don't want her to come yet.

She twists hard seeking more of my touch making herself spin. I can't help my maniacal smirk watching the jeweled nipple clips give flight and her pretty little pussy take the air.

"You're magnificent, little dove."

I find myself disrobing sooner than I anticipate. My clothes are in a puddle on the floor. I kick them aside without thought. My dick is beating its own rhythm demanding to be satisfied.

Grabbing the base, I can't take my eyes off her slick pussy closed to me from the front.

"I've never had your ass, wife. May I have it?" I chuckle, watching her shake her head furiously.

"I could if I wanted to," I say, ignoring the thrum of my dick that wants to bury itself so bad in her hot little pussy.

Spreading her fat ass cheeks, I lick her from the back. She squirms then relaxes into me letting me take her with my tongue.

I pull back. "I'm a nasty motherfucker, you know that." Easing my finger inside, I watch her bottom hole suck me in. Her ass is so tight, come slips from my dick at the sight.

"So fucking pretty, the way you take me back here." My praise relaxes her more. "Look at you taking me in your ass like a good girl," I say, finger fucking her ass. I keep my pace steady covering her hot mound laving and sucking. She arches beautifully as she comes on my tongue.

I take my time bringing her down from bliss. Her pussy gleams like a newly shined diamond. I'm simply captivated. She's a demi-goddess of sex incarnate, and I will gladly yield my devotion. The need to worship her nearly brings me to my knees. She is everything I've ever wanted, needed, and desired. There has never been another since the moment I laid eyes on her at that charity gala, and I will die happy in her arms should she will it. I am hers.

Guiding her body until she is parallel to me, I secure her in a safe position. As delightful and feeding to my power having her hand upside down is, I know how dangerous it is. It has served its purpose of raising her endorphins.

Looking at her closely, I see her pupils are blown with the aftershocks of pleasure.

"Pretty little cumslut, did you like the way I made you my feast?" Making myself eye level with her I take my time unraveling her mouth.

"You will take me down your throat," I tell her. "Then if you're a really good wife I will fill your tight little pussy up." She gasps, taking long pulls of air through her mouth even though her nose remained uncovered the whole time. She's cute in her dramatics.

"You will not speak unless I give you leave," I snap, loving the way her eyes snap with fire.

"Such a naughty fucking girl, aren't you?" My laugh is a low, dark menace even to my own ears.

"Yes," she answers in a way that makes my dick jump. Licking her lips could be a reaction from having the stretch of my rope but I don't think it's that. She wants to taste my dick. Her eyes track from my face to my distended member. She sucks her little plump lip into her mouth, the way she does when she wants what only I can give her.

"Perhaps, I'm asking too much of you," I tease, stroking myself bringing my seed up to the tip. We both watch as it drips over the edge of my head.

Dejection fills her eyes as it falls to the floor. Gotdamn. To have someone want me this much shoots my ego into another stratosphere. Makes me want to be worthy of the pleasure she'll eventually give and return it by double measures.

"Something wrong, little dove?" Taking a drop with the tip of my finger, I press between her sumptuous lips, watching her suck the drop, feeling her tongue wrap around my finger drawing me into the warmth of her mouth.

I could come right now. Retracting my finger, our gazes meet. So much want, so much need, so much fucking promise.

Still, I have more work to do.

Repositioning the claw clamp to the center of her back, I fold her in two. Hands to ankles, bound beautifully for my sole use and her guaranteed pleasure.

Her pussy presses out to the back, freely exposed to me. Hot, glistening, and ready.

It takes everything in me, every bit of the samurai upbringing my beloved father tried to instill into me, the discipline of my mother, and the thousands of hours of the most brutal therapy to hold *Him* back and keep me from burying my face in her fat ass pussy that's beckoning me with pretty promise.

If I truly believed in the deity who abandoned me so many years ago, I would call on him now for fortitude.

"Such a pretty pussy," I muse, loving this position as I watch her spin suspended before me. All her pressure points are covered. Her nipples confined. Her clit trapped between the press of her thick thighs. Every time I wind her, more pressure is placed on her erogenous zones.

Idly I spin watching the transformation take place. The stress on her body in this position is evenly balanced, however the consistent rubbing of the rope on her tenderest flesh is like I'm caressing her all at once. The simultaneous pleasuring does in minutes what individual attention attempts to do in an entire night of hedonistic gratification.

Essence slips over her tight little pussy, she's

biting back moans yet rubbing against the robe partnering in her torture. She's loving it.

Mesmerized watching the exquisite torture I slowly stroke my dick from root to tip until I find myself stopping her and bringing her mouth to cover me.

Eagerness has her taking me a touch too fast making her gag. "Slow the fuck down and take this dick down your throat like I taught you," I ground out, not wanting her to hurt herself but loving that shit all the same.

"Yesssss," I say fucking into her mouth as she catches her rhythm. Slowly I fuck her throat, letting her gag a little then holding her in place pushing farther knowing she can take more. Withdrawing I do it again and again loving the heat and the hot suction she gives me. "Just like that, little dove. Please your man," I say.

"Motto namero." Pulling back, I give her only the head, wanting her to wet me up for different purposes.

Stepping back, I spin her watching her binds tighten against her flesh.

She's at the perfect height to take my dick. And she does —beautifully. The positioning of her in the ropes bends her body perfectly. Easing my dick in, I feel the infernal heat of her pussy cascading over me as I drive inside. Her muscles squeeze me to an almost strangling degree.

"I love how tight you are yet still taking me so well," I tell her on a groan as I bottom out.

The pulleys help when I push her away as I withdraw. When I release her gravity brings her back with a heavy slam making her ass jiggle when she comes into contact with me.

"Look how she loves me splitting her open," I tease, looking down at how she's drenching my dick with her want. "Juicy ass motherfucker," I say more to myself fucking into her deep.

Nirvana couldn't offer me better pleasure than me fucking my little dove. Push and relax, letting her ass cushion the slam as I fuck her. I take her, take everything she has to give, unrelenting and without remorse.

"Ahhh," she cries her pussy gushing around me, hot drops of her girl come dripping on the tatami mat. I don't relent, I fuck her through her orgasm, chasing my own.

My body is hard and slick with sweat as I piston my dick in the soft tight pussy that pulsates with the aftermath of her pleasure. She takes me with the soft encouragement of more, please, and sweet mention of my name. Who am I to deny my goddess? She is my mission, my ministry, my mantra.

Steady long strokes are met with groans of passion, demands of desire.

"Give me this fucking pussy as only you can," I

grunt, pressing hard into her spot again and again knowing she's about to break and ruin me.

"So good. So good, Hisashi," she whimpers.

"Another," I demand, finding her clit swirling, keeping pace with my thrusts. My sac tightens just as her pleasure breaks across my fingers again.

"Good little wife," I praise. My own nut almost forces me to my knees as it shoots out in hot jets filling her pussy until it's overflowing.

Sinking to my knees, I bathe her with my tongue taking both of us down with long sweeps of my tongue.

Rising to my feet I take her mouth sharing our essence.

"Beautiful, little dove."

CHAPTER

TWENTY-TWO

T aylor

~

THERE IS no part of me not sore when I wake in Hisashi's dark shrouded room. I can't tell if it's day or night, vaguely remembering him bringing me in here after he released me from the kinbaku knots and took me into the shower where he washed me and then himself before drying us both and wrapping us in warm robes.

Taking in the darkness of the room, the sparseness of it is not lost on me. I wouldn't be surprised if the rest of this house is just as bare. Hisashi was never very fond of clutter. His apartment at university had only the essentials. At first, I thought it was because he hated the distraction of it. Once I learned more of his condition, I think he did it more to calm his mind.

His body is warm next to mine. I can feel his breath soft against my nape. I don't know what woke me. Maybe the strangeness of the room, maybe being held by him, triggered a memory from long ago since he finally decided to come back to my bed or rather bring me to his. Why he's been back three days and didn't bother to see me is not lost on me. He went to work. His mother is fine from the little I could glean from Aiko. Not that we had time for conversation during the kinbaku session when he was so determined to exert his dominance and test my limits. The type of pleasure he visited upon me was so freeing. For a moment I thought his guardian would emerge, but he didn't.

Hisashi's control last night during our time together was breathtaking. When he goes into the mode of being a kinbaku master his skill is incomparable. In the time we have been together I have seen how he has grown. His experience and maturity have changed his technique. He's still removed from the experience except for the passion he unleashes in order to ensure both parties find pleasure. That's his nature just as feeling emotional is mine. As long as he is touching me and focused on me, I feel safe, cared for. When he withdraws then I feel alone, abandoned.

"Go back to bed," he mutters in my ear. Arm tightening just under my breasts he draws me closer and I can't help the wiggle I give as I nest my body deeper into his warmth. He feels so good. He feels like home. Knowing he's dangerous, more than unhinged, takes none of his appeal away. "A soul mate is yours no matter their flaws. The God of the universe will make it so that you alone are equipped to love them through any situation." Are my mother's words true? Will I be able to care for Hisashi no matter what? How delusional am I to even consider being with a person who nearly killed me. It's not like I will ever be free. The question has become do I want to? And I don't think I do.

"I woke up," I say, kissing the arm that wraps around my upper chest. He's holding me like I'm a lovie. Does he find his safety in me too? I know he once did. Now I feel the urgency in having that again.

"Can I ask you something?" I turn to his sleepy face. He looks at me for a long pensive moment then gives me a hesitant nod. "Hai. Tay-chan, you may ask me anything."

Snuggling closer, I breathe deeply inhaling his fresh clean scent. "I know my leaving is the cause of all this. You know a little of the state your brother found me in, and I don't know how in depth you spoke to him about it but I only left at his insistence. It wasn't my choice." He goes stiff as lead against me.

In one swift moment he shoves away from me. His hair falls in inky black waves over his forehead. His eyes blaze hot with rage as he looks at me through the fall of his hair. Disbelief clouds his gaze. Astonished anger spills across his face. His cheeks flush. The muscle in his jaw tics like a bomb and I swallow knowing I'm the one that will be caught in the fall out.

"Are you saying Kiyoshi forced your hand? That my brother who searched for me for years after you had me committed to one of the harshest asylums in Japan for the criminally insane was the one to make you leave?" He scoffs, shaking his head in disgust. "You've got to be fucking kidding me."

Scrubbing his hand across his face he looks back at me. I'm not just seeing disgust, disbelief, and anger. He's hurt. My heart breaks at the pain I see in his face. I wait for his guardian to appear all full of rage and vengeance but he doesn't emerge despite the war going on inside my husband at my words.

Then I play back what he's saying. "What do you mean I had you committed?" I shake my head. "I would never do that. I left. I thought you were mad because I left," I say, leaning toward him when I know I shouldn't. The volatility of this moment can spiral out of my control at any second. "I didn't do that."

Slowly shaking his head, he pulls away slowly until his nude body rises from the bed. He pauses like he's debating something before he pivots heading deeper into the recesses of his suite.

Moments later I hear a door sliding open then ambient light shines through an open door. He's gone long minutes. Regretting like hell that I even spoke I scoot back to the head of the bed. The tufted pillows behind me give excellent support. Pulling the covers and duvet up and tucking it around my breasts I wait, trepidation warring with wanting to set the matter straight. Briefly I wonder if he's calling his brother. If that's what he's doing he needs to get him on speaker. Getting ready to move to the edge, I pause seeing him coming back with sheets of paper. He's taken the time to pull on some silk lounge pants leaving the rest of his body nude. Still, I feel vulnerable and exposed sitting here before him waiting for the guillotine to drop.

Sitting on the edge of the side he slept on he takes time to go through the papers seeming to organize them. "Here. These are the papers you signed with the power of attorney I gave you. I trusted you. I know I hurt you and I deserved to be punished for what I did. I understand that now. I never thought you would go to such lengths."

Taking the papers he hands me I immediately recognize my signature on the first crumpled page that Kiyoshi and I argued for days over until he told me of his mother's plan to have me arrested for fraud. Carefully I take that page and set it aside.

Despair and disbelief coalesce as I read through the pages and pages of documents where it seems I've given a sworn statement of what I claimed Hisashi did to me.

I, Taylor Love Takeda, hereby swear to the following statement. My husband, Hisashi Takeda, did on the date with malice and forethought. Kidnapped, sexually assaulted, and choked me into unconsciousness several times. He deprived me of sustenance, clothing, keeping me bound for deviant sexual practices.

Tears cloud my eyes as I read the details and the see the pictures of my body lying prone on the floor where Kiyoshi found me. There is a close-up of my face. It's sunken in from lack of food. My lips are chapped and bleeding. My expression is spaced out and deadened. I shake my head in denial about what I'm seeing. I don't even remember Kiyoshi taking pictures of me. But it must be him. He is the only person who knows what really happened. I never told a soul.

"No." I shake my head vehemently. "This wasn't me. Dummy that I was, I still didn't want to leave you. I wanted you to get help. That's all." My fingers blanch around the papers from holding them so hard. Shaking my head I say, "This is bullshit. Your brother—"

"Saved me," he grits out between his teeth the nods to the papers. "Isn't that your signature?"

I look down at the forgeries of my signature. "The first one is mine. I remember fighting with Kiyoshi over signing it. The rest of them —especially this," I wave the affidavit in his face, "is not me."

He looks like he expects the bed to open up and swallow my lying ass whole.

"It's. Not. Mine," I say through clenched teeth. Then. "Call your brother."

"It's late even for him." Shaking his head his refusal is final.

"Uh-uh, call your fucking brother, Hisashi," I urge, raising my voice. Heat flushes my face. I hate coming between him and his family, but Kiyoshi obviously did this and left me to hang. He probably thought he was doing the right thing keeping us apart. Though he never thought I was a gold digger he made it no secret he blamed me for his brother's mental decline. Maybe he thought Hisashi would be done with me for good, divorce me and that would be it. I'm sure he'd be shocked to know his brother not only stalked me but is holding me captive in his house right under his nose.

He could have gotten me killed. He and I are going to have some fucking words. "Please," I implore him cupping his face. "Let me clear my name."

For a moment I think he's going to say no again. Reaching over he retrieves his phone from the bedside table. The phone lights up as Kiyoshi's icon fills the screen. It rings and nothing. Several more times he calls his brother with no answer. Then suddenly there is a message that pops up.

HISASHI. Krie is gravely ill and I have to take care of her. I need you to step in until this situation is resolved. ~K

. . .

SITTING BACK down I let the disappointment wash over me. I don't bother saying it's not me. Handwriting changes over time, so it's not like it would be fair to compare it with my current journal. Slumping against the headboard I let disappointment wash over me. I don't worry that we'll get to the bottom of it. I just hate so much having one more day go by with him thinking that I betrayed him so horribly. Even not knowing the full extent of what he was having to endure with his mental challenges I would have never wanted to have him committed.

My father's brother's my cousin Kandie's dad had a horrible experience at a mental institution and it ended up ruining his family and having Kandie and her sister Karaina being lost in the system while their younger sister, Nikki was taken with their parents. Poor Karaina ended up dying in a fire that burned down the group home they lived in with Kandie being able to barely escape with her life. Their sister, Nikki, who was an infant was forced to live away from them and our whole family until her dad died when she was sixteen.

The trauma behind that experience is something my cousins still have to live with, not to mention what the loss of their parents cost our entire family.

"We could drive over to his home." My eyes perk up at his words but then I think. "The note sounded like he's really concerned about my cousin, do you think he will even see us or let us on his property after he's already told you to take over things?"

"No." He shakes his head. He looks down and my fingers still gripping the mountain of lies.

"This is why you debated killing me?" I ask, waving the papers between us.

"I wasn't." He rolls his eyes.

"No, but *He* would. *He* spent years watching you suffer at my hand as you both believe. *He* definitely would," I say, locking onto his eyes with my own, wondering if I can reach his guardian through the dark onyx of his gaze.

"Perhaps," he concedes. "Definitely."

"Thinking all this you still watched over me. Did things to people who hurt me, when you thought I'd done the unforgivable to you. Why?" Looking at the confusion playing on my face he shakes his head obviously amused by whatever I'm missing.

"You're my wife. Mine to protect, always. I failed in that once. Even thinking you betrayed me I still protect what is mine."

His gaze is unwavering as he regards me. Swallowing against the lump forming in my throat and the ache that's taken up residence in my heart I release the papers.

I'm sorry you thought this for so long. I hated myself for a long time for leaving. I'm not going to lie. I was scared that you hated me for leaving. When I saw pictures of you later in the news you looked at peace. I thought I was bad for your well-being. You were fine before me." I stop him when he shakes his head.

"I thought your intensity was how it was supposed to be. I admired your unwavering focus on nothing but me and your work. Maybe that's all I wanted to see." I shrug. "You weren't honest, but neither was I. I just never wanted us to end. Then when it did, I ran and hid going on with my life. I abandoned you. I will never forgive myself for my actions, so I understand if you can't." He says nothing but moves back beside me taking the papers out of my hands redepositing them on the table.

He pulls me into his arms. "We won't solve this today."

It's not lost on me that he's not saying he believes me. He has too much loyalty to his brother for that. I can imagine the debate warring between him and his guardian about Kiyoshi's part in all this.

I know he thought he did it for his own good. Did he know he was making himself the villain in our story? Probably. Did he care? Not if it meant saving his brother and protecting the Takeda legacy. I know that is what matters most to people like the Takedas. Not only had he married an American and a Black one at that he further thumbed his nose at society by being less than the perfect specimen of the elite society, manhood. How dare he?

One infraction they could barely look past let alone more. I remind myself this was years prior to Akchiro setting them on their ear by marrying Flower. Yet, his mother stood in solid support of him and his new wife. I remember meeting her that night and how kind she was. Yet, Hisashi's mom let it be known she was not a fan of me the moment we met. She was deeply upset when he brought me to the theater.

Knowing her husband had just passed away probably spurred Kiyoshi to do the only thing he could not to cause her further heartache.

He proved to me when he took care of me in his brother's stead there was nothing he'd not do to protect his brother even deepen the chasm between us.

I rack my brain trying to think but there was no one else. It was Kiyoshi who picked me up off the floor, bathed me, gave me water and food. He nursed me back to health until I was strong enough to get out of his brother's life.

Then he made sure the deed was done.

"We'll just wait to see what he has to say," I murmur against Hisashi's chest. There is nothing I can do and the helplessness eats at me. I honestly detest it.

"Hai." He's noncommittal otherwise. "Hungry?"

It's a peace offering. "Yeah, but I want grits, eggs, and Conecuh sausage," I tell him tired of European styled food. We are in the south and I need some home cooking.

"We have your sausage just so you know. You're the one not eating as you should," he informs me swinging his feet to the side. "And my chef can rival your cousin's southern cuisine."

"Really?" I quirk a brow at him letting my skepticism shine through.

"Sure, Jan," I tell him, rolling my eyes then laughing at the confused expression on his face.

"Don't worry about it. It's an American thing." I giggle.

"Well, clearly I was more helpful with Nihongo when we first got together." He gives me an irritated look that doesn't last.

"You're just upset because you always have to know every little thing. I gave you a good head start go figure it out," I tease.

"Brat," tugging me close, he whispers roughly dragging me under him stopping when my tummy growls in protest.

"Un-un fella, you have to feed me first." Giving him a little peck I push aside the angst of having to wait for his brother to come out of his lair before I get any answers.

CHAPTER
TWENTY-THREE

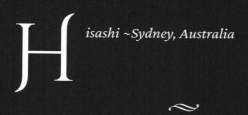

H*isashi ~Sydney, Australia*

I'M TRYING to reconcile Taylor's denial with what I know to be true during that time in Tokyo. So much during that time is lost to me. Most of what I remember is shrouded in the despair of losing father. The guilt that surrounded me by what he was driven to do in no small part because of having to constantly care for me rides me like the wind in a storm.

Then for Kiyoshi to be involved? Does she realize I would be honor bound to kill my brother for such a betrayal? That he would have me confined. Forge her signature?

It's simply not how he operates then or now. My brother is afraid of no man, neither am I. The only thing that kept us from annihilating Akchiro for what we believe was his part in father's death is him keeping mother a Kana captive in his home. He boldly took them in the night informing us by his very actions that he had no qualms about harming them if we dared move against him or Flower. From our visit I could tell that his wife was surprised to find them as guests on the vast estate. I could see how she brimmed with questions even as she tried to present us with a united front as most couples do. The shock on Flower Takeda's face was really something to behold. Yet her husband, much like my brother and I, faced her with a stoicism born from having the samurai drilled into us from an early age.

The night is beautiful as we drive through the city following the performance of *Things Hidden Since The Beginning of The World*, a dramatic mystery about the murder of a 1970's pop icon. Even I was intrigued by the story that incorporates true crime podcast and the current social media to solve the cold case. Fascinated, I watch Taylor watching the show with appreciation for its fresh approach.

"I'd love to have one of my plays in such a beautiful theater," Taylor muses, her back to me taking in the lights whizzing by as we make our way to the hotel.

"I can make it happen," I say softly, drawing her to

look over her pretty shoulder at me. A small smile plays at the corner of her mouth. "You could couldn't you?"

"Well, it's not like I sit on the board like I do several others but I believe my cousin's wife does and I know how much of a fan of your work Flower is." Idly stroking her jaw I'm lost in the beautiful brown hues of her eyes.

"We'll see." Her face clouds a little bit at the words. "This is the first thing I've written since before the pandemic and I'm not sure if it's any good. I mean, I like it. I'm not one of those writers who never thinks their writing is good enough. But if tonight showed me nothing else it's that I need to always be looking at fresh new approaches to the work. The way they integrated podcast and social media was so smart. I loved it," she sighs. "I know there hasn't been a major work addressing how people struggled and overcame loss during Covid and I want to give voice to that. Tonight, they showed me what was nagging at me. What is missing." The passion in her is incandescent. Her eyes are alight with a new passion I haven't seen up close since the fellowship as Sofia. Her generous smile highlights the deep set of her dimples casting her face with an innocence I long to corrupt.

"And what's that?" Her excitement bleeds into me like vapor. My curiosity is peaked.

"How much social media and misinformation shaped everything. The whole time we were getting two opposing narratives and it led to so much tragedy. I'd been focusing too much on the economic part of it in the story and though that did shape a lot of the narrative for people who owned Mom-and Pop-businesses like my characters. Social media and conflicting information also impacted everything." Throwing her hands up in frustration she flings herself back against the cushions. "I missed the mark."

I look at her for along moment. I press the intercom. "Pull over," I tell him. Reaching under the seat's compartment I get the slip-ons she prefers when she's not trying to wear those ridiculously high heels she says make her legs look good— okay they do but they aren't serving any purpose right now.

I slip them on her feet. "Walk with me back to the hotel."

"Um, okay." She shrugs. It's such a pretty night and I want to see her beautiful skin and soft curves against the backdrop of the Sydney skyline. I get out waving the driver away as I open the door for her. Her dress is an Atelier Fe Noel Tulip Fleur Plump dress she fell in love with. The cool night breeze immediately lifts the layer of silk chiffon. She looks like a dancing fairy among the lights. I can't take my eyes off how beautiful she is. How I ever went without her I can't fathom. It was a hell I never want to revisit again.

The fierce urgency of right now has me reaching for her small hand. Lacing petite fingers between mine we walk in silence for a while.

"Your talent has always amazed me," I tell her as we near the hotel. It seems absurd that we'd travel half the world away for a play yet promises kept lead to trust earned. "Now that you know what you need to do, you only have to execute it."

"I know," she says, dragging the last word out. Her mouth is cast in a cute little pout.

Pulling her into my arms, I turn her to face the harbor. Resting my head atop hers, I ask, "Tell me, Tay-chan. Can you ever be happy doing anything else? If I gave you the babies you say you want now would that be enough? I doubt it."

"You'd be right. I'd be miserable. I remember some of my aunts taking jobs that gave them safe careers and were miserable. My father always said his sisters are the backbone of the family. I know they found joy in the family but they missed out following their dreams. I think they push us so hard in the opposite direction because they didn't have those chances back then with all the gatekeeping."

I nod because I know my wealth afforded me privileges that many in my own country didn't have especially people like me with mental illness. I tend not to care about others outside of Taylor and my siblings and in a way I know that has protected me. I am not blind to it though. Far from it. The clarity gained from being imprisoned for three years cannot be ignored. Which is why that particular facility is no more. Reporting them to the state as my brother did and using his considerable influence to have them shuttered. I would not rest until I saw it reduced to ashes and rubble. Not until every motherfucker who abused and raped me were dead by me and Kiyoshi's hand once he found out the extent of my abuse.

I remember the horror and grief on his face when he found out. Now I wonder if it was guilt. Did Kiyoshi betray me? A pang stabs in my solar plexus at the thought.

My face heats. Burns. I have to step away for a moment. Thoughts start to spiral.

"Hisashi," her quavering voice reaches me.

Swinging my head toward her, I look trying to get my shit together. I'm disassociating. I try to focus but I can't. Shaking my head, I try to focus to bring my mind back to the moment. I breathe only to realize I already sound like I'm running a fifty-yard dash.

"Hey." I hear the litany of denials and recriminations blazing through my skull.

Then a gentle but firm squeeze of her soft delicate hand. A hand I could crush if I wanted to. Sick selfish motherfucker that I am, I let her.

"I got you," she whispers. "We are almost back to the hotel. Let me help you, Hisashi." She pauses trying to catch my gaze but I won't let her. I'm too raw right now.

"Do you want to call you guardian? Will that help?"

"No," I scoff through gritted teeth and give her one

truth at least. "*He* wants you. I think *He*'s in love with you." It would be laughable if it weren't so bizarrely pathetic.

"*Damn straight,*" *He* mutters. "*But both of you are mine to protect.*"

Ignoring him, I let Taylor lead me back to our suite overlooking the harbor and the opera house. She dims the lights when we enter. The room is spacious and sparsely decorated with monochromatic soft tones that give a peaceful like feel the to the space. So vanilla, not either of our style but pleasant enough for a brief stay.

My mind is calm. My monster lies in wait in case I need him. His presence is not oppressive, it's as if her softness has calmed even him.

"Do you want to talk about what happened?" she asks as if I'm a man who talks about things. I want to remind her that men like me — psychopaths, don't waste a lot of time talking. We act. Yet my little dove is looking at me with such earnestness. She matters, her feelings matter. She always has mattered to me and that is part of the problem. Why do I even countenance her wild assertion and denials about my brother rather than simply snapping her neck? I'd feel something. It would pain me. Just as having to kill my own fucking brother for treachery would.

"I thought of the possibility of having to kill Kiyoshi." I look at her unwavering then seeing sympathy force myself to look away. She knows better than to try and sway me.

"You won't do it," she says. "You may never speak to him again, but you won't kill your brother."

I scoff making a sound in my throat.

"You didn't kill me," she asserts so boldly I have to correct her.

"I came to the States with that exact intention. I slept under your bed for a week waiting until you slept. I was going to fuck you to death. Choke the fuck out of you while you came on my dick," I growl, stalking to her until her back is pressed against the window.

'Y-you didn't." I feel her breath against my neck we are so close. I'm looking out to the harbor, gritting my teeth remember how fucking weak I felt and for the first time glad I couldn't bring myself to murder the woman I thought betrayed me because she keeps so steadfast in her declaration she didn't betray me so heinously.

"No. I didn't but you are different," I say, finally dipping my head down to look into those luminous eyes of hers. Captivated I can't look away, not even for a second. I find myself not wanting to. I want to drown in them.

"How?" she asks. I think it's quite adorable that she doesn't know. "I will burn this whole fucking world down for you, little dove. I would pierce my heart with my Katana just as my father did for his dishonor before I would allow harm to come to you by my hand. No one garners that type of affection from me. Not Kana, not Kiyoshi. Only you." She watches me then shifts a little. I — not my monster like that. I drag her ass back. "Do you understand what that means?"

Her hand rises. For a moment I think she's going to try to push me away. Instead her hand covers my chest her petite fingers just reaching my heart. "Y-yes. I think so."

"Hai," I say, letting the gruffness of emotion fill my voice.

Quiet surrounds us as we go out on the balcony and look to the night sky.

"It's so pretty here," she muses. I'm noncommittal not because I want to be contrary only that even in all its natural beauty nothing compares to her.

SHE LOOKS BEAUTIFULLY TIED. The kinbaku knots were her suggestion this time. I'm sitting in the chair beside the bed in the early morning of our third day there watching her supine form twist within the binds. She looks as if she's been encased in a spider's web. From the pose it looks as if I've denied myself access to her body but that would be a novice move. Strategically placed I've left her pussy exposed beautifully. The ropes scissor across her breasts leaving her distended nipples exposed.

The white jute gleams against her brown skin. Her curves are lifted and confined in a way that accentuates all of her most delicate bits. She's my masterpiece. My design. Every time I tie her up, restraining her my dick gets painfully hard. It's like a reward for all the years I waited and watched over her without her being aware. Now she's paying the penance for our separation the most delightful way, not as punishment though that could be my due if I so decide, but the draw back to the pleasure she know only I can deal out in the measure she so desires.

"How are we doing, little dove?' I ask nonchalantly, looking over the screen of my laptop watching her writhe. I haven't touched her yet the anticipation building in such a delightful way.

"I need to come." Her voice is thready with need.

I allow a cruel smile to kick the corners of my mouth. "Not yet, love." Turning back to the computer I smile when I see her bite her lip arching against the restraints knowing my naughty girl is pressing her clit against the rope but it's not enough to make her come. "I like your determination." Glancing up from the screen I notice how she struggles not to berate me. So clever she knows by now that will get her nowhere.

I'm patient. Ten years of longing, watching, waiting. So many nights of fucking my fists thinking about her pretty ass pussy and how well she sucks me in.

She squirms. Inhaling the fragrance of vanilla, rose, and her natural musk a growl rises in my throat.

"Please, Hisashi, Please I need you." Snapping the laptop snaps closed, I rise sitting it on the table. I'm between her legs and her fat puffy lips press against the rope. They are squeezed so tightly they protrude slickly wet and glossy.

Just as I bend my phone vibrates. I press my finger to my mouth hushing her. Without looking I answer. There are only two people with this number. And It's not Kana.

"Hai?" Answering the phone, I wait surprised to hear noise in the background. Has Kiyoshi returned to work? He's probably wondering where I am.

"Takeda." The heavy baritone of Angel Cruz fills the line. I know he could have only gotten my number from one person so I know this is serious. We use his trucking and logistics company to ferry our product throughout the country. All of this has been disrupted by the strike and the slowed production.

"Mr. Cruz." Putting him on speaker I give her a hard silencing look and bend to my task. Running my mouth between the seam of her pussy lips, I keep my eyes on her watching her thrash and swallow back a moan.

She's being such a good girl. Taking her hard little nub I work her viciously between my lips. I lap the delicious essence seeping from her as he gives me detailed information about how he plans on helping us and the little chef re-establish business in Shelby-Love.

"Sounds good," I say against her hot glistening flesh. "Send my assistant the details." I'm already depressing the button returning to my task.

My dick is throbbing. I hadn't bothered disrobing because I expected to exert more fortitude while teasing my little dove.

"You make me give face one too many times, wife," I chide, rising and placing a slight but steady smack on her pussy. She arches and shies away from my touch but I'm undeterred. Soon the wet sounds of her punishment resound in the breezy room in Australia.

Her cries of pleasure make my heart burst with pride and I bring forth an orgasm with my steady attention. "See, when you're bad she has to suffer? Such a good pretty girl being spanked because of you. Should I let her come?"

"Please," she pants.

"Such a needy little thing aren't you?" Grinning I expose her clit to the air. Bending my head I flick, lick, and spear deep until I find enough purchase to suck her. My dick kicks as my name breaks apart on her tongue.

Her girl come floods my mouth. I close my eyes as the ambrosia spills across my tongue coming closer than I have ever to embarrassing myself.

Pulling up I take out my knife. Her bindings don't serve the purpose I have for her at the moment.

Eyes flaring with fear she pulls away. "Be still. If you make me nick you by mistake I will punish you afterward." Because we both know nothing will stop me from riding her on my dick right now.

Making fast work of it I slice the bonds free from her curves. She's still as a statue as she's freed.

At the last minute maybe it's an exhale but I nick her anyway.

I still, watching the blood bloom just at the crease of her breasts. Following my gaze, hers follows, watching the crimson chase the sweep of her body sliding down over the curve of her round tummy pooling in her navel.

Dick thrumming at a painful degree I cover the pretty indentation, delving my tongue inside loving the briny taste flooding my senses. I feel my come seeping out as I follow the trail up to the spot of the slit.

Gasping Tay-chan arches closer as I suck and suck and suck.

"I can't wait." Freeing myself, I feel my way to her entrance and line up, not wanting to take my mouth from the font of blood on her chest.

"Ahhh," she gasps and I drive my dick into her stretching her, making her take every inch. Her wet heat surrounds my dick like a greedy fist squeezing and pumping the life out of me. I may like blood but her pussy is the vampire.

"Goddamn, the way your tight little pussy sucks me in —" Words die on my lips when she pulls me to her tangling our tongue. Surging I bring her legs up angling her to take every inch. I fuck into her lush little body. Withdrawing I give no quarter on my return taking everything she's so willingly giving me.

"So good," she whispers against my neck, "so good to me, Hisashi." Looking down, our gazes lock. Then she clenches around me so hard I see stars. Her climax shatters me, pounding past her pleasure. "Come again," I demand, gritting my teeth reaching between us playing with her pussy until she arches again and I let myself go in the deep recesses of her beautiful body.

CHAPTER
TWENTY-FOUR

T aylor ~ Shelby-Love

~

MY PHONE IS on my bed when I get out of it the morning after returning to Shelby-Love. Looking around I think it's some kind of trick.

"What's going on? Why is this here?" I ask Hiru because Aiko is on leave for the next few weeks visiting her daughter in Nagoya, who is due to give birth.

"I wouldn't have thought her old enough to have an adult daughter," I tell him. "But I guess Asian don't raisin." I smile when I get a chuckle out of the normally stoic servant.

"Takeda-san also says you are to have free rein of the house and property. A driver has not been assigned yet, but he has sent for one who is exceptionally trained from Takeda headquarters in Tokyo."

Woah, my heart skips a beat hearing this news. In no way do I feel like Australia was a breakthrough but maybe to him it was. Maybe he believes me now.

Hiru gives nothing away as he busies himself with his tasks of the day. I know that he and Aiko have been with Hisashi for a long time. They along with his father made sure that he stayed on his meds for a time. Hisashi told me. They were his family's most loyal servant. When I asked him how long they'd worked for him he quietly shook his head with a soft laugh.

"Generations. Their families have been with mine since we ascended into the Samurai. My ancestors were protectors of the provinces from which theirs hailed. We served them and they served us. It is a symbiotic relationship. There is nothing I will not do for them or they me and my family. Such loyalty is rare."

The pride in his voice as he spoke about his people prompted me to say, "The people of Shelby-Love are like that if you give them a chance, they will show you."

Pulling away he shook his head. We came here in good faith to bring work and build the economy as charged by my cousin and FADE and Ghadi Carrington. We uprooted key staff and brought them here with their families in order to make the greatest effort and in return we have faced sabotage and claims of grievance. Just by being here we have raised the standards. Shelby Sugar knew they couldn't take advantage of their workers any longer when we came to town paying a fair wage and offered healthcare."

"Then maybe y'all should start looking at the competition as the source of the problem," I told him not letting him get in a snit after we had such a lovely time.

Easing back, he sighed pulling me closer on the seat we shared in the jet. "They were the first we suspected but haven't found anything that leads back to them."

He didn't say anything more about Thad, Mariah, and their shenanigans. I know he only did it to keep the peace. I just pray for my cousin's sake he's not doing anything else to disrupt Creative Chaos.

THE FIRST THING I do is look at all my notifications. I message my parents assuring them I'm okay after seeing all the tags of Hisashi and me my mom sent about us being a couple and a close up of my ring. Ugh, I'm going to have to do some serious explaining when I see them. I'm saving that headache for another day. I read all the news reports, legit and wild speculation. None are even close except the one from my cousin, Joy, saying we met here and it was rumored we knew each other at Sofia University but it's obvious to me that she simply put that together by us being there at the same time. Still, I admire her putting it together.

I have over two hundred messages on the family thread. There are several from Joy asking if my number changed with several shrug emojis appearing except for Kandie telling her {mind your own business. You just want mess for that article}

The rest of the thread is filled with gossip about Krie in the beginning then Ezakiel-Jane having a boyfriend that she won't tell anyone about for the most part. A lot of it is about Thad getting in trouble and a long thread of support and rationalization about him making good trouble with some of the family saying he has no proof of wrongdoing by the Creative Chaos management and they aren't like the Shelby's. Interspersed among all of it is Thad thanking and defending his actions. Krie is silent for the most part after asking everyone to pray for them during the arraignment followed by multiple thanks and praises after Mr. Takeda dropped the charges.

I don't know how long I'm wrapped up in the family drama, but I do notice the moment it turns to more concern for my whereabouts followed by responses from my dad and Xander-Rafe Leroy saying I'd let them know I was going on a sabbatical because of the writer's block I'd been suffering from. Gee thanks, Dad. But I guess his candidness should be no surprise.

It's Joi again who breaks the news to everyone I'd

been spotted in New York then again in London with Hisashi Takeda. She also blasts a news release from the Tokyo Times saying it was announced by his spokesperson that we are married. Then she shows the ring.

Again Kandi comes forward demanding: Ain't you tired of being in other folks business after all the mess you caused with Santiago and Mimi —something else I have obviously missed. Because while we were rehearsing the play, I felt like it was odd that Mimi, who I know is super busy being one of the few doctors we have here, found time to come to rehearsal every day, but it only took me seeing Santiago with Mateo one time to know that he was her baby's daddy. I just kept my mouth closed because I know more than anyone about keeping secrets and I have more than a few. Now it seems that they had a shotgun wedding which Krie disappeared after, and Joi wasn't even allowed to come. Yikes.

I feel like my whole life has passed in a blur and I've missed out on so much being held captive here. My cousins have always been there for me. Supportive and always lending a shoulder when I struggled in some way. Without question they built me up. Kandie with her funny little check-ins. Easy with her gentle words of inspiration and bible quotes. Krie with recipes she thought simple enough for me to try.

Now because of this gilded jade palace of a cage I haven't been there for them when they've needed me.

My stomach sinks when I look at the individual thread with my cousins. They are questions that continue on till this day, Kandie in particular not believing my dad when he said I mentioned going on a sabbatical. Probably because we spoke of my plans to head back to New York as soon as possible and get to work on a new play. She even invited herself for a visit. So, I know why she's not buying it. Joy, on the other hand, is asking for an exclusive for her blog and the newspaper. She even promises to take it easy on me and gives what I'm sure she thinks is assurances not to run with any unfounded accusations after having learned her lesson with Mimi and Santiago situation.

I cradle my phone for a long time before I have the courage to search Hisashi's name.

That brings us the headlines.

THE MOST ILLUSIVE RECLUSIVE OF THE TAKEDA LINE SEEN OUT ON THE TOWN WITH TONY AWARD WINNING PLAYWRIGHT.

He is described as everything from possible investor to lover. It's not until the Tokyo article comes up that things become unhinged. The press in Japan goes into a frenzy with yet another possible betrayal by the Takeda men marrying American women. There are whole think pieces about what has come over the elite Japanese line's men, and what we are doing to ensnare them some unofficial sources even hinting at witchcraft. I don't read too much more knowing it will do nothing but distress me.

"I see you are enjoying your phone back." His dry tone has me looking up into a face that barely hides the savage grace residing within him.

"Not really," I mutter, sweeping my tousled hair from my face.

"Why?" I can tell he's just being polite and the whole thing bores him and why wouldn't it? I'm sure it's far less exciting than tormenting members of my family.

"Well, for one," I sweep my legs off the bed coming over to face him, "your bastard of a brother is holding my cousin prisoner like you are doing to me. My whole family is in an uproar because no one knows where she is. I can't very well pop up out of nowhere and say he's taking care of her." Frustration eats at me. "Not to mention my parents were beside themselves about me and then they got news secondhand about me possibly being married to you. The fuck, Hisashi? Why would you have your people release that without letting me tell them first?'

His gaze drops half-mast at the barrage I toss at him. Hard eyes meet mine. "It is my right. My reasoning is my own. You should have already told your people about me. It's been ten years."

"We weren't together all those years," I clap back. Like what did he think I was supposed to do? Go skip around saying I was married to a Japanese billionaire with no evidence of it? Then both of us would have been locked away. I didn't even have a copy of our marriage license.

"That wasn't by choice, at least by me," he says his voice cold and accusing.

I guess time at the job, the mounting frustration, setbacks happening every time he turns around and the seeming nefarious —though unproven— hacking this time by my cousin has given him more incentive to find fault in me. To doubt me. I can sense it already happening without him even saying the words.

"Have you talked to your brother?" I dare to ask knowing this is the only way to convince him.

"No," comes his stony reply.

"But you're willing to give him the benefit of the doubt?" Incrementally his face hardens until I'm looking at a marble mask — beautifully unmoving in its coldness.

"He's earned at least that." He shrugs daring me to suggest otherwise.

"And your wife doesn't?" It feels like my heart is being squeezed under the callousness of his gaze and the cruelty of his words.

"As you were so eager to point out, you haven't been a wife to me for ten years." He might as well have scooped out my heart with his rusty spoon of truth.

"No, I haven't," I concede. "But that doesn't mean that I'm lying when I say that I didn't sign you away, Hisashi. I left because I was forced to. Two things can

403

be true just like with Thad." His gaze sharpens at my defense of my young cousin. "On the thread Thad proudly admits to hacking Creative Chaos with his friends but the second hack of the message board he denies. And he goes into detail how he and Mariah are trying to discover the real culprits." He looks at me a long time before he scoffs shaking his head not bothering to give me the benefit of an answer.

"What's going to happen when you are forced to let go of your little vendettas?" My challenge is met with a look of incredulity.

"Little dove," he softly chides. "The Takeda never releases a debt. Your cousin cost us millions. There is no one in your family who can allay that debt. Not the doctor for all her good works, not the little chef despite her devoted service to my brother, and not you. It is not our way."

His words are final. Something pierces me then. How could I ever think we would come back from this? Even if his brother told him the truth of why I left — even under duress was a dishonor to our marriage and him. Vengeance is so ingrained in him. He will never forgive me.

"Then let me go. If you hate me so much just let me go. I will give you all my future earnings on Thad's behalf. I can make three million in a season, no problem. Just let me leave." I'm begging and I don't care. All I know is I can't be around him anymore knowing this chasm will never be crossed.

The muscles in his jaw jump as he regards me allowing my words to settle over him. He gives a hard shake of his head. Cold eyes, hard mouth, implacable resolve, and a hard body face me. His hand whips out and I can't help the flinch but his hand is gentle as it touches my curls almost like he's going to muss them in a playful way. His hand settles on my crown.

"You won't be allowed to abandon our marriage again, Tay-chan. Marriage to a Takeda is for life." His smile holds no sympathy, yet no malice. "I understand your western sympathies however, our time of separation is no more. You will honor your vows, our marriage, and me going forward."

"How do you expect us to go forward when you don't trust me and probably harbor this deep resentment toward me? For something I didn't do. I'll remind you." My words are hollow and full of despair. I already know it's hopeless.

To my words he simply shrugs. "It is the only way. I will be back this evening and we will have dinner and speak of our new future together."

He leaves me looking after him and this outrageous pronouncement.

Later that evening I am sitting in the formal dining room awaiting my husband as instructed. Mercurial as ever he comes in as if he's been aggravated since the moment he left harassing me. I don't feel an iota of sympathy for his mean ass. "I know you're probably giving those poor executives hell at the job," I quip, taking a sip of the plum wine I've liberally imbibed.

He pauses his eyes skating over me with a mild quirk of his brow before he takes the seat at the opposite end of the obscenely long table. "We came to an agreement with the workers tonight to end the strike."

"Wow." That's great news. I'm eager to know what this means for my cousins but he still seems like he's more than perturbed. Maybe he feels like they gave up too much and the company will suffer.

"Come here," he demands, his eyes holding dirty promises.

I shake my head. "This is where the lady of the house sits."

"When we have guests. Regardless, you will sit where I desire." Nodding to Hiru, he takes his whiskey as the servant without further instruction sets a place beside him. Silent as a wraith the man comes over to me to hold out my chair.

Not wanting to cause a scene or make Hiru uncomfortable, I pick up my glass and walk over to the seat beside the one Hisashi is lounging negligently in at the head of the table.

He nods to Hiru who disappears, I assume to get our food.

"How was the rest of your day?" Mild curiosity lights his eyes.

"You mean you didn't watch me?"

"Didn't have time. Your cousin and his little friend are still wreaking havoc amongst the employee's message boards at the plant. I've had to put out fires all day. Then met with the strike leaders and other interested parties at The Camellia. Thankfully we were able to come to an agreement and find one of the people who was spreading misinformation and strife. It's all settled now," he says with cold finality, leaving no question exactly how it was settled.

Giving me a low steady look he takes a long sip of his Yamazaki, single malt. Allowing his head to drop back he closes his eyes savoring the taste. The delicate oak aroma bathes the space once he sits the glass between us.

"Have some." He indicates with an open palm.

"I don't want to mix. It may make me sick later," I say.

"Taste it." He's daring me.

Turning the glass, I turn it so the side from which he drank is facing me. Eyes on him, I lick the glass placing my lips over the exact spot his lips were moments ago taking a small sip.

Smooth heat slides over my tongue as I watch his eyes flame. "It's too bad."

"What?" He takes the glass I hand back in tradi-tional fashion with it resting open palm supported by my other hand.

"This is our last meal together."

He pauses looking at the food like I've poisoned it.

Shaking my head sadness settles over my heart like an old familiar hug. "You think I'd poison you, husband?" I ask, taking my glass and downing the rest of the wine before sitting the empty glass away.

"I never thought you a coward before. How is it that you think you'll ever leave me little dove unless I no longer breathe?" he inquires, making a big production of eating his steak.

Taking my utensils, I eat alongside him. The food is delicious, rivalling that of my Michelin trained cousin. But there's no point in having all this money if you can't have the best of everything. Even the linen shift dress I'm wearing with handmade embroidery is one of a kind.

We eat mostly in silence until finally he sits back, and Hiru comes in just as silently as before taking our plates away.

"Would you like dessert?" Hisashi asks me, courteous as the night we met.

"I'm fine, thank you. Though more plum wine would be nice." Hisashi nods to Hiru who takes the plates seemingly a short distance and doubles back to pour.

"Leave the bottle," I tell him, not bothering to give Hisashi a chance to say anything as I take the bottle from the servant and plunk it down. "That's all, Hiru," I tell the man, tired of the pretense. I'm aching for a fight.

"I spoke to my parents. They want me to come for a visit." Since he didn't listen in real time, I'm sure he missed the part where Mommy said both of us and I'm not about to tell him either.

"I don't have a problem with that. When do you want to leave?" Mild curiosity and amusement play across his face like he's ready to have his assistant pencil a visit to my parents in despite everything going on.

I don't for a second believe he'll let me go alone. My mouth twists and my tummy threatens to sour when he gives a low chuckle.

"You can go but you will return to me, or you will be returned to me." He crosses his arms over his chest. "Your parents don't deserve the trauma you're going to visit on them, little dove should you try to leave me. None of your family will survive the hell I will visit upon them if you even try."

Shaking my head, I look down at the glass of liquid courage knowing he's right. "How can we be happy if you ever hurt my family or if I'm not free to leave?"

"Do you want to leave me? Really? Don't tell me how you think you should feel because of how I brought you back into my life. Tell me how you want to leave when you take me into your body. How much you want to leave when I'm buried so deep inside you, and you don't know where you begin and I end. Not only that, the quiet times of us just being together. When we hold one another deep into the night.

There's no way you cling to me like that and want to be free of me. You need to get real with yourself, little dove. You can't even sleep the entire night without me."

Springing up from the chair I almost knock it over as the wine glass hits the table spilling the deep burgundy liquid over the surface.

Hurrying to mop it up with my napkin, I turn furious eyes on him.

"We'll see about that." The words are like a curse.

For his part Hisashi doesn't react just regards me with a chilling impassivity.

Attempting to walk by him I stop when his hand brushes against mine. He doesn't grab me. His fingers idly stroke the back of my hand. I look down into an onyx abyss of glacial intensity.

"Am I going to have to kill you to keep you with me, little dove?"

CHAPTER
TWENTY-FIVE

isashi

~

MY DICK IS hard as fuck pressed against her plump soft ass when I'm awakened well past midnight. Hell it could be early morning for all I know. I shift my nose buried in the bonnet she wore to bed, and my face on the silk pillow I purchased to protect her hair.

Reluctantly I pull away from the softness of her form to answer my phone. I can't tell who's calling since my brother has given my number to several of the contesting parties involved in the strike since before he showed up tonight he couldn't be reached. Bubba-T being the latest addition though I must

412

admit of all the people I've had to deal with in this debacle caused by mere children, he's been honorable. He's proved that tonight outing the woman who'd been misleading the other employees about the concessions we were willing to make for our workers.

I'm surprised to see my brother is the person calling me. "Hai," I answer drily. "It's good of you to pull yourself away from your little chef to give me a call since you can't find the time to meet with me at work." He's been back to work but we've been so swamped with various responsibilities and him leaving me to handle a lot of the accommodations the staff have demanded.

I'm sure the purpose being so we present a united front though we are the farthest we have been on an issue since I first became involved with Taylor.

"They're torching The Camellia." Hard words come across the line, spurring me to pull on my joggers. I barely notice Taylor shifting in the bed as I head out of the room.

"Who is they?" I ask, grabbing my keys and heading toward the garage to pick a car to drive.

"I have no idea. We are heading over there now," he says.

"I'm on my way." Entering the garage, striding over to my G-Wagon, I open the door getting in.

"Hisashi, you don't have to," he starts but I cut him off.

"It's my honor to serve you for once, Kiyoshi-oniichan." Hanging up I rev the engine, clicking the button to lift the underground doors.

IT TAKES me more than twenty minutes to get to the burned-out husk of The Camellia. People are standing around looking helpless. The majority are Krie's family the Loves. Solemn eyes watch as Krie is by her cousins Easy and Mimi. Even from the closed windows looking on I see the devastation on her face. Kiyoshi looks equally shattered as he watches her vibrating with fury at what's been done to her. It's then I realize just how far gone my brother is for his little chef.

I'd assumed she was an obsession that he needed to get out of his system. The first inkling I was in error should have been how he reacted to our mother's treatment of her. I chalked it up to guilt and simply caring for his little toy. The way he took care of her during her illness himself instead of delegating it to one of his trusted staff made me think. Now there is no mistaking the love planted on his face as he watches on as she cries with anguish over the arson of her business.

Moments later her nuisance of a brother comes along with Mariah. The boy has the nerve to rail at my brother. I almost get out the car when Krie comes between them. Kiyoshi reaches for her and she snatches away from my brother. I step outside the door. His eyes meet mine and he gives a small shake of his head.

Giving him my back, I give him the respect of not witnessing the repudiation of the woman he so obviously loves.

Walking around the truck I look out to the vast darkness still able to catch the scent of honeysuckle in the air. There is so much beauty but there's blood in the soil and poison in the soul that's been fed by generations of animosity that brought this night to pass. It almost pains me that Kiyoshi's little chef is a casualty. To have to stand by and watch your life's work go up in smoke is devastating.

Just like that the answer slides into place. I send the text without even thinking so sure I don't have to run it by my brother. The protestors, the employees spreading misinformation on the message boards. The same anonymous posters highlighting Krie's relationship with my brother. It all led to the demise of her business.

Everything we solved at her restaurant could be jeopardized if this isn't handled with care. Her brother didn't help with his inane accusations.

"You are not to harm anyone," comes the dry tone of my brother. It's just us and smoldering ash. Krie left with her cousins and Thad with his little friend.

"I make no promises," I say, looking over to him coming to stand beside me as I lean against the truck.

The black silk of his Henley matches mine. "You will require my skill set to avenge her."

Cold eyes meet even colder ones. Stepping away from the truck I bow with solemnity. "It would honor me brother, if you allow me to aid you in your quest for vengeance for Krie-chan who is under your protection."

"You honor me, Hisashi-niichan." Low words fall to my ears. I don't stand until he walks away. We do not give into shameless emotional displays. We are warriors, raised hard to withstand any turmoil. Takedas don't bend and we definitely don't break. Should someone attack us we come back with fivefold vengeance.

We nod to one another as we go in different directions to our perspective homes. We chose our homesites for the very specific purpose of safety. Keeping them far apart with Kiyoshi making new alliances with using local construction companies and local materials. While everyone was so focused on my brother being such a good neighbor with all the industry, he was bringing to the town, I was having my home made in a secret location known only to me and Cruz and his most trusted lieutenants. He even blindfolded the workers coming to the property as to not reveal its location, which they didn't balk at because of the extra pay incentive.

I watch Kiyoshi pull off in the direction of his home. There is no ache in my heart for my brother, even if I were to feel such juvenile emotions. He will prevail as he has in all things. I saw how she looked at him in return. They aren't over by any measure by my estimation, I think hitting the road to my hidden mansion.

Taylor is standing before the TV. The room is bathed in the glow as the reporter talks about The Camellia being burned to the ground.

Her gaze flies to me as soon as she notices me standing just inside the room.

"Is this you or your brother?" My head tilts at the absurdity of the question.

"Do you hear yourself?" I ask, my memory of her cousins demanding my brother's face in similar fashion.

"Yes, I hear myself, do you fucking hear me, though? Did you or your evil ass brother do this?" She demands. I notice then she's pulled on jeans and a t-shirt like she thinks she's going somewhere.

"Why would I when everything was resolved and the strike your cousin and little friend caused is put to rest?" Stating it with a calmness I don't feel, I step out of the slippers and pull my Henley over my head.

"Why are you answering a question with a question? You're supposed to be a genius but then you act like you don't know that now that y'all can't hold that over us you do something else to keep us under your thumb. Like, I don't know — burn Krie's business." The forcefulness in her voice makes me pause. I wouldn't be surprised if the servants on the property in their own bungalows don't hear her absurd ranting.

"You will not disrespect me in our home." My voice is cold and implacable. To which her little wild ass rolls her eyes and fumes more. "You mean like you busting the fucking window? Making me have sex with you?" Higher and higher her voice gets until she's screaming.

"Oh, I made you?" I scoff. "Even the first time you were begging like the needy little thing that you are." I laugh because it's actually funny. "You were scared all of ten seconds when I put your ass in that trunk. The moment you knew it was me your pussy got wet. I could smell it on you, little dove."

The undertones of her brown skin flush with anger.

"Wow." Turning from her, I rake my hand through my hair. "The way you avoid responsibility — no wonder you ran. Still trying to run. You will do anything not to take responsibility for your own actions. We both know how much you like what I do to you. You beg for it. Push me almost daily for correction."

A hard shove sends me forward several feet. Wheeling around, I feel a sharp sting across my cheek and then another hard shove. Stunned I right myself just as I avoid crashing into the TV.

Looking up I see the door to the garden has been open the entire time.

Rubbing the sting from my face I go in search of a length of jute.

Stepping out I listen. I don't hear her running. I don't even know if she has shoes on.

It's not hard for me to turn predator, I've hunted her for years. Instinctively I know where she will go. Where she will try to hide. The places of refuge she thinks I don't know about. The places she thinks are weak.

"Violence is never the answer, little dove," I call out into the night no longer listening but looking to the shadows. Humans have particular tells when they are hunted. They for the most part hide as long as they can until fear overtakes them and they do something idiotic like dart out and end up facing the very monster they thought to run from.

"Let me help. You know I excel in this," He pleads. I almost give in but —

"No. You want her for your own." I chuckle as he slithers back but I can feel him watching, waiting for his opening.

"I will fuck you where you stand. I look forward to breaking you," I call softly, almost feeling the tremor going through her on the current in the night. The garden is heavy with the scents of jasmine, gardenia, orchid, rose, and a local favorite camelia. There is no vanilla planted here so that will give her away. In this place she and I match perfectly. The garden has grown exponentially since I built it. Was even able to trade rare items with the apothecarist though she made me promise to never tell I was in possession of the vanilla-rose that only the Loves are allowed. It took persuading but her desire to have my heirloom blooms and herbs was just too enticing. She surmised correctly that I wanted the body butters and lotions for one of her cousins, but she assumed I was procuring those scents for my brother not her other cousin, Taylor. Which worked in my favor when she went missing.

Diabolically evil and unapologetic is what my father claimed when I let myself not be tamed by messy emotions of conscience. None of that matters when it comes to Taylor. I've proven I will stop at nothing to have her. Yet still she tries to run. She's cute to try.

It's still in the southern most part of the garden. "There are snakes out here," I say. We shipped them in to keep rodents under control. "You better be careful, little dove. Although they may not be poisonous, their bite still stings."

My head swings around at a whisper of move-ment. Just a few feet away is a dogwood tree indige-nous to the area. We brought in Japanese maple and cherry blossoms but the arborist from Auburn Univer-sity advised to have local trees planted as well so that they would grow in harmony. It almost seems fitting that she sought refuge there. So there she will be fucked.

"Ah there you are," I muse not at all surprised when she tries to throw dirt in my face. "Clever girl, my wife." My chuckle sounds maniacle to my own ears. She doesn't make it two steps before I snatch her back to my chest. Her breast rises fast like a hummingbird's wing.

Dipping my head I whisper, "Pretty little dove. I never told you about my sister's collection of doves did I? Kana always loved birds but didn't understand they like to fly away. They caused her so much despair. I figured I would help. I snapped their wings first but she didn't like birds with broken wings. They made her cry. She barely noticed the broken legs and thought the wrapping I put them in was pretty. She never cried over a bird again." Watching the way her breath stills lets me know I have her attention. "I never wanted to clip your wings. In fact I simply watched you and gave you the time you needed to find your passion. Still, you seek to dishonor your vows." I shake my head. "I'm tired of trying. You are the most vexing woman."

"I don't have to be. I don't have to be anything to you." She sneers at me. "You don't love me. You don't care about my happiness. All I am to you is a thing. Something you can fix up, put on display, and fuck whenever you want to."

"Indeed." Pulling her arms up so high she has to get on her tiptoes I throw the length of jute over the lowest branch. After several winding motions her hands are secured in the most rudimentary of knots. If she had leverage she could be out of them in mere minutes. However, having her small frame stretched high has compromised her balance. She has to put all her effort into standing on her tiptoes.

Taking my ceremonial dagger, I slit the fabric of the t-shirt. Then clamp the blade between my teeth like a barbarian and rip the shirt from her body with my hands. My dick kicks at the sight of her breasts spilling free. "No bra, little dove? It's almost like you wanted to get caught," I tease. Unable to stop myself I lean in a take a distended nipple into my mouth. Sucking on the diamond hard tip, I groan. "Damn you taste better than you look."

"Fuck you, Hisashi," she hisses at me.

"Who am I to deny my woman anything? But first a correction of sorts." Stepping away I let my palm fly then watch in fascination as her juicy globes jiggle in tandem as I mete out my punishment. I'm lost in fascination as color slowly blooms.

"Such a brave girl," I praise when she doesn't cry out just takes it like she deserves. "Such a naughty brave girl, who knows she needs discipline."

Again and again I spank her ass. Slowly she twists like a ballerina doing a pirouette.

Taking my time I circle her giving her no relief.

"I wonder if you're ready for me?' I muse stopping her. Stepping between her deliciously fat thighs I hoist them up until she's locked them around my waist.

She's open to me her nub distended and glistening. I stroke the protrusion methodically watching her defiant glaze. I can see her struggle even admire it to a point. "By the end of the night, you will be begging me to take all your holes, my brave little brat."

Slipping one finger then another into her tight sheath our eyes meet when her muscles squeeze me. "Look how she's sucking me in. You see how badly she wants to play."

Slowly I fuck her with my fingers watching them all glossy and wet. Never taking my eyes off hers I watch every emotion filter across her face and register in her irises. I watch as her pupils blow and she comes on my fingers.

Taking my fingers out I give her one watching her eyes close in pleasure as her mouth encases the digit. My dick flexes like she's wrapped her mouth around him. He kicks hard in my joggers wanting out, wanting inside her.

She pants so prettily as she watches me lick my finger clean, greedy motherfucker that I am I even dip into the crease to gather the moisture there.

Shifting her, I pull my dick free and with an easy upward thrust I take her to the hilt. My sac slapping her bruised bottom has her gasping. Her pussy floods all the same.

"Good little cumslut of a wife taking me so well," I say, thrusting deep and hard making her take every turgid inch of me.

Fishing for the knife, I set her free. I know my movements are erratic and I don't want to hurt her unnecessarily. She's still bound at the wrists, so she loops her arms around my neck for leverage.

Bracing my feet wide I grip her hips, bouncing her up and down on my dick. The way her muscles squeeze me is breathtaking. The smell of our bodies coming together its own aphrodisiac.

"So fucking good. So fucking mine," I grit, feeling my climax rushing forward. I pull her off dropping her to her knees. And just like a good little wife she opens her mouth to take my come.

I watch it hitting her tongue and face in thick creamy ropes.

She licks her lips, watching me. "Dirty little freak."

Coming, I pull her down with me taking her mouth, tasting myself on her lips.

"Up," I command, dragging her over me until my face it level with her pussy.

"Thank your husband for letting you come even though you tried to run from me," I say, darting my tongue to swipe her slit.

"Arigatō, otto. For letting me come even though I tried to run away from you," she replies with quick words. Her thighs tremble with anticipation.

Covering as much of her drenched pussy as I can I drink her dripping essence down, savoring the unique taste of her. Her hips buck, her hesitance enrages me. "Sit on my fucking face, if I wasn't man enough to take it, I wouldn't have told you to do it." She descends with slow deliberation. "Fucking smother me," I growl, burying my face in the soft flesh of her delectable cunt. She tastes like heaven.

Tongue fucking her with deep strokes I guide her hips as she rides my face. With rapid twists she moves adding a swerve to her hips that has me nearly coming again.

Reaching down I grip the base of my dick in a stranglehold the next time I come will be in her sweet little pussy.

When I have more control, I bring my hand up grasping the flesh of her ass slipping my hand into the crevice. Taking some of her moisture, I ease my finger into her ass.

"Ahh," she cries, her muscles clenching. Maneuvering so that I can reach her clit, I flick in slow intense laves as I finger fuck her ass. In seconds her come spills on my tongue bathing my face in the luxurious essence.

Pulling up, I turn her forcing her to her knees. "I'm done being nice," I ground out driving my dick hard into her.

My name breaks apart on her lips with every thrust. My heart leaps as she takes me rawly, opening to me so beautifully. She gives me the submission I require. Looking over her shoulder our gazes lock. She lets me have her the way she likes best.

Gripping her hips so hard they may bruise, I fuck

her among the posies, crushing so many of them. She's lovely like a little fairy made dirty by a demon. She's every dream, ephemeral and forever being pleasured by me.

"Pounding into this pussy is my favorite pastime. How dare you think to deny me of such pleasure, little wife." Steadying her with my hand, I slap her ass in tandem with each thrust I serve. She arches into me taking everything I give.

"Fuck yeah. Why do you let me fuck you like this, Tay-chan?" I demand, doing my best to find my home in her.

"Because it's yours," she pants between my hard drives. She's taking me like a motherfucking champ. My heart kicks up. I can't take my eyes off her when I find her spot. She clenches her eyes blooming in pleasure.

"Take all of it." Thrusting, I make sure I hit the soft raised tissue inside. A shudder shakes my body just as she convulses around me taking every drop of my seed.

I KNOW she's gone before I'm even fully awake. I don't know when she drugged me. Maybe at dinner but then Hiru would have been complicit. Groggily I rise scanning my surroundings seeing nothing out of place, but my spirit knows. She's fucking gone.

Taking the late-night tea she requested I take my cup she gave me and sniff it. Gardenia. I was so far gone, lost in her I didn't notice she laced my tea. I'd never fathom she would do that. Fucking clever little —

"Uh, uh. We don't use that word anymore," this motherfucking monster snickers.

"Wife," I say. "I was going to say wife."

"Sure, Jan." He chuckles evilly.

"She's going to regret it." Throwing off the covers heading to the shower so I can wake up more, I let fury lead me as I wash my body letting the stinging hot spray further ignite the fury coalescing in my veins.

Hurrying through my ablutions, I step into her closet going to the shelf where I have put some of my clothing since I've started sleeping the night with her.

Wasting twenty minutes I look for my keys realizing she's taken them.

"This little motherfucker took my keys." Shaking my head I look to see which one of my whips she took.

"She made it easy for me, there's a tracker on every car." Laughing to myself, I suddenly feel good about the hunt.

"Leave her be," He says with cold finality.

I shake my head before I even begin to respond. "Hell, no. She's mine."

"If she's really yours, she will come back."

isashi

"I NEED YOU, BROTHER."

The message is all it took to drag me out of my stupor of losing my wife the second time —at least for the moment. Kiyoshi's call to do as he termed put work in, an Angel Cruz term he now uses.

I took the time to go by the bungalow Santiago leased making sure she's safe. There is a tracker on all my vehicles not to mention the one I had inserted beneath her skin years ago which led me to her exact location. I know why she stayed close — to try and protect her family.

Pulling up to the antebellum mansion that harkens on days long gone by, I get out of the dark van that blends into the scenery. I know my brother is waiting inside.

Pride fills my heart. It is my honor to aid him in this manner. He's never asked much of me, other than I stick to my medicine and therapy regimen in a manner that would put our most revered Buddhist monks to shame. I know why he asked this of me. Only for me. My well-being. Because he cares for me. As hard as that is for me to extrapolate. I don't know if he's even capable of love any more than I am but he values me. Therefore my well-being matters to him. Which is why the concern in his eyes these days when he looks at me is not lost on me.

He knows I went too far taking her. He thinks he gave his little chef a choice. I don't bother to remind him that threatening to kill her brother or imprison him does not give the indication tender care is being served.

The same can be said of me when I regard him. This event with his little chef had taken something from my brother. I would seek vengeance if he did not care for her to the degree I suspect.

Leaving all essentials I see myself into the final house on our mission.

In the few weeks since Krie's restaurant burned we've exacted brutal vengeance on all who dare touch her. Leaving none of them unscathed.

~

"More sad news for Shelby Sugar. Two days after the CEO Mathias Shelby Sr.'s plane crashed in the Swiss Alps killing him along with his personal secretary, Monica Sellers, Tobias Slaughter, third husband of Clara-Lee Shelby, was found drowned at Smith Lake. Mr. Slaughter was a Bronze Medal Olympic swimmer but is said to have been a sleepwalker. Foul play is not suspected.

"That was some of our best work," *He* praises and I preen inwardly.

"It was almost as satisfying as the reviewer," I say, stepping into the darkened entrance of the mansion, recalling how the racist sonofabitch hurled every slur our way before I slowly drowned his ass in his own pool, after Kiyoshi poured enough liquor down his throat to make it look like an accident. "Kiyoshi insisted on not bleeding him out which was unfortunate." I press my lips tightly at the thought of having my fun interfered with.

"She's his to avenge. He's giving you this tonight." I know. My brother looks on from the man he's standing over whose chest is puffed out in false bluster.

"I can small his fear." *He* snickers. A smile plays across my face as I focus on the words the dead man is spouting from his lying lips.

"Now wait one minute." Scrambling up from his overstuffed leather recliner, he stumbles, dropping the tumbler in his hand. His eyes go wild searching for an exit. Both are blocked. One by me the other by Kiyoshi, who stands as calm as the eye of a tsunami.

"Why are you running, Lance?" I tsk, my voice alight with deadly mischief. "When you were so bold in destroying my future sister's restaurant?"

"I-I didn't have anything to do with that," he screeches. His face is purpling with anger and overindulgence. "S-She's a Love, of course they're gonna blame us Shelbys."

A low chuckle leaves me but I don't miss the amusement in my brother's eyes. Though it's not the good kind, no. It is too filled with malice and the delight in killing.

"You're not even a real Shelby, are you? Your mother married into the Shelbys. Everyone knows only the direct line gets anything. You did all of this for what? Crumbs?" Shaking my head, I step forward reaching under my coat.

Lance decides in that moment to make a run for it by barreling through Kiyoshi, who, I assume he foolishly thinks is the lesser threat, since he remains silent this entire time.

In one swift move, Kiyoshi makes smooth, controlled cuts with precision.

At first glance Lance thinks he's stumbled, only to raise his hand in disbelief to his neck now awash in crimson. First there's a stream then a river of red washes from the wound in bright beautiful stream. It's almost comical as a macabre surprise plays across his face. He stumbles toward my brother, his eyes wide in horror as he meets his reckoning, his mouth gapping like a fish flopping on the Shelby Catfish Farm we set ablaze, before his knees give way falling to the floor dead.

"Well done," I say, slowly clapping as I watch him wipe his blade before returning it to the scabbard. Cool satisfaction washes over me despite the fact I've had no fun yet.

"Hai, although I never thought I would get to it with you playing with your food." He watches as I shrug. He steps over the body, heading to me and the door. "Has the infrared signature been double-checked on the property?"

"Yes. We will run it again just to be certain," I assure him, trusting my team to have done the job done to perfection just as they did the private jet of Mathias Shelby Sr. Along with the ready approval of his son. Though we came to him thinking to appeal to the avarice that seems innate in the Shelby den of vipers after Angel Cruz revealed that not only did he owe the man a blood debt, but he is also his best friend. To say he surprised us with his aid but also his commitment to make sure there is no more interference with Loves or Creative Chaos going forward would be an understatement. Our dispatching the various nuisances in his family goes both ways.

He nods, following me as we make our way to the nondescript black van I drove here.

"The third scan shows the only heat signature is Lance's rapidly cooling body," I inform him, looking at the device we used to run the scans on the residences of our various marks.

It's what I've used to keep me from losing my shit since she's left. With it I can watch over her making sure she's not left the state. As well as know she's resting even if not peacefully in the cottage the rock star leased but has no use for.

"Well, let's rectify that. We wouldn't want him to cool off too much before he enters hell. Light that bitch up." Coolly, he watches as I press the button on the remote devices pre-triggered to create the mini explosions throughout the Shelby estate belonging to Lanceton Shelby.

The flames lick up the sides of the house. Within a minute, the whole thing is ablaze.

I've never had an affinity to fire but cool satisfaction fills me as I watch the mansion go up in flames.

"Are you going to her?" Looking over to my brother I ask after we take the highway back to Shelby-Love.

Grimacing, he shakes his head absently rubbing away the tension I'm not at all surprised he feels.

I commiserate with him. I feel much the same. Unable to do anything other than watch over a woman who no longer wants me. My dreams are plagued by sweet smiles and bruised eyes watching me as I continued to doubt her. She stood so bravely asking me to believe her, for a second chance but I just couldn't open myself up to being abandoned again.

"Not only that. You were afraid to be hurt, so you hurt her instead." He slides that in but I'm not in the position to respond. My brother's had too many run-ins with the monster. To say they don't get along is an understatement.

Thanks, I know that now.

"She won't want to see me," he tells me in the ensuing quiet.

"Why? Because you handled all this business for her? She knew who you were and took you to her bed, Kiyoshi, even knowing the worst of it with our mother."

"She safe worded me. Out of bed. She felt it was the only way to get me to leave her alone. A hard stop. I have no other recourse but to respect her wishes." He lets out an exasperated, no defeated sigh. It's over. Just like Tay-chan and me.

"I need to visit home and see how Kana is doing under Flower's guidance."

"And take up with your mistresses again?" I say with deliberation quirking an amused brow at him. "Word of advice big brother, that shit won't work. Once they have wormed their way under your armor there is no way to get the chink out." It sounds like an omen to my own ears. Only it's more for me than him. He's never caused her harm. I did that and more the first night I took her. And fuck it I'd do that shit again. The only thing saving her ass is the so-called guardian who's now decided she's also his to protect. Motherfucker.

"I heard that," He slithers through on a whisper.

Good, bitch.

Sighing ripping my hand through my hair then looking out the window, I tell him, "You think you're obsessed now? Wait until time passes and you can't see a clear way back. It'll make you do some unforgivable things. Things can never come back from. And you'll be so crazed by the very sight of her you'll never want her out of your sight."

"What the fuck did you do?" Turning a hard gaze on me our gazes catch.

"Too much, not enough." He shrugs looking out the window. "She did the breaking this time."

"What happened, Hisashi?" Never before have I sensed true sadness in him. He has me worried.

"Later, just think about what I said."

Eventually, I ask, "Why didn't you tell me the truth about Taylor's leaving Sophia?"

"You mean when I found you a broken husk of the man I knew a year and a half after I sent you home to be cared for?" He looks at me with horror playing behind his eyes.

"You didn't even know your own fucking name, Hi. We almost lost you. Mother was beside herself when we found you."

"Tay-chan swears the only thing she signed was the affidavit signing over the power of attorney back to the family which she said was under duress" — My heart stops when he nods.

"Hai, mother was determined to have her arrested for fraud. And father—" He scrubs his face, then looks at me with sorrow in his eyes.

I go cold waiting as the words wash over me.

"Father had — contingencies in place in case he passed away so you would be cared for. Unfortunately, he didn't do enough research about the old school facilities he chose."

"How did her signature get on the papers?" I demand through clenched teeth. Hearing that the man I respected more than anyone living betrayed me.

"Maybe he saw how close you were getting. Maybe he had spies checking on you and saw you get married and had them drawn up. It wouldn't surprise me. He probably anticipated mother's actions."

His head falls on the headrest exhaustion eating away at him.

I exhale a shaky breath not trusting myself to speak.

"I can't believe he knew what they'd do." He fists his hand rather than touching me. I'd probably break his hand. I feel my monster, my protector, my guardian seething.

He roars in my mind. He howls, he claws.

The anguish I can't feel but watch with cool resolve.

Never again.

"Hai," I manage to get out.

Nodding more to reassure him than anything else, I speed us back to the small town we once hated but now feels a little like home. To watch over the one person who's suffered more than me over this entire situation.

PULLING up two blocks away from the bungalow Taylor's living in, I skirt around the neatly manicured yards carefully avoiding the ones who keep their dogs outside.

The flak jacket fits snugly on my body, the infrared scanner pressed against my chest.

I make quick work of the magnolia tree. The white blooms contrast with the black I'm wearing but I'm soon swallowed up behind the thick leaves.

I sit midlevel the tree positioning myself so that I have an unobstructed view of the little house.

Following the infrared signature, I watch her form highlighted in blue as she sits on the sofa watching the television. Several hours tick by and I'd assume she was asleep if not for the periodic trips to the bathroom and the kitchen for snacks.

She always was a good by herself person having learned to do well being alone as an only child.

However we both know that difficulty lies when she's alone in bed at night. I know she's back to having nightmares. She won't take a sleep aid knowing I will come and hold her all night. I know she knows I'm here, which is why she closes her blinds and her curtains.

Like I said my wife is clever. She learned from my past behavior. She's not left. Not visited her people. I assume she wants to keep it to herself. From what I could tell from the texts I read that she doesn't want to worry her family. I understand that she didn't tell her fellow musical theater colleague; she doesn't want them in my sights. She knows I won't allow anyone to come between us. She doesn't need protection from me, despite what she thinks. However, I will eviscerate any motherfucker brave enough to step between me and what's mine. I don't care their relationship to her.

I made sure to keep her father away for this very reason. The ambassador is very busy putting out various fires with his government and mine. Much too busy to ride to the rescue for his only child. Especially when she keeps assuring them she's okay. When I get her back —

"When she comes back, you will not force her this time," He chimes in.

When she's back, I'm going to talk to her about putting others before herself. Silly little dove.

"You mean like you." He sneers.

"Fuck. You." I sneer back.

And she knew not to go to them. She understands me like no other. I knew what she meant to me the moment I met her at the Sofia University charity gala. She saw me even when she was unsure of the monster that lay beneath.

Closing my eyes, I knock my head against the trunk of the tree. "Fuck. Fuck. Fuck," I mutter seeing her face when she begged me to believe her, the coldness of my response. I will myself to feel nothing so I wouldn't snap her neck. Thinking she was lying, never doubting my brother let alone my father for a moment.

I always felt like I was something my parents hand to handle, had to deal with. The knowledge settles around me along with what it cost Tay-chan and me.

Finally she gets up her from trailing to the bedroom. I watch until she stops moving. I finally allow my eyes to drop. The wind is pleasant. I'm used to sleeping in this tree. Taylor for all intents and purposes knows I watch her but she doesn't know how or where. This is my only option since she hasn't left the house since she left me.

I'm here every night watching over her since day one. I stave off the rage of learning of my father's actions and Kiyoshi's complicity in Taylor leaving me though I know he'd not yet come in the power he wields within the family now and did what he thought best to keep her safe. Understanding doesn't mean that I can forgive his actions and never telling me.

"I knew from the moment you met she would be a problem. She makes you feel something," He speaks into the quiet of my mind.

I fire off a quick text before I can stop myself.

"Perhaps." Raising my lids I look at the darkened house and the scanner to reassure myself her small form hasn't moved before I close my eyes again.

TWENTY-SEVEN

T aylor

~

I CAN'T SEE him but I can feel him watching me. Blinds closed, windows shuttered, me not daring to peep let alone step outside, yet I know he's out there watching. Oddly it comforts me.

I try to reason with myself that he knows I couldn't come back despite it hitting the news who was really behind the arson of The Camellia. I'd been awakened the night of the fire to find my phone buzzing with back-to-back messages from family all aghast at Krie's restaurant being burned to the ground.

Thad immediately came on saying how the Takedas were determined to exact retribution and how Kiyoshi was obsessed with his sister and practically had made her his concubine and locked her way in his Samurai mansion. The jet exploded afterward. I went back and forth between the messages from family much of which were broad speculation. My thoughts ran more along the lines of how Hisashi promised retribution if I attempted to leave him. Did I really think he'd done it? Or did I use it as fuel to finally do what I should have already done? Leave him.

After Sydney I was dying on the vine of his disbelief. There was no way to get past it and I know I can't live like that.

Then there was a ping on my phone with a simple message.

H🪔: I spoke to Kiyoshi. I was wrong. Ore o yurushitekure

I don't know how long I stayed up looking at the words on the screen. They shouldn't mean anything to me. I should use them as leverage to get as far away from him as possible but I haven't moved. Not an inch. My bladder pulses with intensity getting me to finally get off my tail and go to the bathroom. I take the time not only to shower but take down my protective style of two simple braids with satins scrunches wound around the ends to prevent breakage and wash my hair.

The shower is hot and again I'm thankful that Santiago asked no questions when I asked him if he still was leasing the cute little house right off Main Street.

Taking my time I wash my body thoroughly hoping I can scrub away the memories that I can't seem to shake.

Now that my mind and body have had a chance to sync up once again memories I've suppressed or long ago pushed to the far recesses of my mind come to the forefront.

$\sim$

"TELL ME LITTLE DOVE, *what does your dream date involve,*" *He muses, pressing soft kisses along the back of my neck. He was working late and I was irritated so I came to drag him to bed so he could hold me. Selfish I know.*

"*Umm, you mean like a bucket list type date?*" *Seeing his confusion, I add,* "*Like the best date I could have before I kick the bucket?*"

"*Hai, if you're choosing to be morbid about it.*" *Nodding, he rests his head on my shoulder but doesn't stop the code he's still managing to write though I've plopped down in his lap.*

"*Simple. Take me to the theater,*" *I say.* "*Maybe dinner before or after. I'll wear a nice dress.*" *Shrugging I watch his long, elegant fingers fly across the keyboard forming numbers and formulas with a dizzying amount of speed.*

"*What's your favorite theater?*" *he asks in bemuse-*

ment, when I have to look away from the busy display I in no way understand.

"Well. That's a harder question. I love Broadway theaters because of all the excitement and openness. I love Drury Lane in London because it's so stately. I've never been to the Sydney Opera house but would love to go. And the Théâtre Des Nouveautès in Paris was lovely when my parents took me there on my high school graduation trip." I turn to find him smiling at me. "But I think the one here is now my favorite because you took me there."

Heat rises to my face. I try to shy away but he doesn't let me. He holds my face not letting me look away. "You would do me a great honor if you allow me to take you to those places, Tay-chan." I can't help but smile hearing those words, seeing the solemnity in his dark onyx eyes.

"Hai. I would love that."

FINDING myself sitting on the edge of the bed like I've just come out of a fugue, I jump up and rush to detangle my still sopping wet hair, not recalling even finishing my bath or washing my hair.

Recalling in more detail other things matched up in his samurai mansion and things I'd told him I liked or wished to have. The color purple being my favorite and how it was the highlight of the room. How so many of the plants in his garden were of that shade. Even the silk pajamas were and my sheets lilac.

Okay he overdid it on the purple. Looking at my reflection, I notice how I've changed so much since the night I came here. That night I looked rested, well fed. Now, I look like someone rode me hard and put me away wet then left me to starve. My cheeks are hollowed out even for a curvy girl. My mom would be aghast. You'd think he left me.

No I left him. Accusing him of heinous shit very much the same way I feel he did me but only I didn't have the proof. He'd been going off forged documents and at least they were good forgeries. If I didn't know myself better I would have thought I'd done it.

Looking at my hair even it looks limp. It's too wet to pull back in a ponytail, I just tie it up and away from my face. I have no energy to diffuse it.

I can tell by the way the light is streaming it's still morning but well past dawn. Feeling like I lost time I grab my phone and check the time. After eleven a.m.

I'm so startled when the phone buzzes that I drop it and somehow it answers.

"Hello, Helloooo, Taylor?" The heavy twang of my cousin Kandie comes out over the line shaking me out of whatever state I'm in.

"H-hello?" I answer into the speaker after sitting it on the bed.

"Girl, are you still in town? Ulysses says he caught one of them Takedas sitting in a tree in Mrs. Earline's yard. That's right by that bungalow Billy and them fixed up as a get rich quick scheme to make it an

Airbnb for Santiago. I guess it worked though since he leased it a year, so he could see his baby by Krie. Anyway, Ulysses' lying ass says you're living there for the time being. Why didn't you tell nobody?"

"Well," I hurry to cut in." It's a long story but yes. I just got back in town. I can concentrate better down here."

"Um-hmm," she says with skepticism dripping from her voice. "So why that real quiet one — and you know that's saying something when Krie's man don't talk at all, is sitting in trees with night scopes and shit?"

Stunned silence builds around me. So that's how he watched me.

"We are together," I lie, my tummy in knots not wanting to make it sound worse than it is.

"Then why is that motherfucker sitting in a tree outside the house instead of in it with you?" She quizzes like she's Judge Mathis or something.

"We had a fight and I locked his ass out," I hurriedly explain wanting to be done. Something tells me everybody is going to know about this.

"Ohhh, I get that." She chuckles a little. "I hope you blocked his ass on everything."

I join her laughter because even though the situation is not funny the way she talks about it is.

"Don't tell anyone."

"You have to make me promise on my momma and daddy for me not to." She sounds bored.

"Okay then promise on your parents, that you won't tell anyone." I force out laughing.

"Chile, I guess." She sighs. "Well let me go get these sweet cross buns out the oven."

"Okay, bye."

"Bye, honey," she coos.

I know she's going to keep her promise right up until she's had one too many shots of Remy Martin then it's all going to come out. Plus it's a Friday night. Yep. My phone will be blowing up by tomorrow morning.

"Ugh," mumbling to myself, I wonder how long he's been out there watching me. Probably from the day I left knowing him. He could have been arrested for goodness' sake or shot knowing how much people down here love their guns.

He really needs to stop. Shaking my head I try to think of what I want to eat, no it's pointless. Hisashi has taken up all my energy.

How are you?

I wait twenty minutes for an answer thinking maybe he's busy or not left work.

Trying his phone there is no answer. Then I wait feeling like my heart is skipping every other beat and not in a good way. He just got the most terrible news, has he lashed out to his brother? What did Kiyoshi tell him? Did he admit to the whole thing?

I know I can't wait around for an answer I'll never

get. I call the one person I would consider an ally in this situation.

"Hiyo, Tay-chan," comes the thick rumbly voice of the one person who struck fear in me all those years ago — Kiyoshi Takeda, not anymore though. My main concern is his brother.

"Um, hiyo," I don't know where to begin. I'm pretty sure between me rushing Hisashi with a hug bomb at the airstrip and the press reports he's well aware of my return to his brother's life. I don't know if he knows how we came to be though. I will never betray Hisashi so I'm trying to be careful with my words.

He sighs gently. "Do you need help, Tay-chan? As I understand it, you are still my sister."

"He's not answering his phone. I didn't want to bother him at work," I say, feeling more than a little silly. What if they are there together?

"I believe he's taking the rare day off," he says, then I hear shifting and a soft murmur of a familiar woman's voice whispering okay.

I cringe when I realize it's my cousin. Krie just probably heard me asking after Hisashi and now knows I'm married to him. Why else would her boyfriend call me his sister?

A litany of profanity laced admonishments fly through my mind. "Well, okay."

There is a long silence on the phone, so long I pull back to check that he didn't hang up.

"Taylor are you going over there?" Concern is etched in every word.

"I don't know," I say, wondering when I started lying so much. "Ah, probably. He never not calls me back. Last night he texted while I was asleep saying he talked to you and found out everything that happened when I left," I hedge, hoping he'll fill in the blanks.

"Hai." The one word stony response lets me know just how false that hope is. Then he says with cold precision, "You will call me when you get there and when you leave. If I don't hear from you or my brother within two hours of your call I will come to get you."

"Kiyoshi-oniichan," I say softly not wanting to be overheard by Krie if she's near. "He's never hurt me, not even back then."

"Ah, bishōjo, I know. He's not who I'm worried about," comes the solemn warning. "I would never forgive myself if I let anything happen to you again. Promise you will do as I instructed. I trust my brother but his monster as he calls him is another thing entirely."

"I trust them both. His monster as y'all like to call him only reacted to what he thought was a threat to Hisashi. He only wants to protect him. I promise to call." I add the last part just to reassure him.

After a few more questions and reassurances he gives me the estate's passcode: TAYLOR.

∽

452

"Hey," I say, my way of introduction, entering uninvited into the darkened bedroom belonging to my husband.

He's the perfect villain in his lair reclining in a dark gray nearly black chair, his face a mask of despair and anger.

Why that makes my heart clench is not lost on me. I will never stop the feelings I have for this man. I accepted him as he was long ago. He's deserving of love. He's deserving of mine. His mental challenges haven't made him less but so much more. He had the courage to face them and me. I have to have the courage to do the same and show him I won't fail him again.

"What are you doing here? You wanted to leave, I let you go." Swirling the whiskey just so it catches the light, Hisashi takes a long swig before resting the crystal highball on the arm of the chair slowly rotating it in his hand.

"Did you really, though? I heard you were hanging out in trees by the little bungalow." Popping one hip out, I toss his keys on a console by the door, they clang loudly before settling somewhere in the center.

"Leave," he snarls like he's about to spring.

Maybe not the best idea but I continue until the smell of blood and a clearer view of my husband stops me cold.

He's cut through the tattoo signifying me coming into his life and our marriage.

"Oh," I bemoan the destruction of his beautiful body but manage a simple tsk. "Never thought of you as a quitter. You've shown so much dedication thus far."

Shaking my head, I walk into the bathroom and get the medical kit. My heart feels caved in. A brief glance in the mirror has me clearing my expression because I look as devastated as I feel.

Ignoring the rivulets of blood running down his body I take the peroxide saturating the pristine white cloth. He has the nerve to rear back when I sit on his thigh.

"Sorry," I say not sorry at all as I gently apply the disinfectant to his self-inflicted vivisection.

"So, you done with us then?" I push verbally while simultaneously cleaning his wounds with smooth precision.

"Maybe, I'm tired of being someone else's burden. My parents, my brother— yours."

"Did I ever you say you were a burden to me?" Looking up from one particularly deep laceration I meet the dark onyx of his gaze. "Love is never a burden. You aren't a burden to me. You are a blessing."

He looks away first. His jaw flexes, hardens. Head swinging back so fast he nearly jostles me off his lap. Strong hands stop me from tumbling. "How can you say such things?" Incredulity spikes every word.

"I don't think either of us has much of a choice in

the matter." I shrug. "The God of the universe has spoken."

He grips my shoulders giving me a rough shake. "Do you know what the fuck you are agreeing to? The life I live. The bad days..."

Shaking my head, I take his face in my hands. "The bad days were the ones when I didn't have you. Didn't know you were watching over me. Protecting me."

Eyes searching mine he whispers, "I was a shadow, a shadow existing outside of the living. The only thing sustaining me were glimpses of you."

My eyes fall to the streak of blood on his lips. Pulling his lower lip out I see where he's sliced the inside of his mouth.

"There will be no more bleeding outside of a scene." He looks absolutely mutinous for a moment at my admonishment then gives me a gruff, "Hai," with a bow of his head.

"I can't believe your guardian allowed you to do this." Shaking my head I glance up from his handiwork to catch his flash of jealousy.

"Well, I threatened to silence *him* permanently," he grumbles. "*He's* taken a particular interest in you. I think he's in love with you." He looks at me steadily. His gaze speaks volumes, but I don't push. I know he wants to say more but distrust is hard to unlearn. Just as trust is hard to gain. Patience, I remind myself, he's just been dealt a severe blow in that regard.

His head dips touching mine forehead to forehead.

"I don't want to share you, Tay-chan. Not with my guardian, not with any potential kids, not with anyone. You are mine and mine alone." I can't help but smile at his possessive words.

"I am yours alone. Your guardian only emerges to protect you. Now, *he* knows I won't ever purposefully hurt you. You have not relinquished control —not once since that night, even when you wanted to. I saw you fight for control and win that night in the garden. I trust you, Hisashi."

He pushes back. "You shouldn't. You can't just let your guard down like that. Not just with *him*. With me. I'm dangerous."

"So is your brother, so are some of my cousins. I'm not a stranger to dangerous men. Stop trying to push me away. Unless you realized during our time together you don't want a forever type of thing with me." I shrug with fake nonchalance, rolling my eyes for good measure.

"If anything, I realized that I couldn't live without you. I won't live without you." His dead ass serious- ness gives me pause.

"Is that what this was?" I wave at his neatly bandaged torso. He looks at me stonily.

"Hisashi." I swat his chest hard the same time I yell his name. He grips my wrist as I am shaking my head tears welling in my eyes. "How fucking dare you?"

"You left," he grits out. "I didn't know if you'd ever come back." He tosses my wrist away like it's nothing.

"I will always come back to you." Taking his hand I put it over my heart.

"Because you love me," he says but it comes out like a question.

"No. Because you love me. Not only that. The way you love me. I realized at the bungalow you took me to all the theaters I spoke of when we first got together. I didn't even realize..." I trail off when he won't meet my gaze.

"It was the first thing I remember when my brain and body had healed from everything they'd done to me." His words are low and rife with pain.

Leaning in I kiss his cheek letting him tell me the rest of the story.

"I thought I was losing touch with reality again when I kept having dreams and memories of this pretty Black girl with an American accent. Yet, every time I focused too hard it would give me a migraine or I would just draw a blank. When medication didn't help Dr. Inoru intervened reaching out to Kiyoshi, who confessed the truth of our relationship. He kept it from me because he obviously didn't realize that he was doing more harm than good."

"Oh my goodness, babe." Just thinking of how he suffered fearing I was a figment of his imagination breaks my heart.

"How did they make you forget?" Immediately I regret asking. "No. You don't have to tell me. I don't want you to have to relive anything horrible." I wave for emphasis. But he's already grabbing my hand, kissing my palm.

"No. It's okay. I want to tell you." He draws me close and I don't even mind the smears of drying blood on the pretty rose gold dress I decided to wear.

"Lobotomies, drugs, so many drugs. That's why I stopped smoking blunts everyday. After that experience I never wanted to feel altered, I also didn't need them anymore to self-regulate. It took me a long time to get my body back after all the torture they called treatment. They took so much from me, Tay-chan." His eyes are pools of sorrow and shame. "I can't believe my dad did that to me. I thought he was always on my side." Looking away he roughly wipes the glimmer from his eyes.

"My monster would emerge and fight for me. The monster attacking anything that tried to touch me but one thing our sensei taught us in samurai training is that you aren't going to win every fight and when you are losing a battle just survive another day. Eventually with all the beating, tortures and, and—" he trails off not meeting my eyes, his cheeks flushed with a shame not its own saying, "Rapes."

He looks at me fully. "They raped me to break me. Eventually they did. And I just existed until my brother rescued me from that place."

Stroking his hair, I pull him into my arms. He buries his head in my neck and silently sobs.

"I needed you so bad. While I could still remember,

I just wanted to hold your hand like I did in the beginning," he whispers brokenly in my arms.

Lacing our fingers together, I hold him absorbing all he's told me.

"I'm here now, Hisashi. I'm here forever."

"I love you so fucking much. Aishiteru yo. Tay-chan." His voice is so raw, so guttural, it flays me as I sit in his arms.

Then for the first time since his father's death we hold each other and cry.

Later, when he pushes inside me, loving me so sweetly he whispers to me again and again, "Aishiteru yo, Tay-chan."

His lips take mine, our kiss is bloody, yet I take everything he has to give holding nothing back and I feel his monster watching.

I say the words back knowing monster or not, psychopath and all, he deserves love and I'm going to spend the rest of my life giving him all of mine.

CHAPTER
TWENTY-EIGHT

isashi

~

"LAST ITEM ON THE BUCKET LIST-O," I told Taylor earlier as we sped through the Tokyo night to the Kabukiza Theater to see the drama *YOWA NASAKE UKINA NO YOKOGUSHI*, an adaptation of the film, *Scarface*.

"It's just bucket list." She laughed softly, leaning the way I love giving me a soft kiss just under my jaw.

She asked no questions when I told her I had a surprise in Japan a week ago. In the time we've been here I've finally met her parents and sat through the interrogation they gave us on our relationship.

Candidly telling them about my struggles with my mental health and our forced separation seemed to soften them a bit, well her mom. Her father on the other hand was quick to remind me of her intensely problematic cousin Ozymandias Savelle who handles certain situations for the family. My remaining unflappable at this threat garnered a little more respect. Now that I'm on this radar I doubt I'll ever get off.

The rest of the week is us reacquainting ourselves with Tokyo. Since my business requires me to come home my residence at the Toranomon Hills Residential Tower comes in handy. Her love of the penthouse makes me happy since I judiciously had the designer incorporate her love of purple throughout the space. She let me make love to her on the purple chaise after I draped her in her body jewelry. Biting back a groan I try not to think of how she looked coated in my come and diamonds and the way she allowed me to lick her clean.

As we watch the story unfold of the mob boss and the geisha we're both riveted. She on the production and me I was simply spellbound by her joy.

Her love of theater is incandescent. I can't help being won over by her enthusiasm. The over-the-top experience she happily claims is by far her favorite of all she's seen.

"Really?" I ask with delighted skepticism. "We have been to Broadway, London, Paris, and Sydney and you love Tokyo most. Are you just trying to please me, wife?"

"Nope. There's something hugely appealing to me about an artform that traces back to its origins. We were told to hold off on visiting the theater because they wanted us to be authentic in our approach in writing so that we used our lived experiences to create. I'm so happy you brought me," she says just as the door is opened by the driver. Rushing around to my side, I feel anticipation fuel me and not a little bit of hunger because we decided to eat after the play.

Just as the car pulls off, I hear a loud screeching of tires. Instinctively I dive over Taylor dragging her to the floor of the Rolls Royce.

"Go, Go, Go," I shout to the driver just as a hail of bullets lights up the car.

"You drive," Monster shouts. *"He's in on it."*

Not once in the thirty years have I ever doubted my guardian as Tay-chan loves to call him. Kogi has been my driver for years.

"Anyone can be gotten to," He assures me. *"You must protect your wife."*

Arguing no further. I move.

"Get the fuck over and if you move, I will kill you," I snarl to the trembling man.

Training my ass. He may have pissed himself. Taking the wheel I drive over the curb, driving into oncoming traffic, with precision I find the spaces to take my car between the cars racing toward me. Keeping calm, I make a U-turn crossing the divider so that I'm now going in the right direction.

The assailants have long been since left behind. I see Taylor trying to sit up.

"Stay down, little dove." My words bely the adrenaline pumping through my veins as I take safety maneuvers drilled into me for years until I arrive safely at my penthouse at Toranomon Hills Towers.

"We own this building. No one on staff can come and go without our express knowledge," I say to Taylor even as I type in and send for lockdown procedures as we ride up the elevator to our floor. Aiko and Hiru stand at the ready as soon as we enter.

"Take care of your mistress," I say to them before turning her to me.

"Listen, go take a shower. I will be back in a little bit."

She's already shaking her head.

I stop her when my phone chimes making her fume but in this case, it can't be helped.

"Cousin," I say as soon as I see the other person on the phone is Akchiro, who holds the position as The Takeda, the head of our family and our vast business interest including a multibillion-dollar conglomerate.

"What the fuck is going on?" he snarls in the background.

"That's what I'm wondering," I tell him. "I was at

the theater with my wife and someone tried to kill us in the most dishonorable way. With guns."

Hearing the disgust in my voice he sighs. "I'd have thought he'd have been appeased but it seems Tatsumoto is still miffed your brother chose another over his sister."

"You mean she chose her female assistant over Kiyoshi. It seems like a win for everyone," I say, reminding him of that little missed gem.

"He could have still had them. Had them both if he so chose you know that."

"I believe he loves his little chef," I throw the winning salvo because didn't my cousin also choose love.

"You will take care of this for me. Try to resolve it without bloodshed if possible since we have many mutual business interests. However, you will do what you must to stay alive. It would upset my wife and I don't want to see her more upset than she already is," he grumbles with the resignation of a married man. I suppose she's giving him fits after discovering he's kept my mother and sister captive in his mansion in Osaka for the last few years.

Seconds later — Tsuyoshi Tatsumoto's location is sent to my phone. Heading toward the elevator I pause when a small, delicate hand grips my arm. Pivoting I turn catching her waist looking at the lovely lilac petal rose couture dress she's wearing.

"Tay-chan," I begin.

"Hi—" she cuts in.

Shaking my head, I silence her pulling her close. "You are making me give face in front of others, little dove," I growl, frustration lacing my words making them come out as a growl.

"S-sorry. I will gladly give you mine. I was so scared." I can feel her trembling. I watch her with my heart swelling, and she bows before me before coming back clutching the lapel of my suit pressing her face into my chest. "Please just stay here."

"The head of my family gave me a task. It would be a great dishonor. It would require my life if I fail his order," I tell her with cold finality making it more than clear what the expectations are.

"Going could cause that." Her eyes are wild with worry.

"You know who I am. You have always seen me, me little dove. You know there is nowhere I will go and nothing I will not do to keep you safe. They didn't just target me. They attacked you too." Canting my head, I chase her gaze until she locks in with me. "And that's when they fucked up. They sealed their fate. Now, give me the grace of having one less thing to worry about. Please shower and have Aiko make you a calming tea." I press a kiss to her forehead silently communicating to my staff what I need to be done.

～

I would have thought as head of the most powerful Yakuza clan Tatsumoto would have had his men ready to cut me down the moment I approached his property. Taking a few precious moments, I cloned his security system masking it with video from an hour ago.

The entire space is eerily absent staff as I navigate the expanse of the mansion made in the style of the Edo Period but still has the new money flash and bang that the syndicate so loves. Yet these paintings are less garish and more provocative in their social commentary than you see the Samurai in the murals being hunted and expunge from society when they are no longer needed by the government going on to form their own clans which led to the rise of the Yakuza.

Looking at the art, I don't miss the message. I know he doesn't do business here so this is only for him and those closest to him. His belief in his organization is as strong as any Takeda. I almost regret having to kill him but taking the vendetta to my beloved sealed his fate.

Taking one long corridor after another I pass the inner sanctum of the head to the Tatsumoto Syndicate. My hackles rise, there should be more guards. More protection. I feel for the false wall that's in the plans my cousin sent me. The doors slide open silently. I am arrested by what I see inside.

The yakuza sits before a painting that runs the

expanse of a wall. The canvas is stark white. Until you get to the bottom and there is a black pool of liquid that runs along the bottom of the canvas that gradually turns crimson. The blood trail leads up and up until it is shown to be spilling from the slit neck of a beautiful woman draped in a silk kimono.

I step closer to further inspect her beauty. If he's aware of my presence he doesn't bother to look up from the crimson he's mixing. Beneath him on the floor is the very same woman her hair tied back as depicted in the painting. Her mouth is gagged with his foot on her neck. A pet. Yet her eyes burn with something akin to hatred. She looks at me and that look does not change.

"Did your cousin or your brother send you to kill me?" comes the bored question from the man who doesn't bother to even glance away from his work.

"Cousin," I say, giving him that much.

"Ah," is all he says as he smoothly rises moving in the opposite direction going over to the painting. He makes broad strokes on the canvas to the red kimono, occasionally looking at the woman whose head is turned in my direction.

"It's unfortunate. I would have thought the presentation of such an extravagant gift," he nods toward the woman, "after my sister's abrupt end to the engagement upon finding out about your brother's attachment would have settled things nicely between our families. Or is there a business situation I have not been made aware of?" Quirking an uninterested brow at me he turns back to his work with an intensity that borders on mania.

Absently I wonder if he saves all his passion for the canvas.

"I would inquire the same after tonight's incident. Guns are a tad bit gauche don't you think, old friend?" I keep my tone as bored as his though I feel only rage simmering as the monster prowls the edge of my mind.

"Kill him. Kill him. Kill him," He urges.

All in good time.

"Guns? No one in my organization is allowed to use such crass tools. We are of silence and blood when we put work in. You know this. Why have you come?" All pretense falls away. A cold killer stands before me ready to draw his weapon the moment I do. He may even do it before me since I came into his home uninvited.

"My wife and I were attacked by a Yakuza swarm as we left the theater tonight. Nothing happens in this city without your approval, my friend. So you tell me. Why have I come?" If not for the brief moment of shocked outrage on his face I would have thrown my ceremonial blade into his throat.

"Apologies, for the incident to you and your wife. I hope she is well." He bows deeply. "I take full responsibility for any harm that has come to your wife because as you say I run this city and if someone within it has acted in such a dishonorable way then it falls to me. May I ask, were any survivors interrogated?" Deep concern etches his features as he pulls out his phone shooting off a series of texts.

"My wife is fine and resting at home. She is a brave woman delicate but far stronger than any other I have ever met." As the words leave my mouth I watch as his gaze skates over to the woman lying prone on the floor before he drags them away and continues to let his fingers fly across the keypad.

"Then the gods favor you, Hisashi Takeda." He bows then silently reads as a flurry of text responses come in. "All my chiefs have confirmed their teams' whereabouts as well as time stamps on their daily schedules. I will of course conduct an audit and if found I will bring them before you myself."

Frustration rips at me but something tells me that he is not lying. Tatsumoto has never acted without honor in our dealings. We found out after his sister eloped with her assistant, he'd only previously opposed the match because he knew she was in love with her assistant and wanted to honor that. Mai's love for their father is what led to her duplicity. All indications point to his non-involvement. However, Takeda's are not so trusting.

"There is time to kill him later," He advises.

Since when did you become the voice of reason?

"When she came back. Still, we get to kill the actual wrongdoers."

Perfect.

"I await your findings." I bow briefly to him.

He bows briefly before walking over to the woman. "Up," I hear him snarl as I enter into the darkened corridor.

As I leave, I notice the servants are back out in their usual positions. One even opens the door as I exit the mansion.

When I get inside my black Maserati there is a black velvet case sitting on the passenger seat. A vellum card has Mrs. H. Takeda emblazoned on the outside. Opening the lid, I spy purple diamonds all the size of almonds in a beautiful platinum choker with matching teardrop earrings.

"Motherfucker," I mutter, pulling off anxious to get back to Taylor.

"How is Mrs. Takeda?" I ask as soon as I enter the penthouse.

"I believe well, Aiko went in with her tea several hours ago. She said she was going to sit with her until you return." Hiru bows deeply. "Please accept my deepest regret for what transpired tonight."

"Arigatō," I say, bowing slightly in return feeling nothing but the need to see my wife, though I appreciate the sentiment. Taylor's name played through my mind nonstop as I drove home. I even brought the gift from Tatsumoto in hopes to see her smile. Something tells me all she wants is for me to hold her. I will do so gladly if it brings her any solace.

I know by morning I will have the name of the culprit.

The matter is all but settled in my mind when I stop dead in the bedroom. Two smells assault my nose, human waste and the distinct smell of cyanide.

"Taylor," I yell, picking up my wife's crumbled form that is half lying off the bed.

"Hiru," I yell. In seconds the man is there. "She's been poisoned. Get the guards." He's gone before I can even finish the words.

"Taylor," I urge checking for a pulse, my heart plummets when I don't feel one.

Pressing my head to her chest I listen. There. Barely and with way too many empty beats between them.

"Listen, you have to fight. I'm here now, Tay-chan. You have to fight."

My phone buzzes.

"I'm on my way. I've sent all our best people," Akchiro says over the line. I'd already updated him on the status with the Tatsumoto Syndicate on the way here.

He hangs up without me responding.

Seconds later people are swarming in. The apothecarist comes in hurrying over to us. Swiftly she checks Taylor's eyelids, tongue, nail beds. "Help me strip her," the woman commands. Without hesitation I get to work removing Taylor's clothes. I don't have to look up to know the guards posted have turned their backs.

After a swift assessment the woman pulls put a syringe so long it makes my blood curdle.

"It's a tiny needle," she assures me. "Open her mouth." As soon as I do she sticks the needle under Taylor's tongue. Grabbing another she distributes the antidote at various places on her body. When the last shot is administered Taylor shoots up in the bed into a sitting position and screams, "Hisashi," before collapsing in a heap against the pillows.

The apothecarist sits back shaking her head. "This was made to torture. Whoever did this hates your wife very much. Hire a food taster," she advises.

"Who do you know that can make this type of poison and what is it?' I demand.

"No one living. That's why it took me many precious seconds we didn't have to look for punctures. This is an old imperial poison not seen in centuries. It combines breathing restriction with systematic organ failure. You are very lucky it is slow acting making one feel malaise. Your servant there must have been prepared to end her own life." Raising her hand in the direction of Aiko, whose mouth is filled with so much foam it has spilled from the sides. The scent of almond and urine waft from her.

"What happens now?" I ask my gaze tracking back to Taylor, who looks too fragile in the bed.

"It's hard to say." Slowly she drapes the covers around her. "Her body must first continue to fight the poison so expect a fever. I will leave you remedies. Do not give her any other medicine. I don't know how this poison will react to them. The process can't be rushed. Once she awakes then we will be able to ascertain the level to which any damage has been done cognitively. If she's been spared in that area the rest of her body should be fine."

"Arigatō." I give the healer my most respectful bow.

Scooping up Taylor I stride out of the room. "Please have the room cleaned and sanitized," I say to Hiru who bows in response.

Laying her down I watch the rapid eye movement. Willing her to wake, terrified she won't.

Kneeling beside the bed I tell her, "Come back to me, little dove. If you want me to beg, I will gladly beg you not to die. Leaving me to this wretched existence alone. I will gladly give face to you. I will take yours and you may have mine."

THERE IS a soft knock on the guest room door. "Enter," I say, not looking away from my sleeping wife.

"Sensei, I found this clutched in Aiko's hand." Giving me the note he bows and leaves the room.

Carefully I peel open the sealed and somewhat crumpled envelope.

"You disappoint me, yet you always have. I will however not stand for your dishonor." 母

I put the note with my mother's kanji in my pocket and return to watching over my wife.

CHAPTER
TWENTY-NINE

H isashi ~ 4 days later.

~

"THE FIRST FLUTTER of her lids was two hours ago," I say to my brother and cousin standing like sentries in my freshly cleaned bedroom. I hesitated to bring her back here where the poisoning took place then decided we aren't cowards, and we will face this together.

"I sent Aiko's family her pension and handled the cremation and the memorial service as you requested," Kiyoshi says in disapproving tones.

"Always so ruthless, brother," I chide him uncaring he's just performed a task that would have fallen to me.

"If this is what love does to a man than I want no part of it." Kiyoshi scans the room with a critical eye his eye landing on the color purple as if it offends him personally.

"The emotion stops with her — and Kana." I turn back to her sleeping form.

A low chuckle from my cousin has me turning back to them. "You realize you were not included?"

Kiyoshi's eyes narrow on the man who looks uncannily like him. "Nor you or did you miss that?"

Akchiro shrugs. "I'm the same way and so are you despite what you have said, they are different." His gaze takes on a faraway look. Uncomfortable knowing the challenges he's having in his marriage I ask, "What would you have done?"

His face turns glacial. "Buried them all, the entire family except maybe for the daughter's baby."

Kiyoshi's nodding lets me know I am by far not the most bloodthirsty of the lot despite my monster.

"Guardian, motherfucker," He rages.

Monster.

"Bitch," He hisses. *He's* been beside himself since we found her.

"The ultimate responsibility lies with the one who sent her." My low response has both men nodding.

"Hisashi." The soft crack of her voice has me spinning wildly in her direction.

"Little dove," I say, rushing over to her side.

"We are glad you are better, little sister." Kiyoshi

and Akchiro bow deeply in respect before leaving us alone.

Pouring her a glass of water, I hand it to her. "Just sip it. We've been putting ice chips on your tongue for the last three days." I don't tell of the first twenty-four hours of sheer hell watching her thrash and fight which the healer said was a good sign, though she was delirious.

At one point I broke and just got in the bed and held her.

"You came back," she said, her eyes bright with fever then we both slept for hours.

"Day two we started an IV to keep you hydrated. I drew the line at a feeding tube but gave you little sips of broth." Looking at her body beneath the covers I almost hesitate to add, "Day two you started bleeding badly like the last time but it's too early to tell. I preserved a sample if you want to find out."

Pressing her hand to her lips, her eyes fill with tears, but she shakes her head, "No'.

"I'm so sorry, little dove, so sorry for all this." I pull her into my arms, trying to be careful of her IV. I hold her.

In the minutes that follow I hold her telling her what happened the night I left her, telling her Aiko's part and my mother's treachery.

"Hisashi, no." She pulls back then her eyes go wide giving me enough warning to turn just in time to face my attacker.

Within seconds I disarm him of the blade turning it on him plunging the ceremonial dagger in Hiru's chest.

"Why?" I demand, watching as blood bubbles up from his lips.

"Loyalty. To madame. She is the matriarch. We are all loyal," he gasps drowning on his blood. "More will come."

"Fuck." My shout makes her jump. "Sorry." I bow to her then again and again. "Sorry for failing to keep you safe. For dragging you into my family's mess. Please forgive me."

As I say the words rage from a thousand days pours through me like a legendary river of lava from Mount Fuji.

"What happened?" My brother and cousin burst through the door.

"One of mother's minions." Giving a negligent wave of my hand I indicate the loyal retainer I've had for the last thirty years.

"I never really liked him," comes the soft voice from the bed. Which brings forth a rare low chuckle from the two killers beside me.

"He said more are coming." I meet The Takeda's eyes.

"Indeed?" he asks his voice deadly. I nod.

"It seems we need to pay mother a visit," Kiyoshi says, all emotion wiped from his voice.

"Iie," I tell him. He had his chance. "I go alone."

. . .

THE GARDENS of our family estate have been neglected. I wonder if she did it out of spite because they always brought my sister so much joy. After what she pulled with Krie, Kana won't speak to her. Kiyoshi and I worried what impact living with her on Akchiro estate had on our younger sister. Yet, Kana remained a delightful kind girl, who is now enjoying her life at university.

"I knew you would come," my mother says looking up from the watercolor she's painting. Her eyes are dead. Psychopath she is not. Malignant narcissist? Yes.

I never felt love from her only disdain. When my mathematical skills brought accolades that was the only time, she showed any interest in me. Otherwise, I was my father's to deal with.

"Your brother had his chance. That American has made him weak. I really think he cares for her." She laughs like that is the most ludicrous thing in the world. "Such disappointments. At least there is Kana. Well, when I bring her back into the fold."

"Kana is lost to you. I hear she's been spending time with an Al – Rasheed's cousin." I smirk seeing the rice powder on her cheek stain crimson underneath.

"What?" She snaps, gripping the brush so hard it vibrates. Then like magic her expression cools. "You and your brother are useless just like your worthless father." Shrugging one shoulder she turns back to her painting.

"I suppose you're here to kill me?" Laughter low and mean emanates from her entire body. "I guess it was inevitable once you discovered the truth about your incarceration." More laughter but his time with sheer delight. "The fact that I made you hate her for it was like dessert. I'd hope you'd kill her, but know you became enamored again threatening to spoil our line with more defectives like yourself and halfu on top." Scoffing she turns eyes full of hatred on me. "Three miscarriages to ensure it didn't happen. There will be none of your spawn ever if you let me live. Yet, like your weak brother. I know you won't." She tuts turning her back to me.

"Your words have never meant anything to me Mother yet knowing Father did not betray me has given me peace. As for Taylor she has filled those empty ravaged places inside of me your hired tormentors wrought." The Tatsumoto assassin, my brother, cousin, and I agreed to do the job steps out of a thicket of brushes but I shake my head in the negative.

I always knew it would be me.

"Allow me," He cajoles.

"I got it," I say aloud, startling my mother along with the sing of the Katana right before I slice her throat.

THIRTY

T aylor ~ Weeks later..

~

"It's quiet out here," I tell him, kicking my feet in the pond. It's warm enough for us to enjoy being outside but only just.

"Not if you keep splashing and talking," he grumbles, face turned up to the sun. He likes it despite me having to drag him out of that tomb of an office of his as he coded in new algorithms for new Creative Chaos software.

"Well eat something then," I say, handing him a cornbread muffin.

"They are too sweet," complaining around a

mouthful, he narrows his gaze on me before turning his face back to the sun.

"How can you be so gross and cute at the same time?" I ask, leaning in to kiss a crumb on the corner of his mouth away.

Stilling for a moment his head swings back in my direction. Giving me a hard look shifting away, his long body folds forward as he discreetly adjusts his erection.

"Mimi gave me a clean bill of health," I tell him, watching that information sink in.

"When did this happen?" He shifts to his side resting on his elbow taking some fried catfish and eating it.

"Right before you came back from Western Cape." I don't look at him then turn to look out at the pond instead.

"That's nearly a week ago," he says lowly. "Why did you wait so long to tell me?" Gaze skewering me he takes a wet nap wiping his hands clean.

Sucking my lower lip in, I feel heat rising to my neck and cheeks. Unease ripples through me as words fail me.

Long, unyielding fingers capture my chin making me look at him. "Why, Tay-chan?"

Still, I hesitate, my nose stinging.

"Are we good?" I blurt out the question that's been eating at me since we came back from Tokyo, and he's buried himself in work every day since not coming to bed until well past the time I'm sleep and gone before I wake. The only reason I know he's been there is his scent clinging to his pillow.

I don't even think he wants me in his room even though he had all my things brought into the subterranean space. I feel the slow creep of distance insinuating between us.

I can't stand it anymore which led me to impose on his work from home day. I miss him.

"Are we good?" He asks as if there is something lost in translation.

"Yes." I nod. "Between you and me? Are we good?"

He studies me for a long moment then sighs, shifting so that now he's facing the pond. He stares out at the pond for a long pensive moment. "No."

My tummy drops.

He tilts his head to the side looking at me with somber onyx eyes. "How are we supposed to be okay after everything that happened to us? After my mother tried to make me believe you betrayed me, so I would kill you out of spite. How are we supposed to be good after I kidnapped you and took you from your life for months? Tormented, and tied you up? How the fuck are we supposed to be good?" His eyes bore into mine waiting for an answer that I don't know how to give.

"We're in therapy for all that —together and separate," I tell him. "Dr. Inoru says the process will be slow and frustrating at times. To help each other when we see the other having a bad day. None of which we can do if we are never together. You are here but you're not." All of which he nods yet his expression is unwavering, like I'm not giving him the answer he wants.

"I don't know what else to say." Shaking my head, I look away then back at him, feeling powerless. "It's like you're mad at me."

"Then I guess there is nothing left to say." He rises but I grab his hand stopping him.

"Hisashi, what's going on?" I try to tug him back down, but he pulls his hand away.

"Why are you still here, Taylor?" He sounds so angry — at me.

"I'm sorry?" Confusion has me stumbling in the rush to get to my feet. "Where else would I be?"

"Anywhere but here." Shaking his head like I am a lost cause, he rips his hands through hair he's let grow past his shoulders. "You have an entire family that loves you. A mother and father who adore the ground you walk on. Yet you're here being a nursemaid to your mad husband."

"Don't." Charging him I shove him hard. He stumbles twice before catching himself. "Don't you ever say that in reference to yourself again. You will never disparage yourself for things outside of your control," I seethe, teeth clenched.

His face flushes but he gives me a rough nod.

"Are you in a bad place?" I softly ask.

"Are you?" he demands in a hard one. "Why didn't you say anything?"

"Because of this, I think." Waving my hand, I indicate the distance between us. "And yes, I was in a bad place when I saw the pictures from Western Cape all over the internet of you having such a great time when you wouldn't spend time with me. That was a huge party." A huge party hosted by my cousin Oz with beautiful models and shapely South African tech executives. "You seemed in your element around your peers."

I spent more than a few hours scrolling through all the reports. I saw him in some of the shots actually seeming to have a good time. Smiling like I haven't seen since the night in Tokyo at the theater. I never felt so alone and unwanted.

"That worried you?" This time the question is soft.

"I mean you take me everywhere but not there. I don't know why." I shrug, hating this feeling and kind of hating him for making me feel this way. It's like now that he has me, he doesn't want me anymore.

"Your cousin's home may seem like a paradise and he is the top facilitator of business in that region, however his compound it not safe. After Tokyo and as much as I want you with me always. I cannot risk your well-being. Ever." There is no mistaking his sincerity. "As for distance I wanted to give you time to heal from everything that happened and get some therapy sessions behind us before we went fully into this whole healthy relationship thing we're trying." His laugh is rough almost doubtful but he's really trying.

"Little dove." Warm hands touch my shoulders bringing me into the depths of his arms. "Understand this, right now we are not good." Somber eyes meet mine, everything stripped away but the truth. "Does that mean I don't want to touch you, taste you? Fuck no. That's all I can think about. Why I needed to stay away and hell yes it made me cranky." Pressing a soft kiss to my brow he whispers, "You can feel how badly I want you, can't you?" I absolutely can feel his hardness pressing hot and strong against me.

My body responds immediately. I melt into him.

That's all it takes for him to sweep me into his arms.

HE COVERS me with his body not allowing us to separate when he presses me into the soft down.

"Eyes on me," he commands, stripping off his shirt. His chest still bears the faint scaring of his time with the knife but none of the tattoos were marred. With every movement his muscles ripple and I can't take my eyes off him and I watch in fascination as he takes the rest of his clothes off then starts with mine. "Up," he says, pulling the deep purple whimsical day dress over my head.

"No bra, no panties." His eyes skating over my body snag on the apex of my thighs. "Why are you wet for me, little dove?" His voice rumbles over me like a warm wave heightening the feeling of anticipation flooding through me since he showed me how much he wanted me in the garden.

He doesn't touch me though. He crawls over me, his long body caging mine.

"Do you know how I've longed for you? Wondering if you'd still want me after what I'd done." He stills me with a finger to my mouth giving a slow shake of his head. "Knowing the heinous shit I'm capable of. How I will annihilate the world for you."

His sharp onyx gaze cuts into me like his blade. "Such a pretty girl. Will you come prettily for me, little dove?"

"Yes, sensei," I bite back when his dick jumps at my words.

Sitting back on his hunches, he grips the base tightly stroking up. A dollop of come pearls at the tip. He swipes it with his forefinger.

My mouth is already open when he brings it to my lips.

"Hmm," I moan around his fingers. Withdrawing it slowly he rubs the tip over my bottom lip. My thighs squeeze, I squirm.

"I love that shit," he mutters.

"What?"

Onyx eyes flare. "When you squeeze those juicy ass thighs and squirm letting me know just how much you need me." He bites down on his bottom lip shaking his head.

Suddenly he's face to face, his arms bracketing my head. "Aishiteru yo."

"I love you back," I pant, meeting his unwavering gaze.

"May I kiss you, little dove?" It's more of a tease than a real request.

"Oh, we're asking now?" I quirk an eyebrow.

"Iie." He shakes his head in the negative for emphasis. His mouth covers mine. His body sinks onto mine. He's heavy but I welcome his weight. My legs open making room for him.

He takes his time kissing me. I savor every drag and swipe of his tongue against mine. He tastes spicy, sweet, and like everything I ever desired.

Our tongues wrap and swirl, suck and glide. He pulls back leaving me panting. His breath saws in and out like he's labored all day.

The heavy press of his dick against my tummy is both torturous and delicious.

Kisses move to my throat. He sucks the flesh on my neck then harder leaving a bruise I don't have to see to know is there.

Placing little bites along my collarbone he sucks every sting away. It's like a reminder that he's a barely tamed animal even with the monster in his mind mostly quiet these days.

When he gets to my breasts he mutters, "Pretty titties. So neglected." Pushing them together he sucks them then pulls back skeets then begins lapping them like a cat in cream. My pussy clenches in anticipation.

Moving down he groans sucking the flesh of my tummy burrowing his face. "Whatever they put in that cream is addictive. I think it makes me feral." Growling for emphasis this motherfucker bites me. "Sorry." He chuckles when I smack him on the shoulder.

The moment he reaches my pussy he pulls my legs over his shoulders rising to his knees. He has me almost vertical. "I said eyes on me, little dove." I can feel his lips moving against mine. Nodding, I shiver.

"Ahhh, Hisashi," I cry when he covers me. Holding me by my hips he gives me no mercy as he devours every inch of me. Beginning with the outer edges he traces every inch of my pussy. His tongue is soft, wet, leaving no part unattended. His eyes are determined as he watches me daring me to look away. I couldn't if I tried. I admire his dedication.

Arching I give him more access. He rewards me by delving his tongue into me. My muscles clench trying to capture the invader. Only he has another purpose — to tongue fuck me into oblivion. I happily fuck his face in return uncaring that my cries can most likely be heard all over the estate and probably five miles out. I haven't had the pleasure of my husband for weeks and my body is determined to have its due.

Swiping his tongue from hole to clit again and again, he holds me in a bruising grip as my climax sends my body arching and pumping while he licks my pussy clean.

Gentle arms ease me down. He doesn't give me a chance to catch my breath. In one smooth thrust he drives his massive dick into my needy and still pulsing body.

A hard hand presses along with the driving force hitting my spot over and over. Another climax hits me before the other one has fully subsided.

Hard driving sends me higher up the bed. "Take it," he grits fucking me like he means it. "Take me. All of me." Taking my thigh and angling it higher, he fucks me deeper. I can feel him in my chest.

"Too much." I shake my head whining not from pain but fear from the intensity of what he is making me feel. Deeper than he's ever been. That's when I realize he's been holding back all this time even with the intensity of what we've already had.

Feeling a pressure build I reach for something — anything to ground me. "I've got you. Kimochi ii." And I want him too. I'm just scared of this intensity.

"Tay-chan," he commands, his eyes glinting. "Trust me."

Unable to form words I nod.

"Yabai, gammon dekinai." Ohmygoodness, he's right it feels so good. I can't hold back either. It's like a dam bursts when I come this time. He keeps fucking me through the orgasm his dick hitting the spot deepest with me. My pussy gushes as pleasure makes me see stars.

Fingers spearing through my curls he anchors me making me take all him as his face hardens. "Aishiteimasu, chīsana hato." Throwing his head back on the guttural cry he stiffens coming deep inside of me.

He stays buried inside me until he softens. Moving to my side he pulls me out of the way from the saturated side over to his.

Curving behind me, he idly brushes my messy hair away from my face. "Do you worry I don't mean it? Can't mean it when I say I love you because of how I am?"

Turning in his arms I look into his beautiful solemn face. "No." I shake my head. "I love you for the man you are, every aspect of you. You — Hisashi, the monster, guardian. You showed me from the start that you do. I don't miss all this purple, how you come hold me through the night making me feel safe even when I wasn't ready and the dinnerware? I thought it was cruelty until I realized you didn't remember. They took so much. We're not going to let them take anymore. Why? Do you doubt me, that I'll leave again?" I ask, knowing he has every reason to doubt me. "About the way I failed you?"

Rising on his elbow, he shakes his head. "You never failed me. You did what you had to do to survive. You are a courageous woman. I will love you forever. You stayed beside me until they forced you away. I know that now. Never say you failed because when I needed you most you were here."

Shaking his head in wonder he strokes my cheek back and forth with his thumb.

"Loving you was inevitable. The night of that gala might as well have been foretold. I don't remember a time when I didn't love you. I knew in that moment you were going to be my everything, completely, unequivocally, mine. I know I'll never be worthy but I'm just selfish enough of a motherfucker to know without you my life has no merit, no purpose. The way you love me makes me realize there is hope for someone as broken as me."

"You are not broken, Hisashi. You are more than worthy of my love. You are my everything, completely, unequivocally, mine."

"Mine," he whispers in agreement dragging me under him again.

EPILOGUE

PENING NIGHT

TAYLOR ~ SYDNEY OPERA HOUSE.

I WAS tired after the fourth ovation but the look of pride on my husband's face is enough for me to endure. Who am I kidding? I live for this. Seeing my creative hard work coming to fruition. He flew my entire family out to see the play so no one would miss it. The residency here will be a year. Kiyoshi supported him working in a satellite location and Akchiro grudgingly agreed but is too busy with his new baby girl to put up much of a fuss.

Mama and Pa-Pete made the journey without one bit of complaint. So much has changed in our family since the Creative Chaos plant has come to Shelby-Love.

"I'm so proud of you, little dove." He whispers to me as soon as I reach him backstage. The love in his eyes surpasses all understanding.

"Aishiteru yo," I whisper in return feeling the hot press of emotion rising in my chest.

"You've accomplished so much tonight. A play that explores mental challenges during the pandemic, how social media misinformation was particularly harmful and how the lack of real time services impacted people and how you characters still managed triumph in a way that was real to them." The pride in his voice has me pulling back to look into the dark onyx of his eyes.

"Sounds like us." A smile pulls at the corner of my mouth.

"It does. Only with no babies in the mix." A frown plays around his lips.

"Well, you were right." I raise my hand when he shifts. "We just got here and we need to still relearn each other like you said. It doesn't have to be ten years. I can have it removed anytime. Just not right now." Getting on my tips toes, I press my lips to his.

Finding out his mother was behind my miscarriages caused a shift in his perspective. Really listening to his concerns about us needing time to relearn each other and navigate this relationship changed mine.

"Maybe in a couple years." Touching his forehead to mine, he says.

'Definitely," I smile.

LATER AFTER THE celebration that nearly had Hisashi climbing the walls and a kinbaku session to help him decompress we're cuddling looking at the Sydney Skyline. My phone starts buzzing.

"Who is it? Your family needs to learn about time differences." He grumbles in my hair.

"Says the fella who talks to his brother at all times of day and night."Shrugging his arm off, I grab my phone my eyes rounding at the text.

> Kandie: Sorry I couldn't make it cuz, this dirty ass cop locked me up and I just escaped. TLL.

"Babe." I turn to Hisashi showing him the text.

"Hmm?" He mumbles sitting up then reads the text and starts laughing.

"What is going on with Kandie and Ulysses Shelby?" My heart is speeding up because our families are mortal enemies.

"A lot and not our business." He says, placing the phone back on the nightstand. "They will work out their toxic shit just like we worked out ours."

"Ohh." Instantly, getting his point. Well meaning

and bad actors alike had cost us a lot of time. "It was hard but we did work it out."

I kiss the tip of his nose. "But worth it."

"So worth it," he agrees.

His eyes feather close, his insomnia and my night terrors a thing of the past.

THE END

And you thought your mom was bad...

ALSO BY KENYA GOREE-BELL

THE MOGUL SERIES

Rappers Delight

Lotus Flower Bomb

California Love

The Kronic

Always Be My Baby

BLOOD LEGACY SERIES

BAD GUY

EASY LIKE SUNDAY MORNING

DARLING NIKKI

THE KANDIE SHOPPE

DESPARADO

THE HAREM DIARIES SERIES

Adored

ONE LAST THING

Ummm...
     What's going on with Kandie? And how does she keep escaping the county jail? When I tell you there is a huge story behind it just wait and see.

BLURB
     Ulysses
     "Dirty ass cop."
     It's sheriff but fine whatever.
     Kandie Love is a fūcking mess.
     The town tipsy,
     The town baker,
     The town gossip,
     The town —
     It doesn't matter because her little nosey ass has

510

rolled up on something that's not her business but definitely interferes with mine.

So now I have to put my foot on her throat to keep her from telling everyone what she thinks she saw.

I don't have time for her, the wildness she makes me feel.

Now, the more I make her bend the more she makes me break.

I left here fifteen years ago to get away from her crazy ass, now I can't get rid of her.

And now I'm not sure I even want to.

Damn.

SHE TOLD me to tell y'all to go ahead and preorder her book KANDIE SHOPPE it will be out around May 2024, by now you know how i set up the preorders. 🌐

ACKNOWLEDGMENTS

This book poured out of me.

Hisashi is Japanese. My friends, Mami Tagani and Lica Nichols helped to make this possible with sharing their language and culture with me. I love you to bits! Any mistakes are mine as well as the artistic license I took throughout the book. Kiyoshi is a fictionalized over the top, obsessive hero , who is proudly a villain and has no problem burning shit down for Taylor. This in is no way to represents any man or any culture, so don't think you are going to go out there and find anyone this darkly perfect.

Naima Simone is always the best friend that any person can have. Who accepts me and occasionally lets me cry, listens to me tell her the whole book over the phone before I have even written a word. Thank you, for giving me honest advice, truth and unconditional love and friendship. I cherish you. Like for real. Welcome to the Dark side, bestie.

Bethan Hagan is the best person on the planet. Her heart is gold. She uplifts me and helps me soar. I'm honored just to know her. When I send her little bits of vague naughtiness she is always and forever like,

"DOOO ITTTT" and "That's HOTTT". I wish everyone had a Bethany but you cannot have mine. Vampires forever!

Elle Kayson who is the first person to read my books and gives me smooch encouragement. Such a gifted person taking to time to read my words always so humbling and very much appreciated.

My little family hugs me everyday and leaves me alone to write. They ask me how my writing is going and tell me I'm great when they haven't read a word of my naughty books. My husband is world class and creates a life where my dreams come true everyday by being with him.

My dear readers thank you for letting me entertain you. Thank you for the kind words and for encouragement. Writing is solitary and can be lonesome. That's hard for an extrovert like me but every time I put work out you guys more than show up, you show out. I promise to always give you my very best. I love you all.

About the Author

Kenya Goree-Bell lives in Alabama with her former warrior husband and three kids. She is the author of the Harem Diaries Series and the bestselling Mogul Series and Blood Legacy Series. When not writing she is a romance novel influencer, lifelong bibliophile and can be seen weekly on Instagram and Facebook Live interviewing other authors on her IG: TheKGB — The K's Grown and Sexy Book Club. She believes that Happy Ever After belongs to everyone and writes about worlds where everyone deserves love.

Follow me on all social media @kenyagoreebell

Sign-up for my newsletter to get more information

The Naughty List

Join My Patreon to read my current WIP as I write it!

Kenya's Patreon

facebook.com/kenyagoreebell

instagram.com/kenyagoreebell

tiktok.com/kenyagoreebell

patreon.com/kenyagoreebell